2 00

THE

SHENANDOAH

SPY

a novel by

Francis Hamit

BRASS
CANNON
BOOKS

Brass Cannon Books
brasscannonbks@earthlink.net

Typeset in Georgia font, a TrueType font.

ISBN 978-1-59595-902-7

Printed in the United States of America

BOOK DESIGN BY LEIGH STROTHER-VIEN

Dedication

for Leigh,

with Love.

FOREWORD

Belle Boyd was a real person, and became world famous as a spy for the Confederate Government. That may seem like a contradiction in terms, but the Civil War was one where amateurs predominated and passions overruled common sense. Common sense would have prevented the whole tragic episode in our history.

Belle, in September 1862, became the first woman in American history to be formally commissioned an Army officer. A Captain of Scouts at the age of 18 (wrong army, but who really cares about that?)

Looking backward there is a tendency to dismiss this ceremonial acknowledgment of the key role she played in Stonewall Jackson's Valley Campaign as so much propaganda; a gloss to promote the Lost Cause of the Confederacy. But surviving documents, of which there are very few (the Confederate Secret Service archives were burned when the Confederate Government fled Richmond on April 2nd, 1865) indicate not just a very sophisticated and active intelligence service, but one which used female spies like Belle to great advantage.

The central event of this novel, where she ran across a battlefield under fire is verified by eyewitness accounts. Belle's reputation was savaged at the time and later by people with their own agendas. This book is a fiction, but closer to the truth about her than many a history written about her. She was a passionate rebel; a patriot for her cause. Recently she has become something of a feminist icon, and perhaps a model for the modern military woman in many respects. Her cause was in doubt. Her courage, never. For that reason her story must be told.

The Union thought enough of Belle's spying to jail her several times, and there is one reported episode where she appeared to a reporter wearing the uniform of a Confederate Army Lieutenant Colonel. Unlike most of her female colleagues, Belle was a scout as well as a spy. She could ride and shoot better than most men, and her work with Turner Ashby was the least of it. She also served with John Singleton Mosby, and may have been at Gettysburg. The documentary evidence for any of this is very thin. An indication here and there, and by anecdote rather than official document. It's a mystery — but one that fascinates. What is important is how Belle saw herself. She signed her letters "CSA" during the war. Confederate States Army. She saluted her old friend David Hunter Strother when she told him that she was once more being arrested and jailed by the Union Provost Marshal. Strother was a Union intelligence officer and the salute is the exchange of courtesy between soldiers. Her heroism at the Battle of Front Royal is documented by two eyewitness accounts. There is a historical marker where she gave her report to Jackson.

So this is my framework for this novel. I have some experience of intelligence organizations and how they function. I applied that to what is known and began making up the rest on Page One. This book is neither fact nor fiction, but something in between...and something closer to truth than you could get with either on its own.

This book is about just the first year of Belle Boyd's remarkable career. Since she did not exist in a vacuum, the series becomes a faux history of the entire Confederate Secret Service, which had the services of many remarkable individuals

Let it be noted that I hold no brief here for that cause, which was founded on an evil principle and fully deserved to fail. However to ignore the heroism and courage of these women would be to ignore an essential and much misunderstood part of American history, which might help us better understand some of the current problems that confront us as a nation.

In the spirit of the film **Sunset**, I will say "It's all true, give or take a lie or two". Devotees of pure historical fact may find much to argue with here, but they are not my audience. This is an entertainment, one that I hope will also provoke thought, discussion and a new way of looking at the Civil War.

DRAMATIS PERSONAE

SOUTH

Isabelle "Belle" Boyd, Confederate Army nurse, scout and spy

Ben Boyd, Belle's father; a Confederate soldier
Mary Boyd, Belle's mother
William Boyd, Belle's little brother
Eliza Corsey. Belle's personal servant and sub-agent
Ruth Burns Glenn, Belle's grandmother
James Glenn. Militia Captain of Scouts, Belle's uncle
Alice Stewart, Belle's cousin and sub-agent

and
(LTC>BG) H. Turner Ashby (aka Henry Turner, Veterinarian), Commanding Officer of the 7th Virginia Cavalry
Doctor Ben Ashcroft, Belle's supervisor at Front Royal General Army Hospital
MAJ George Henry Bier, Confederate artillery expert
Alexander Boetler, Congressman, and local Secret Service chief.
Lucy Buck, a young woman in Front Royal
William Buck, a prominent merchant in Front Royal
MAJ Reverend Dabney, Jackson's Adjutant General
MAJ Henry Kyd Douglas, Deputy Inspector General, Valley Army
CPT Harry Gilmour, cavalry officer under Ashby
Antonia Ford, Belle's friend, fellow courier and spy
James Harrison, an actor, Confederate scout and spy
(COL>MG) Thomas "Stonewall" Jackson, Commanding Officer, Valley Division, Confederate Army
Major Hunter H. McGuire, Jackson's Medical Director
Jules St. Martin, Confederate Secret Service code section chief
BG Jeb Stuart, Confederate Cavalry Commander
BG Richard Taylor, Louisiana Division Commander
MAJ Robideaux Wheat, Commanding officer, Louisiana Tigers Battalion

DRAMATIS PERSONAE

NORTH

La Fayette C. Baker, Chief, United States Secret Service

MG Nathaniel Banks, Union Army Commander

CPT Bannon, Assistant Provost Marshal, Winchester

(COL>MG) David Birney, 23rd Pennsylvania Volunteers

COL Thorton Fleming Brodhead, Commanding Officer, First
    Michigan Cavalry

Mr. William Clark, special correspondent, *New York Herald*

Alfie Cridge, United States Secret Service field agent

MG John Adams Dix, Union Army Commander, Baltimore

LTC James Fillebrown, Provost Marshal, Tenth Maine

MG John C. Fremont, Union Division Commander

BG John White Geary, Brigade Commander

CPT James Gwyn, 23rd Pennsylvania Volunteers, Provost Marshal

CPT Daniel Keily, Irish mercenary recruited to the Union Army
    and Belle's lover

(LT>MAJ) Michael Kelley, former police detective and Provost
    Marshal/ Inspector General

CPT Myles Keogh, Irish mercenary recruited to the Union Army

Ward Hill Lamon, Boyd family friend, lawyer and political
    operative for Abraham Lincoln

Lt. Douglas Preston, Assistant Provost Marshal

LT Hasbrouke Reeve, Co. L, First Michigan Cavalry

BG James Shields, Union Army Commander

(CPT) David Strother, better known as the *Harper's Magazine*
    artist and humorist, **"Porte Crayon"**, topographical
    engineer and intelligence officer

MAJ Hector Tyndale, Provost Marshal, Winchester

COL Sir Percy Wyndham, mercenary soldier, Commanding
    Officer First New Jersey Cavalry

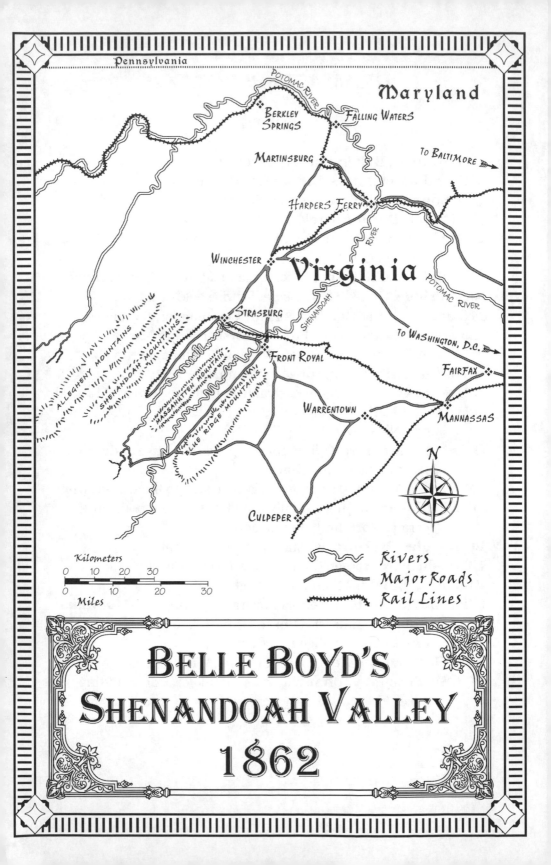

CHAPTER ONE

July 3, 1861, Martinsburg, Virginia

Dick Ashby is dead, and the war has come to Martinsburg, Belle thought. Her heart filled with grief but the rest of her was just numb. On the verge of tears, and yet unable to find any, she swore to be revenged on the Yankees.

She peered out the window, looking up Queen Street towards the turnpike that led past Tuscatora Creek to Williamsport. From there the weary Virginia regiments had fallen back after failing to stop the Yankees at Falling Waters the day before.

She growled, "Damn them!" Her maid, Eliza, looked at her with reproof. Belle was a young lady now, and young ladies of her class were not supposed to use profanity. Ever.

Eliza danced nervously side to side, her eyes wide and white in her dark face. This was not safe. The rest of the family had taken refuge in the cellar.

"I don't care," Belle said defiantly. "I'd like to kill them all. Why are we letting them in?" Anguish and rage fed on itself. It was a useless question; one to which she already had the answer.

Her view was obscured by the miasma of smoke that still issued from the yards of the Baltimore and Ohio Railway, where three weeks before hundreds of railway cars had been set alight, and still burned fitfully. More than forty locomotives were removed and hauled away, by men using teams of horses and mules, down the turnpike toward the railhead at Winchester. The cars had been burned to keep the Yankees from using them.

That right there should have told us that Martinsburg would be lost, Belle thought bitterly.

"Miss Belle, you come away from dat window," Eliza's voice was soft but insistent.

Belle made a sharp, cutting motion with her hand, signifying both that she had heard Eliza and that she had no intention of doing any such thing.

"You can go," she said. Eliza shook her head and remained

where she was. Her place was at her mistress's side.

The house shuddered from the rhythm of marching feet outside the house. Suddenly the mirror on Belle's dresser fell forward, off the nail that secured it to the wall, and slipped to the floor with a crash.

Eliza walked over, picked it up and said mournfully, "Sebben years bad luck."

Belle looked. It was cracked straight across, from top to bottom. *An ill omen indeed*, she thought. "Put it back up when they've gone."

Her mother's voice floated up from the kitchen, filled with anxiety, "Isabelle, you get down here right this minute!"

Isabelle. I'm in trouble now, she thought. Her mother only used her full name when she wanted to chastise her. Still, she did not move.

The house rattled again as heavy wagons passed. It was a mistake to build so close to the street, but that was the fashion now. It was a new house, less substantial than the one her father had built on Race Street across from the train depot when she was 12, and given up almost immediately when financial matters went against him.

Peering out the other window gave Belle a view up the street. The wind had come up and momentarily cleared the smoke from the sky.

"There," she breathed out, "There they are!"

Eliza, hugging herself, crowded in beside her to look. In the distance Union soldiers moved like ants, in two columns of four, taking up the entire width of the Williamsport Turnpike that led from the battlefield at Falling Waters, six miles away. Behind them came another long double line of wagons. On they came, thousands of soldiers.

"Lawdy," Eliza said softly.

South of town, the Second Virginia Regiment, was in orderly retreat, screened by cavalry drawn from the ranks of the younger gentry, the so-called "chivalry", who provided their own fine horses, under the command of Captain Henry Ashby, whose Mountain Rangers militia had been taken into the new Confederate Army wholesale.

Belle wanted nothing more than to be on a horse, riding with Ashby, saber in hand. She'd been taught to ride by the Ashbys. One glorious summer she had demonstrated her skill at tournaments, riding as Dick Ashby's "squire" when he played at being a Knight by collecting small wooden rings on the tip of a lance at the gallop — an indulgence on his part that cemented her mother's determination to ship her off to Baltimore to learn the arts of being a "lady". Her acquiescence in this plan was purchased with a fine black stallion that she rode every chance offered to her. She knew herself to be a better rider than most men; so good that she could stand on a saddle at a full gallop, amazing the crowd.

That was five years before, when she was a skinny twelve year-old and still allowed to wear boy's clothes for the occasion. Before she was a "lady" — a term she disliked more and more. As the war grew closer, Belle felt the disability of being a woman more keenly than ever. She chafed at the limits it imposed on her even as those limits were eased.

Under her apron she now carried a new Colt Navy .36 caliber revolver, with the holster tied up with a strip of rawhide so that it lay flat across her belly and could be easily drawn with her right hand.

"You women may have to protect yourselves from these Yankees," her obviously worried father had said, when the war had started ten weeks before, as he pulled two pistols from the store's stock.

He had not only taught Belle and her mother, Mary, how to shoot them, but made them practice. Mary did so with a grimace, wincing, which gave her an unerring ability to miss the target at any range greater than a handshake.

Belle soon learned to puncture tin cans from 20 yards, never missing one. She took to it right away, and laughed at having found a delightful new game. Not ladylike, but no matter. Women of her class were reputed too delicate to handle firearms, but with so many men away in the Army, what choice was there?

Martinsburg wasn't the West, but now that the war was on, Belle was not the only young woman who carried a pistol to protect herself. Civility, like civil order itself, was noticeably absent of late.

Ben Boyd had returned for a few hours the previous night, weary and footsore, looking far older than his 44 years. A "gentleman private" in Company D, all Martinsburg men, he had stepped up with the same will as his teenaged neighbors, only to have his body betray him.

Hard marching and some fighting in recent days along with scant rations had shrunk his belly to the point where he'd punched two new holes in his leather belt.

Once home, he was properly spoiled by his wife and daughters, as his eight-year old son William cautiously touched the new Enfield musket he now carried. The servants ran back and forth, fetching him cold drinks, removing his already badly worn boots, pouring a bowl of warm water to soak his feet, taking away his gray uniform to be brushed, finding him fresh linen to change into. For a few hours he was master of himself again.

"This is no easy thing we've gotten into," he said over dinner. "You remember when we set out, all the presents and goods, we were given?" The initial fitting-out, with uniforms and muskets purchased from England, had been a huge party, with bands playing, speeches given and small comforts pressed upon the brave men off to defend Virginia. These gifts included fierce Bowie knives, and extra shirts, cans and jars of delicacies, and scarves and mittens for the cold evenings. Many of these items were purchased from their own store.

Ben drew on his pipe. Belle was shocked to see that there was suddenly lots of gray in his beard and hair that was not there when he enlisted.

"Problem is that no one thought of how we'd have to carry all that. You need rations and a canteen and a bedroll and your musket and sixty rounds, but all that other stuff just gets in the way, so first you try to give it to someone, but he's just as footsore and tired as you are, and wants to give you something he don't want to lug, and so you leave it by the side of the road, both of you, and then you got to hurry and catch up because this Colonel we got, Tom Jackson, is death on straggling, even if he does set a pretty fierce pace."

He leaned back, smiling ruefully. "I could stock our store five times over with what got thrown away out there. Nice goods, most of it."

For Belle, the crisp spring days just past were an extended picnic, with family and friends making the long trip to Harper's Ferry, where young men postured while young girls giggled and flirted with them, and older men, in new gray uniforms, tried to make an army to defend Virginia.

The big picnic was over. Harper's Ferry was given up without a fight by the West Point men who had defected to the South.

How much more would they surrender without a fight? Belle wondered bitterly.

Martinsburg was vital, a place where the railroad met three turnpikes and brought commerce every day. Those who promoted the Southern cause said it must be defended against Northern aggression — but, again, that was not to be. Yankees were too thick on the ground.

Bragging, the men who signed up for the militias in the first rush of patriotism said that a Southerner could lick any four Yankees they sent. But the Yankees sent more than four. Many more than four.

Her father told them the hard truth. "We can't hold Martinsburg. The whole brigade will come through tomorrow, falling back. Yankees sent thousands of men. Don't seem that they amount to much, but with that many of them, they don't have to. We couldn't hold them off at Falling Waters and we can't do it here. The town will be utterly destroyed if we try."

Now the Yankees marched, regiment by regiment, thousands

of them, off the turnpike and right down Queen Street.

As Belle watched the Yankees from the high window, rage and grief threatened to consume her. She blinked back tears, thinking of Dick Ashby's tragic end. He was only the secret desire of her heart, the man she had hoped one day she might marry. By foul chance, one of the first to die defending the South.

Her father tried to keep the news from her, but failed. Oh, how he had tried not to tell her, she recalled.

"You should have joined the cavalry, Daddy," she'd said at dinner the night before. The comment, light and teasing, provoked his laughter.

"You got a better chance of joining the cavalry than me, daughter. I don't ride hell-for-leather the way these young bucks do, never have."

Her mother frowned, "Don't give her any ideas."

Belle smiled, "Well, Mama, I might meet a beau." At seventeen, Belle already risked being thought of as an old maid by the locals. Her mother had married younger than that. Most did.

Ben frowned as well, "They don't let women in the Army, Isabelle. Put it out of your mind."

Belle pouted, "I don't see why not. I can ride and shoot as well as a man. Dick Ashby said so. About the riding that is." Her eyes shone brightly with the pride she felt. Even side-saddle, she had a remarkable seat and could gallop full out.

"And could you cut someone down with a saber?" her father asked heavily, serious now. "Butcher him like a hog?"

That grisly image quite took the fun out of it. Everyone stared at him in the silence that ensued.

Belle's face became grave. "I think I could," she said after a moment, causing her mother to throw up her hands. Her grandmother merely chuckled, drawing an irritated look from her father. Glenn clan women rivaled the men for savagery, it was said.

"To protect you or Mama or the children — or anyone from the Yankees. Yes — I could!" Belle looked to her Grannie Ruth for support.

Ben Boyd regarded his mother-in-law and his daughter solemnly, "Don't go looking for trouble. It'll find you fast enough." He sighed, frowning, "This may seem like wonderful fun to you youngsters, but, when you see someone shot down, bleeding his life away...," Ben fiddled with his pipe, looking downward, away from them, as he did when the news was bad.

Belle asked, "Wasn't the whole purpose of forming companies and regiments and making an army to protect the border areas and keep our homes safe from the Yankees?"

Ben just shook his head wearily, "We learned a sharp lesson at Falling Waters," he replied. "Big difference between saying a thing and doing it."

"Ben," his wife asked suddenly, "Do you need to be a soldier this bad?"

"Well, hell, Mary, it ain't like I can up and quit it. They call that desertion, and they hang you for it. I said I'd do it, and I am going to do it," he said ruefully, as if he had once more been caught on the bad side of a bargain.

"But look at you," Mary protested. "You're not a young man. You look as tired as I've ever seen you. Can't you be an officer and ride a horse at least?"

"I don't know a thing about leading men in battle. That's what officers do. Colonel Jackson graduated from West Point and fought in Mexico. He teaches at the Military Institute. Jeb Stuart's another West Point man, and he arrested John Brown. These men know the trade of soldiering. The rest of us are rank amateurs, even Henry Ashby."

"But you're a Master Mason. Surely...."

"That don't mean anything in the Army. That kind of politics don't matter there," Ben replied. "I'll be marching till Hell freezes over or we lick the Yankees."

He was obviously uncertain which would come first.

Belle tried to cheer him up, "Daddy, what fun is that? Given my druthers, I'd rather ride with Dick and Henry."

Ben sighed and looked at her sadly, "I'm very glad you're not able to do that, Isabelle. It's no summer tournament, playing at Knights and Ladies. It's war. Men die out there."

He paused a long time, searching for an easy way to say what came next and then, unable to find it, blurted out, "Dick Ashby is dead — killed by the Yankees!"

Belle, shocked, sat frozen. "How?" she managed at last, in a whisper.

"I wasn't going to say anything about it," Ben replied slowly. "I wanted a happy evening before I went back."

Staring at her, he licked his lips, unsure of himself. That was a worry. Ben Boyd was a cheerful, ebullient man in normal times, a back-slapper, a political animal.

Her grandmother, in a moment of uncharacteristic delicacy, collected the younger children and took them off to bed.

Belle sat very still. "Tell me," she said. "Who killed him?" Her eyes were very bright, her jaw set. Her father stared at her a long moment.

"Well, I wasn't anywhere near, so this is just what I heard," Ben said, tamping a fresh load of cut tobacco into his pipe with his thumb. He puffed it into life with a coal from the fire and looked at his oldest daughter curiously. "You and him weren't...?"

"No, Daddy. Nothing like that. He'd just come back, so there was no time for that, but I did have hopes."

Her mother choked a bit at this, as Belle knew she would. Her mother and grandmother had other plans for her, and looked down on the Ashbys.

Ben leaned back, frowning. "What I heard is that he was out by Luray, leading a patrol after some Union spy, and they was ambushed by Union cavalry. Regulars, they were. Whole thing might have been a trap. Most of his boys' horses got flummoxed by a cattle guard and his horse was shot dead and fell on him. He was all alone in the middle of the meadow, with Yankees all around. They called for him to give up, but he wouldn't, not with the rest of his patrol looking on. He kept slashing at the Union troopers with his saber every time they got close. They shot him a few times, but he wouldn't give over. Then Captain Ashby rides up very quickly with the rest of the company and drives the Yankees off. It took them awhile to get that dead horse off him, but he was still alive. They carried him back to camp for doctoring, but Doc Funston couldn't do much but give him something for the pain. Hip broke, legs broke, and gut shot. He finally died yesterday. Hard way to go. Henry was awful tore up about it. Stood over the grave with Dick's saber, broke it in two and threw the pieces on top of his coffin, swearing a blood oath to be revenged on the Yankees."

"As was his right," Belle said stiffly.

"As was his right," her father agreed; "But it isn't your right, so you be sensible about this. We have troubles enough."

Belle wanted to scream, but that would be unladylike. Instead, she sat silently, making herself not cry. Not making a sign, her face closed.

Ben pulled on his boots, saying to Mary, "Tell Sam I need a new pair, but just the one. I don't want to lug extras." He got up, put on his coat and forage cap, picked up his musket, slung his rucksack over his shoulder and let Mary come into his arms.

"You take care of yourself, Old Man," she said.

"Old Man, yourself," he replied with a grin; "I'm as good as any man in the regiment." He looked over to where Belle sat and said, "Isabelle, you mind your mother, heah?"

Belle looked at him, surprised.

"I mean it," he said. "You always were a willful child. Don't mess with these Yankees. Leave it to us soldiers."

Belle saw no point in argument. She truly didn't wish to have anything to do with the Yankees, and only hoped to be left alone in her grief. "Yes, Daddy," she said.

Ben kissed his wife and went out the door to rejoin his company. Belle's mother, tears in her eyes, went to her room without another word.

Belle pulled her pistol from its holster, checked the action and the caps, then wiped it down with a rag. She'd sat up, holding the Colt, for a long time.

Now, as she watched the Yankee invasion, she felt the weight of the pistol and did not wipe away the tears that finally coursed down her face for Dick Ashby. To her dismay, some of her neighbors were lined up on Queen Street to greet the Yankees, one holding a big Federal flag. She was hurt and astounded. Many were good friends. Some had cheered as loudly for the South. The indignity of it all!

I will go mad, she thought. "Leave me alone," is all she said to Eliza, and the maid, for a mercy, did so. She continued to watch the Yankees marching past below, wanting nothing better than to shoot a few of them, but understanding how useless and stupidly dangerous that would be.

The itch was there, for Dick Ashby's sake.

Just seventeen years old and already, in her own mind, a widow, or if not that, the next best thing, even if nothing had been said between them of love, much less of marriage. A young girl's foolish fancy? She rejected the notion out of hand.

Dick Ashby would have suited her very well. She liked the size of him and the smell of him, and the way he laughed, and his kindness years before at tournaments and parties. She could have persuaded him now that she was all grown up.

"Gone. All gone now," she cried softly to herself, as she wiped her tears away. Her right hand wrapped around the grip of the Colt firmly, drawing strength from it. "But not forgotten. Never that."

CHAPTER TWO

Later that day, her close neighbors, Virginia and Betty Doll, came to call. Belle invited them into the parlor while their maids went into the kitchen to chat with Della, the cook.

"Y'all want tea?" Eliza asked, pretending this was just a normal day, rather than one when the world had been turned upside down. Belle went along with the pretense because she didn't know what else to do.

Her mother and grandmother were in the "store"; actually a long narrow room that ran the length of one side of the house. They were taking an inventory of the remaining stock.

"Yes, Eliza, tea would be very nice," said Belle, and went back to her guests. Virginia and Betty were close enough in age to be taken for twins by strangers. Both had light blonde hair and dark blue eyes and, at fifteen and sixteen respectively, neither lacked for beaus.

Belle liked them anyway. She was not an envious person. She stood taller than most men by two inches, and would simply have to wait to meet a very tall man. Like Dick Ashby.

She had a classical face with a strong profile and a Roman nose that marked her as a Boyd. Not a beautiful face like those of the Dolls — they lived up to their name all too well — but she had a spectacular figure which had blossomed in just the past two years, with such a narrow waist that wearing a corset was simply a bow to convention rather than a necessity.

She was often unnerved by the way that some men looked so admiringly at her as she walked by. Her hearing was very good, and their comments to each other often made her blush. Not that she didn't know how to play the game.

In Baltimore, during the night-time sessions at Mount Washington Female College, she had learned to flirt, to listen attentively to men as they postured, to dance, and all the other skills required to land a husband. These were as much a part of the curriculum as French, literature, music and singing.

Here the process of molding her into a proper lady by the

older girls began. Not just for everyday wear in Martinsburg, but suitable for the salons of Washington. Her mother and grandmother thought her smart enough to find a husband there, among the powerful. When Ben Boyd went broke in the Panic of '57, they still found money for Belle's school and fancy clothes.

The year before, she had been taken to Washington to stand along with her cousin Alice Stewart to have a "season". Alice's family lived there and had "connections". The war changed all of that. She would have been there again, but now those hopes were dashed, and all she had to show for it were a few fine gowns made by Elizabeth Keckley and some wonderful memories. She pitied the Dolls, whose own season would likely never come now.

Belle understood, with gratitude, what her mother had done for her by sending her to Baltimore for a proper education. Girls who stayed in Martinsburg settled for men from there or another rural town. Their futures were safe and certain — and dull.

"Settling" for Dick Ashby wouldn't have been settling at all, but the realization of her heart's fondest wish. No other man made her feel that way, but she'd kept her feelings secret, even from him, and waited until the time was right. Waited for him to return from the West.

With the Yankee invasion, everything changed and nothing was right. She regarded her two neighbors cautiously, unsure of their feelings about the war and the Union. They looked at her, distantly polite, showing none of their usual girlish manners nor enthusiasm. This was new. No one knew who to trust now.

Belle thought of the way she had shown off the display of flags and patriotic emblems in her room to them before the fighting began and hoped she would not regret it. Their father was employed by the Baltimore and Ohio. The arson in the yards gave them no reason to love the South. Their hopes had gone up in smoke, in more ways than one.

The three girls looked anxiously at each other. Virginia Doll took one of the little cakes Eliza had brought in on a plate, and nibbled it delicately. Betty sipped her tea reflectively.

"We were going over to the Masonic Hall," Betty said at last, "To do some more hospital work."

"I thought all the wounded had been evacuated?" Belle asked in surprise.

"It wants cleaning," said Virginia.

"And we thought our maids could do that, while we look in on those two poor boys with fever who couldn't be moved," said Betty.

"Lucy Glenn is with them now," said Virginia. "She sent word that those Yankees are getting rambunctious. Said they're a rough mob and all look like penitentiary convicts. We need to get those poor boys out."

"Where's Mrs. Pruneface?" asked Belle, sending the Doll girls into giggles. Even Eliza had to smile at that. "Oh, I am sorry," Belle continued with a straight face, "I meant Mrs. Pruitt."

The day before, Mrs. Pruitt had upbraided Belle for waving at the men of Company D as they marched past.

"I am waving to my father," Belle had replied with some spirit, after Mrs. Pruitt, one of those self-appointed guardians of the public mores, had called her 'an immodest little tramp'.

Given Belle's height, the term 'little' was in doubt, and it was hardly her fault that some of the younger men waved back.

"We thought," Betty spoke in that delicate way of hers, "That we would make up a party. Mrs. Prune...Pruitt has gone off to her farm, and...."

"...And you're so brave, Belle," finished her sister. "You can keep the Yankees at bay."

"There are thousands of them," Belle demurred, "Perhaps...."

"You're very strong, Belle," said Virginia reasonably, "And, there will be six of us altogether. We should be safe enough with you as our Captain."

Belle thought hard for a moment. She didn't fear the Yankees, but didn't want her anger with them to lead her into difficulty. Still, it would be doing a small thing for the Cause, and a way to distract herself from her grief over Dick Ashby. She was also terribly curious about what was going on in the town. The Masonic Hall was five long blocks away, at the center.

"I need some exercise," Belle said, as Betty shot her sister a relieved look. "Just let me tell Mama." She got up and went into the store.

"Be careful," was all that her mother said, motioning significantly to the revolver under her apron. Her grandmother shot her a worried look, but said nothing.

Outside, formed up with Eliza and the other maids in tow, they began a slow, cautious walk down the graveled street. The trees along the way were scraped and cut, with broken limbs, as if some great beast had passed by. The road dipped, following the earth, so that they were a bit out of breath by the time they reached the hall.

Virginia Doll noticed that Belle still had her apron on. "How practical you are," she smiled, spinning her parasol gaily, "We should have thought of that."

Belle said nothing about the hidden revolver. She walked along with her friends, the three of them chattering gaily.

Most of the Yankee soldiers had passed right on through and were setting up camp on Israel Robinson's farm on the other side of town. A small group of them were posted between the Catholic church with its tall spire and the three-story Masonic Hall. These two brick faced structures rivaled each other for the title of the tallest building in town.

The soldiers started whistling and clapping as they approached. Betty and her sister looked at the ground, but Belle stared defiantly ahead.

"Gawd, Harvey," said one of them loudly, "Look at the teats on that big one!" The rest of the men laughed. Belle flushed with embarrassment. This was not admiration, but an assault on her dignity. She heard Betty and Virginia gasp, while the three servants girls muttered to each other. Belle lengthened her stride and the other women rushed to catch up.

"Pay no attention to that trash," Betty advised, her voice trembling. Belle blinked back the sudden tears coming to her eyes. *How dare they*, she thought helplessly, *how dare they outrage me that way? If I were a man....*

Behind them Father Bannon, the old priest whose parish this was, came out and remonstrated with the Yankee soldiers.

"This is a decent town," Belle heard him begin in a thick brogue that matched their own, "And the women here are to be treated with respect...." Glancing behind her, she could see the Yankee soldiers standing half to attention as he lectured them.

They walked quickly out of earshot. At the Masonic Hall, they paused. The streets were empty in the middle of the day, and no wonder, if decent women couldn't walk abroad without being insulted by ruffians in Yankee uniform. The lowest level of the building, open to the street, was a marketplace where farmers and merchants sold their goods and produce all days except Sunday.

This was Wednesday but it was deserted, except for some Yankee soldiers unloading wooden crates of supplies from several wagons. A sentry stood nearby, a bayonet fixed on his musket. A crude, hand lettered sign nailed to one of the posts that supported the overhead wooden shed roof said "supply depot". A tough looking man with many stripes on one sleeve was obviously in charge, and no untoward comments came their way. Some of the men doing the unloading stopped to stare at them for the two seconds that passed before a sharp word put them back to work.

Double doors led up to the Masonic Temple. They stood open. Everyone stood uncertainly. Was it safe to go on? Belle squared her shoulders and touched her revolver for reassurance. She saw that Betty and Virginia were rather scared.

"Let's go," she muttered, and the other women followed her inside. Up the broad staircase to the second floor they went, all together in a group. The large room on the second floor, which was sometimes used for public dances, was empty. In one of the small rooms to one side, they found Lucy Glenn and two other women,

Rebecca Peterman and Dottie Strother, trying to calm a young man who was deliriously tearing at his clothing and trying to get up from the straw pallet on which he lay. Nearby, another boy, no older than Belle, moaned softly.

"We are here," Belle announced. "What can we do?"

"Grab an arm or a leg," said Lucy Glenn, one of Belle's multitude of cousins, and a practical girl. She was kneeling, pressing both hands against the sick boy's shoulders. It was a struggle. He was delirious and combative. Belle could see that Lucy's hair, normally impeccable, was disarrayed, and she was breathing hard.

It was the kind of physical contact that the censorious Mrs. Pruitt had worked so hard to prevent the day before — until one of the older ladies had pointed out that nursing was not possible without it, and that the wounded were hardly a threat to anyone's virtue. At which point Mrs. Pruitt had declared her unwillingness to be a part of such an immoral enterprise, and had gone off in a huff.

Belle knelt down and captured a flailing leg. Betty caught the other one. "Goodness," said Virginia weakly. "What's the matter with him?"

"We're hoping it's not Typhoid," said Rebecca Peterman grimly. The thought gave them all pause. Typhoid, like Yellow Fever, was a deadly killer. And no one knew what caused it.

"What should we do?"

"Well, they can't stay here. The Yankees want it for their own men," Dottie Strother fretted.

"Give me a hand here, Ginny," Belle said, and Virginia sat down just as the boy stopped moving suddenly.

"Has he passed?" asked Betty fearfully.

Belle got to her feet and looked around. "No. Honey, you and Missy go and get Sam and Nathaniel and two other hands. Tell them to bring small beds or something else we can move them on."

"Yes, Miss Belle," the servant said and ran out the door followed closely by Missy, who belonged to Betty Doll.

"Oh, look," Betty said, giggling.

They turned and did so. The other boy's blanket had slipped down and revealed a lack of any clothing besides his linen shirt. Virginia and Betty stared, fascinated.

"Oh, for pity's sake," Dottie Strother snapped. "Haven't you girls ever been on a farm? "

Virginia and Betty had loosened their grips on the first boy's legs, and were blushing furiously. Suddenly spasms shook his body and they grabbed on again.

Dottie, married and the mother of several children, knelt and touched his forehead. "He's burning up!"

Suddenly, from below, came the sound of booted steps, marching up the stairs like thunder and entering the room. Three Yankees. A Union Captain, who held a large American flag on a standard, and two privates with muskets.

They paused in the middle of the large room and then turned as one and advanced to where the women and their patients were. They wore Zouave uniforms with bright red baggy trousers and tight dark blue waistcoats and kepi caps. Volunteers, rather than regulars.

"I heard there were Rebels here," the Captain said, waving the flag over the prostrate bodies of the two boys. "I arrest you on charges of treason, and hope you get the hanging you deserve, you damned Rebels!"

Belle stepped forward angrily, "Why, sir, these boys are as helpless as infants and have, as you may see, no power to reply to your insults."

The Captain, a very short, dark-haired imitation of Napoleon, with a mustache that stood sharply out from the sides of his head, stared up at her. "And, pray, who may you be, miss?"

Suddenly too angry to speak, Belle simply stared at him as if he were a particularly loathsome bug.

"A Rebel lady," said Eliza, with heat. That startled the other women in the room. Servants did not speak that way.

"A damned independent one, anyway," said the little Captain. He bent over the delirious man and looked closely.

"Well, he's no threat," he admitted. "Neither is the other one. What do you ladies propose to do with them?"

With difficulty, Belle regained her composure. "We must move them. Perhaps you could provide the means."

"I'm not detailing my men to carry Rebs, even sick ones."

"Our servants will do that," Belle said.

"Your slaves, you mean!" said the little Captain with a sneer. Obviously an Abolitionist.

"We don't call them that," said Betty Doll, and looked at him in a way that made him flush and stammer. "Captain," she said, taking his arm, "Can't you simply lend us some of those folding beds you have?"

The Captain, dazed, said, "They're called litters, Miss."

"But couldn't you?"

Belle watched this exchange with growing amusement, as did the other women, as Betty sank the hook deeper still. "We would be ever so grateful," she simpered, fluttering her eyelids.

The Captain puffed up like a young rooster then, and ordered the privates to go get two litters. The two sick boys would be moved to a large room in the Peterman house across the street from Belle's home.

Walking home beside the litters, each born by two strong Negro men, Belle wondered if this was how sick Confederate soldiers were to be treated when they fell into Union hands. It made her furious.

The Doll sisters were uncharacteristically silent for much of the walk. Finally, Betty said, "He was quite handsome, wasn't he? That Captain."

Virginia looked at her sidewise and smiled, "Yes, he was. Do you fancy him?"

Betty twirled her parasol once more and smiled just a little. "I don't know. He looks interesting."

"By which you mean you can wrap him around your little finger," replied her sister with a laugh.

Betty pretended to inspect that finger through her glove and said, "You think so? Yes, he might fit."

Belle couldn't believe what she was hearing. "You can't be thinking of consorting with these invaders?" she asked indignantly.

Betty and Virginia looked at each other, and then at her. "Some of us don't see them that way, Belle. Our family is for the Union. As far as we know, they are here to put down a rebellion by vandals like Ashby and Jackson. Look at the damage they've done. Must be millions," Virginia inclined her head towards the smoking rail cars that crowded the B & O tracks at the end of Race Street.

"Don't speak ill of the dead," Belle said.

"Who is dead?"

"Dick Ashby."

Betty paused and bowed her head. "Poor Harriet," she added.

Belle turned her head and stared at her, "Harriet?"

"Yes, Harriet Caperton, over to Fauquier County. He came back to marry her."

"He came back to fight for Virginia!" Belle replied, a bit angry now, "Nothing more."

Betty and Virginia looked at her and then at each other, their faces quizzical and their minds obviously racing. Gossip was their favorite sport.

"He wrote her from Fort Cobb, in the Indian Territory," Betty said. "Perhaps he wrote to you as well?"

Oh, she's quick, Belle thought, *and looking for scandal*. She managed an easy smile. "No, but I saw him two weeks past when he came up from Richmond to join Henry's brave company."

"I see," Virginia smiled maliciously, "And what did you talk about?"

"Horses," Belle replied and saw how disappointed they were that she told the truth. Then she ventured to ask the question that buzzed at the back of her mind. "This Miss Caperton — did they have intentions?"

"No, more like intentions to have intentions. He hadn't asked her father or anything like that. It was early days for them," Virginia said.

"And now it's too late for them, which is so sad," Betty added.

And for me, Belle thought, and then, *did I wait too long?*

Virginia, always the practical one of the pair, observed, "If all the good Southern men are going to go off and get themselves killed, we need to be nice to the Yankees."

"Yes," Betty agreed, very serious now, "Husbands are hard enough to come by. Good respectable ones, that is."

"So just the officers, then?" Virginia said.

"Oh, of course," Betty agreed.

Belle shook her head in dismay. "I thought you were both true to the South. You went to do hospital work...."

"Those boys are our neighbors, so that was simple Christian charity," said Betty.

"And very educational," added Virginia slyly, glancing sideways at the boy whose shirt had ridden up. "One does not normally see that side of a man."

She and Betty giggled together.

Belle simply didn't know what to think. She had known these girls all their lives, and now felt as if she didn't know them at all.

"With all due respect to Dick Ashby, that brave handsome man," Virginia added softly, "Some of us still love the Union and hope to see it stand."

Belle stared. "You never said so."

"Captain Ashby and the other Rangers arrest men who speak out. They put poor old John Strother, who never did anyone any harm, in jail simply because he's an old Whig who spoke up for Lincoln." Betty returned Belle's stare until she looked away.

"That was wrong," Belle admitted. "The passions of the moment...."

"Overrule judgement and fairness," Betty finished.

"But we are still friends?"

"Certainly," said Betty with a smile.

"How could it be otherwise?" Virginia asked.

Behind them they heard someone running. The three of them turned to look. Eliza, who had stayed behind to help the other servants clean the room where the sick boys had been, caught up with them.

"Dem Yankee soldiers," she said, between gasps for air, "Dey broke into de distillery and took de whisky."

Belle looked over to the railyard towards where the distillery was. It was too far away to see with all the houses in the way. How many men would a barrel of whiskey serve? There were thousands of them already in the town and lots of barrels.

The hollowness of fear bloomed in her stomach. "They will all be drunk tomorrow," she said, and added, with considerable understatement, "That does not bode well."

CHAPTER THREE

July 4, 1861, Martinsburg, Virginia

Belle woke, not to the rooster's crow, but to the sound of distant gunfire. Groggy, because she'd slept badly, she groped for the revolver on the nightstand, found it, and struggled to her feet. The thin cotton nightdress clung to her stickily in places. The room was already oppressively hot and humid.

Eliza glided into the room, carrying a pitcher of very warm water. At the sight of the pistol in Belle's hand, she laughed.

"Ain't you a sight!"

Belle frowned, stepped over to the mirror, still holding the Colt, and smiled ruefully at the way her hair was disarrayed.

"Would you bring me a cup of hot coffee and a bit of bread?" she asked, falling into her morning routine.

"Ain't got no coffee, Miss Belle. All gone."

Belle sighed, remembering. There was none, not even in the store stock. "Tea, then?"

"Yes'm," said Eliza.

"What was that shooting?" Belle asked, as she pulled the cotton shift over her head and prepared to wash herself.

"Yankees. Dey all Pennsylvania boys, mostly Irish and Germans," Eliza said with a disdainful sniff. "Drunk."

Belle examined her image critically in the mirror.

The Doll sisters might tease her and call her "our Amazon", but men now took immediate notice. Most didn't seem interested in her face all that much. Their eyes usually rested further down on her most obvious attractions. Who needed "pretty"?

Pouring a bit of the lavender-scented warm water into a basin and taking a clean rag in one hand, she began to carefully wash herself, wiping the accumulated sweat from under her heavy, full breasts, and then scrubbed her neck, face and under her arms.

More ragged gunfire came from the center of town, along with the bleating of a brass band badly in need of practice.

"Goodness," asked Belle, "What's all that?"

"It be the Fourth of July, Miss Belle. Independence Day."

Belle looked around her room, at the new Confederate flag and the banners displayed along with portraits of Jefferson Davis and General Beauregard, unframed, which she had put up when the war started. It was a tasteful array.

Belle was suddenly angry again at the Yankees, and also at Dick Ashby for getting himself killed so foolishly and for writing Harriet Caperton all those years he'd been gone, and not remembering her.

She turned to Eliza as the Yankee brass band found its musical footing and began to play a recognizable march.

"Their independence, not ours," she said. "We are invaded and occupied and I see nothing to celebrate about that."

"No, ma'am," Eliza said, her face impassive. Belle turned back to the mirror, picked up a brush and began to angrily brush the tangle of long red hair. This hurt, but excused the tears in her eyes.

Once dressed, she hefted the Colt and slid it into the holster across her belly. It was more than fourteen inches long, weighed more than three pounds loaded, and spoiled the line of her dress, but she wore it anyway. She went down the back stairs two at a time into the kitchen, making quite a bit of noise. Her mother looked up with a frown at her unladylike descent. William could get away with this as a small boy, but better behavior was expected of her. Her mother sighed and went back to the work in front of her. She was going over the accounts.

Belle sat down at the table, saw there was coffee after all and poured herself a cup. One taste of the bitter brew told her that it wasn't anything close to coffee. "Gah! What is this?"

"Chicory," Mary replied, "And roasted wheat hulls. Something that Mrs. Peterman told me about. Do you like it?"

"Not much," Belle choked, "It's awful!"

"It is what we have," Mary replied calmly. "We will have to make do. In fact, there will be a great deal of making do in the times ahead. We are not getting our regular supplies from Richmond, or even from Shepherdstown, and I'm not sure how we would pay for them, if we did." Mary looked at her daughter and sighed, "We have people who owe us money and can't, or won't, pay." She slid a small stack of stiff cardboard account forms across the table. Belle recognized the names.

"What do these triangles in the corner mean?"

"Masons, like your father. Part of the grand brotherhood. He gives them better terms and prices, and they pretty much buy all they need from him. It's good business. Or it was. With all of them off in the Army, it's left to their wives and servants to take care of their business affairs. The servants can't read or figure, most of 'em, and the wives mostly aren't up to keeping track. It's a mess. Last night I told Sam and Nathan to take the store sign down and hide it."

"We're closing the store?"

"Yes and no. Our neighbors know where we are, and since we don't have that much on hand, we'll save it for them. I neither want nor can afford to seek Yankee custom. I 'spect that we're going to be doing a lot of barter to get by."

Belle looked over to where her brother William sat, sulking and tearful. "What's wrong with Willy?"

Mary shook her head. "He can't get it through his head that, Fourth of July or no, he can't go out and ramble around today with his friends, not with all those drunken Yankees everywhere." She sighed again, exasperated, "Can you do something with him?"

Belle tried very hard to think of a reason why she couldn't. Failing to find one that would past muster, she smiled brightly, and said, "Certainly. We can read together. Would you like that, Will?"

"Not much," he said sulkily.

"It will have to do, William. None of us are going out today, much less to a Yankee celebration," Mary said, her patience clearly at an end.

"None of us?" Belle said with dismay.

"None," said Mary. "Betty told me about the rude attention you got yesterday — she was quite concerned. And about Harriet

Caperton."

"Who? " Belle asked innocently.

Mary reached out and took her hand. "Darlin', you were a child when Dick Ashby went out west. Whatever made you think...."

"He carried my favor at tournaments," Belle said, again feeling tears well up, "And I'm a woman now."

"Yes," Mary agreed. "Impulsive, heedless, but not wanton. You don't need to be throwing yourself at no-accounts like the Ashbys. Tournament." She shook her head and bent to her accounts once more, "That was a game. Just a game. How could you imagine...?"

She sighed and looked up at her, speaking very firmly now, "I don't want you further exposed to the kind attentions of our Yankee guests. If we leave them alone, they'll leave us alone. You help William with his reading."

And that was that. Belle tried to put the best face on it that she could. She even let William choose the book. It was Fenimore Cooper's **"The Spy"**, an old boy's tale set during the Revolution, ornately written, which, as Belle read aloud, with the proper dramatic flourishes, began to pique her interest. Its theme of partisan warfare — men protecting their homes and families from the overwhelming tyranny of the British — could not help but resonate with her present mood and desires.

It was the very way local men like Ashby and her father proposed to fight this war, as guerrillas, but the West Point men like Jackson, who had been appointed to lead that brigade, had their own ideas.

There were parallels between the scenes in the novel and this new war. Not everyone was on the same side. Some were loyalists, the way that the Doll sisters had declared their family to be for the Union the day before.

William listened carefully for a while and then became bored and sleepy. Belle, her throat sore, handed him the book to read and, as he was less than a polished orator, gave him leave to continue silently, sitting by his side as he traced the lines of type with his finger.

Her own thoughts were on the war. Virginia hoped to prevail by stern resistance, but had been unable to stem the tide of Yankee volunteer regiments marching down from Pennsylvania and New York. The hastily assembled Southern forces were overwhelmed.

Partisan warfare — a guerilla fighter behind every bush and knoll — was supposed to hold them back. Yet it had not. Belle puzzled as to why, but could find no easy answers. Rather than fight to defend Martinsburg, they had fallen back; not running, it was true, but not fiercely resisting the Yankee incursion either.

Belle was still very upset, but maintained an outward calm. Her little sister, Mary, who was four, played with dolls near the fireplace, as William stumbled across the harder words. Belle looked at her fondly, too young and innocent to be caught up in the terrible events that had overtaken them.

The morning dragged on, and then Eliza was in the room, just before the noon hour, her eyes wide and filled with fear.

"What is it?" Belle asked anxiously. Eliza was not given to hysterics or exaggeration the way some servants were.

"Yankees comin' down de street, with guns and whisky."

That said it all. Alarmed, Belle got to her feet and went to the window, while trying to keep William from doing the same thing. She saw a party of men in the same Zouave uniforms as she had seen the day before. Their red trousers were dirty and their waistcoats and hats were askew. They carried their muskets carelessly in one hand, and were passing a jug of whisky around.

They were loud, boisterous, and mean. She watched with horror as one of them discharged his musket right at the Doll's house next door. The front window shattered, provoking feminine shrieks of anger and dismay.

Another Yankee fired into the Boyd's house, breaking an upstairs window. Belle tried to remember if there were any pieces of window glass left in the store. Her grandmother, very alarmed, came running in from the kitchen, followed by her mother and Della the cook. Together, they pulled Belle away from the window.

The Union soldiers laughed uproariously and passed the jug once more. One of them, with the chevrons of a Sergeant on his sleeve, consulted a piece of paper and then looked right at the Boyd's front door.

Belle was outraged, feeling both fear and anger. Someone in town had given their address. The county was more for the Union than against it, so it might have been any sneak or informer seeking favor from the invaders.

The Sergeant lurched slightly and then walked towards their front door with great determination. Mary came into the front room, her pistol in her hand.

"William, git upstairs!"

"But, Mama...."

"Git! Now!"

William got, carrying little Mary with him, just as the Sergeant began pounding on the door. Mary looked at the pistol in her hand and put it aside. Opening a drawer in the hall table, she hid it under a pile of papers. Belle moved into the front hallway behind her, just as Mary opened the door, causing the Sergeant, about to renew his pounding with fresh vigor, to almost fall into the room.

He recovered, lurched, and stared at her owlishly. Belle marvelled that he could stand at all.

"Your pardon, madam," he said, and slurred the words out slowly. "You be the Boyds?"

The accent was Irish. His breath betrayed his breakfast of whisky. Since the Boyd name was carved over the door, there was no point in denying it.

"Yes, what of it?"

"Got orders to search." He waved at the others behind him. "Come on boys."

Suddenly they were all in the house, milling around in the parlor, peering at the pictures on the wall and the books and knickknacks on the shelves. It was the best room in the house, with real wallpaper on the long wall, painted bright yellow otherwise to encourage conversation and filled with all of the little treasures that defined the family as upper class. One trooper, with an unintentional and thoughtless sweep of a rifle butt, brought a vase of flowers crashing to the floor next to the fireplace.

Mary lost her temper, "How dare you! Get out!"

She saw another soldier begin to pocket a silver-framed photograph, "And put that back!"

Belle tried to think of what to do. She felt helpless. And then angry again as she recognized two of the men as members of the detail that had made rude comments about her near the Catholic church.

The Sergeant, blinking and with that great calm that drunks sometimes have, tried to explain to her, "We heard you got Rebel flags and other trash and we come to con..con..con...."

"Con-fis-ticate," said a third soldier, his English markedly accented with German. He leered at Belle and gave a broad wink.

Behind her, Belle felt rather than saw Eliza dart up the front stairs. That spurred her to action. She moved forward and, face to face with the German boy, said, "You men have no right here. Get out!" She pushed hard against his shoulder with little effect.

The boy, also drunk, sneered at her, "Damn S'sesh. We heard about you."

Mary spun around, trying to track all of them. They were opening drawers, looking behind pictures, putting their dirty hands everywhere on her clean furniture.

Upstairs, Eliza ripped down the flags and emblems, bundled them up in her arms, ran down the back stairs and into the kitchen where she threw them all into the big iron stove. They caught fire slowly. Della, the cook and Mary's personal servant, helped her make sure they all burned completely.

Finally Mary was forced to give way, and let the Union soldiers search. It wasn't legal. It wasn't fair. But there were too many of them with guns — and they were all drunk and dangerous.

On the verge of tears, she looked for Belle and saw her just as Eliza came back in and whispered in her ear. Belle nodded and smiled briefly at her mother. The Sergeant and two others ascended the front stairs. Soon they could hear their footsteps overhead, clumsy and wanton, and the sound of another vase hitting the floor and shattering.

Mary gave a wordless cry and bit her fist, almost besides herself. Belle was entirely calm, looking at each man carefully to remember his face, her hands tucked under her apron. Eliza tried to make herself invisible.

Finally, the Sergeant came back down the stairs and into the parlor, sour and dissatisfied. "Okay, missus, yer got no subversive things here."

"Now," said Mary with a calm she did not feel, "Will you please tell your men to put back the items they have appropriated, and please leave?"

The Sergeant gave her a mean grin, "Ah, missus, yer wouldn't begrudge me lads the odd souvenir, would yer?"

Mary stared at him, amazed at the effrontery.

"And there's one more thing," the Sergeant continued and called to one of his men. "Sean, bring that flag."

Two more of the men, one carrying a Union flag which he unfurled, came forward. "We'll just be putting this on your roof, to show how loyal you are."

"You will not!" Mary replied with quiet fury as Belle and Ruth moved next to her. "Men, every member of my family shall die before you raise that flag over us!"

"Have it your way," the Sergeant said, as the German boy brutally pushed her down, knocking her to the floor.

"Ye old bitch," he snarled, and moved to strike her again.

And was stopped by the sound of a gunshot. Looking down, he saw blood running freely from a wound in his belly. Shocked, he dropped his musket, which clattered to the floor. He fell backwards into the arms of his fellows, who seemed extremely surprised at what had occurred.

They all turned and saw Belle, behind a cloud of gunsmoke, pull back the hammer on the revolver grasped firmly in her hand and level it at the Sergeant, who turned white with fear.

To Belle it seemed to take forever for her to draw the Colt and fire it. The whole world slowed down. Everything was tinged with red and she could hear her own voice as a distant echo when she told the Sergeant, "Get out! All of you! And take that trash with you!"

Carrying their wounded comrade, the Union soldiers left in haste, pausing only to pick up the fallen musket. Belle closed and bolted the door, then put the Colt on a side table and knelt down to her mother. Mary stared at her and then hugged her.

The enormity of what she had just done fell on Belle like an avalanche. She collapsed the rest of the way to the floor, in shock.

"What have I done?" she whispered.

CHAPTER FOUR

After a moment, Belle composed herself. She and her mother, with help from Eliza and Della, got up from the floor and began to look at the damage done by the Yankees. Mary's lips formed a thin, angry line. Her grandmother Ruth muttered under her breath, something that sounded very much like profanity.

Mary said, "Isabelle. You have done nothing wrong here. I should have shot one of them myself."

The parlor, usually so neat, was half destroyed. They could not immediately see what had been stolen. Everything was in disarray, and, in their haste to leave, the Union soldiers had knocked over two small tables, scattering their contents across the floor. Della started to pick up some of the fallen items.

"Leave it," said Mary, "I want witnesses to the destruction. Go over to...."

They heard hasty footsteps overhead. William came tearing down the front stairs, very excited.

"Mama, them bastards is getting ready to fire the house!"

"William, your language...," Mary began, and then realized what he had said. She frowned grimly and went to the drawer where she'd hidden the Colt revolver. Belle ran to the window and pulled aside a curtain.

Outside, the man she had shot was stretched out on the street, with two other soldiers attending him. There was quite a lot of blood. One of them stood up, shaking his head.

The sergeant, his face set in a hard frown, stared at the house with absolute hatred. Between swigs from the jug resting on his left arm, he directed the other men as they piled pieces of wood against the house. One kneeled with a flint and steel, trying to get a spark in some dried grass.

Belle drew her own revolver, and moving quickly, intercepted her mother before she got to the front door. "Give me that gun, Mama. You can't hit the broad side of a barn."

Mary started to argue, then looked at her own mother, who simply gave her a short, affirmative nod. Seeing Belle was determined, Mary handed her the other Colt. Belle hefted the revolvers in both hands. She took a deep breath as Eliza rushed up to open the door.

With a nod from her, Eliza pulled the door back and Belle stepped outside. A great calm came over her as she calculated the odds against her. She had only two more shots than there were soldiers.

"You men!" she shouted. "Stop what you are doing right now!"

The sergeant and other Union soldiers gaped at her. One raised his musket. Belle took deliberate aim with the revolver in her right hand and fired, clipping his left ear. Howling in pain, he dropped the musket and clutched the bleeding ear. He was little more than a boy, she saw. Tears came to his eyes.

The sergeant grinned sickly, "Damn fine shooting, miss."

"Not really," Belle replied, her voice almost sweet. "I meant to kill him, as I mean to kill all of you, if you do not leave off this thing right now!"

I must stay calm! I dare not show the panic and excitement I feel! Trickles of sweat ran down her spine. Her heart raced madly. Taking another deep breath, she tried to smile, which made the Yankees regard her even more fearfully.

The sergeant and his men backed away into the middle of Queen Street. They began to whisper among themselves, watching her carefully.

"Nathan!" Belle shouted.

Nathan, a rangy Negro youth of fourteen who was Della's son and who usually helped Sam with his work, stepped out of the door behind her cautiously, gaping at the Yankee soldiers.

"Yes, Missy Belle?"

"Go find a Yankee officer. Bring him here."

"Yes, ma'am," Nathan said. He ran as fast as he could for the center of town.

The sergeant had sobered considerably and had even dropped

his jug of whisky, which clattered on the pavement spinning around and around. He looked at Belle, calculating his chances and saw that they were not good.

"You're a Rebel in arms, miss. That's a hanging offense."

"Are there no laws in your Army? You've attacked innocent civilians. I think you're the one likely to hang."

Belle's mouth was dry. She stood there, both revolvers steady and aimed at them, cocked and ready to fire, willing her arms to not be dragged down by their weight, as the Yankee soldiers watched for any moment of weakness.

Lord above, she thought, *I may have to kill them all.*

If they rushed her....

Virginia and Betty Doll, each carrying one of their father's shotguns, suddenly appeared on their own porch next door. Then Sam, and the Peterman's man, Zeke, were nearby, each holding a shotgun at port arms. Both looked scared, but their presence was a sobering sight to the Union soldiers, who unconsciously began to draw together into a small group, looking all about them, clutching their muskets tight against their chests.

A Union captain rode up on a fine bay mare, followed by a brace of lieutenants, also on horseback, and a squad of infantry moving at double-quick pace. The captain said nothing and took his time getting off his horse, then raised his gloved hands to show that he was not armed. The two lieutenants remained mounted, although one of them leaned over to speak quietly with the sergeant in charge of the squad they had brought with them.

Everyone began speaking at once and the Union captain raised his hand for silence. He looked directly at Belle.

"Miss," he said calmly, "Will you please point those weapons at the ground?"

"I will, sir, if you will guarantee our safety. Who are you?"

"Captain James Gwyn. 23rd Pennsylvania Volunteers. I'm Provost Marshal here." He was dark-haired, neat and clean-shaven except for a large mustache, Belle saw, and completely sober.

"Provost Marshal? What is that?" Belle didn't lower the revolvers. Her arms ached terribly.

"It's a kind of policeman, miss, for the Army."

"If you're the police, then arrest these men."

Captain Gwyn studied her. He took several slow, deliberate steps towards her. "I may, when the facts are known. Now if you would be so kind...," he held his hands out for the revolvers.

Instead of handing them to him, Belle folded her arms so that they aimed straight up. Gwyn looked at the man laying in the street.

"He dead?" he asked.

"I certainly hope so," Belle spat out. "He struck a defenseless woman while house breaking."

Gwyn favored her with a small smile, "You hardly strike me as defenseless, miss."

"My mother, sir. He struck my mother."

Gwyn's face became grave. "That is indeed a serious matter."

"And they were about to burn us out."

Gwyn looked over to the pile of wood and saw that it was so.

"I see," he turned. "Lieutenant Kelley!"

"Sir!"

"Take all of these men prisoners for investigation. Keep them under silence and march them back to headquarters. Separate them there for interviews."

"Sir, I will." Kelley dismounted and, taking some of the men in the detail, began rounding up the men who had invaded the Boyd house. Hands on top of their heads, they were marched raggedly away. One or two, still drunk, complained bitterly and were cuffed into silence for their trouble.

"You need not fear them further," Gwyn said, with a reassuring smile. "Now, if you will give me those pistols."

Belle smiled at him and said softly, "But, sir, how will we defend ourselves? Those men have friends, I have no doubt. They may take revenge."

"We will protect you," Gwyn said.

Belle gave a tinkling, ladylike laugh. "You've done so well so far."

Gwyn smiled again. "Lieutenant Preston!"

"Sir!" said the other officer.

"I want sentries on this house, around the clock. Two men at a time with orders to see that this lady and her mother are not further annoyed."

"Yes, sir! At once, sir!" Lieutenant Preston got off his horse and, taking two of the soldiers, posted one at the front of the house and sent one around to the rear, talking quietly to them, pointing out the boundaries of their patrol. Belle noticed that these men also wore Zouave uniforms, but with dark blue trousers and jackets and a light blue vest. Obviously not from the same regiment as those who had invaded their house. Gwyn and the two lieutenants wore the blue sack coats and straight leg trousers of regulars. She hoped very much that they were.

"Now, miss," said Gwyn, "The pistols?"

Reluctantly, suspecting that she would never see them again, Belle handed them over, reversing them and presenting them grip first and uncocked. "They took items from the house, you know."

Gwyn grimaced. "I will try to recover them for you," he said. "Men of the 7th Regiment discovered a considerable quantity of whisky yesterday and it was ordered destroyed."

"And they drank it instead?"

"The 7th was formed in Harrisburg, mostly of Irish boys. From their point of view, there was no better way to destroy it than by passing it through their bodies."

Gwyn shook his head sadly. "Of course, once other regiments heard about it, the contagion became general. Do not judge us too harshly. These are 90-day men, units raised quickly for the emergency and trained *en route*. There is a singular lack of discipline. They are not regulars."

"Thank God for that," Belle replied. "You will note that our army is a disciplined force. General Beauregard would never permit his men to get so out of hand."

"I know Captain Beauregard," Gwyn said. "He's a fine officer. West Point man."

"You provoke me, sir," Belle said. "He's a General now, if you'll do us the courtesy."

"He may have the title, miss, but does he have the skill? That's yet to be seen." Gwyn hefted the two Colt revolvers. "You have the makings of a soldier yourself."

Along Queen Street, things were quiet now. The Doll sisters had retreated into their house as soon as Gwyn had appeared on the scene. Sam and Zeke had likewise made themselves invisible. Belle sensed rather than saw the many eyes of her neighbors peeking through curtains.

An ambulance drawn by two horses pulled up. The dead soldier's body was placed on a litter and carried away.

Gwyn watched Belle's face carefully. "I will need to put you under house arrest, Miss...."

"Boyd. Belle Boyd. Why? What have I done, except defend my home?"

"You've killed a man," Gwyn said.

Belle suddenly felt weak in the knees. The weight of her act oppressed her, but, feeling Gwyn's eyes looking at her so carefully, she simply shook her head and looked away, offering no excuse and no repentance.

Gwyn said, his voice calm and gentle, "It seems that you were quite within your rights, but the matter will have to be investigated. Until that time, I will trouble you not to go abroad without a written pass from me."

"That hardly seems fair," Belle said.

"Fair don't enter into it," Gwyn said tiredly. "None of it is fair. What it is, is war."

Belle pouted, "But how shall I see my friends?"

"Your friends may call on you, and I will have my Lieutenants call as well. You will not lack for company."

"And your investigation...."

"Will be done with all dispatch. We are awaiting orders for further movement, so it must be."

Belle raised her chin proudly. "I await your judgement then, sir."

Gwyn touched his hand to the brim of his hat in a kind of salute. "Your servant, miss."

The following days were anxious ones for the Boyd household. Virginia and Betty Doll were daily visitors, as was Rebecca Peterman, who reported that one of the Confederate soldiers in her care had died of fever, but that the other was on the mend.

Lieutenants Preston and Kelley also became regular visitors, welcomed with grave courtesy, and grateful that Belle did not immediately show them the door. Preston was a shy boy of 19, and seemed well brought up. Kelley was originally from County Cork, with a droll sense of humor that often had Belle and her mother helpless from laughter. Even her grandmother granted him an occasional amused smile. They all found him very likable, for a Yankee.

Finally, Belle and her mother, along with other witnesses, including Eliza, were summoned to Union headquarters, where a Union Colonel named Birney took charge of the matter.

At this hearing several other officers and a large muscular man in a fine hand-tailored suit and a top hat were in the room. Belle had not seen him much in recent years since she had been away at school, but her mother's indignant gasp of "Hill!" identified him as Ward Hill Lamon, who had been born in Martinsburg, but now lived in Illinois, where he practiced Law. He was rumored to be among the blackest of Black Republicans now; a Union man to his very core.

"Hill, why are you here?" her mother demanded angrily.

"I was in town on other business," Lamon replied, his face sad, his elegant top hat held before him almost like a shield. "I heard about this bit of difficulty Belle has fallen into, and thought...."

"You're a Yankee lawyer now? Are you here to prosecute the case?" Mary asked sharply.

"No, Mary. I am simply here to observe. This is a military court. I have no standing here. But, if I can use my poor influence...."

"For whom?" Belle asked nervously, not liking the idea one bit.

Lamon did not answer, but stared at her in a measuring way that sent a chill down her spine. He had known her all her life, and now seemed like a stranger; no longer the jolly "Uncle Hill" she recalled from childhood.

"Mister Lamon is here for Mister Lincoln," Colonel Birney said. Belle noticed that he, unlike Gwyn and the other officers, was attired as a Zouave, but with a dark blue frock coat.

Mary's voice went slightly higher, "Mister Lincoln! Abe Lincoln? What does he have to do with this?"

"He is the Commander in Chief," said Colonel Birney, "And the ultimate authority over us all."

Belle wanted to refute that idea angrily, but outward calm and grace were the better tactics. She mustered her sweetest smile. "Then let us proceed."

She and Mary took their seats and waited while Captain Gwyn, without notes, gave a remarkably accurate account of what he had seen. Colonel Birney, acting as judge, asked questions of him, of Kelley and Preston, and then of Mary, Belle, and, finally, Eliza.

Eliza was taken aback when her testimony was asked. It would have never happened in a Virginia court, where slaves had no more standing than a horse or a pig.

In the end, Colonel Birney said, "Self-defense, plain and simple. You don't have to be a Philadelphia lawyer to see that." Obviously Birney was a Philadelphia lawyer, since Gwyn smiled politely at the joke and Hill Lamon managed a polite chuckle. Belle and Mary were told that they were free to go.

As they walked home Mary said angrily, "I never thought I'd see the day when Hill Lamon would turn against his own."

Belle, surprised, looked at her mother and saw that she was quietly furious. "Hasn't he always been our friend?"

Mary laughed bitterly. "I always thought so. He courted me when we were younger than you are. I chose your father, and he moved away to Illinois. Became a lawyer, I heard, but was never sure, because no one from his family will admit knowing him now."

"Why?"

"Isn't it obvious? He became one of Lincoln's law partners, and is now his lackey. He's come back to lord that over us and to make trouble." They walked on in silence for several blocks.

As they approached their house Belle said, "Mama, you've noticed how much these Yankee boys like my company?"

Mary sighed, "Yes. I'll be glad to be shut of them, now that the case is decided."

"Maybe we shouldn't be so quick to shut them out," Belle said thoughtfully.

Mary saw the mischief in her eyes.

"What are you up to, Isabelle?" Her tone of voice was the one used when she thought that Belle was doing something wrong.

"Me?" Belle asked with too much innocence. "Why, nothing Mama,... except I was thinking of how they like to brag to one another. I was making a list of all the regiments they're from last night."

"Why?" Mary asked suspiciously.

"I thought that perhaps Henry Ashby would like to have it. Isn't that part of scouting? Finding out which units are on the enemy side?"

Mary looked at her with a mixture of hurt and pride. "You will not be deterred, will you? Spying is a very dangerous game, Isabelle. You won't be able to tell anyone you're doing it, so consorting with those Union boys is not going to be understood by our friends. If you're caught, you might be hanged and will certainly go to jail. Think what you're risking, child!"

Belle had read **"The Spy"** over two or three times, looking for guidance, but could hardly admit that she took her inspiration for such a dangerous course from a novel. Her voice became strained as she searched for the right words to define her new passion.

"Think what Daddy, and Uncle James Glenn, and all the other brave boys and men are risking! Knowing where the enemy is will keep them from being surprised and might save their lives. I have to do this, Mama," Belle pleaded.

Mary stopped and looked away. "You know what they're already saying in town about you keeping company with these boys, even when they are imposed upon us. Think of that! You might never find a husband."

"Oh, what does that matter now?" Belle asked, exasperated. "Any man I would marry is likely to make me a widow, and what then? I cannot stand by and let this invasion go unopposed. If I can worm good information out of these Yankee officers, I might well save one or two of our boys who'll make good husbands. I surely won't marry a man who hasn't served." She set her jaw to show her determination.

Mary stared at her and suddenly threw up her hands in despair. "Lord save us," she whispered. "You're a woman grown, Belle. You must find your own way. All I can do now is pray you'll find the right one."

CHAPTER FIVE

Martinsburg, July 12, 1861

Two parcels were delivered to the Boyd house. They were carefully wrapped in brown paper and done up with coarse twine. One was addressed to Belle.

Mary greeted them with suspicion, and had them laid on the kitchen table. William started to tear at one only to have his hand slapped by his mother.

"Have a care. We need to save the paper and string."

Abashed, William stood back and watched as Mary and Belle picked at the tight knots. In a few minutes, Mary had one open. It was a wooden box with a number of items that had been stolen by the Union troops — and several which hadn't. Not from them, anyway.

Belle separated the things that they recognized and then examined the others. "I think I saw this at Dottie Strother's," she said.

Mary picked up another, a little glass figurine. "I'm pretty sure this was on the mantle at Mae Pruitt's house," she said. "Did they leave no one unmolested?"

"Dem Yankees was everywhere," Eliza said. "Dey break into everyone's houses, take dem things."

"What possible use could they have for them?" Mary asked in exasperation. "It will take weeks to sort it all out."

Belle cautiously unwrapped the package addressed to her. "Goodness!" she exclaimed, and held up a belt and holster with a Colt Dragoon revolver. In the box she also found a small powder flask, a cloth sack with lead balls, a mould for making more and a small cardboard box full of percussion caps. She picked up a note that fell to the floor.

"To replace that which was taken from you," she read aloud. "It's not signed."

Mary frowned and looked at her mother, who had joined them.

"Don't look a gift horse in the mouth," is all Ruth said.

"Well," said Belle, after a moment, "These Yankee officers do not lack for courtesy, no matter how brutish their men might be."

"You should send it back. It may be a pretext for them to search the house again," Mary said.

Belle looked at her mother. "How? I don't know who sent it. This is a fearsome piece of artillery, Mama. A .44 caliber, and almost new." She took it from the holster, rubbed a finger on the handsome brass mountings, tried the action, and then laid it carefully on the table. "What if we hide it and save it for the next bunch of Yankees?"

Mary's frown deepened, "Where would you hide it?"

"I'll give it to Eliza to hide."

Mary couldn't argue with that. She'd entrusted her jewelry and the family silver to her own servant, Della. Della had been with her since her 12th birthday and was "family". Eliza, having married Sam, was now equally trusted.

Della smiled and looked up from her cooking. "Eliza know de good places, too," was all she said.

Eliza accepted the assignment calmly. "Give 'em to me. I find de place," she said and gathered it all up. She went out of the room.

"I must write a note to Captain Gwyn," said Belle, "Thanking him for his kindness."

"If you must," Mary said, looking depressed. "You still propose...."

"Yes, Mama."

Eliza and Della looked at one another, their faces impassive. Eliza left without a word. Della returned to her cooking. Belle found a piece of paper and a pencil and began to write carefully, in the pretty hand that she had learned in school, making her loops full and well rounded. Mary and Ruth took some of the recovered things into the front room.

Eliza came back in a few minutes, just as Belle was finishing the note. "You wan' me take dat?"

"Yes," said Belle as she folded it and wrote Gwyn's name on the outside, and then looked up at her. "Eliza? How would we get a note to my father? Does anyone know where their camp is?"

"Slaves know," Della said, when Eliza hesitated. "We know de camp. It be 'n Darketown. Massas are sending for dem slaves to come to dere."

"Why?" Belle was genuinely surprised.

"Clean dere boots, wash dere clothes, cook. Why else?"

Belle suddenly realized that many of the "gentlemen privates" of Martinsburg had yet to grasp the harsh realities of campaigning.

"Then taking some papers would be no great inconvenience," she said.

"Long way dere," said Eliza, "Sebben miles."

"Who could go?"

Della stirred the pots in front of her, thinking, "We find who go, give dem de papers."

"People go every day?" Belle asked thoughtfully.

"Pretty much. Dem men ain't gonna clean dere own boots."

Belle smiled. "See if you can get someone to carry something tomorrow, Della, and Eliza, when you return, please come up and help me get ready."

"Yes'm," Eliza said, surprised. "Fo' what?"

Belle smiled, a bit sardonically, "Why, Lieutenant Kelley has offered to escort me around the camp on a ride. Being cooped up here — well, some exercise would be very welcome."

"Yes, miss," Eliza said, her voice doubtful and looking at Della, who shrugged and continued to stir. There was no accounting for white folks and their ways.

When Belle came back downstairs, she wore her best riding habit, with her waist drawn in by her corset smaller than its normal twenty-two inches. That earned her a second look from Lieutenant Michael Kelley.

Nathan led Belle's horse, Fleeter, a black stallion about 16 hands high, out from the barn behind the house. He knelt down, cupped his hands for her foot, and Belle hoisted herself into the side-saddle easily. Inevitably, she showed some ankle, which drew Kelley's open interest.

Belle smoothed down her skirts. "Such a bother," she said. "You men have no idea how easy it is for you to ride."

Kelley lifted an eyebrow inquiringly.

"Why, think of what it's like at the gallop, sir. Sitting sideways, like a circus rider. And I do gallop. The animal requires it. He's very spirited."

Kelley grinned. "And in that he matches his mistress, I'll be bound. He's a beautiful animal. Arabian?"

"You know your horses," said Belle, favoring him with a smile. "Shall we go?" She could feel her neighbors watching.

Inwardly she quailed at what she was about to do. Not only would it not be understood, but she would never be able to explain. Already she was the object of unwanted gossip and scandal.

That, she'd learned from Fenimore Cooper's novel, was part of the game played by spies. Harvey Birch, Cooper's hero, was much misunderstood, and deliberately so, since the misunderstandings aided him in his work. She would hazard no less.

The Union sentry in front, bored, rolled a cigarette. He threw a negligent salute to Kelley. His musket was leaning against the porch rail, seemingly forgotten. Irritated, Kelley started to reprimand him.

Belle favored Kelley with a dazzling smile and put Fleeter into a trot. Kelley rushed to catch up, jumping into the saddle of his own mount.

They rode around Martinsburg, visiting all the Union Army camps. She was greeted everywhere with polite interest by young officers, mostly on horseback, all of whom wanted to meet the brave Rebel lady who had defended her home so fiercely. Kelley provided a gracious escort, making the introductions. The younger men vied for her attention, and some seemed awed at meeting her.

Belle displayed all the charm she could muster, and played the game of "flirt". She also made mental note of the names of everyone she met, inquired politely as to just what it was they did, watched troops drilling, tried to count supply and sutlers' wagons, and asked questions that she hoped seemed those of a naive dullard. The "lads", as Kelley called them, were eager to explain, all the while gazing covertly at her body rather than her face. Belle took deep slow breaths to encourage their interest.

That she could do so without choking was perhaps the one good thing about the Yankee invasion. Troops had been mustered, the local fire wagons commandeered, and the burning rubble in the railyards soaked with river water until it smoldered no more. The sodden remains were cleared away, and repairs began by a crew from the Baltimore and Ohio, under the supervision of her neighbor, Mister Doll. Belle felt both cheered and emboldened by the fresh air, and spurred Fleeter into a gallop more than once. Kelley proved equal to the challenge, keeping pace with her.

After one mile-long sprint outside of town, she and Kelley dismounted and walked their horses. "How did you come to be a Provost Marshal?" she asked.

Kelley smiled wearily. "In Philadelphia, I'm a policeman, so it seemed natural enough. I was elected First Sergeant of me company and this carried a promotion. Anything that gets me off me feet on the march is welcome."

"A policeman? How interesting," Belle said. "So you aren't a regular Army officer?"

"Me? As you can tell from the accent, I'm from the Oulde Country. Came here as a boy, half starved because of the famine, and determined that I would be an American evermore. When they called for volunteers, I was first to put me name down. Most of the lads from me neighborhood were eager to join. This is a great fine country we have and her causes are my own."

Belle studied him carefully, "Well, Virginia is my country, sir," she said softly, "And her causes are my own."

Kelley smiled at her, "And ne'er the twain shall meet?"

Belle flushed, but controlled her anger. "I think it

presumptuous of you Yankees not just to tell us how to live, but to invade our country to enforce your will over us," she said quietly.

Kelley nodded, "I can see how you would feel that way. Meself, I don't give a fig if you own slaves or not. I don't see anyone here unhappy with the arrangement, and most of the lads from my company feel the same. And we ain't an army, not yet. This lot can barely do a proper drill."

He looked off into the distance a moment and then met her eyes again. "When I was a wee lad and me pa and ma were put off the land, we lived by the side of the road awhile, shelterin' in ditches...and the British soldiers on patrol, riding their fine black horses, would come thunderin' by, jest to remind us who owned it all, and sometimes they'd leap those beasts right over us."

"You must have hated them," Belle said sympathetically.

"Nay. I was ten. I thought they were the most beautiful things I'd ever seen. I wanted to be one of them — and now I am, in an odd way. Me dad, he would rail and curse them after they were gone. Only after. He feared them too much to do it to their fat faces. Here's the hard truth, miss. We wuz worse than slaves. Yer wouldn't treat a dog or horse the way we wuz treated. We wuz starvin' — starvin' and dying. So we left Ireland, a million of us or more, and came here, to Boston and New York and Philadelphia, and, yes, New Orleans and Mobile, lookin' fer a better life. And even though we do the same kind of work there that your slaves do here, we are free and happy men — and we'll fight to give that gift of freedom to other men and to preserve this great country. That's jest the way of it."

Belle smiled at him in a teasing way. "Are you running for office, sir?"

Kelley laughed, "Not that I know of, but unlike most of me compatriots, I do not think that this is simply a stroll through the countryside. 'Tis a war with hard fighting to be done. A man who keeps his wits about him might well end up a general before all is said and done."

This declaration made Belle stare at him. Surely he could not be serious? She had met many of the officers who had left the Union Army to join that of the Confederacy. He simply was not of their class.

"You are aware that we have many West Point men in our Army?" Belle asked, "And that the homes your troops invaded belong to the men you're fighting?"

"Aye," Kelley said unhappily. "We've stained our honor. I might plead that there are two things that an Irishman could never resist and the first is whisky, but I won't. 'Twas disgraceful. That boy you killed was German, by the by, not one of the lads. His name was Frederick Martin."

Belle concealed a shock of surprise. She didn't care to know his name. It made her remember him too clearly. She was silent for a moment, aware that Kelley had done it deliberately as some kind of policeman's trick and was studying her reaction carefully. She smiled at him brightly, lowering her head flirtatiously, and cooed, "And what is the second thing no Irishman can resist?"

Kelley threw his head back and laughed. "Why bragging to a pretty girl," he said.

Belle nodded at the compliment and asked innocently, "Anything that gets you off your feet is welcome? Did you not have to walk so much when you were making your rounds as a constable?"

Kelley laughed, "Bless you miss, not for some years. I had an aptitude for the work, y'see, and was promoted long ago."

She looking at him, pretending to not understand.

"I'm a Detective-Inspector," he said after a moment.

Her worst fear. She would have to be very careful with this man. "Fascinating," she smiled, and then nodded towards the afternoon sun. "It's getting late."

"And I suppose you'll be wanting your supper," Kelley said, watching again as she used a nearby rock, about the size of a small shipping crate, to mount her horse as smoothly as any cavalryman.

"I'd ask you to join us," Belle said, "But we're short of many things and I'm sure my mother and grandmother would not find it proper."

Kelley mounted his own horse. "And what would you be needing?"

Belle stopped and considered, "A bit of coffee would be welcome." She had smelled hot coffee everywhere they'd been that day. The Union officers seemed to consume it constantly.

"Sure, now, and I'll have a hundred pounds for you in the morning. Me cousin is a quartermaster."

Belle looked at him, very surprised, "Surely you jest?"

"Not at all," Kelley assured her. "Of course, if I might further impose and bring me cousin and young Lieutenant Preston, and if you could invite those charming blonde girls from next door, then we might have a fine old time."

Belle was a bit shocked at his request. *How could I even ask?* she wondered. It could mislead the local people into thinking that she actually liked Yankees and run cover for her true purpose.

"Preston is a shy boy. How did he end up a Provost?"

"Aye, shy he is. He's reading law and his father is rich, a famous judge in Harrisburg. It may be that his father wanted no more than to keep him out of harm's way with easy duty, but he faced down a mob of about twenty men last week with nothing but a pistol on his hip and some words. There's more to him than meets the eye. He has grit."

"I will ask my mother," Belle said, "And send you a note."

A hundred pounds of coffee might go a long way towards mending fences with their neighbors. Or fill their own needs for a year.

Kelley rode with her back to her home and contrived to dismount ahead of her so that he could help her down, his strong hands on her waist, lifting her a bit from the saddle. He was that strong. She felt herself blush. It was not a disagreeable sensation to be touched in that way, but when she looked to see what was in his eyes, she saw not the ardor of young love or even male lust, but the steady speculative gaze one would expect from a doctor — or a judge.

That was unsettling.

Kelley's interest in her and all of his wit and charm and great courtesy had nothing to do with romance and everything to do with being a detective. She smiled graciously, inwardly on her guard now.

The offer of coffee won quick agreement from her mother to the party.

"A hundred pounds? That's a fortune now."

Belle said, "What do you mean?"

"Before all this started, we paid 17 cents a pound for coffee and charged 35. Now I can get three times that for it, if I have any."

"But we'd be trading with the enemy, Mama."

"Nonsense. We have to live — and they owe us compensation for all the damage they did."

Belle saw, not for the first time, why her father had become less and less active in the day-to-day business of the store, and why he had been so eager to join the army.

That night Belle spent several hours writing down everything she had seen on her ride with Michael Kelley, recounting who she had met, what they did and the numbers of troops, horses and wagons she had observed. She called to Eliza as she was sprinkling sand on the last page to dry the ink.

"Yes, Miss Belle?"

"I have a letter for Henry Ashby," Belle said. "Can you find someone to take it to him?"

"I send Sam. Dat good?"

"That's fine," said Belle, got up and started to get ready for bed. Sleepily, she tried to think how she was going to invite the Doll sisters to be at that supper for the Yankees.

It wasn't going to be easy. They might favor the Union, but consorting openly with Yankees was another matter, after all the damage done the week before. Already tongues were wagging along Queen Street about her own scandalous behavior. That she'd killed one seemed almost forgotten. It was yesterday's news.

CHAPTER SIX

Martinsburg, Virginia July 14, 1861

Belle was not particularly alarmed when a half squad of soldiers from the 23rd Pennsylvania Infantry, also known as Birney's Zouaves, marched up South Street, turned onto Queen and came to a halt before the Boyd house.

She now knew the differences in Union uniforms among the various volunteer regiments. Each had its own peculiar glory, and none lacked for style, making the stolid blue uniforms of the Regular Army look dull and pedestrian by comparison. The Yankee volunteers were as much peacocks as patriots. Not that such male vanities were confined to the Union. Zouave units had been raised in the Confederate states as well.

She knew them to be of the 23rd, from the dark blue baggy trousers and light blue vests they affected, unlike the hated men of the 7th, who had invaded her home ten days before. They wore bright red trousers and dark blue coats. No, this was Captain Gwyn's Provost Guard. Belle assumed that they had come to relieve the soldiers who now stood sentry around the Boyd house, as happened several times a day.

Four men stood at ease and the fifth, a corporal, walked up to the front door. His face was grim and unfriendly. Belle retreated from the window. There was muffled conversation at the door, and then Eliza came in, closely followed by the young corporal.

"Miss Belle...," Eliza began nervously.

The corporal cut her off, "Miss Belle Boyd?"

Belle smiled at him. He was quite handsome, well put together with bright red hair, blue eyes and a pale freckled complexion. She rose gracefully from the sofa where she had posed herself and came forward to meet him.

"Yes," she smiled, her voice low, carrying a bit of the siren's call. He stared straight ahead, declining to be charmed or even to meet her eyes.

"Your presence is required at once, miss." His voice was high and sharp.

"Where?" Belle felt a tinge of alarm come over her.

"Colonel Birney's office. I am ordered to take you there under guard."

Belle suppressed the beginnings of panic. *I must be calm*, she told herself sternly.

"Have I committed some offense?"

"That's not fer me to say, miss. I am acting under orders."

"Must I come now?"

"Yes, you must."

"Will you give me a moment to change to more appropriate attire?"

"Me orders are to bring you there forthwith, miss."

Belle studied him carefully a moment. This was serious. She was in some kind of trouble.

"May my mother accompany me?"

"No, miss."

"My maid, then,"

The Corporal was tired of the game and finally looked directly at her. "See here, Miss Boyd. Me orders are to bring you, now, and if screaming and kicking it has to be, then it will!"

Belle put her hand to her throat protectively. "Very well, then," she said. "Eliza, please fetch me my hat and a parasol."

"Yes, Miss Belle," Eliza said, her voice cracking with alarm, and almost ran from the room. Mary came in. Belle could sense Della and the other servants lurking somewhere nearby. Mary's face was more impassive than Della's normally was.

"Mama," said Belle, "Colonel Birney wants to see me."

Mary would not give this Union intruder the satisfaction of seeing her beg or plead. "I see," she said, outwardly calm.

She looked at the corporal coldly. "I will expect her to be escorted home as well."

The red-headed corporal said nothing and would not meet her eyes. Eliza came back with the hat and parasol, and helped Belle out of the apron she was wearing, then put on the hat, pinning it to her mistress's hair.

Mary's face gave no indication of her feelings, but Belle could see panic deep in her eyes. "It will be all right, Mama," she said quietly.

Belle walked proudly out the door, with the corporal following closely behind. The soldiers fell in around her and allowed Belle to set the pace, but deterred any effort of hers to delay or to wave to neighbors and friends.

Her heart beat wildly, like a trapped bird, for a few moments, but the steady walk calmed her. By the time they arrived at the 23rd's headquarters, she felt very calm indeed. Captain Gwyn stood at the door, waiting for her, which put her in a bit of a temper.

"Well, sir," she challenged him, "Am I under arrest?"

Gwyn failed to smile at her or to try to ease her fears. "Not yet," he said, his voice grave, "But you're working on it."

Belle tossed her head proudly to show a bit of defiance. A better choice than stamping her foot and showing temper. That would be childish and unladylike.

Gwyn ushered her into the Colonel's office. Belle tried to recall what she had been told about him. Birney was a plump, if active man, but not a professional soldier. A colonel by election, because of the money he had put into the enterprise.

David Birney, whose normal trade was the law, had recruited and organized the 23rd Pennsylvania himself. He'd purchased its uniforms and arms from his own pocket. The regiment had seen much marching but little actual fighting, and the ninety-day enlistment terms were running out, while the fight looked to drag on far beyond that.

"Miss Boyd. We meet again," he said, and picked up a sheet of paper from the desk. He gazed at her sternly, a parent about to discipline an unruly child. Belle decided she was too old to play that game.

"Colonel Birney," she smiled with a grace she did not feel, "Always a pleasure."

Birney waved the paper at her. "Is this yours?"

Belle knew that it was and exactly what it was: one of the two letters she had sent yesterday to the Confederate camp at Darketown.

Belle took the sheet of paper from Birney's hand, looked at it carefully, and said, "I don't recognize it." Her blue eyes met his with an unbroken stare, and her puzzled expression was a bold denial of its own.

Birney, pouncing like a prosecuting attorney, waved another piece of paper. "This is a note of thanks you wrote to Captain Gwyn for returning the items stolen from your home. Do you recognize that?"

Belle took it, looked at it and smiled, "Certainly."

"Then how do you explain that the handwriting on the first, containing vital military information, is identical to the second. It is your handwriting, is it not?"

Inwardly, Belle felt her stomach drop about a yard. Outwardly, she smiled, and said sweetly, "My dear Colonel, this is the hand all graduates of the Mount Washington Female College in Baltimore are taught to use for such letters. It proves nothing. Many local girls have attended there. It could be any of them."

Birney tugged at his beard, and then rubbed his right ear in frustration. His dark eyes blazed with fury, but he contained himself. "Captain Gwyn?"

"That may well be true, sir. I'd say insufficient proof."

Birney growled like a bear. Belle decided to distract him. "Sir, are you a Southerner? You speak like one."

Birney stared at her a long moment. "I am a citizen of the United States, Miss Boyd, as are you. I was born in Huntsville, Alabama." He rocked back and forth on his feet, "I am also an Abolitionist, as was my father before me."

Belle found this an amazing assertion. It was as though he had declared himself in league with the Devil. Indeed, his spade beard and unruly spiked hair increased the similarity. More amused than afraid, she glanced over at the unsmiling Captain Gwyn and decided this was not a time for rational discourse. These men had her in their power and could do as they pleased with her. Her only defense was that she was a woman and presumed to have neither the sense nor the responsibility of a man.

Birney pawed through the papers on his desk and pulled one out. He cleared his throat and fixed her with a intense, almost hypnotic, stare.

"This is a new regulation which I will now read to you, and after that you may consider yourself on notice that you will be bound by it."

Belle nodded, listening politely, still outwardly calm. Birney was a man of the law. He would follow it and its uses.

"From the Articles of War," Birney began portentously, "Whosoever shall give food, ammunition, information to, or aid and abet the enemies of the United States Government in any matter whatever, shall suffer death, or whatever the honorable members of the court martial shall direct."

Belle's heart increased its rhythm to a gallop at the word, 'death', but she maintained her slight and patronizing smile.

"Do you propose to bring charges?" she asked in a bored voice.

Birney threw up his hands in frustration. Gwyn, perhaps with a twinkle in his eye, replied, "Not at this time."

No, of course not, Belle thought; *if they were going to do that, I'd already be in a jail cell. They wouldn't go on about it so.*

And they were getting ready to move on. You didn't have to be a spy to see that. Everywhere, tents were being collapsed, gear cleaned, supplies distributed. They would be gone in a day or two.

"May I go?"

Colonel Birney sat down heavily, his head in his hands. "Go," he waved one hand, with a grumble, "Go. Now."

Belle bowed low and said sweetly, "Thank you, gentleman of the jury." She swept out the door, followed by Gwyn, who held his kepi cap in one hand. He placed it carefully on his head.

"Let me see you home," he said and offered his arm. Belle took it as they stepped out on the street. This was bold indeed, but, having just been threatened with death, she was beyond caring what the neighbors would think.

"I must inform you, Miss Boyd," said Gwyn, "That I am doubling the guard at your residence and neither you, your kin, nor your servants may go anywhere except under military escort."

"You do me too much honor, sir," Belle murmured.

"Also, I think that Lieutenants Kelley and Preston will no longer be permitted visits to your home that do not strictly accord with their duty, and the same is true of all of our other officers and men," Gwyn added pleasantly.

Belle actually felt a sense of relief. "That's a great pity," she said, knowing that Betty Doll would be more aggrieved than she. She had caught her and Preston kissing the night before. Lieutenant Preston was nowhere as shy as he seemed, Betty reported, her face flushed with excitement.

Kelley had been more reserved with Belle, not even venturing to hold hands when the opportunity arose. He was his usual jolly self, always quick with a joke or remark, and not by any means oblivious to her charms. She caught him gazing at her bosom several times, but he ignored any opportunity to get closer to her. Did he have a wife back in Pennsylvania, or was he just, at heart, a policeman observing a suspect?

Gwyn delivered Belle to her front door and then started to go to speak with the guards in front.

"Captain Gwyn," she called to him.

"Yes, Miss Boyd?" He turned back towards her.

"Would you call this evening and explain all of this to my mother and grandmother? We are not under total restriction are we? We may still receive visits from our friends?"

Gwyn weighed his answer; before he could reply, a horse and wagon stopped in the street and a short, gray-haired man got down from the driver's box.

"Miss Belle," the man said urgently as he rushed over to them, "I got your message."

Belle looked quickly at the wagon, which had the words "H. Turner, Veterinarian" freshly painted on the side, and recognized him at last. It was Henry Ashby.

She felt momentarily faint, but smiled and said cheerfully, "Doctor, how kind of you to come. I think Fleeter may have a bad colic."

Ashby walked right up to where she and Gwyn were standing. "Captain Gwyn, this is Doctor..."

"Henry Turner, Captain. I'm a horse doctor hereabouts."

Gwyn inspected him closely, and then took the hand he was offered.

"James Gwyn, Doctor," he said. "Are you a friend of Miss Boyd's?"

"Son, I am a friend of anyone with a sick horse or cow. Reasonable rates and fast service, that's my motto."

Belle watched, fascinated. Ashby was a gifted amateur actor. Once, a few years before, he had been prominent at tournaments as the Knight of Hiawatha, a theatrical concoction of his own device that allowed him to ride bareback as a half-naked savage Indian — and to still win the Queen's favor with his skill. This sudden apparition as an elderly horse doctor was a guise worthy of Harvey Birch.

Gwyn was entirely taken in. "Well, if you have business...," he said.

"I am so sorry to break off this conversation," Belle said with obvious insincerity, "but Fleeter, my stallion, has been so out of sorts. It may be just lack of exercise." She looked pointedly at Gwyn.

Gwyn smiled, "Well, please remember all that we talked about, Miss Boyd. Good day. Nice to meet you, Doctor Turner."

Ashby looked at him shrewdly, "Would you have anything to do with the care of horses, sir?"

"Aside from riding one," said Gwyn, "No."

"Perhaps you might tell me who does. I'm always willing to be of service."

Gwyn thought a moment. "You want Major Keenan. We have our own veterinarians, but we're moving on to Bunker Hill tomorrow, so some extra help might be welcome."

Ashby smiled his most becoming smile, "Half my usual rates to the Union Army."

"Take that up with Keenan," said Captain Gwyn, somewhat annoyed. He bowed slightly to Belle and walked away.

Chattering gaily, Belle led Ashby back to the barn, where, for appearance sake, he began to examine Fleeter.

"Who was that?" Ashby asked in a low voice, while keeping up a loud patter of horse talk for the sake of the sentry who had followed them.

"Captain Gwyn, Provost Marshal. They just hauled me in and read me the Articles of War," Belle replied, in a voice equally low.

"Hmph! Not surprised you got caught."

He leaned over and did something that caused Fleeter to give a loud, alarmed neigh.

"Uncoded. In your own hand. You are a brave, but very foolish girl."

Belle looked at him unhappily. "What would you have me do?"

"Did it not occur to you that we have scouts and spies for such things?"

"Yes, but...."

"It is very good information," Ashby admitted, "And we need all that we can get, but it does no good if you get yourself caught. They'll be on you now, always watching."

"Then teach me," Belle implored.

"Teach you?"

"You're obviously no slouch at the game," Belle said. "Teach me."

Ashby shook his head firmly. "Impossible. It would

scandalize the men." He looked up and saw the Yankee soldier rolling himself a cigarette. "Say, son," he said loudly, "Don't smoke that thing in here!"

The sentry looked up, surprised. Ashby took a step towards him. "We got hay everywhere here. If you must smoke, then do it outside!"

"Yes, sir," the man muttered and retreated out the door.

"What do you mean 'scandalize the men'?" Belle demanded.

"Men will not accept a woman in the field. Not of our class. We are fighting for our homes and our way of life. Chivalry demands that we protect our womenfolk, not...."

"By that reckoning," Belle interrupted, "It should of been one of you who shot that Yankee ruffian who insulted my mother...but, none of you were handy, were you? So, I had to do it myself!"

Ashby blinked at the venom she put in these words.

"Your parents...," he said, keeping an eye out for the Yankee sentry.

"Haven't a thing to say about it," Belle said sharply. That wasn't quite true, but she was obviously closer to being a woman than a child. "Women carry pistols now, Henry, because you men are all out in the field in the Army. We have no one to protect us but ourselves. Like it or not, we are in the fight as much as you. That is the nature of partisan warfare, is it not? All I ask is to not be totally useless!"

Ashby ran his hands carefully over Fleeter's long legs again. "I will think about it," he said at last. "I've got a lot of ground to cover when I leave. He did say Bunker Hill, didn't he? That's useful to know."

"But, Henry...."

Belle looked towards South Street, where the guard had returned and was now standing, his cigarette done, bored and inattentive.

"I will do what I need to do to fight these horrible people. I heard about Dick," she said, laying her hand on his arm in sympathy.

At the mention of his dead brother's name, Ashby's eyes flashed at her angrily. "What of it?" he growled.

"I, too, feel the need for vengeance. If my sex bars me from riding at your side, let me offer myself as a scout and spy."

"Miss Belle," he said after looking around to make sure no one could hear him, "You mean well, but you lack skill and there is no school for spies, especially ones who have a facility for drawing the attention of the enemy to their every action. Women know nothing about soldiering. Not proper. Not to be thought of."

Belle was dismayed to hear this, but it was true. She should have used a code but didn't know any, and there were probably other tricks as well, not covered in Fenimore Cooper's book. Still she could not leave it alone and be quiet.

"Skills can be learned!" she replied sharply.

Ashby suddenly favored her with a wide grin. "I see they didn't take all the spirit out of you at that fancy school. You're still bold and determined. I have no time to debate this with you now. I will think on it. For now, please, do not send more letters. Stay safe."

"So the information was useless, all for nothing?"

"No," he admitted, "It was very good. Colonel Jackson thought it very valuable. However, you became the talk of Martinsburg, riding around with those Yankee officers."

"Henry," Belle said, "Men like to brag to women. You all do it. Why should our cause not profit from that unfortunate aspect of the male character? It's an even better disguise than the one you wear now."

Ashby chuckled then, and whispered, "It is often necessary to put on a mask. I am two men these days. One is Turner Ashby, the cavalry officer, the other is Henry Turner, the horse doctor, and since both are part of my real name, Henry Turner Ashby, I play either part with equal conviction."

Ashby straightened up, his hands easing his back, acting the old man. He looked around. "I will think on it and I will ask. These

West Point men who have taken over the army have their own ideas. They speak of drills and strategy when all my men want to do is to fight the enemy. We should have stopped them by now, and thrown them back over the river."

He looked quite put out, Belle thought. Ashby had played at being a knight so long that not to be permitted to meet a challenge on the field of honor galled him deeply. He sighed and then patted her hand.

"I am no longer free to do as I wish, having submitted myself and my men to the larger force. They have a strategy...." He grimaced at the word, which seemed hateful to him.

"I will be in touch. For now, just try to stay out of trouble." For the sentry's benefit he spoke in a louder voice as they walked back together to the street.

"I think a hot bran mash will take care of the problem," he said, "He's a little dyspeptic. It will clean him out, but he needs to run more."

"So do I," said Belle.

Ashby smiled and took her hand. "All will be well," he said quietly, and then he climbed into his wagon and drove away.

CHAPTER SEVEN

October 1861, Front Royal, Virginia.

Belle and her whole family were caught between giant opposing forces which threatened to crush them. Ben's service in the Confederate Army allowed them not even the guise of neutrality, and Belle's flirtations with Union officers caused tongues to wag on both sides of the question. In the end, they decided to make a strategic retreat from Martinsburg.

Belle's mother moved them to the resort town of Front Royal as much to get away from the vicious gossip and clucking disapproval as to get behind the Confederate Army's lines. The Unionist faction, no longer suppressed by the passionate advocates of the new Confederacy, treated those who most espoused the cause very harshly. As no one was more passionate about the Cause than she, Belle caught hell from both sides for riding and talking with the men of both armies. Mae Pruitt and her friends fed on this "scandal" like hogs at a trough.

The controversy was felt in other ways. Even old friends stopped buying from their little store. There was little point in staying put. And while they did not move "lock, stock and barrel", it was only prudent to take along anything that housebreakers might steal. Civil authority now tended to look the other way, especially when the perpetrators were the armed soldiers of either side.

As they drove south, Belle and her family saw an eerie and disturbing sight. At intervals along the road the train engines which had been looted from the Martinsburg yards lay tilted into the ditches beside the road. The horses, mules and men who had been employed to haul them were gone, and they were shoved off the hard macadamized road to one side, like shipwrecks in the inlets of green grass that bordered the turnpike.

A crew of Negroes, working under a black overseer, crawled over one of the engines, dismantling it and throwing the salvaged parts into a wagon drawn by a four mule team.

Mary drove past them, not turning her head. Belle's hand reached for her revolver as the entire crew stopped and stared their way.

"Somet'in' not right there," Della murmured from the seat behind them.

Belle pulled her Colt from its holster and checked the caps, not to brandish the weapon but to make it plain that she knew how to use it.

"Jest keep on, keep on," Della said softly.

The salvage crew, almost as one went back to their work, as lackadaisical as jackdaws feeding on a corpse.

Ahead of them they saw a lone rider in Confederate butternut. He stopped and tipped his hat politely as Mary pulled on the reins.

"What is all this?" Mary demanded of this cavalry officer riding along the road in the opposite direction. "Why are these just left to rust?"

The officer, who was perhaps a year older than Belle, swept off his hat, trying to bow from the saddle. He looked embarrassed.

"Well, ma'am," he drawled, "They meant to use them on our own tracks, but it seems the gauge is too wide. They got one to Strasburg, saw the difficulty and gave it up as a bad job."

"Did no one think to measure first?"

The young officer shrugged. "Seems not. Colonel Jackson never thought much of the idea anyway. But at least the Yankees won't be able to use them against us."

He donned his hat, nodded and went on his way. Mary and Belle stared after him. Mary shook her head. "Men," she said.

Belle nodded. "Any woman would know better."

Her cousin Alice had been her collaborator during the season in Washington the year before. Like all girls their age and class, they had gone to formally enter the glittering world of Washington society, and to eventually find suitable husbands among the political class, under the supervision and guidance of the famous hostess Rose Greenhow and the leadership of her close friend Antonia Ford, whose father was in business at Fairfax Courthouse. Alice, whose father was practicing law there, had been at school with Antonia, and looked to her as a mentor. Belle was a "country cousin", but interesting enough to be accepted by Mrs. Greenhow as a junior member of her circle

So Belle was "on the market" that season, but the war had ended all of that. Rose Greenhow's power and influence evaporated when her close friend James Buchanan left the Presidency. A protegee of John Calhoun's and a strong advocate for the South, she fell not only out of power but out of fashion. Belle's and Alice's hopes of another season in the Capital also evaporated, along with that of a "good marriage".

Alice's family, the Stewarts, retreated from Washington and took over the Fishback Hotel in Front Royal. It was a profitable resort located almost directly across from the train station. Belle had spent several pleasant summers there as a child. The building was as familiar to her as the Boyd home in Martinsburg.

The Stewarts welcomed them gladly. Belle's cousins Alice and Fannie were, at turns, teasing and awed over her adventures in Martinsburg. She had shot a man! There was no escaping the notoriety that followed her from that deed.

If Belle thought that her reputation as a Confederate was enhanced by it, she soon discovered the limitations of her influence with other women.

The idea of nursing only met resistance in Front Royal, even as every spare room, barn and shed filled up with patients for the general hospital. What passed for "polite society" there discouraged and disparaged the entire idea of women nursing soldiers.

"It's not proper for a lady to mingle with common soldiers," Fannie Stewart said, parroting the opinion of her friend Lucy Buck.

"Do they not see what is happening?" Belle asked in exasperation. "We have so many who need care."

"But they have male nurses and slaves," Fannie said.

"Few of whom know what to do, and none of whom are capable of keeping track of the supplies, or making sure that everyone has proper food and medicine," Belle said.

She smiled when she said this, but inwardly felt only a growing fury at the trap she had fallen into. She had proceeded boldly, without consultation, and had already been given charge of an entire ward and dubbed a "matron". when these objections were raised.

It was her ability to keep a set of books that won over the surgeon in charge. Having neither the time nor the additional trained staff to comply with the new Confederate Army Surgeon General Regulations, he was happy to have someone, even a girl, take on the paperwork.

"Have you had the measles?" he asked her, finally giving in to her entreaties.

"When I was a child," Belle said. "It is important?"

The doctor, Ben Ashcroft, had leaned back in his chair and looked at her in a measuring way. "It is."

Suddenly he rose, put his hand on her arm, took her outside and steered her towards what had been a tobacco drying shed.

"Measles is a very mysterious disease," he said as they walked, with Eliza following behind. "No one knows what causes it, or how it spreads. But we know this: if you've already had it, you won't get it again. We have entire regiments sick with it since the battle at Manassas. These seem to be from remote places in the country. In the regular Army, it's pretty rare, and doesn't seem to be very infectious. With these country boys, it's virulent. The disease itself is not so bad. Usually, it burns itself out in a few weeks, although a few die of it. What most die from is the pneumonia that they catch because the measles weakens them. So, we have established a ward just for men with measles. This shed has the virtue of being well-ventilated, but it has a packed dirt floor and will be hard to keep properly clean. It is apart from the other patients. These men need rest, clean linen, hot food which has been well prepared and is nutritious, and they must be made to keep everything clean, themselves most of all."

His hair and beard were somewhat tangled and wild, and his neck was dirty, but his hands were white from scrubbing. He looked very tired. Belle looked in the door of the shed and counted fifty beds and pallets, some with more than one man on them. She turned and looked at Eliza, who simply nodded.

"We are not amateurs, sir. We've done this before."

"Have you?" He wanted to doubt her. "Then perhaps you can identify that odor?"

"Dysentery or diarrhea," Belle replied seriously. "The men suffer from loose bowels."

"And that does not disgust you?" he said.

"Part of the job," Belle said calmly. "Haven't heard of a hospital without it."

Ashcroft stared at her a long moment and then said, "By God, Miss Belle, you're something out of the ordinary."

He escorted her into the improvised ward. "We want to discourage visitors for several reasons. Most are silly girls looking for a husband. These boys ain't what they want, by far. Most of them are poor farmers who don't even have shoes. The young ladies don't know what to do, so they wash their faces, which is nice, but not as useful as washing other parts. They won't do that because it would be shocking and sinful. All in all, their attentions don't do much besides annoy everyone."

He looked over at her to see her reaction. Belle simply smiled.

"Some of them, not surprisingly, have gotten the measles," Ashcroft said. "Then there are the families, some of whom descend upon us en masse and set up camp. They interfere with their loved one's care, inconvenience the other men, and argue with the doctors. They try home remedies which, combined with what we're giving them, just make them sicker, even kill them."

Ashcroft looked particularly haunted for a moment, "One girl loosened her fellow's bandage because he said it was too tight. He bled to death."

He turned to Belle, "Take charge of this ward and prevent such things."

Belle turned and looked at Eliza, who simply looked around. "How many slaves you got?" she asked.

"Five. Two for nursing, two for cooking, and one for general work. He's old and can't do much."

Eliza nodded, muttering to herself. She couldn't read, but she could count. "T'aint enough, but we kin start."

"I'll take it," Belle said.

"What was your name again? Stewart?"

"Boyd. The Stewarts are my aunt and uncle."

Ashcroft stopped and stared at her a long minute. "Belle Boyd. You're the girl who shot that Yankee soldier."

Belle nodded gravely, "Yes."

"Why do you want to do this?"

Belle laughed, "It needs doing, if we are to have an Army. I'm a patriot, sir." She looked around the ward, "Perhaps if I do it, the other girls in town won't think it's beneath them."

It did not work out that way. Young ladies were expected to be patriotic and support the war, but not to undertake work foreign to their "delicate natures". The only thing Belle had going for her in this controversy was that no one had ever described her as delicate.

Even Alice Stewart declined to work in the hospital. "You come and go at will, Belle. I have to live here, and so does Fannie. I'm sorry, I just can't. I don't see how you can."

"What do people say about it, anyway?" Belle asked, although she knew the answer.

"Oh, Belle," Alice said sadly. "The cruelest things. All those men...."

"Who are sick, some near death, and none able to hurt a fly, and who have never treated me with anything but the utmost respect," Belle replied briskly. "Those that aren't going to die, are needed in the Army. How do people think we're going to win this if we don't do everything we can?"

"Surely there must be something else a young lady can do, Belle," Alice said. "Nursing is work for men and Negroes."

Belle's mother, Mary, was, on the other hand, entirely supportive. "These folks haven't seen what happens when the Yankees take over a town," she said with a bitter smile. "You do what you can."

Mary, although feeling poorly herself, sometimes came to the ward to take a turn as matron simply so her daughter could get some rest. Eliza took the other slaves in hand and the ward was kept clean, the linen changed as often as possible, the food cooked. It fell to Belle to obtain rations, fresh vegetables, soap, and other supplies, and to deal with the patients' families. A rotating roster of convalescent soldiers assisted her with the heavy work, and if a family member got too obstreperous, would draw that person aside and whisper that Belle was the girl who had shot that Yankee in Martinsburg and not to be trifled with.

Belle's size also helped. She was polite, charming even when dog-tired, which was most of the time, and firm. She was also strong and agile enough to prevent a determined sister or daughter from forcing her way past her into the ward.

She and Eliza put in very long days and saw little of the Stewarts. Sometimes they slept in the ward, which simply added to the gossip floating about Front Royal.

At the end of two months, when Major Hunter H. McGuire, Jackson's Medical Director in the Valley Army showed up and inspected the ward, he was impressed.

"Who is the matron here?" he asked Belle.

"I am," said Belle.

He looked up at her, saw how young she was, and said, "No, I meant the person in overall charge."

"That would be me," Belle replied sweetly.

Major McGuire blinked, looked up and down the long shed, looked at her again and said, "Well, young lady, this is one of the best-run wards I have seen here...or anywhere. Even your reports and tallies are done correctly."

Belle felt a rush of pride. "Why thank you, sir," she said. "I have excellent help, of course."

"Your mortality rate is low, too."

Belle frowned, "To me, one is too many. Most die of the pneumonia. We had one boy whose leg had been cut off, died of gangrene."

"Was having the measles a factor?"

Belle hesitated. She knew that if she ventured a medical opinion, he would upbraid her. Doctor Ashcroft certainly did.

"I couldn't say, sir," she answered at last. "I'm sure it didn't help."

He blinked and then laughed. "Very good! A very good answer. Well, you've done outstanding work. I shall so report. What was your name?"

"Belle Boyd."

He looked up from his notes. "The spy?"

Belle didn't know quite what to say to that. "What do you mean?"

"We get some Yankee newspapers in Richmond. A girl of that name was reported to be spying in Martinsburg. She shot a Yankee soldier who broke into her house and got off, and then turned around and tricked Yankee officers into giving her information."

Belle blushed, "I wouldn't say that I tricked them."

McGuire chuckled, "No, but they did."

He pulled a cigar from his inside coat pocket. "Do you mind?"

Belle cleared her throat, "I don't allow smoking in here, Doctor. Doctor Ashcroft emphasizes the need for fresh, clean air. Perhaps we should go for a walk outside."

He smiled. "Yes, just so." He gathered his papers into his portfolio, stuck it under his arm and stepped outside. He was lighting his cigar when Belle joined him. She'd stopped to have a word with Eliza and to get her most reliable convalescent to man the desk. This one could actually read and write.

"I never smoked before the war," McGuire said. "Filthy habit."

They walked side by side through what had been a meadow three months before. The first brown and red leaves of the fall season crunched under their feet as they walked. On every side were large tents, some with wooden floors. These, the tobacco sheds and the barns, made up Front Royal Army General Hospital.

"Why did you take it up?"

"When I'm not going about criticizing the work of my betters," he replied sardonically, "I'm a surgeon, or as the men would put it, a butcher." He looked at the cigar reflectively, knocking off a bit of the ash, "These things deaden the sense of smell. There is nothing laudable about 'laudable pus'."

Belle felt herself gagging a bit at the memory of the surgical wards, where she was sometimes pressed into service. She had seen more surgery in the two months past than most doctors saw in two years. Blood and pus no longer dismayed or disgusted her, but the very mention of the carrion smells they produced made her nauseous. He was an observant man.

"Would you like one?" he asked with mock seriousness.

"No, thank you," Belle replied with a laugh. "My reputation is enough at hazard."

"I take it that you've been unjustly criticized for your role here?"

"You might say that."

He looked at her carefully, "I doubt that there is much that could deter you from a course of action, once your mind is made up. However, I am going to give you some medical advice. You're a strong young girl, but you need to spend less time here, perhaps take a furlough. I've seen this elsewhere. The strain of social disapproval and lack of polite society would be enough to wear you down, but you've also been working like a field hand. If you continue on much longer, it is you who will be in the hospital, and hospitals are very dangerous places. People die there." McGuire looked at her kindly, expecting a response.

Belle, caught off guard by this speech, which was neither patronizing nor avuncular, but said with the utmost sincerity, said, "But, the men...."

"Need you? They certainly need someone like you, Miss Belle, but they don't need you in particular and in detail. You are obviously not well, and, unlike many of my colleagues, I do think that women can play an important role in caring for the sick and wounded. We need more; many more. That won't happen if we kill off the few that have stepped forward with overwork."

"Perhaps if we had more slaves...."

"Slaves must be paid for. For that matter, when we hire civilians of any kind, we pay them a wage. Volunteers such as yourself help lighten the load. We need more. However, I am going to tell Ashcroft that you are a resource to be husbanded, not used up, and that he needs to give you leave."

"Are you suggesting I need a husband?"

"I am sure you will find one, Miss Belle. If I weren't a married man already, I might adventure it myself." There was honest admiration in his eyes.

"You're very kind," Belle murmured, looking around at the tents on the meadow. A distant scream from one of the surgical tents told her that another amputation was about to be performed. She knew now that it was horror of losing a limb, not pain, that had caused the man to cry out. Chloroform was readily available. The doctor was Ashcroft, who made a point of washing his hands before every procedure — not knowing why, but knowing that it had something to do with the fact that fewer of his patients died of infections after the operation.

She felt torn. She was more tired than she had ever been. Bone weary. At the same time, if she left, she and Eliza would not return. The ward would become someone else's responsibility.

Well, what of it, she said to herself, *you've done a job. The man just said so. Now you need to rest or you'll be sick yourself.*

She tried to remember the last time she had gone riding and couldn't. *Poor Fleeter*, she thought, *he must miss me so.*

So, after another week, she took Doctor McGuire's advice and left the ward in the hands of a male nurse with one arm; he had left the other at Manassas. He was smart, a school teacher before the war, who had been elected First Sergeant of his company. He understood the paper work and had an air of authority. This lessened her regret at leaving. "Her" patients would be in good hands. Or at least "a" good hand.

When she left, Doctor Ashcroft presented her with a leather satchel of medical instruments and supplies. "You may find use for these," he said gruffly. "Life is uncertain and war is more so."

Belle accepted them graciously as an accolade for her service, but hoped not to need them.

Her mother returned to Martinsburg to see to business there. Mostly this was to urge old customers to pay what they owed. They were in need of money and prices were rising like a signal rocket. Fortunately the Fishback Hotel provided a living for them all.

Belle slept for most of three days, and then found that she remained the target of much ignorant gossip. At a party Lucy Buck ventured a snide remark in her hearing, and Belle, turning with polite ferocity, reduced poor Lucy to tears by simply saying that being a camp follower was certainly better than being a useless stay-at-home. Lucy had brothers who were clerks on Beauregard's staff. She made much ado about this and how important it was.

Belle sweetly agreed and hoped that the young men would never find themselves wounded, and without the comfort of a sympathetic matron in whatever hellhole of a hospital they ended up.

Lucy Buck ran out of the room, wailing. Belle, not feeling particularly good about herself, made her excuses, pleading fatigue and went home to bed. She was on the verge of tears herself, regretting her hasty words, but also feeling much abused. Why did no one understand? Why would they not leave her in peace?

CHAPTER EIGHT

Virginia, November 1861

Belle returned to Martinsburg to rest and recuperate. The local Union Provost insisted that she not walk through the town without an escort, and such was seldom to be found. Michael Kelley called once to take her riding, but carefully steered her away from the Union encampments.

It was a game of cat-and-mouse, with him trying to get her to admit she was still spying. Belle would have liked nothing better, and was distressed it was not so. Gossip about her spread like a cancer through the town, poisoning relationships with everyone outside her family.

Belle made excuses the next time Kelley called on her. There was no point to any of it. Even if she obtained information, there was no way to get it to anyone who could profit by it.

People in the town avoided her politely. Even her neighbors, the Doll sisters, did not call. Local sentiment was no longer leaning against the Union, the ninety-day men having been sent home and replaced with new regiments, often with the same number, whose men had enlisted for three years and whose officers were appointed, rather than elected. Many of them had transferred from the Regular Army to gain higher rank and responsibilities. Others, like Kelley, simply continued on as volunteers.

Belle learned that one of her distant cousins, and her family's dear friend, David Strother, better known as the **Harper's Magazine** artist and humorist, "Porte Crayon", had been seen in town quite a few times. But he was reported to be riding around behind Confederate lines near Johnston's Army, possibly making maps for the Union Army. Belle reflected that, while he was Virginia born, he had lived up in New York City for many years and was likely to be a Union man.

Even more so since his father's arrest by Confederate bullies because he had spoken up for Lincoln. John Strother owned a resort as well, at Berkeley Springs, but closed it in protest against the war. He was an old man but still eager for a fight. Defiance was in his blood, as it was in Belle's.

Belle felt torn apart. The Strothers were family, and she liked David tremendously. She had danced with him and practiced her flirting with him at Mrs. Greenhow's parties in Washington. He was too old for her by far and now remarried, but still a very attractive man.

Damn politics anyway, she thought, *how will I ever find a husband with all of this going on?* The supply of available men had dramatically increased, but the complications also grew apace. For instance, she liked Michael Kelley and his wry Irish way of looking at things. But he was Union and she was "Sessesh" and that colored everything. It seemed to her very unfair and made her both sad and angry. Her loneliness increased.

Most of all, she missed her beautiful black stallion, Fleeter. She'd left him in Front Royal to keep him safe from Yankee Quartermasters. She needed exercise and fresh air and not the confinements of the Boyd house. It was with a glad cry then that she greeted her mother's announcement that they would be going to Manassas.

A large house, convenient to Beauregard's headquarters, had been set aside for the use of officer's families. Her father was a Captain now, a paymaster. His Masonic connections proved of some use in the Army after all.

They went by carriage, stopping briefly at Front Royal, where Belle found Fleeter in pasture, fat and happy. He caught her scent and nickered a welcome, trotting over to let her scratch behind his ears. She examined him carefully. His hooves needed trimming and he would have to be re-shod. Her cousin Alice Stewart had walked out to the pasture with her.

"Did no one think to ride him?" Belle asked, a little irritated.

Alice laughed. "How? He wouldn't let anyone near him with a saddle. He's your horse, Belle. He might let me on, if you gave him leave, but he'd not be thrilled about it. Won't pull a wagon, either."

Belle pursed her mouth in amusement at her horse's rebellion and bestowed a kiss on his forehead. Alice said, "A Provost came around, trying to get horses for the army. That's a very smart horse, Belle. He suddenly had the worst limp!"

"A Union Provost Marshal?" Belle asked, very surprised.

"Confederate. We have them too, now, and they seem to all be the same Irish ruffians, just like up North."

"Why would we need them?" Belle felt a little dizzy and confused by the notion.

"Not everyone is the kind of die-hard patriot you are, Belle," Alice said. "When it became obvious that the war would not be resolved quickly, many people began to think anew. There have been desertions, there have been thefts and frauds in the camps and the hospitals, and I'm told that straggling on the march is a particular problem."

Belle sighed, "That is so disappointing. No one said this would be easy."

"Actually," Alice pointed out, "Most of them did say that. Braggarts and liars, my mother calls them. I'm glad my Daddy had sense enough to stay out of the Army. No offense," she added hastily as Belle turned quickly.

Belle stared at her for a moment and then sighed again.

"None taken," she said.

She petted Fleeter on the neck. "Look how fat you've gotten," she crooned to him. "Well, we'll soon put that right. I need exercise, and so do you."

After a trip to the local blacksmith, she rode him from Front Royal to Manassas, calming him with long gallops along the road. There was a happy family reunion with her father and her uncle, James Glenn.

Captain Glenn, Mary's oldest brother, was a militia scout, as were her cousins William Boyd Compton and John Boyd and John Singleton. Glenn had experience, fighting the Cherokee in Georgia and Florida years before. He led a company of scouts. His specialty was scouting the enemy lines.

He greeted her with, "I hear you want to go into the family business, Belle."

Her cousins laughed at that.

"Well, why not?" Belle shot back, a bit angry. "I can ride and shoot as well as any of y'all!" Her cousins, realizing that it was not a jest, stared at her, surprised. Not that they would deny the truth of what she said, but she was, after all, just a girl.

Glenn tugged at his graying beard, a twinkle in his blue eyes. "Well, Jeb Stuart was complaining about how all of his young officers are tied up on courier duty. The Army is getting ready to go into winter quarters and he needs to have them training, not hanging around headquarters. I could put in a word."

Belle was elated, "Oh, would you, Uncle?"

"I will," he said. "And me and the boys can take you out and show you how to scout a bit. Jeb is real impressed with that friend of yours, Antonia Ford. She was at Manassas. Did a fine job, he said. Went where she pleased, and the Federals never suspected a thing. He's given her a commission and made her an aide."

"That's just Jeb puttin' on airs," John Singleton said. "He likes pretty women. They flatter him. He can't make someone a Major anymore than I can. Department of War does that."

Belle smiled, "Well, he might know something you don't, John. Antonia is pretty, and smart enough to use that well. Women can do this work, too. It isn't all about riding a horse."

"No, but that was the reason he gave it to her," James Glenn said. "She scouted at Manassas. Did good work behind the lines, as much as any girl could."

Glenn poured himself a pre-dinner glass of whisky and lifted it in a toast. "That's the wonder of it. You girls all look so sweet. If you get arrested by the Yankees you'll be treated like queens. Me and the boys here, we get caught, we get imprisoned or hung. Probably hung." He tossed back the whisky and waited for the warmth of it to spread through his body. "Don't hardly seem fair," he laughed.

"What about Henry Ashby?" Belle asked. "I'd hoped that he

would give me employment."

Glenn frowned. "He calls himself Turner now, after his father and grandfather. The men like him, but he's in a bit of trouble with old Stonewall just now."

"Stonewall?"

"That's what everyone calls Tom Jackson now, since Manassas. Cause he held the Second Virginia there and stood like one. You was there, Ben. Wasn't that how it was?"

Ben Boyd looked around solemnly, "It was. General Bee's men panicked, but he rallied them behind us and we stood off the Union assault until they gave up. Bee got killed that day, but he left Jackson a name that's stuck to him like glue. Wasn't nothin' like we thought it would be. Smoke and noise everywhere, men crying for their mommas, screams...and the blood, the blood, the blood...." Ben Boyd looked away as his voice trailed off, tears in his eyes.

Glenn looked sympathetically at his brother-in-law. Not every man was a warrior born. He went on as if nothing had happened.

"Anyway, ol' Turner Ashby, as he calls himself these days, don't exactly suit Stonewall's book when it comes to being a cavalry commander. He got's the dash and the fire, but his whole brigade or regiment — and no one's quite sure which it is, because he just keeps adding on companies as the Chivalry enlists — is disorganized. Stonewall's a West Point man, fought in Mexico along with Lee and some of the others, and he wants it done proper, which means reports, and the proper staff, and all that. Ashby and his men just want to ride around and kill as many Yankees as they can."

"Isn't that the point?" Belle asked, a bit confused.

"Don't do no good," said James Glenn, "If it don't win the battle. And he holds himself above the grunt work. Doesn't write reports, nor will he drill."

"Doubt if he could," Billy Compton said. "The Chivalry ain't much on such things. Wouldn't cotton to it, and woe betide the man who tried to make 'em."

"Yep, they'll just up and go home. Partisan rangers, they'd say, ain't regulars," said Glenn, with a ferocious grin, "And that puts them 'bout one step up from bandits as far as the West Point men are concerned. They don't care for Turner Ashby and the political hold he has on his men."

"But he can lead," Billy Compton said.

"That he can," Glenn agreed. "And he's good at scouting behind the lines, but he's supposed to be leading the band, not playing the trumpet or beating the drum. Last I heard, he's got eleven companies in his regiment and one poor bastard of a Major to run his staff. No, Stonewall ain't pleased."

"But, what's he going to do about it?" Ben Boyd asked. "Henry is a politician, and he's got friends in Richmond like Al Boetler."

"Stonewall's a good soldier," Glenn replied. "He'll take orders from the next man up and do his damnedest to git the job done, but he ain't going to be second-guessed by civilians who never served a day in uniform. If Jeff Davis weren't a West Point man himself, he'd just go home. He ain't fond of lawyers, that's sure. Most men knuckle under, looking for that next promotion. Not Stonewall. He's the best we got, and he knows it. This is his time."

The servants started bringing in the food and the conversation moved on to other things, but Belle had cause to think a lot about her uncle's assessment of Turner Ashby in the months that followed.

Two days later, Belle, in her best riding habit, topped with a stylish winter coat, and with her Colt Dragoon revolver strapped around her waist, reported for duty at General Beauregard's headquarters. Jeb Stuart, now a Brigadier, greeted her fondly.

"Hello, Cousin," he said. "Good to see you."

Belle felt herself blushing. She looked around the room. Beauregard had taken over a plantation house whose owner had been fond of balls and parties and had actually built a large hall for the purpose. The walls, once sumptuously decorated, had been stripped and there were large dark rectangles where paintings had hung. The wallpaper, hand-printed, and from France, was already damaged by the many papers and maps that were pinned to the walls.

Beauregard had a private office in a small room to one side. His staff was in the big room, working at tables strewn around the room at odd positions.

Everyone stopped what they were doing and stared at her until Stuart, with a wave of his hand, put them back to work. General Pierre Beauregard came out of his office and stared up at her. He was an elegant little Creole, very handsome with a short mustache and dark eyes, Belle saw, but not much given to smiling. He looked sharply over to Stuart. "This is she?"

"Yes, sir."

Beauregard looked Belle slowly up and down, and unlike every other man she had met recently, did not seem impressed by her figure. His gaze was cold and analytical, like the engineer he was.

"Can you use that thing?" he asked, nodding at the pistol.

"I can. Would the General care for a demonstration?"

He frowned, "Some other time, perhaps. This is already too much of a circus."

"Belle is the one who shot that Yankee soldier in Martinsburg," Stuart said, a touch of pride in his voice.

Beauregard nodded, "I did hear of it." He looked at Belle again, "Can she ride?"

"Like the wind!" Belle said, irritated at being spoken of as if she were not there. "And I have a very smart horse."

Beauregard, making up his mind, clapped his hands together. "Private Buck!"

A young sallow-faced boy with a touch of acne and a cowlick in his hair, came running up, "Sir!"

"Are the dispatches for General Johnston ready?"

"Yes, sir."

"Sign them out to this courier."

Young Private Buck gaped at her and then recovered himself.

"Yes, sir. Right away, sir!" He ran over to a table and picked up a leather satchel with a long strap. He brought it back and handed it to Belle along with a receipt and a pencil. She signed it with a bit of a flourish, aware that he was looking at her very oddly.

"Johnston is at Centerville," Beauregard said. "Do you know the way?"

"Yes, sir," said Belle.

"Very well. Dismissed."

Belle, shifting the satchel to her other hand, drew herself up and saluted. Beauregard gravely returned the salute. Then he took Jeb Stuart by the arm and drew him away to look at a map which had been spread out on a beautiful walnut dining table.

Belle, seeing no reason to linger, walked towards the door. Private Buck kept pace with her. "How is it you are doing this?" he asked peevishly. "T'ain't proper."

"Where are you from?" Belle asked, as sweet as she could, but not breaking stride.

"Front Royal."

"You know the Stewarts and the Fishback Hotel?"

"Yes, and I know about you. My sister wrote me all about it."

Belle stopped then and looked closer at him. "You're Lucy Buck's brother?"

"Yes, what of it?"

Belle laughed. "Oh, nothing. Nothing at all." She started walking again, with him following. She turned and smiled, "Do tell your sister I send my fondest regards," she said. She left him there, fuming.

At Centerville, there was a satchel of dispatches to go to Beauregard, so Belle was able to give Fleeter a long hard workout. The roads were mostly empty and the leaves mostly off the trees, so that she could go quickly without difficulty or fear of being surprised. The next day her muscles told her how out of condition she had become, but she reported for duty and was given another courier run, this time to Jackson's headquarters. That took some finding, as Jackson was on the move. Still, she got there, albeit well after dark.

There, Jackson's Adjutant General, Reverend Dabney, looked at her pass, trying to hide his surprise.

He took the satchel and examined its seal, finding it still intact. Belle braced herself for another rude comment, but he smiled at her graciously, and said, "I remember you, Miss Boyd. My regards to your parents. You are quite a patriot, I understand. Does this work suit you?"

"Very well, sir," Belle replied. "I consider it a great honor."

"That's a fearsome bit of artillery," Dabney said. "Are you any good with it?"

"I can knock a man's hat off at fifty yards," Belle said. "Would you care for a demonstration?" Belle drew the revolver, upended it and began reloading, juggling the powder flask and lead balls expertly. He realized that the weapon had been fired. Recently.

He laughed, raising his hands in mock surrender, and then regarded her more seriously. If she could knock off a man's hat, she could split his head like a melon.

"You had some difficulty on the road coming here?" he asked.

"Some men, not in uniform, wished to stop me. I was required to discourage them a bit." Belle flashed a wide mischievous grin at him. "They were riding very poor horses and gave it over when I shot at them."

Dabney nodded, trying to conceal his surprise. "You must have been very frightened."

Belle smiled again. "Actually, sir, I found it quite exhilarating."

He shook his head, a bit amazed, "How old are you?"

"Seventeen, sir. Were I a man that age, I'd be riding in the Seventh Virginia."

"But you're a young lady, and too delicate for the horrors of battle."

"I wasn't too delicate to run a ward for fifty sick and wounded men. And I'm not too delicate for this riding around. I've done twenty miles today. Men underestimate the strength of their ladies." Belle wasn't smiling now, but looking at him in a most pointed way.

Dabney's face said that he found the whole line of conversation very disturbing. "Perhaps, but we have a tradition to uphold."

"And to that end, we need everyone in the fight, sir," Belle said, her eyes bright. "It is war, isn't it?"

"Are you a lawyer, too, Miss Belle? You argue like one."

"No, sir, not yet," Belle replied charmingly in a low sweet voice, dropping her eyes. She was dirty and sweaty from the long ride, but at that moment Dabney got a glimpse of why men found her so attractive. He cleared his throat.

"Hmmm. Well, yes. We won't have any dispatches for you until morning. I suggest you get some dinner, and you may use my tent to rest tonight."

"Thank you, sir. I will have to tend my horse first, of course," said Belle, and startled him by rendering him a proper salute, which he returned before he could think about it.

CHAPTER NINE

Front Royal, Virginia, December 1861

"Law is a system that trains the mind," Alexander Boetler said, and looked around the dining room of the Fishback Hotel at the five men and two women who sat at the long table. Colonel Turner Ashby sat in a chair at the back of the room as a silent observer.

"Law requires its practitioners to keep their clients' secrets. It requires us to be zealous in their behalf. When you try a case before a jury, you deal in facts as well as law, because law can interpreted, but facts are immutable."

Boetler, recently a U.S. Congressman from Harper's Ferry and surrounding areas, was about forty-five, and had been a witness to the John Brown raid. He now served in the Confederate Congress and did double duty as a field commander for the Secret Service.

Sometimes known as "Colonel" Boetler, he looked too old and fat to be in the Army. Rather than a uniform, he wore pince-nez glasses, a well-tailored black frock coat and trousers, and a boiled white shirt with a removable paper collar.

"Sir," asked a young, very short and slender blond man named Frank Stringfellow, "What has all that to do with spying?"

Boetler took a sip of hot coffee before answering. Belle Boyd and Antonia Ford looked at one another briefly, also puzzled.

"Spying is also a system, Mister Stringfellow — and it deals in facts. Many facts." He waited for another question, but none was forthcoming.

Billy Compton and John Singleton were restive. This was too much like being back in school for their taste.

"When we scout the enemy, we need to know what?" Boetler asked, playing the schoolmaster once more.

"Where they are," said James Glenn, who was present to keep his younger kin attentive and respectful.

"Where they are going," said Billy Compton.

"How many they are, and what kind of unit," said Antonia.

"How much ammunition and supply they have," said Belle.

"How many horses and mules," said Sam Boyd.

"Who their officers are," Frank Stringfellow said.

Boetler spread his hands, obviously pleased. "Yes. All that and more. We also need to know if the men are sick or well, how close they are to a town, a railroad, a bridge, or a ford. We need to know more than the names of their officers. We need to know where they were educated and what their experience is."

"That's a bit more than usually comes up in casual conversation," Belle observed.

"Well, a lot of it you can get just scouting a column," James Glenn said. "You can count off their wagons and have a fair idea of how much supply they have. If you look close, you can see if the wagons are riding light or heavy. You can count regiments on the march by rank and file and come up with their strength, and so on.

"And you can tell where they're headed and how fast. Yankees got their certain ways of doing things, so you need to look for where the cavalry is screening the column and where the artillery is in the line of march. But that's easy.

"To get everything, we need to get right inside the lines and go for the goods. We need to spy, to ask, to find and steal their marching orders, rosters, orderly reports, and maps; anything that will tell us their intentions."

Boetler listened to this long speech and nodded. "Think of it this way. An army on the march is like a huge animal, say an elephant. In battle, everything is chaos and we look to the cavalry to tell us where that elephant is. We rely upon you scouts to tell us where the elephant is going to be. Problem is, it's a very big elephant and each of you only sees a little bit of it, the ear or the tail. No one can see the whole elephant." He nodded in appreciation of his own metaphor. "But you get back here and tell us what you've seen and we can put together a pretty good picture of that elephant, where it's going, and maybe how we can kill it, or, if we can't kill it, how we can get out of its way."

"Well enough, but what does that have to do with practicing law?" asked Stringfellow.

"Just like law, it's a secret," said Boetler. "One you take to your grave. How we do it, when we do it, who we do it with, these are things you can never reveal. To do so is more than a sin, it's a crime against the state." He slowly moved his hand around the room. "You will have to develop your memories. Nothing you see should be written down. It must all be remembered and reported. And just the facts. What you saw and know to be true. Not what you think it might mean. Leave that to Stonewall and Ashby and the other officers."

Boetler put the tips of his fingers together, his brow wrinkling to show great mental concentration. Belle recognized it as bit of theatre, a politician's trick.

"You've all heard about my dear friend, Mrs. Greenhow?" he asked at last.

Everyone nodded.

"Rose's mistake was trying to give us more information than we could conveniently use. She developed so many sources we were hard put to manage it all, or to understand it properly. For all of that, she deserves full credit for allowing us to anticipate McDowell's movements. That won us the battle at Manassas. Her eagerness to collect more and more information got her arrested, and now she's no longer of use. Her network is gone."

Boetler sighed. "Use discretion," he said. "Bring us only what we need, and don't muddy the waters. Let us see that elephant clearly."

"How are we to remember it all?" Billy Compton complained.

Boetler looked at him thoughtfully. "I will give you a model for the mind," he said, "From rhetoric. Think of your mind as a large house where you keep certain things in certain rooms. Pots and dishes in the kitchen, for instance. How many do you have and how many will you need for dinner? That kind of thing. Apply the same principle to the Union Army. Put the soldiers in one room and the artillery pieces in another. How many do you have of each and of what kind? You can practice this by going through this hotel and looking at each room to see how well you remember all the objects in it. Look at the room carefully, go away for a hour, then make a list of what you have seen: every plate and bowl and picture. Then go back and see what you've missed. Repeat the process until you can do it perfectly at a glance."

"From rhetoric, you said?" Antonia Ford seemed amused.

"Yes," he said. "This is how a lawyer recalls all the points in a summation in court, or how a politician remembers his stump speech."

"Why not just write it all down?" asked James Glenn. "Be a sight easier."

"Papers are proof. They will get you hanged," Boetler replied grimly. "You're not much use to us dead."

Glenn chuckled, "No. You're right about that." He scratched his beard gently, and then pointed at Belle and Antonia. "What about these girls?"

Boetler grew very serious. "It's even more important that they not be caught with anything that can be used against them. Miss Belle's been lucky so far. But they know about her and they watch her when she is in their lines. She's a worry to them."

"Why send her, then?" John Singleton asked, a bit angry.

"The more they watch her, the less they watch out for other spies and scouts. Belle can be a big noisy parade. She draws them off, while we pick their pockets."

Her uncle chuckled at this, very amused. Belle felt herself blushing as Antonia regarded her with a smile.

"You make it sound like a criminal enterprise," Billy Compton objected.

"By their lights, it is," said Frank Stringfellow, "And they catch you out of uniform, they'll hang you right quick."

Alexander Boetler and Turner Ashby, who had stayed completely silent until that moment, looked at one another. Ashby shifted in his chair, his brow furrowed from following the lecture, his expression wary. Boetler gazed at him, and silence filled the room as everyone waited for a response.

"Couldn't have said it better myself," Ashby said. "Now you men will be servicing our army on the march, scouting deep behind the lines of the Union forces. Sometimes you'll do that in civilian clothes or in Yankee uniforms. The ladies," he nodded at Belle and Antonia, "Will be 'in residence'. Agents in place, who will build their own networks among the locals.

"Fairfax Court House is a Yankee headquarters, and Front Royal may well be when things start up again in the spring. We don't have enough of an army to defend little towns against Yankee incursions and still maneuver properly. Yankee officers like taking over fine houses and big hotels for their headquarters. Miss Belle should help her kin run this place. That way she becomes part of the scenery and less likely to be noticed.

"Are we all agreed on this plan?" Ashby asked. Everyone murmured their assent.

"Good. Mister Benjamin is sending a man up from Richmond to work with you on codes and ciphers. Jules St. Martin, who, I believe, is his brother-in-law. Meantime, Captain Glenn, I would be most grateful if you could give your niece and Miss Antonia some practical work on scouting."

"I'll do er, Colonel," said Glenn. "We'll go out in parties of three and see what the Yankee positions are like. Pack a lunch. We'll be out for awhile."

With that, the meeting broke up. Belle and Antonia walked out together down the long hallway and to the front door. Antonia took a deep breath as they continued outside on the veranda that fronted the hotel, and said, "It's very refreshing, isn't it?"

A company of Ashby's cavalry was setting up camp in the village square next to the train station. Young men glanced their way, but there were no rude comments or catcalls of the kind they had both suffered from Union soldiers.

"The air here is wonderful," Belle replied. "So clear."

"I don't mean that, silly," Antonia said. "I mean the way they treat us. We are not petted or patronized."

"No," Belle said. "We are employed."

"We are soldiers in the Cause," said Antonia with complete satisfaction and happiness.

The next day, Belle went off on a scout with Billy Compton and John Singleton, while Antonia went in a different direction with Captain Glenn and Frank Stringfellow.

Just before dawn they assembled for Ashby's inspection in front of his tent.

Antonia was riding her favorite horse, a sure-footed dun mare named Princess. Fleeter had pulled up lame and Ashby, looking at the injury, said he needed a few days rest and pasture. He provided Belle with a gray two-year-old colt named Teddy.

"He's a little rambunctious," Ashby said, "So, keep a tight rein on him."

Before they parted, James Glenn had a word with his niece. "You remember when we'd go camping, all the things I taught you?"

"Yes," said Belle. Her uncle was a woodsman straight out of a Fenimore Cooper novel. From him she had learned the ways of the forest, much plant and animal lore, and how to hunt and fish. "I can still hide in the bush."

Glenn laughed, "Do try to stay out of the poison oak this time."

Belle blushed. Billy Compton and John Singleton chuckled.

"As if you didn't make the same mistake yourselves," she said.

"And none of your circus riding, Belle," Glenn cautioned. "This is serious business."

"Uncle!" Belle protested. She was embarrassed and wished that she could be gone.

"Circus riding?" Antonia queried.

"My uncle exaggerates," Belle protested.

"I seem to recall an incident a few years ago," Alexander Boetler said, "When I was campaigning and your father invited me to dinner. Was it not you, already as tall as a fence post, who rode your pony into the dining room, after being told that you could not sit with the adults at table? How old were you then?"

Antonia regarded her with amusement. She had never heard this tale.

"Eleven," Belle admitted.

"No wonder they sent you to Baltimore to civilize," Antonia laughed.

"Well, I did think my pony was old enough," Belle said, her voice artful, her eyelashes fluttering, "And if that was true, so was I."

Everyone laughed.

John Singleton added, "I've never seen anyone, man or woman, who can ride like Belle. I've seen her make a run, full gallop, standing on the saddle."

"Well, that's bold," Antonia said. "But what was the point of it?"

"Why, to prove I could," Belle said simply. "And I was the only one. The boys couldn't manage it, not one of them."

"That's true," John Singleton added. "I was there."

Glenn said sternly, "Well, you forget all that showing off, young lady. Scouting is about stealth. Be like an Indian brave," he glanced at Ashby; "A real one, not a tournament fiction. This ain't no show. Don't forget that, with all the leaves down off the trees, you can be seen from a long way off by a picket laying quiet."

"Yes, sir," Belle said, hoping to end the lecture.

Glenn nodded. "See that you do, then."

Belle started to turn and gallop off.

"Don't call attention to yourself," Glenn called after her.

Belle hauled in the reins, causing Teddy to buck a little. She and the others moved off at a trot.

"Better," Captain Glenn called after them and then turned and made a motion to Antonia Ford, who urged Princess forward in the other direction with her right heel.

Belle looked across a field covered with dead grass, towards the camp of a Union infantry regiment. The camp was new, and she was trying out Boetler's mental trick, first counting the tents, and then trying to determine which one was the headquarters.

John Singleton and Billy Compton were a few feet behind her. Belle was just inside the tree line, ducking to avoid limbs, and trying to control Teddy, who was snorting and fidgety.

"Be careful, Belle," Billy Compton whispered. Just what he wanted her to be careful of, she never found out, for, at that very moment, Teddy neighed loudly in alarm, half-reared, and took off across the field, directly towards the Union lines.

"Teddy!" Belle shouted. "Damn it, horse!!" She sawed at the reins, but Teddy had the bit in his teeth and ran full out, directly for the Union pickets, one of whom was raising his musket. Seeing that the rider was a young woman, he lowered the weapon.

Two Union officers quickly mounted and moved to intercept her. One was a good enough horseman to be able to grab the reins near Teddy's mouth and pull him to a stop.

It all happened in a matter of seconds; Teddy was shaking, blowing white ropes of saliva from his mouth, gulping the air. Belle held up a hand while she caught her own breath. Infantry pickets came running up and were waved away by the other officer.

Belle sized them up. Both were blonde young men who had the physical build of farmers or laborers. Both wore second lieutenant's rank. Both regarded her with intense interest. Finally she caught her breath. One of the officers offered a drink from his canteen, which she accepted gratefully.

"Thank you, kind sir," she said, after taking a few delicate lady-like sips and handing the canteen back. "As you can see, my horse has run away with me and carried me within your lines. I am your captive, but perhaps you could restore me to my friends?"

One of them looked at the other and winked, "We are very proud of our beautiful captive, but we could not think of detaining you. Permit us to escort you."

"I had scarcely hoped for such an honor," Belle said, eyeing them cautiously. "I hoped you would give me a pass, but since you are so kind as to offer your services in person I cannot but accept them."

"I suppose that we need have no fear of these cowardly Rebels," the other said, making a joke.

Inwardly, Belle's anger bloomed at the insult, but she managed her most charming smile, "Why, no fear at all. I am with my cousin and a friend."

"Then lead the way," said the first officer.

"At a lesser speed," said the other, with a laugh.

Belle turned Teddy around and went back across the field at a slow canter. "What regiment are you boys from?" Belle asked loudly.

"Third Illinois," said one.

"Really," Belle replied. "You've come far."

They reached the woods on the other side and then went through them to the road beyond. "Lots of snakes in here?" asked one of the Illinois men fearfully.

"Tons," Belle replied cheerfully. "Probably what set my horse off." That made both men watch the ground ahead very carefully and not the areas on either side. Belle could see her cousins ghosting in behind them out of the corner of her eye.

Stopping in the middle of the road, the two officers looked up and down. "Where are your friends?" asked one.

"Billy? John? I've brought you something."

The two Confederate scouts burst out of the brush behind them, one on each side of the Union men, each with a revolver in his hand. The Union officers, with amazed expressions on their faces, slowly raised their hands in surrender.

"These are the 'cowardly' rebels you feared, gentlemen. Your pistols and swords, please," Belle said, still with the same charming smile. The young men from Illinois were stunned at the turn of events and made no effort to resist.

"May we know the lady's name?" asked the first officer.

"Belle Boyd, at your service," Belle said sweetly.

"Good God! The Rebel spy!"

"Since your journals have named me that, so be it," said Belle, as John Singleton took strips of rawhide and tied their hands to their saddle pommels. Billy Compton now had two revolvers trained on them and looked like he might bust a gut laughing. Tears were streaming down his face and his shoulders shook.

"See here," said one in an aggrieved tone of voice, "This is really quite unfair. We were simply trying to help you out of a predicament."

"Ah, boys," said John Singleton, in high good humor. "All is fair in love and war. You know that." Belle smiled sweetly at them and then led the way back to the Confederate lines where the hapless Yankees could be turned over to a Provost Marshal.

CHAPTER TEN

Front Royal, Virginia, December 1861

Eliza Corsey surprised Belle by accepting her request to become a spy as the most natural thing in the world. What else would she do but what her mistress asked? Helping her dress or helping her spy, it was all one. And, Belle realized, without her help the job would be difficult, if not impossible. Nothing got done without the aid of servants; not by women of her class.

Which raised another issue, "Who among the Negroes here can we trust? Who will help us run messages to the Army and smuggle supplies?"

Eliza, her dark brown eyes looking steadily at her mistress, replied, "You leave dat to me, Miss Belle. I know which be de ones do de job. Better you not know."

Belle was taken aback. "Why not?"

"Buckras only tink dey know black folk. Dey watching all the time, feared of us rising up." She shook her head. "Dat John Brown, he a fool, but a holy kind of fool. De Yankees, dey never watchin'. We like cows or maybe dogs to dem, dere, but nothin' to worry 'bout. Dey don't know us. Some colored folk, dey see de Jubilee comin'. Dey sell you to de Yankees, right quick, smiling all the way. De rest, we know, come what may, we be living here. War don't change nothin'. Life go on de same ol' way."

Belle was amazed. It was the longest speech that she had ever heard Eliza make. "What do you suggest?"

"We fool de Yankees good. You leeb it to 'liza. I find de right ones do de work."

Belle's mind raced as she calculated her chances. She flattered herself that Eliza was family, and loyal. That made trust easy and essential. She looked carefully at the Negro woman's eyes. Nothing sly or hostile lay there. She took her chance.

"If you need money...."

Eliza laughed, "Dat do make it easier. Dem little gold pieces. Easy to hide."

Belle felt a bit lightheaded. She had expected resistance, the passive attitude that slaves were famous for. Yet, everywhere she looked black men and women were working hard, as they always had, to do their white masters' bidding. They were teamsters and laborers and nurses; she would not have been able to run that hospital ward without them to do the cooking, laundry and cleaning. The Abolitionist promise of freedom for the slaves had been a hollow one so far; a cruel hoax as far as she was concerned. The Underground Railway offered them new lives up north, yet most stayed as they were, where they were born.

Belle thought, *We women play our little games to get what we want from men. Why would slaves not do the same?* In some households, the maneuvers between the butler and the lady of the house would do a general proud. She saw Eliza was still waiting for her to say something.

"Well then, that's what we'll do," Belle said brightly and took Eliza's hand, and then hugged her. Eliza gave her a broad grin, and then went back to her work.

Jules St. Martin came up from Richmond to teach her codes. Elegantly turned out in a black velvet suit, he was quite unlike any other man she'd ever met. His manner was delicate, yet decadent.

He had the Creole good looks shared by many men from the old families in New Orleans. Dark hair and eyes, olive skin and the most perfect white teeth she had ever seen. There was a musky, but not unpleasant, scent about him.

"Please do not ask me why I am not in the Army," he said after he introduced himself.

Belle blinked. She had been about to do just that.

"They also serve who stand and wait," he continued smoothly, "And my part of this war is to sit in a little room and do codes."

"All by yourself?"

"No," he admitted. "I have some young ladies to help me."

"No men?"

"Oh, it's quite impossible. The Provost Marshals are always

stopping them and asking them why they're not in the Army. Of course, they cannot answer that they are employed by the Department of State, because then they are asked for other explanations, and it becomes incredibly difficult. I gave it up as a bad job, and surrounded myself with young ladies."

"Quite a sacrifice," Belle said drily.

"You have no idea," he sighed in a world weary way, and then winked at her, set down the black leather portfolio he carried, and untied the ribbons that secured it. "Codes have always been a hobby of mine, so, naturally, J.P. wanted me to take charge of it. Before this, we had been using the Masonic code books, which are, of course, also available in the North."

"My father is a Mason," Belle said.

"Is he? Which rite, York or Scottish?"

"I don't know. York, I think."

"You see, that's another problem. These are secret societies whose true loyalty is unknown, and which are supposed to be above politics, although that's seldom true." Jules leaned back in his chair, regarding her with interest.

"Women cannot join, of course. Negroes have a separate lodge, and even white men's lodges don't all recognize each other. I cannot join because I am a Catholic."

"They accept Catholics," Belle said. "I'm sure of it."

"Yes," Jules replied, "But the Catholics do not accept them. It's heresy and automatic excommunication. And, should that befall me, who then would I confess my many sins to?"

He was trying to charm her — or worse. The foppish attire concealed a dangerous rogue.

"I am sure your sins are minor ones."

"Alas, no," said Jules, and shook his head sadly.

"Really?"

"I have an unfortunate predilection for other men's wives," he confessed. "And I've killed three men in duels."

Dangerous indeed, thought Belle, and wondered if it were all invented to impress her, but he didn't seem like a man who felt the need to impress anyone. She cleared her throat, amused but not prepared to dismiss him lightly.

"Perhaps we should return to the matter at hand?"

"Yes, of course. We were talking about our chief, J.P. Benjamin. He's just finished writing the Army Regulations, and one of those mandates that we have a uniform system of codes in use for scouts. That includes spies behind the enemy lines and that, my dear, includes you." His manner was brisk and business-like now.

Belle watched as he took out several sheets of paper and laid them on the table along with two pencils.

"This system is simple to use," he said.

Belle blinked, "Won't it be easy to undo, then?"

"No, as a matter of fact," Jules replied. "Decoding relies upon detecting the frequency of certain letters in the message and then finding which letters they really are. In this system that changes constantly, making it much harder. We start with a Vigenere alphabet square."

He slid a printed table across to her. The letters A to Z went across the top and also down the left-hand side. The square was filled with letters in alphabetical order running left to right and top to bottom.

"You will not need to carry this around with you," he said, "You can make one yourself anytime. It's very simple. Now you need a code phrase. This must have exactly 15 letters, but you can have the same letter in more than one position. It must be something that can be remembered and not written down, so it is never more than two words. You do not put a space between the words."

Belle frowned in concentration. "Can you give me an example?"

"The phrase this month is 'Manchester Bluff'," Jules said. "So we take each of those letters and number them from one to 15. Then we put those numbers along the right hand side of the code table next to those letters. We use only those rows for coding. Then we convert the letters in the message to the letters in the table. You see?"

Belle stared at it a moment. Then she saw how it worked. "Yes," she said. "It's simple. Easy to do."

"But you see how the letters change from word to word as you move across the table?"

"Yes," said Belle with growing excitement.

"Good," Jules said. "Now encode these messages."

He got up from the table. "I will be back in a few moments."

He left the room for half an hour. Returning, he found the three messages he had given her encoded. He examined them carefully.

"These are correct," he said, smiling. "Now, decode these."

He sat and watched Belle, one finger tracing across the Vigenere square to find the correct letters. She solved the three messages quickly.

"Very good," he smiled. "I seldom see anyone grasp the matter so quickly."

Belle felt a rush of pleasure. This was not flattery but honest praise.

"Why are we just using this now? I would think anyone could do it."

Jules laughed. "Hardly. Not from memory. Which is how it must be done. Bad spelling can undo the whole thing. Devising memorable code phrases is a major problem. We do not want to use the same one for everyone."

Belle smiled, "In case a code phrase becomes known?"

"Yes," Jules enthused. "Without the code phrase, the alphabet square is useless. So by using different ones we protect our messages. They won't all decode the same way."

He smiled at her. "Can you think of a code phrase?"

"Black Republican?" Belle teased.

Jules laughed, "Memorable, I'll give you that. But impolitic. My brother-in-law has enough problems."

She stood up and offered him her hand, "Thank you so much for what you've shown me today."

He looked at the hand, amused. "I normally do not shake hands with beautiful young ladies," he said.

Belle, puzzled, replied, "No?"

"No," Jules said, putting away his papers. "I have sat here all this time, looking at those luscious lips and wondering if you kiss as well as you talk?"

"Sir!" Belle protested, her face turning red. She was both flattered and outraged. Quickly she stood up and retreated towards the door. He did not follow her, but gazed at her hypnotically, as a snake might at a small bird.

"I've come so far and worked so hard," Jules said, his eyes filled with mischief. "Surely you can spare me one little kiss?" Belle looked away and suddenly her was at her side. Their eyes met. Like most men, he was a bit shorter than her.

To demand such intimacy on such short acquaintance was very wicked of him, yet he was so charming and persuasive about it that, Belle, almost against her will, found herself bending her neck and meeting his lips with hers. What happened then literally took her breath away. She found his tongue inside her mouth and, rather than disgusting, it was thrilling. An electric shock went down to her toes and tingled her nipples and the place between her legs. Confused, she stepped back, breaking away from him, suddenly short of breath.

Jules studied her carefully, a slight smile on his face.

"What...what did you do?" Belle stuttered.

"I wanted to see if the things they say about you are true."

"And are they?"

"Not by half," he assured her. "You flirt well, but you've never been with a man, not totally."

Belle felt outrage at the intimate turn the conversation had taken. "Is this how you test the women who come to work for you?" she demanded.

"*Mai oui*," he said, laughed, picked up his portfolio, put on his hat and went out the door. He paused briefly, smiled and said, "Another time, *cherie*."

It took her several moments to recover her natural manner, such was her confusion. She sat down, her body still filled with the most peculiar feelings, realizing that she had, in effect, been seduced; all of her defenses swept away by a single kiss, from a skilled libertine. It was the very stuff of melodrama and romantic novels. Why had he not followed his obvious inclination and completed her seduction?

A phrase of her uncle's about "shooting fish in a barrel" came to her. Jules St. John was, she decided, a sportsman in his own way, and declined the easy mark.

Belle told Ashby about the training, leaving out the kiss. He seemed to view the entire idea as yet one more unnecessary measure imposed by what he called "the West Point crowd."

"Westpointism will choke out every brave and chivalrous soul in this army," he grumbled. "All this talk of 'strategy' simply hinders our efforts to protect our homes and way of life. It's not necessary and not wanted."

There speaks the Cavalier, the Black Knight of tournaments past, Belle told herself, *The man who will always lead the charge*. She admired him and feared for him in that moment.

They were out by the stable. Fleeter was able to run again, and was being exercised. Ashby was also teaching him a new trick.

"Why would I want him to kneel?" Belle asked.

"You are a very tall woman on a very tall horse. Sometimes the woods and the brush won't be enough to conceal you entirely, especially in winter. At the same time, you must stay mounted. Mounting and dismounting a side saddle is awkward and time consuming. If he kneels with you on him and you lean forward, then it becomes much easier to conceal yourself."

"You will turn me into a circus rider yet, with all of these tricks."

"Miss Belle," said Ashby, "We are about to embark on dangerous work. Your life may depend on such tricks. This particular trick, I hope you never have to use. But, it will be there if you need it."

"All right, then." Belle knew better than to try and charm Ashby. It was refreshing to dispense with feminine artifice and work with a man who treated her as an equal.

It took a day to teach Fleeter to kneel and another to make it easy and natural. He was a very smart horse, and she was lavish in her praise of him.

Ashby said, "There is another man you need to see before we embark on this deep scout behind the lines. Someone who will teach you to be less like yourself when need be."

What's wrong with the way I am? Belle said to herself, but knew the answer. She was not just tall, but easily recognized. Her manner was both loud and flamboyant. All of which got her noticed at the wrong moments, by the wrong people.

Her next instructor was impossibly handsome, she thought, and well-turned out in a new hand-tailored Confederate Cavalry uniform. Ashby introduced them, and because there had been a protest from Belle's aunt, Frances Stewart, about the impropriety of her being alone in a room with a single unknown man when Jules St. Martin was there, Ashby sat in this time.

Belle actually felt relieved about that. It would keep her mind on business and her virtue intact.

"My name is James Harrison," the new man said, "And I'm an actor by trade."

"Oh, my word," Belle said. "Don't let my aunt hear that. She would never welcome an actor here."

"Vagabonds, liars and thieves," Harrison said cheerfully. "But also the arbiters of the classic works of Shakespeare and his fellows. Something of a contradiction, is it not?"

Belle looked around nervously. "I've read Shakespeare," she

said.

"Every schoolgirl does," Harrison said dismissively. "But have you seen it performed?"

"No."

"Let me illustrate," said Harrison. "You know Hamlet? King Lear? Julius Caesar?"

"I read them once."

"Once?" exclaimed Harrison with mock outrage. "Once! Watch this."

He performed those roles, becoming each of those characters in turn. Hamlet as a young prince, Lear as a mad old man, Caesar as a proud general.

Belle's mouth fell open in amazement at the transformations. She started to clap like a school girl and then caught herself.

"You are going to teach me that?"

"Not at all," said Harrison genially. "I didn't even use my stage voice. Usually I have to get those words out to a few hundred people in the audience. This was very pale by comparison, and I didn't use the style that one must with a large audience. No, I was playing for an audience of one, which is what you must do."

Belle leaned forward, "Acting?"

Harrison chuckled, "Is that not what all you belles do, Miss Boyd? Play the role of pretty simpletons and flatter men with their importance? Seek to draw attention to yourselves?"

"I suppose," Belle said with a pout, dismayed at the accuracy of his perception.

"Not all men are taken in, Belle. Some of us play the role right back at you and enjoy the dance. You should know that." Harrison was no longer smiling. He looked at her gravely. "This is dangerous work. Acting, as most people do it, will not serve. Learning it properly takes years. I am not going to attempt to train you in that, but rather teach you a few tricks for concealing your identity and your true nature."

He sprang to his feet and walked around the room,

transforming himself into a man many years older simply by changing the way he walked.

"Can you do the same?" he asked. Belle got up and attempted it. Badly, as it turned out. Quietly and firmly he made a few suggestions. At the end of a hour she had learned not just how to walk like her grandmother, but all the other actions that went into being a woman that age. Then he taught her how to change her stride, how to walk with a limp, and most importantly, how to keep her actions consistent with the role assumed.

Over the midday meal, he regaled her and Ashby and Alice Stewart with tales of his life and the curious people one met in the theatrical trade. Alice was quite taken with him. He had real charm.

During the afternoon, he showed Belle how to change her face by using a few wads of cotton inserted under the cheeks, by applying a few lines of charcoal, and how to dress in ways that concealed her femininity. Belle found herself enjoying the entire idea of changing into another person.

"Careful," Harrison mockingly warned when she confessed this. "That way lies madness...or an acting career."

"Sir," said Belle. "You go too far! I am a well brought up and very proper young lady."

Harrison held up his hands, "No offense meant. This war seems to be changing women. They want to be spies and detectives, for instance."

"Only a few," Ashby said. "Actually, we could use more."

"But we've unleashed the whirlwind, haven't we?" asked Harrison. "They also want to be in battle."

"You mean the vivandieres? Those ridiculous women who sell tobacco and candy to the men? Just another kind of sutler as far as I'm concerned," said Ashby sourly.

"They also carry water to men on the line and messages to and from the officers. A valuable service," Harrison said.

Ashby looked uncomfortably away. "That does free up men for the fight," he admitted.

"Oh, they fight, too," Harrison said. "It's becoming something of a scandal in Richmond. One was discovered wounded in hospital. She had been taken for a boy all along, passed herself off, and been in several pitched battles. She got gut shot and sent to hospital. It was when the surgeons went to work on her that her secret was discovered."

"How did she get away with it so long?" Belle marveled.

Harrison looked at her simply and said, "She acted like a man and did a man's things and a man's work. She wore her clothing loose to conceal her obvious female attributes and since these country boys don't bathe with any regularity and are private in their toilet habits, it wasn't all that hard."

"A lesson there," Belle said, her mind opening to the possibility. "What became of her?"

"She died. The wound was too grievous. There have been others caught. They are quietly discharged and sent on their way. One said she simply wanted to earn a bit of hard money, another was following her man."

"So, she's not the only one?"

"No. I suspect there are many."

Harrison shook his head and favored her with a wry smile. "In Shakespeare's time all the roles, male and female, were played by men. It was a man's trade. Now we have women who do quite well, and I think they may use the war to do well in other domains formerly reserved for men."

Belle looked at Ashby who was tapping his finger on the table, taking all this in. "Do you agree, Henry?"

"I see no way to prevent it," he grumbled, and stood up, offering his hand to Harrison. "Perhaps we'll meet again. Where are you bound?"

"General Longstreet's headquarters. I will be working for him."

"As a scout?"

"As a spy. The Yankees have rolled up another of our

Washington operations. I'm to see if we can't form another among theatrical folk."

After Harrison rode off, Belle turned to Ashby and asked, "Is there anything else we need to do?"

"Come up with a disguise for yourself, Belle. One totally away from your public character. Show me that, and then we will adventure it." Ashby walked away, swinging his arms, a bit angry at something.

Belle watched him go. She wondered what kind of young lady would be so unlike her that no one would know it was her in disguise. An idea came to her later that night.

CHAPTER ELEVEN

The next morning Turner Ashby received a note from Belle, asking him to call on her at two that afternoon. He rode from his camp with Harry Gilmour whom Belle had known as a dashing young policeman when she'd been in school in Baltimore, and who was now a Captain with his own cavalry company in the Seventh Virginia. They were admitted to the front parlor by Eliza, who seemed to be laughing to herself about something. She went off to get them some refreshment.

A tall sallow-faced woman in a plain everyday dress entered the room. Her graying hair was up, and she looked like a school teacher about 40 years old. A large black enameled wooden cross hung around her neck, and she had some pamphlets in her hands.

"Please, sir," the woman said in the tired, resigned voice of someone accustomed to being rebuked, "Would you take just a moment to read our tract about the Lord? Are you a Christian? Do you feel the injustice of this terrible war and its effect on innocent women and children? If you could just take a moment...."

The two officers sat transfixed at this unexpected apparition. Then Harry broke into laughter and began to applaud.

"Bravo," he said. "Bravo. Why it's as good as a play, Henry!"

The woman stopped at this outburst, apparently hurt and confused, "Sir, cannot you contain yourself and come to the Lord?"

Turner Ashby stood and stepped up right in front of her, staring into her eyes. Her expression changed little, except to become more perplexed. He looked her up and down and then lifted her hands and examined them carefully.

"Almost," he said. "The hands don't match the face, but damn me if it isn't a very good caricature, Belle."

Belle didn't smile, but continued to blink in apparent perplexity until he said, "It will do for our first mission."

Then she smiled and bowed very slightly, "Your servant, sir."

Ashby turned her around. "How have you done this?"

Belle replied, "The dress is larger and therefore very loose. Since the thing men seem to recall most about me is my figure, I thought it well to conceal that. The rest of it is tricks Mister Harrison taught me. That, and imitating Lucy Buck and playing her as a missionary. She is such an earnest and delicate soul that I could think of no one more unlike me."

"You do not care for Lucy, I gather."

"Actually, I like her quite well," Belle replied thoughtfully. "It is she who doesn't care for me. Calls me 'vain and hollow', but not to my face. She is very dedicated to the Cause, but not so much so that she would stir herself to actually leave her house and do a spot of work for it. Sometimes, I just want to shake her and wake her up."

"Well, this was not Lucy, but someone else entirely," Turner Ashby observed.

"Lucy was where I began, but I had to change it. I wouldn't mock her. That would be too cruel. She is great friends with Cousin Fannie, and we don't need her to be upset."

"I would not show this to anyone else," Turner Ashby cautioned. "Save it for the work."

"Most assuredly," Belle agreed. "I wouldn't want it to grow stale or false."

"Are you prepared to argue your case?" asked Harry shrewdly.

"Have I not been dragged to church, willing or not, every Sunday of my life? I can preach a sermon as well as anyone."

"You haven't been to a Negro church, have you?" Harry asked with a twinkle in his eye.

Belle stared at him a moment. "That occasion has not been made available to me," she said after a moment.

"Ain't nothing quite like it for zeal and intensity. They work hard at it."

"Where have you...?"

"Two Sundays ago. I went with General Jackson and some of his other officers."

Belle looked at him doubtfully, "Really?"

Ashby held up both hands, "No, it's true. Stonewall is a very devout man. Always tries to avoid movement or battle on the Lord's day. Doesn't always get it done, but he tries. And, he goes always to the church closest to the camp, and that's after the Chaplain has had his service for the men. Wants to let people know that the Army is led by godly men."

Belle, still suspecting a joke, for Ashby was notorious for his pranks, looked at Harry questioningly.

"At home, Stonewall teaches Sunday School to the little black children and teaches them to read aloud from the Bible," Harry said, his face quite serious.

"Oh, now I know you're making this up, the both of you," Belle said. "That's against the law, teaching slaves to read."

"No, he just don't care about that law is all. Thinks everyone should be able to read the Bible, regardless." Harry Gilmour looked thoughtful. "I'd love to see him tried on a charge of breaking that law. It would be a courtroom spectacular."

"He'd lose," said Ashby looking uncomfortable. Before the war his Mountain Rangers had set out to enforce such laws and to catch runaway slaves and agents of the Underground Railway that aided them. That was their official duty. In reality they were simply a Democrats' political club for the Chivalry, and funded by rich men like Alexander Boetler. The Baltimore police force that Harry Gilmour belonged to was another such club. Harry loved politics and argument for its own sake, so he cheerfully continued his line of thought.

"Well, Colonel, winning ain't everything, and I'm not so sure he would lose. If a slave is property and a master can do anything he wants with it, including rape it and murder it, then teaching it to read, if that's his choice, ain't illegal either, not if it confers a benefit — and who is going to argue that learning to read the Bible is a bad thing?"

Ashby frowned, "Stonewall don't say much about his thinking on any subject, much less that one, but I've the idea he don't exactly favor the Peculiar Institution. I think he's a Virginia man first and foremost, and if Virginia had declared for the Union we'd all be wearing blue and fighting Beauregard."

Belle was shocked at the idea. This was a stunning admission for any Southern Gentleman, much less a slave catcher like Ashby, to make. She tried to speak and couldn't. Finally she managed it. "You'd follow Stonewall even if he was a Yankee?"

"Into Hell itself," said Turner Ashby, and Gilmour nodded in agreement.

"But that's talking over kitchen whisky time," Ashby continued. "You've got a final bit of schooling before we set out."

"What, yet more?" Belle said, unhappily. "What more could there be?"

"Well, we won't be sending you to VMI, but it would be useful if you knew a thing or two about artillery."

Belle thought a moment and nodded. "It would," she agreed.

The next day Ashby invited her to meet him at the headquarters of the Seventh Virginia Cavalry. There he introduced her to Jackson's Ordnance officer, Major George Henry Bier. He was a lean, muscular man in his mid-thirties, with close-cropped brown hair and beard, and lines near his eyes as if he had spent a lot of time staring into the sun. His face was tanned to a nut brown which made his green eyes more startling. He smoked, without apology, a corncob pipe. Belle had seen another face like this before in Washington, when she had been introduced to Catesby R. ap Jones, who was then in the Union Navy.

"You look like a sailor, Major Bier."

He smiled at her. "I am. But we don't have much of a navy yet, so I thought I'd come up here and help out. Cavalry is natural for these country boys, but artillery is a bit of a mystery, and ordnance more so. We don't want them blowing themselves up. Powder is too hard to come by."

He seemed like a very good humored man and Belle liked him at once. She also noticed that he wore a simple gold wedding band on his left hand.

He noted her glance and added, "I believe you're acquainted with my wife."

"Am I?"

"Susan Berkeley?"

Belle remembered her at once, a very pretty blonde-haired girl who had also attended Mount Washington Female Academy, and who had talked of a mysterious beau who Belle and the other girls were half sure was an invention of her imagination. Obviously not, because Major Bier matched what Belle remembered of Susan's descriptions.

I should be jealous, Belle thought, but I'm not. No, I'm happy for her; for them. "You must remember me to her," Belle said.

"I will, but she has already instructed me to tell you how much she admires you." Belle looked puzzled. "The newspapers," he explained.

Belle found that she very much wanted to change the subject. "Perhaps we should begin?"

Bier led her outside, where an artillery piece and its crew waited. "Note, first of all, the red stripe on the trousers," he began. "That is how you know an artilleryman, in our army or theirs. Next, the carriage which carries the piece; this is a six-pounder, the most common item in the inventory. It's called that because it fires a six pound solid iron ball — a shot, we call it. Against infantry, we use case shot or shrapnel, which is a hollow shot filled with lead or iron balls like buckshot. It explodes in mid-air and can stop an infantry charge in its tracks. When the charge gets too close to use case shot, we switch to canister, which is a can of smaller balls packed in sawdust. This turns the cannon into a huge shotgun."

Bier paused and looked at her, "Are you with me so far?"

"Yes," said Belle, frowning in concentration.

"Good," said Bier with a wide grin. "Now, behind the carriage is the limber, also on two wheels, with an ammunition chest on top. Hooked together with the carriage, the whole assembly becomes a sort of four-wheeled cart. Behind that we have the caisson, with two more ammunition chests. The gun crew can ride on top of these if need be, although we save that for moments when fast maneuver is called for, because it's hard on the horses. Horses are even more important to the artillery than they are to the cavalry, and they are older, more settled, and stronger, usually plough horses or the like. There are a lot of tools and implements which must be carried, and these are usually in the battery wagon."

He stopped and peered at her a moment. "Which of all of this do you think is the most important?"

Belle took a long moment to think about that. "The horses. You can't move all this without them."

"Not a bad answer," Bier admitted. "But the horse can't serve or position the gun, so we need the men in the crew as well, and of course without ammunition the gun is useless. Every bit of it is important."

"Of course," Belle murmured. "Is there anything else?"

Bier laughed, not unkindly, "Miss Belle, we've just begun. Get your horse and I will show you how a crew serves a gun."

Belle, a bit put out because she had thought the lesson would be a short one, had Fleeter brought up, and reported back to him a few minutes later.

Bier looked at her horse doubtfully. "He looks high strung. He may bolt when he hears the gun fired."

"Not if I am with him, and he should become accustomed to the sound, given where he and I will be going," Belle said.

With Bier riding at her side and the gun crew following, the six-pounder behind, they traveled a short distance to a small wooded valley where no one lived. There she watched the artillery crew pull up, dismount, detach the gun carriage from the limber, maneuver it into position and then load and fire one round. The noise was not as loud as she had expected and while Fleeter jumped in alarm, she was able to quickly calm him.

"What you see here," Bier said, "Is how every man has his

part to play in the operation of the gun. If a man is lost, the others in the crew can manage, but the rate of fire goes down. Likewise, if the carriage, limber and caisson are not all present, the amount of time and number of shots the gun can fire is much lessened."

"I can see that. So the crew must be protected?"

"Artillery is usually a defensive rather than an offensive weapon unless you are laying siege to an enemy position. You use the solid shot to break down their fortifications, and the case shot to kill and wound their men. So, yes, we need the protection of some infantry. Otherwise we could be overrun by enemy cavalry or infantry and the guns lost, the crews killed."

Belle tried to put it all together in her mind. "Artillery can kill many infantry, but can be killed by a few of them?"

Bier nodded. "Essentially," he said, indecently cheerful at the prospect. "And the gun is not easily turned; it can be flanked and overrun. It is only effective against what is in front of it, unlike a man on the ground or on horseback. Our sharpshooters are trained to identify and kill two kinds of men: officers and cannoneers."

"May I see the drill again?" Belle asked.

"No, unfortunately, powder is in short supply just now. We need to save it for battle." Bier signaled to the crew to start getting ready to move. He waited until the men had remounted and let them take the road first. It was still wet from rain the day before, and the wheels of the carriage, limber and caisson threw up sheets of mud to either side as they moved.

Bier pointed, "Note that. Artillery uses special wheels for six- and twelve-pounders, which are forty-six inches high, and shaped to keep mud and moisture away from the powder and crew. It also leaves tracks that are unlike those of an ordinary carriage or wagon. A scout needs to know the differences."

Belle simply nodded, trying to take it all in. Bier said nothing more until they were in front of the Fishback Hotel. There he dismissed the crew of the six-pounder and watched them ride off.

"Well, thank you...," Belle began.

"Oh, we've hardly begun, Miss Belle," he said, grinning wider still. "There is much more."

"Of course," Belle said with a sigh. "Let me have someone see to the horses. You will stay for dinner?"

"Thank you," Bier replied, still smiling in a most irritating way.

After dinner, situated in a side room under the watchful gaze of her Aunt Frances, Bier hauled out books with drawings of other kinds of cannon to show her. Belle had never known there were so many ways to kill people. Mortars, howitzers, and something called a Parrot rifle.

"Why is it named after a bird?" Belle asked, thoroughly confused.

Bier choked with laughter and then recovered himself. "It's named after its inventor. It's iron rather than bronze, with a reinforcing ring of cast iron at the muzzle...and it's rifled."

"Rifled?"

"There are spiral grooves cut into the barrel, which cause the shell to rotate. This has several advantages. It's more accurate and can travel further with the same charge of powder. Rather than round shot we can use a long shot or bolt which is tapered at one end and which can be fused to explode when it strikes the target; and because it's made from iron, we can make it bigger so that it can throw many times the weight — one hundred pounds or more."

Bier tapped his finger on the paper with the illustration. "This is the future of artillery. Greater power at longer range. This is what we will put on our navy ships when we have them."

"I thought we were building a navy," Belle said.

"We are," said Bier, "But for defensive purposes on brown water. Rivers," he added, seeing confusion in her eyes once more. "But, we need a blue water navy as well, for the deep seas. We must break this blockade that the Union is imposing on our ports, and we need to be able to attack their commerce even as they are attacking ours."

Bier fiddled with his pipe once more, "Everyone looks to Britain and France to intervene, but a few realize that our nationhood cannot be dependent upon such things. We must be able to protect our merchant fleet the way that Britain protects its own, and that requires warships. Mister Benjamin is working...."

"You are from Mister Benjamin?" Belle was startled. She stared at him.

"Oh," replied Bier. "I thought that was understood. The blue water navy and the Secret Service are all one. Measures are underway, and I hope to be to sea again very shortly. In the meantime, Stonewall Jackson, being an artillery man, knows the value of it, but has no time to drill troops himself, so I've been loaned for a few months to the Army at equivalent rank. Jackson understands artillery. He will always be anxious to know about the artillery on the Union side; therefore it's fallen to me to give demonstrations and instruction. And to see that our own is well managed."

Bier leaned back reflectively, "You Virginians are demons for cavalry, but not much on the other branches. Too much complication, not enough glamour."

"Do you think we can win?"

"Oh, yes," he smiled, "For the Yankees are in far worse shape than we are. They use horses to pull wagons and plows and not much else. No cavalry worthy of the name. Artillery crews are not made overnight either. We can win, but we'll have to be quick about it."

CHAPTER TWELVE

Romney, Virginia, December 1861

Three days later Belle, in her religious missionary garb, and Turner Ashby, in his guise as Henry Turner, the horse doctor, set out to scout the Union forces at the village of Romney, some forty miles away. Starting before dawn, they went by different roads and at different times.

Belle drove a small wagon pulled by a two-horse team, rather than ride Fleeter and risk having an envious Provost seize him, and left her pistol behind as well. It might give the lie to her pose as a religious worker.

Belle had never been to Romney and knew no one from there. There was little risk she would be recognized.

It was a cold, sunny day and all the leaves were off the trees. She could see quite a way into the woods along the road, which meant that they offered poor concealment.

She carried a Union pass issued by Lt. Col. Fillebrown in Winchester to someone else entirely. Fillebrown had been careless and not entered an expiration date. The name on the pass was Eileen McCorkal. Outside Romney, she gave it over to an alert vidette, a picket on horseback, who squinted at the signature and handed it back.

"Are you a Christian?" Belle inquired in a low voice. "Would you care to read of our Lord?"

She proffered one of the pamphlets, but he waved it away. "Can't read," he grunted. That surprised Belle. She wondered how often a Provost guard or picket might see a pass and not know what it said. "Well, God bless you anyway," she said, and drove on into the town.

Union troops were everywhere. Normally, Romney was another railroad town, but Jackson had had the tracks torn up months before to prevent the Union from using it. Belle saw that several wagons were loaded with cut lumber for railroad ties. The teams that had hauled them had been detached and sent to other duty, and the wagons just sat there, lining the side of the street next to the depot for a quarter mile or so. No one who had grown up in Martinsburg could be ignorant of railroad equipment. She took it all in at a glance and remembered it.

In town, she took her team of horses to a livery stable and paid a Negro boy about twelve years old to watch them and the wagon. Pamphlets in hand, she set out to survey the Union camp. Several times she was stopped by inquisitive Provosts who, when presented with a pamphlet and an earnest question about faith, beat a hasty retreat, allowing her to proceed unhindered.

These Union forces seemed more professional than the ones she had met before. Wisconsin and Indiana regiments, and no ridiculous Zouave uniforms. Lingering near a sutler's wagon, she overheard a few interesting tidbits, but that worthy, afraid that she would hinder trade, asked her politely to move on. He was selling cards and dice and, she suspected, whisky. Men would buy small bottles of "medicine", conceal them in their sack coats, and hurry away.

Her attempts to actually enter one of the camps were rebuffed, but she had better luck at the hospital. There, a nice Quaker woman from Pennsylvania allowed her to help change some bed linen.

"Have thee been long on thy mission?" she asked as they turned over a mattress together.

"I began but today," Belle replied.

"Thee will have a hard time, I fear," the Quaker said. "These are rough men. The war has coarsened the most gentle spirits among them."

"If I can save but one," Belle replied in the resigned voice she had heard many times from her own mother. She looked around the half-empty ward. "Not many patients."

"The camp fevers have run their course. Good sanitation and good food is all it takes. Everyone is preparing for the winter now." The Quaker woman, who was about forty, gray-haired and ruddy-faced, looked at her curiously. "Thee has nursed?"

"Once," Belle admitted. "But my people did not approve."

"Ah, that would be hard," the Quaker said sympathetically.

"Why are you here?" Belle asked.

"We do what we can. I came to work among the colored people, but they have all been moved to Winchester."

"Why?" Belle tried not to seem too curious.

"To rebuild the railroad. They plan to use the escaped slaves, the 'intelligent contraband' as they call them, and are gathering two thousand of them there."

Belle was taken aback. "Why so many?"

"They plan to organize them along military lines. Men and boys to do the heavy work. Women and the rest to keep camp and cook and do laundry."

"Just another kind of plantation," Belle sniffed.

"Thee has hit the nail on the head," the Quaker woman said, nodding grimly. "For there is no talk of paying wages or doing any other thing that will lift them out of bondage. Pure hypocrisy."

Belle agreed it was a terrible thing, and after accepting the woman's kind offer to share her dinner and listening to all of her gentle complaints about the Yankees, left her there. She walked on, looking carefully about, counting tents.

Several times she stopped and engaged men in conversation, starting with a pamphlet and the matter of religion. Officers had no time for her, but some enlisted men, simply glad for an excuse to rest for a few moments, were all too happy to talk to her. Oddly, Belle noticed, all of them treated her as they would a sister. There was no flirting or innuendo or rude attention. They were respectful, and if she simply listened, she could learn a great deal.

One even undertook to explain to her the workings of a cannon. Inwardly Belle was amused, but also careful to note that it was part of a defensive line that was being dug in. Everywhere men were building huts for the coming cold weather. Some had brick fireplaces.

Finally, late in the afternoon, she saw the Henry Turner,

Veterinary wagon parked near the center of town. Ashby stood there talking to three Yankee officers. She waited until he had parted from them, which involved much back-slapping and expressions of mutual esteem.

She approached him, as they had arranged, with a pamphlet in hand.

"Please sir, would you...," Belle began.

"Of course, Sister," Ashby said and drew her aside, pretending to read the pamphlet and discuss it with her. "What have you learned?" His breath smelled of liquor.

"They plan to rebuild the railway from Martinsburg, using contraband labor for most of it," said Belle. "And they are building up here for the winter. Quite a bit of supply on hand. Hospital is in very good condition but not much used. Haven't seen much artillery, but they are digging fortifications that will protect the town and supply depot. These are three-year men, and some militia, but I can't tell how many."

Ashby glanced around, making sure that no one was within hearing range, "About six thousand, in six regiments, with very little cavalry, but quite a bit of artillery. They mean to make this a base for operations next spring."

He chuckled, "One thing I learned today. I have more traction with these Yankees if I bleed them a little for money. They respect that, being avaricious themselves. I saw fifty horses today, all in shameful condition. They simply have no idea that you have to take care of stock and to rest it. They barely know how to feed and water it."

Belle was amused, "And how much did you gain?"

"Five dollars a horse. But I set them right on how to care for them. They got their money's worth."

"Was that wise?" Belle asked. "Would it not be to our advantage to have their horses break down?"

Ashby was shocked by the notion, "Perhaps, but it ain't the horse's fault he's working for the Yankees. He don't know blue from gray, and wouldn't much care. Most horses ain't all that smart and only ask that we treat them well for their service. Besides, Doc Turner's reputation ain't something I'll hazard lightly."

Belle felt rather apologetic and was about to say something when she suddenly spotted a familiar figure walking towards them. She turned quickly, transmitting her alarm to Ashby, who tensed, but did not move.

"What is it?" he asked quietly.

"Kelley, the Irishman I knew in Martinsburg. Provost Marshal, coming right for us. He mustn't see me here."

Ashby nodded and turned, as Kelley hailed him.

"Doctor Turner, is it?" Kelley called.

"Turn and walk away slowly," Ashby said in a whisper to Belle. "Leave him to me."

Belle, trembling inside, nodded, and moved away, walking deliberately slow.

Ashby turned and said with more cheer than he felt, "How can I help you, Captain?"

"I'm Michael Kelley, Chief Provost Marshal for Romney. I wonder if I might see your pass?"

"Certainly," Ashby replied, fumbling in his pockets. "Here it is."

Belle walked on, no longer able to hear their conversation. She went directly to where she had left the wagon and team, gave the Negro boy another coin, climbed aboard and drove out of town towards Winchester.

Once well clear of the town, she took a little-used farm road that the Union scouts had not yet found and waited at a pre-arranged rendezvous at a cross roads. Fortunately, there was a good moon and not many clouds.

While she waited, she tended to the horses, feeding them from a nosebag with some dried corn she had brought for that purpose. She resisted the temptation to build a fire and sat there cold and hungry, waiting.

Finally, about midnight, Ashby came along the other road, pulled up along side of her wagon and said, "Your friend is no fool."

"No friend of mine," Belle replied with an edge in her voice. "He's a charming rogue, but Yankee to the core."

"And with that brogue," Ashby chuckled. "He was charming, but very much on point about where I'd come from, where I was going and so on. Fortunately, my answers satisfied him. But he'll remember me."

"That he will," Belle said. "He was a policeman, and I suspect a good one."

Ashby noticed that she was shivering, "Have you eaten?"

Belle shook her head miserably. He looked in a leather satchel and handed her a slab of beef between two slices of stale bread. It was wrapped in brown paper. "No coffee, I'm afraid."

Belle tore into the sandwich hungrily. "Water will do," she replied between bites.

Ashby lit a cigar and peered at a pocket watch. "Near midnight. We could camp here, but I'd rather not risk it. Front Royal isn't that far. We can be there by dawn."

"Fine by me," Belle said.

"You know," Ashby said, "Stonewall and them may be right. It may be time to give over Doctor Turner and stick to being Turner Ashby."

"Why do you say that?"

Ashby puffed on his cigar a few moments trying to form the words to express what was on his mind. Finally, he said, "When all this started, it was this or nothing — and the Yankees were incautious fools. Now they've learned some discipline, it's too much to risk. I am a Lieutenant Colonel now. I have five hundred men in my charge."

He chuckled. "The extra money was nice, or would be if I could spend it."

"I'll buy those greenbacks from you," Belle said.

"What would you do with them?"

"I suspect I'll find a use for them," Belle said drily.

Ashby laughed, pulled a roll of bills out of his pocket and handed them to her. "For Secret Service work. Of course. Take them and welcome."

He looked up at the sky.

"We're losing the moon."

He reached under the seat of his wagon and handed her a revolver. "In case there's trouble. Follow my wagon, but not too close. Let's go home."

Belle hefted the revolver, checked the caps and asked, "Did we do a day's work?"

Ashby replied, "And then some. I suspect that Stonewall will want to break up this Union formation right quick."

Ashby picked up the reins and urged his horses forward at a slow trot. After counting off a full minute, Belle followed.

CHAPTER THIRTEEN

Front Royal, Virginia, February 1862

After three mysterious stops that no one bothered to explain to the passengers, the train arrived in Front Royal at four in the morning. Antonia Ford, stiff and drowsy, alighted to find a patient young Negro waiting with a wagon drawn by a single horse. He held a lantern. It was pouring rain, and wind made her umbrella useless.

"You be Missus Jessup?" he inquired, shivering under the rubber cloak he wore..

"I am," said Antonia. She was traveling under a false name again. Secretary Benjamin had provided papers for Amanda Jessup, a widow. General Winder, the Provost Marshal in Richmond, now required passenger lists from the railroad and he did not want to excite that man's curiosity about a young woman who traveled alone to and from Richmond on a regular basis. Antonia had been a half-dozen young ladies recently, as she shuttled between Benjamin's offices in Richmond and various points in the field, carrying messages to and from Alexander Boetler and Jacob Thompson, his principal field deputies for the Secret Service.

A Negro porter brought her one small bag from the baggage car, and handed it to the boy.

"Dis all you have?"

"Yes. You are from the Fishback Hotel?"

"Yes, ma'am," said the boy, and placed her bag in the wagon. He pointed to a two-story building across the street, which was covered with rapidly flowing water several inches deep. Antonia saw that she could cross, but only at the expense of her fine boots and the ruin of her dress. The Negro boy silently offered her his arm and helped her onto the front seat, and with the lantern held high to light the way led, rather than drove, the horse pulling it.

"Dey had artillery pass by yesterday. Done tore up de road somethin' awful, den the rain came," he said over his shoulder.

It was a one-minute ride to the hotel, already brightly lit from within, as servants prepared for the day. Several large tents were pitched on the other side of the road. Officers in various stages of dress squinted into cups of something that might be coffee but probably wasn't. They looked as if they had perhaps drunk too much the night before.

"Who are they?" Antonia asked, as the boy helped her down from the wagon.

"Sebben Virginia. Ashby's I Company."

Antonia nodded, and went through the door into a pleasant room with bright yellow walls accented with polished wood, several short couches upholstered in bright yellow burlap, and a high desk.

Antonia's heart sank as she recognized the girl at the desk.

It was Alice Stewart, Belle Boyd's cousin. Alice was writing a list of some kind. Antonia would be recognized and it was very important that Alice not call out her name. Men in gray homespun were coming down the stairs. Cavalry officers. Ashby's rather than Jeb Stuart's, but she still ran the risk of being recognized by some old friend on liaison duty. Tucking in her chin and hoping the bonnet would cover her face and prevent someone else from recognizing her, she stepped up to the desk, and spoke softly.

"You have a room for Amanda Jessup?"

Alice looked up, startled, recognized her, started to speak, and then saw the urgency in her eyes. "Mrs. Jessup," she said slowly; "Yes, we got your telegram. Your room is ready." She looked up and saw the boy bringing Antonia's one small lonely bag through the door. "Nathaniel. Take Mrs. Jessup's bag to number twelve."

Inwardly, Antonia was relieved that Alice was so quick, but also concerned. How much had Belle told her cousin?

"Please sign the register," Alice said, sliding a large cloth-bound book over to her, "And may I see your pass?"

"Certainly," Antonia produced it from a fold in her cloak. She took the quill pen from its holder and signed 'Mrs. Amanda Jessup' in a bold, flowing hand.

Alice looked at the pass carefully, handed it back, and smiled.

"Welcome to The Fishback Hotel. Is there anything else we can do to serve you?"

"I'd like a bit of breakfast if that can be managed."

"Certainly. I'll bring it myself. Give me a few minutes to roust the cook." Alice held out a large key. Antonia could feel the curious glances of the young officers coming down the stairs as she went up and found her room.

"Who is that?" she heard one of them ask Alice.

"That is Mrs. Jessup, a widow traveling alone."

Inside the room, she took off her cloak and bonnet, and saw her bag sitting on a narrow bed. There was little other furniture aside from a table with a wash basin and two small towels, a mirror and a small dresser. An old chair and a table were near the fireplace, which glowed with the remains of a fire.

She took a few pieces of coal from the scuttle and added them carefully. She opened her bag and took a small photograph from it and then kissed it before setting on top of the dresser.

A few moments later, there was a tap on the door. She opened it to find Alice holding a tray. She stepped inside and Antonia closed the door behind her.

"I suppose you want an explanation?" Antonia said nervously.

"No," said Alice seriously. "I've learned from Belle not to ask too many questions. I assume it has something to do with the Secret Service."

As Antonia delicately sampled the breakfast, Alice spied the picture on the dresser. She picked it up and examined it carefully. It was of a young man with dark curly hair and beard, and liquid dark eyes, wearing a Confederate Army uniform.

"How handsome he is," Alice exclaimed. "Is he your beau?"

Antonia smiled, almost wriggling with pleasure at the words. "He is. His name is Tom Rosser and he's on Stuart's staff."

Alice said, "You're very fortunate to have so many men pursuing you."

"Just the one," Antonia said primly, "And, in the beginning, t'was I who pursued him."

Alice seemed taken aback, "Really?"

"Well, I'm almost twenty-three now, and not destined to be an old maid. And I wanted him the moment I saw him. But he was all business, like most West Pointers. A little shy."

Alice sat on the bed, drinking in every word. "Oh, tell me, more," she begged.

"As you know," Antonia said, primping a little, "I am accounted a great beauty. Does that sound vain and hollow? Perhaps, but it is not an easy thing. Some men are put off by it, you know."

"Why?"

"They think they won't have a chance. Or they think their mothers won't approve."

Alice shook her head in disbelief.

"Oh, that last is very true," Antonia assured her. "Very few men have the intestinal fortitude to defy their mothers in the choice of a bride — and who wants to marry into a situation where she does not approve of you?"

"That would not be good," Alice agreed. She looked at the photograph again and gave an admiring sigh. She looked very young.

"Sometimes, it becomes very clear," Antonia said. "The moment I saw him, I knew he was the one. Most of Jeb's staff are well-favored boys, but Tom is no callow youth. He's a man." She smiled, remembering. "He paid me no mind at all. It was very aggravating. I'm not used to that."

"What did you do?" Alice asked excitedly.

"I sent him flowers."

Alice's mouth fell open in shock. "Oh, my, that's bold," she said after a moment.

"It was, but all's fair in love and war." Antonia looked very pleased with herself. "And it got the job done. Jeb and the others teased him about it, but he took note of me then."

"Why not Jeb?"

"Aside from the fact that he's married and his wife is a dear friend of mine?" asked Antonia teasingly. "Only that much of my work is with his headquarters. It's not proper to mix duty and romance. Tom's with the artillery, so our paths don't cross that much. Jeb is my employer."

"As Belle's is Ashby," said Alice.

"How much has she told you?" Antonia asked, alarmed.

"Not much. But one can observe things and draw one's own conclusions, and she's asked for my help if the Yankees come in here."

"As they likely will, once things start up," Antonia said sadly. "We don't have enough men to hold them off."

"Belle says it's a war of bluff and maneuver, whatever that means."

Well, that's nothing she couldn't find out by reading the Richmond newspapers, Antonia thought.

"Where is Belle?" she asked.

"Winchester or Martinsburg. Supposedly, she's helping her mother get goods for their store."

Antonia looked at her thoughtfully. "Would you be a dear and help me loosen my corset? I need to rest for awhile. If Belle is not here, then I will be taking the train tonight to Centerville."

"Certainly," said Alice. "I'll make sure you're not disturbed until supper,...Mrs. Jessup."

Once she was gone, with the now empty tray, Antonia got under the quilt on top of the bed, drew it close about her and tried to sleep. *Alice would be all right*, she thought. *She is young, but then, so is Belle. Could I have done this work at that age?*

Her hand rested on the heavy envelope concealed within her corset. Letters were smuggled through the lines by many women. Usually in small bundles, often hung beneath their hoop skirts.

She had been sent to take one letter all the way to Washington by a most indirect route to Baltimore, still a hotbed of Secession sentiment, and then work her way back west to Washington. The letter was from Judah Benjamin to Lord Lyons, the English Minister. That was all she knew about it, and all she wanted to know.

The noises from the yard, the camp across the road and the railroad station grew louder, but she fell into a deep dreamless sleep which lasted until late afternoon. When she woke, it was already dark, but there was a tapping on the door.

Oh, won't they let me sleep, she thought, as she got up and stumbled to open a it crack, to see Belle Boyd, in a riding habit, standing there, grinning at her with suppressed excitement.

Antonia drew back as Belle slipped in and enfolded her in a big hug. Disoriented, she said, "Alice said you were not here."

"I've just returned," Belle said.

"What time is it?"

"Seven," said Belle, and Antonia realized that she had slept the day away.

Oh, my," said Antonia. "I've got a train to catch."

"Not tonight. The track's come undone. Washed out by thawing mud." Belle added, "It is so good to see you."

"And you. Where have you been?"

"Martinsburg," Belle said sadly. "It seems to be going for the Union now."

Antonia went to build up the fire again. As it glowed brighter, she saw that Belle was wearing a pistol at her side.

"Scouting?"

"Yes, with Uncle James Glenn and the boys, a little, but many women are wearing them now. There are stragglers and bandits everywhere along the border." Belle sat on the bed and motioned for Antonia to take the chair.

"Tell me the news from Richmond," she said. "We hear so little here, and the newspapers are wrong more often than they are right."

Antonia was still trying to wake up. "Well, Jeff Davis is confirmed as President now for six years, and Beauregard is being sent west to Tennessee."

Belle, surprised, said, "How can that be? He's our best

general next to Stonewall."

"And he and Jeff Davis hate each other. It goes back several years to when Jeff was the Secretary of War. Beauregard always speaks his mind, and is even more vain and arrogant than our dear President."

"I see," Belle sighed. "It seems rather silly."

Antonia began to put her dress back on. "It is silly. Men are silly and vain creatures, even more so than women. It's very aggravating sometimes. All that posturing and maneuvering for position."

"I don't see that much out here in the field," Belle said.

"Oh, surely you do. Just look at these uniforms they've put on. Zouaves are a chorus from the comic opera, and Jeb Stuart, as much as I like him, is very much the peacock. Gold lace on the sleeves, a cape lined with red that flutters as he rides, and that hat with the big black feather. And the circus at his headquarters, the young pretty acolytes, the musicians, the dinners. It's quite amazing that he gets anything done."

"Well," Belle said pointedly, "Ashby doesn't go in for such displays."

"No, because Stonewall Jackson sets the style, although one hesitates to use such a word to dignify his ancient uniform and forage cap. It's all one. Ashby has a different kind of drama, but he's seriously jealous of Jeb." Antonia sighed. "He's intriguing to get promoted to Brigadier, too. Seems to think it his due."

"Well," said Belle reasonably, "Jeb is a bit of a Davis pet; a favorite."

"Only because he's, pardon my language, damn good at what he does. He knows his business, having been to West Point, and he served in the Army out west. Ashby is simply a talented amateur." Antonia said this without heat and Belle listened carefully.

"Ashby is in mourning for his brother Dick still," Belle said. "It's changed him. He's blind with anger about the Yankees coming into Martinsburg and taking over. Folks tried to make it up to him."

"How?"

"Various ways. They made him a Master Mason. He went from Entered Apprentice to Third Degree in a single night."

"I didn't think that was possible."

"Exigencies of war. My father is the Grand Master of that lodge and arranged it."

"I see," Antonia said slowly. "Did he tell you this?"

"Oh, no. Tell a woman?" Belle smiled. "They had Eliza's husband Sam standing watch for 'cowans and eavesdroppers'. Everybody wanted to be there for the ceremony."

"Sam is a member of that lodge?" Antonia was very surprised.

"No, but he's a Prince Hall Mason, and they stretched a point. Masons are supposed to admit any worthy male, and while no one here would extend that to a Negro, Sam knows what to do. It's a difficult time for that lodge, whose name is Equality." Belle smiled sardonically. "Ward Hill Lamon was there."

"Lincoln's man? How so?"

"He grew up in Martinsburg. It's his Mother Lodge from when he was eighteen. He and my father both courted my mother."

Antonia was nonplussed, "How very odd."

"David Strother was there, too. Porte Crayon?"

"My word. Is he from Martinsburg, too?"

"Yes, and he's a close friend of my family's, not to mention that everyone there is some kind of cousin to everyone else."

Antonia looked at her shrewdly, "What's troubling you?"

"Oh," said Belle, suddenly holding back a tear, "Just that I really like him, and not just because he's so funny and droll. He's been riding around, spying for the Yankees."

"But none of that matters in the Lodge."

"Politics stays outside, my father always says," Belle said.

"As does mine," Antonia looked at her shrewdly. "How do you know he's been spying?"

"Well, he's the one, as the good book says, to 'spy out the land'. You've seen how he draws; very detailed. He can do that from memory and he knows this area better than most, having not just grown up here but written all of those books, which he illustrated. Besides, we caught one of his partners in the enterprise."

"Really?"

"A Mr. Luce, who my cousins caught riding along a road, with a map and notebook in one hand and a compass in the other. He's been sent down to Richmond."

"Well, it seems like we have big problems in Martinsburg," Antonia said. "Perhaps you should send in a report."

"Already done." Belle got up, now a bit agitated. "We don't have enough men to hold those counties, and I think they're going to split off in favor of the Union. Hill Lamon is sure trying to make that happen."

"Can we get more information?"

"We're stretched pretty thin now. It's a job for cavalry now, and we don't have enough."

"Ashby's got 26 companies, I hear, in his regiment." Antonia was fixing her hair in the mirror.

"Where did you hear that?" Belle asked. "Nothing like. He's got eleven, but keeps changing the flags and guidons to make it look like more." She took a man's watch from her pocket. "Almost dinner time. Alice said you were traveling incognito?"

"Yes. She was very quick on the uptake."

"Then I shall be gracious, but supercilious when we are introduced," said Belle.

"And I shall be a little mouse," Antonia replied with a smile, "And say nothing. That's my way; quiet as a mouse always. Not making a big show like some I could name."

Belle laughed, "We'll get you through. Where are you bound?"

Antonia looked at her in a measuring way.

"No, you're right," said Belle after a moment. "I don't need to know that."

She slipped out the door and went to her own room to

change.

Antonia waited several minutes and went downstairs as Amanda Jessup, prepared to answer few questions and to resort to tears when the matter of her "late husband" was raised.

CHAPTER FOURTEEN

February, 1862 Washington DC

Antonia made her way to the offices of the English legation, and asked to see Lord Lyons. One clerk superciliously rebuked her for not having an appointment, and another asked her to wait in a small ante-room. Within minutes another man, well-dressed, but with the aspect of a clerk, came in and asked her name. When she gave it he was startled.

"My word. Are you from Missus Greenhow?"

"No," said Antonia, confused. "I'm from Mister Benjamin. Who are you?"

"Harry Mouton," he said. "Do you have a communication for his lordship?"

"I do."

"May I see it?"

"My orders are to hand it to him in person."

Harry Mouton looked at her speculatively, "I recall you from Missus Greenhow's balls, Miss Ford. How did you come through the lines?"

"By way of Baltimore."

He raised an eyebrow at that.

"Excuse me. Let me see if his lordship is available." He slipped out of the room and returned moments later.

"His lordship can indeed see you now."

Antonia smiled her best smile, "Do you have a place where I might freshen up first? The journey has been long and difficult."

"Certainly." Mouton led her to a door behind which there was a water closet. Antonia gasped at the beauty of the furnishings and the luxury of the hangings and curtains.

"Take your time," Mouton said.

"It's beautiful," Antonia said. "I might well want to take up residence here."

"Yes," said Mouton drily. "It's things like this that make us a great nation — or so I am told."

Lord Lyons accepted the thick, ornate envelope from Antonia's hand, turned it over and examined the wax seals carefully. "Are you to wait for a reply?"

"No, m'lord." Antonia resisted the impulse to curtsey.

"Very well. Thank you for bringing this. I cannot, given my position here, reply directly in any event. Do you need an escort?"

Antonia smiled and shook her head, "I have my friend Sam with me."

Mouton looked alarmed. As far as he knew she had come alone. Lord Lyons looked at him and got a helpless shrug in return.

"Sam?"

Antonia was wearing a winter ensemble which included a muff, from which she now pulled a small revolver.

"Sam Colt," she slipped it back inside and smiled again.

Lord Lyons laughed loudly, with genuine warmth, "By God, madam, I admire you frontier women. You are so...." Words failed him.

Shaking his head, he bowed, and kissed the hand she extended.

Mouton saw her to the door. She flashed a dazzling smile and was gone.

It was a rather large room, and Lyons had his desk in the center, with all of the oil lamps lined up to provide enough light to read by. The fire glowed dimly, but most of the room was in deep shadow. Antonia had not observed that there was another man sitting in the room, unmoving in those shadows.

He waited until Mouton returned to the room and watched Lyons pick up the envelope and smell it as he might a rose. "Carried it next to her heart, I'll be bound," he said. "Ah, the scent of a woman. Eh, Sir Percy?"

Percy Wyndham struck a match, illuminating the hard face of a professional soldier as he lit his cigar. He was careful to keep the flame away from the long luxurious mustaches that were his hallmark. He puffed the cigar into life and drawled, "A very dangerous woman, m'lord. Who is she?"

"Antonia Ford. One of La Greenhow's ring of amateur spies," said Mouton. "She's the daughter of a prosperous tradesman out at Fairfax Court House, about twenty miles from the city, and a society belle. Hasn't married yet."

"Humph," Wyndham replied. "Be tempted to give her a run myself. Quite a beauty."

"I'd say she's not quite the amateur anymore," Lyons said. "I see evidence of training and skill, not to mention considerable determination. The South, being poor in resources and singularly without friends, has been forced to innovate. Girls like her are one of the innovations."

"Aren't we their friends?" Wyndham asked, raising an eyebrow.

"Alas, no," Lyons sighed. "This isn't Italy. Can't take the risk of being drawn into this. The North has raised a considerable army and, in McClellan, found a great organizer."

"That does not mean that they are ready to use it yet," Mouton observed.

"Well, McClellan is not the man for that anyway, and Lincoln has erred in making him General of the Armies," Wyndham said.

"I rather thought so, too," Mouton said. "But why do you say it?"

"He wants to be ready before he moves. Shows his lack of real experience," Wyndham said, blowing out a cloud of fragrant smoke. "It ain't never ready, not really. You just have to be ready when the moment comes. He keeps putting it off, which makes Lincoln a bit mad. Makes me wish Garibaldi had accepted the command when it was offered him."

"The Catholics made quite a noise against it, and Garibaldi is an Italian patriot, not an American one." Lyons opened the humidor and selected a cigar of his own, a fine Havana. "It's a different game here, Percy. There, we were seeking to unite a nation. Here we're trying to divide one."

"Too deep for me, m'lord," Wyndham replied. "What's become of my old friend, Russell, of the Times?"

"Going home. Damn near died of typhoid and then found that those new friends of his in the Union government weren't so friendly since his articles about them got published. Didn't like the way he told it. Cut him off at the knees, so to speak."

"Well, anyone who trusts a reporter is a damned fool," Wyndham said.

"You have volunteered?" Lyons asked.

"I have," Wyndham said. "McClellan wrote me and begged me to come. They are desperate for professional officers. Based on my record in Italy, I'm to be made a Colonel right away. Couldn't quite manage Brigadier, and mine is some young pup out of their West Point, who may know his business or be a complete fool."

"Or both," said Mouton.

"Given my druthers," Wyndham said, "I'd much rather be on the other side with my old friend Wheat and his Louisiana Tigers, but the pay is adequate. The uniform is new and I can make something of it. First New Jersey Cavalry."

"How do you know Wheat?" Mouton asked.

"We served in Italy together. Good man. Brilliant soldier—had a brigade like mine."

"Mason?"

Wyndham's hand went unconsciously to touch the metal pin on his vest, "Yes. That might save my life, but it won't give me any slack if I come up against him in battle."

"Nor him?"

"Certainly not. We're professionals...and we have a wager to settle."

Lyons nodded. "We have placed a few people in McClellan's intelligence establishment. Mouton?"

Mouton cleared his throat, "Yes, m'lord. Little Mac as, they call him, is a cautious sort, one might even say timid. Missus Greenhow realized this and recommended to her government that they practice some deceptions on him. In fact, they had already done so, with the Quaker guns at Manassas and so forth. Now they are planting false information as to the number and strength of their units. The Union spies are under Pinkerton, who lacks military experience, although he's a first-rate detective. You will see estimates that will immediately strike you as ludicrous."

"And what am I to do?"

"Simply say nothing. Don't draw attention to yourself by disputing them, one way or the other."

Wyndham nodded, "I will have a well-bitten tongue."

He rose lightly from his chair. "Well, at least I'm in the cavalry this time, instead of the bloody infantry. Shouldn't be too difficult, given the nature of the opposition."

Mouton grimaced, "Don't be too sure, Sir Percy. I came to this post with Lord Napier and have seen many remarkable things. One of the most remarkable are the summer tournaments held down in Virginia where the locals have taken Sir Walter Scott's 'Ivanhoe' to heart, and pretend to be knights and ladies from the Middle Ages. These gentlemen have even taken to calling themselves the 'chivalry'."

"What does that have to do with the military situation?"

"They more or less live on horseback anyway. Until recently there were no good roads and one could travel no other way. Moreover, they play at horsemanship at a level that must be respected. It's very entertaining to watch a man pluck a wooden ring on the end of a lance while riding at breakneck speed for the favor of a lady, but it bespeaks a level of training that must be reckoned with."

Wyndham raised an eyebrow, "Really?"

Mouton pressed his case, "They only do this in the southern states. The North is industrialized, and people hardly ride horses at all, anymore. You will be hard pressed to find an equal level of horsemanship in any civilized nation."

Wyndham shrugged, "That's why we have training, my lad. With all due respect, I will put a trained, disciplined force up against a bunch of farmers any day. And win."

He crushed his cigar out. Lyons came around the desk and took his hand, "Now, don't be a stranger, and write often, old son. We value your efforts."

Wyndham seemed to grow two inches, "Thank you, m'lord."

Mouton escorted him out and returned a few moments later. Lyons had opened the envelope delivered by Antonia and was looking at the letter within.

"Bother, it's in code," he said.

Mouton looked at it, felt the paper, and found a pattern of pinholes he knew. "One of the York Rite Masonic ones, I think. Give me an hour and I'll have a clear text."

CHAPTER FIFTEEN

Northern Virginia, March 1862

Belle whispered sweet nothings. Unfortunately the recipient was not a beau, but her stallion, Fleeter, as he tried to rise from the snow drift he was kneeling in. The snow was damp and uncomfortable, and Belle herself was chilled and shivering.

She could sense Yankee cavalry bearing down on this little-known and unmarked crossroads between Winchester and Front Royal. It had been a long two days in the field, and she wanted nothing more than to be gone from here. But first she had to evade the trap she felt closing around her.

Draped over Fleeter's neck, she wondered if the naked branches of the small trees in front of her provided enough concealment. She could see the crossroads a little too well. She whispered again in his ear. It twitched and he snorted in apparent disbelief at her offer of a rubdown and hot bran mash when they returned to Front Royal.

From her left came the mild thunder of hoofbeats. It was echoed by similar sounds from the other direction. She watched as Union cavalry came into view. Eighty of them, led by a Captain. A full company, perhaps. Riding with them was a tall bearded man, in civilian attire and a rubber cloak, whom she recognized at once. *Porte Crayon*, she thought with dismay.

Here was proof at last that David Strother had gone over to the Yankees entirely. She picked up the binoculars that were in front of her and took a closer look. Yes, it was he. Her heart sank. He was in charge of this expedition.

From the other direction, a smaller patrol of five men appeared. They had galloped some and their horses were sweaty, which was unwise in such cold weather. Again she recognized their leader. It was Michael Kelley.

He had actually been in pursuit of her, she realized. Some Unionist spy or sympathizer had betrayed her. She had been collecting messages left in secret mailboxes by Confederate agents who lived between Kernstown and Winchester. Some were in code, but most were not, and often little more than hasty scribbles on half-sheets of paper.

Michael Kelley and the captain in charge of the company of cavalry exchanged a few words. Through the binoculars, Belle could see that Kelley was dismayed and confused. No, the other captain seemed to be telling him, they had passed no riders on the road, especially not a very tall woman on a very tall black horse. Kelley actually took off his hat and scratched his head in confusion. Strother unfolded a map and pointed at something, probably pointing out an unmarked farm road that she might have taken.

Kelley put his hat back on, wheeled his horse around and took his patrol off back the way he had come. Belle knew that road. It was four feet deep in drifted snow at the moment and treacherous. She waited, hoping that no one would look her way. They didn't, and after a few moments the company of cavalry moved on at a mild trot. Belle shivered, but was also exhilarated. Once more she had slipped through the Yankee's fingers. She kept Fleeter in his rather uncomfortable position only a few more moments before allowing him to stand, and then, picking her way over ground that was still frozen, but relatively free of snow, made her way back to the road. She dismounted, took some dried brush, and groomed the snow back into something resembling its natural state. It wouldn't fool an expert tracker like her uncle James Glenn, but it would the average Yankee. Even David Strother.

He's lived in New York too long, become too citified, she thought.

Back on the road, she cautiously walked Fleeter a few hundred yards until she found a stone wall where someone had struck a sulfur match and left a black burn mark. She counted five stones over and five down to find the stone that was loose. She pulled it out and was gratified to find the folded bit of paper behind. It was damp, but still readable. She tucked it between her breasts.

She waited a long time, listening carefully for sounds of other Yankee patrols. Since the weather was still cold and damp, she was only worried about Yankees on horseback. Finally she began to walk Fleeter again and then mounted and rode him slowly back to Front Royal, something which took much of the rest of the day. The roads were very bad, and she couldn't stand the thought of him being injured. *Easy does it*, she told herself.

Once there, she made sure that Fleeter was well-rewarded for what had been a long and difficult mission, and, finally, took her dinner in the kitchen. Alice Stewart bounced in, anxious and eager with anticipation.

"Well?" she said.

"I'll need to account for my whereabouts this day," Belle said, her eyes bright now that she had food and warmth.

Alice thought a moment. "We could go annoy Lucy Buck."

Belle frowned. "Must we?"

"It will be perfect. She's had a hard day teaching school and will only want to get away from us. We will insist that she play and sing with us. It will get us complained about."

Belle nodded thoughtfully, "She will write about it in her diary." The prospect of making small talk with Lucy Buck dismayed her, but she could not ask for a better alibi. Lucy had come to cordially loath both her and Alice, while remaining firm friends with Alice's younger sister, Fannie.

Belle had been mystified by this, since she had always tried to be kind to Lucy. She had discussed the problem with Antonia Ford during her visit.

"She's jealous," said Antonia when Belle described the frosty relations between them.

"Good Lord," said Belle. "Of me? Whatever for?"

"Style and the advantages you've had," said Antonia. "I have been similarly treated by women my age in Fairfax Court House and Alexandria."

Belle looked doubtful. Antonia shrugged. "Lucy was not afforded education at Mount Washington in Baltimore," she said, "Nor was she presented in Washington the way you and Alice were, and she's plain."

"I'm the plain one," Belle protested. "Lucy could be quite pretty if she tried."

"If she knew how," Antonia replied. "Which she does not, and which she would not attempt for fear of censure by her own family, who give the Quakers a fair run for plain modesty. Style is important, Belle. But so is discretion."

Belle frowned again. "What do you mean?"

"Did you, by any chance, show off that very expensive dress from Elizabeth Keckley?" Antonia smiled as if she knew the answer.

"Only at Christmas parties," Belle said. "And it's last year's dress anyway."

"Alice, too?"

"Yes. We wanted to dress up and have a good time."

"And you rubbed Lucy's nose in it, didn't you?"

Belle had to think about that. "I didn't intend to," she said at last. "But, then again, she has been rather cruel, talking behind my back about what a flirt I am."

Antonia shook her head, still smiling, "It was a mistake. You need all the friends you can get here if you are to be successful in the work — and you are a flirt. Outrageously so."

Belle blushed slightly. "I do enjoy it," she admitted. "It makes men pay attention."

"Which only invites more jealously and censure from the Lucy Bucks of this world." Antonia patted her hand, and half-whispered, "She will never be your friend now, Belle, so the best you can do is to try and not turn her into your enemy."

Belle shook her head sadly, remembering this good advice. Necessity made all of her efforts with Lucy annoyances. Part of the problem was that the Bucks and the Ashbys were related, and she had to take special pains to conceal her work for Turner Ashby. Lucy was not only the worse kind of casual gossip, but also had taken to keeping a diary since Christmas. Belle wanted no documentation of her real work in Front Royal.

Feeling considerably misunderstood and put upon, Belle went up to change her clothes and fix her face. She removed all of the bits of paper she had collected on her scout from between her breasts and read them one by one.

The Union Army was getting ready to move; that was plain enough. One seemed to be a letter from a female cousin, but she recognized the handwriting as Alexander Boetler's. She looked at it carefully, first at the date of 2/1/62. She added the digits together to get eleven and counted off the first eleven words. The next sentence was "How do we define gallantry?" Define Gallantry was the new key for coding and decoding messages. Two words, 15 letters. Nothing else in the letter fit.

She took a few moments to decode the two messages written in code. One was to her. "My dear child," it said, "The enemy forces will soon invade along the rail line from Manassas to Front Royal. We need you to be a listening post among them. Please remain where you are and give us complete information. Your father is well. T.J."

Thomas Jordan? Belle wondered briefly, knowing that he had gone west as Beauregard's Chief of Staff, and then realized, feeling a bit of a thrill, that the message was directly from Thomas Jackson. Stonewall himself!

She was tempted to keep it tucked away as a souvenir, but reluctantly threw it in the fire with the others. Alice bounced into the room again. "Aren't you ready yet?"

"In a moment," Belle said, peering in the mirror and seeing that the shadows under her eyes made her look years older than she really was. "Is Fannie going with us?"

"No. She thinks it's a terrible idea."

"She's probably right," Belle admitted. "Lucy is such an earnest little soul. She won't take kindly to our invasion."

Alice smiled wickedly, "It's for the Cause, no?"

Belle nodded, wondering, not for the first time, if anyone would ever know or appreciate her efforts. Lucy called her and Alice false and vain. It was unfair, but something they had learned to live with.

CHAPTER SIXTEEN

March 1862, Washington, DC

At a military tailor shop, David Strother was being measured for his first officer's uniform. After months of work as a topographical engineer and unpaid aide, he had finally applied for a commission. He now held the rank of Captain, which he found gratifying.

Still, it did not fill him with joy. His elation was tinged with sadness. Many of his dearest friends and family were confirmed and passionate Rebels. He hoped that they would someday understand his decision.

Ward Hill Lamon had persuaded him to make this final commitment as they rode back together on the train from that remarkable ceremony in Martinsburg where they had seen Henry Turner Ashby, a Colonel in the Confederate cavalry, elevated to the rank of Master Mason in a single night.

The rattle of the train's wheels and the shaking of the cars discouraged conversation, so Lamon was silent at first, sipping from a pocket flask of very good whisky, which he offered to share with him.

Strother took enough to clear his throat and said, "The world turned upside down, eh?"

Lamon shook his head ruefully, "World has changed, David. Ashbys didn't used to be so respectable."

"It makes Ashby a solid citizen, that's for sure. I see Alex Boetler's hand behind it. Politics is all it is."

"Not every politician thinks it wise to join the Nobel Craft, especially not up north, where there is still strong sentiment against it."

"Lincoln?"

"Oh, no. Abe don't hold with secret societies. He always figured on being somebody big someday and, given the way some folks feel about Freemasonry, he didn't think it would help."

Lamon took another swig of whisky, "He was invited, more

than once. Be a bit difficult for him now, given what we just saw. It's bad enough to have his wife's brothers going for the Rebels. Being obligated to give relief and protection to lodge brothers who are Confederate officers would be just too much, I think, even for him."

He leaned back and regarded Strother with a steady eye, "You've got to make a decision."

"I'm for the Union, Hill. Always have been."

"Then get yourself a commission and let everyone know where you stand."

Strother tugged at his beard, wistfully, "I guess I've done all the scouting and mapping I can."

"Regardless, you don't want to get caught behind the lines as a civilian. Get yourself hanged, right quick."

Strother nodded, "It's a risk."

"More of one now," Lamon said, "Thanks to that fool, Fremont."

"How so?"

"He has this company of scouts he brought back with him from Missouri. You know his wife Jessie travels with him? Sort of a 'daughter of the regiment'. Well these fools wear Reb uniforms and scout deep. Call themselves 'Jessie Scouts' in her honor. The Rebs won't even bother with a trial if they catch them; just string them up. Rebs are already pretty stirred up about spies."

"The Rebs picket their lines really well," Strother admitted. "We've had to be very careful, especially since Luce disappeared."

Lamon looked at him, an eyebrow raised in inquiry.

"Captured, most likely. He was in uniform, but he hasn't shown up on any prisoner parole lists."

"They ain't going to exchange him. He's seen too much."

Strother sighed, "Hard to believe that no one had a decent map of Virginia when all this started."

"That how you got involved?"

"Partially. I wrote all those books about Virginia, and I draw. I could give them a rough one from memory alone, but they kept asking questions about how the land laid down, where the heavy forests were, how this river or creek flowed and what kind of bottom it has — all that kind of thing where you just have to go and see for yourself. So Luce, who has a West Point education and could see it from a military perspective, and I just went and did the best we could. B & O had some maps, but only where their rails run. It was a mystery."

"And now?"

"Less so, although I'm sure we missed half of what's there. But at least we know which roads go where. Rebs took down all the signs."

Lamon nodded. "We're about to tear off a chunk of Virginia for the Union, including Berkeley County. Make it a separate state if we can hold it. Capital will be Wheeling."

"Martinsburg ain't strong for the Union," Strother observed.

"It ain't strong for the Rebs either," Lamon replied. "We get a good civil guard going and raise some volunteer regiments and it'll hold. And maybe we'll have some cavalry that ain't a total and complete disgrace."

Strother laughed, "New York regiments aren't that bad!"

Lamon took another swig from his flask. "Damn cold in here."

"Damn cold everywhere around Martinsburg," Strother replied, "Or hadn't you noticed?"

"You mean our kith and kin? Yep. Mary Boyd, who was the great love of my youth, looks at me like she wants to kill me. Very slowly at that."

Strother sighed, "Then she'll treat me the same. Ben is with Jackson's army, I hear."

Lamon grunted. "Belle's a proper rebel, too. Shot and killed this fool volunteer from Pennsylvania who invaded their house. Drunken fool struck Mary, and Belle just up and shot him."

"I read about that," Strother replied. "It was in the papers."

"I was there at the hearing," Lamon said. "She had every

right and Birney let her off."

"Birney?"

"He was a volunteer 90-day Colonel, but also a member of the bar. He's proven to be a good officer, so he's advanced. Major General now."

Lamon put the flask aside and drew a pistol from an inside coat pocket. He checked it carefully. Seeing Strother's surprise, he said, "Sometimes the Rebs try and stop this train."

Strother looked around, and then out the windows into the dark.

"I've another, if you want to hold it," Lamon said after a moment.

"Thank you," Strother accepted the revolver and held it awkwardly in his hands.

"You'll need to practice some, I see," Lamon said, laying the first pistol on the seat beside him. He produced another one and began checking it.

"Damn, Hill, you got an arsenal under that coat?"

"Damn near," he grinned. "You'll need to be cautious around Belle."

Strother nodded, "Yep, she's all grown up, but I'm married again."

"That ain't what I meant," Lamon said after a moment. "They caught her spying in Martinsburg and now she's traveling a lot, and always seems to have lots of money."

"You think she's spying? Come on, she's a child!"

Lamon looked at him patiently. "Where did you meet her last?"

"A ball in Washington given by Missus Greenhow."

"And where is Missus Greenhow these days?"

"Old Capitol Prison."

"I rest my case," said Lamon. He looked out the window into the dark night, obviously expecting trouble. Strother shook his head. *Belle, a spy? Ridiculous. She is much too young and flighty.*

Spying isn't something women should do. Look at what had happened to Rose Greenhow and her friends when they tried it.

"We're done, sir," said the Negro tailor who had been measuring him. Strother snapped out of his reverie. He watched as the tailor, a strong young man about 28 years old, used a piece of chalk to mark up the blue wool.

"You have a good eye," Strother commented.

"Thank you, sir," he replied. The bell on the door signaled the entrance of another customer. The man entering sported a remarkable set of mustaches that seemed to extend nearly a foot from either side of his head. Strother knew him at once for a professional soldier from the way he held himself and the hard, careful way he surveyed the room.

"Suh Wyndham," said the young Negro with a wide grin, "I gots them all ready for you." He went into the back.

The man looked Strother up and down. "You look fit enough. Can you ride a horse?"

Strother realized with surprise that he was English. "I can ride," he replied, both edgy and amused. "Why do you ask?"

The man gave him an engaging smile, "Because I am saddled with farmboys from New Jersey who have only the barest notion of how to ride a horse properly without breaking its back. I could use some help."

He pulled out a *carte d'visit* and presented it. "I'm Percy Wyndham," he said, "Colonel of volunteers."

Strother patted his pockets until he found his own cards, "David Strother," he said. "I'm on Nathaniel Bank's staff at the moment."

The young Negro came out of the back carrying hangers with two uniforms, followed by a young Negro woman carrying two more. Wyndham unbuttoned the coat on his suit and took it off, draping it over a nearby counter. The tailor held a fresh uniform coat open for him as he slid into it.

"Fits like a glove," Wyndham said happily.

As he tried on another uniform coat, Strother had a chance to look at the card in his hand.

"Sir Percy Wyndham?" he asked in surprise. "You're a knight?"

Wyndham looked at him ironically, "Only in Italy. King Victor Emmanuel insisted. I led a brigade in the recent Italian War."

Strother, impressed, said, "I see. What brings you here?"

"War is my trade. This looks to be a good one for someone of my talents."

Strother didn't know what to say. He'd heard of soldiers of fortune, and even met a few. He didn't approve of them, mostly because of their reputed eagerness for battle and bloodshed. Yet, he didn't want to offend this man, who had come so far to join a good cause.

Wyndham looked at him with piercing black eyes, seeming to read his mind. He stepped forward and grasped his right forefinger between his own thumb and forefinger. It was the grip of an Entered Apprentice. "Does this have any meaning for you?"

Automatically Strother returned the countersign grip. Sir Percy was a Mason, and so was he. That made them theoretically as close as brothers, despite the fact that they had never met.

Strother decided not to go through the rituals in front of the tailor and his wife. Percy Wyndham looked at him with one eyebrow raised, seeming to instantly understand.

"Perhaps a drink later?" he murmured.

"The bar at the Willard Hotel, say at six?"

"And then dinner?"

"If you like," Strother agreed. "See you there."

A few hours later, in the long bar in Willard's Hotel, found Strother seated at a corner table, a glass of beer at his right hand. In front of him he'd spread open a leather-bound sketch book, and was sketching the crowded scene before him, when Hill Lamon came up, carrying a glass of his own.

Strother, focused on the drawing, made a brief gesture of welcome. Lamon sat in the chair to his left. Neither man said anything, as Strother continued to work at his sketch, his hand making short rapid strokes. After several minutes, he put the pencil down and looked at Lamon.

"Something wrong?"

"No," Lamon replied. He did not elaborate, and Strother continued his work. After a few more moments, he stopped again and took a sip of beer.

"Supper?" Lamon offered.

"I'm waiting for someone, but yes."

Lamon raised his eyebrow in inquiry.

"English. Professional soldier just made a colonel of cavalry. He's a lodge brother."

"Ah," said Lamon, "Should be interesting. How would I know him."

"Look for the mustaches," said Strother with a grin. "He looks like he's wearing a bird in flight under his nose, which is a monument in itself and completes the effect."

"I see," Lamon smiled.

Strother fished in a vest pocket and came up with the *carte d'visit* he had received earlier. He passed it over. Lamon looked at it and passed it back without comment.

Strother resumed work on his sketch. A moment later, Percy Wyndham walked up. Lamon raised his glass in silent greeting. Strother stared in a measuring way at the scene before him rather than acknowledging Wyndham, as he continued to draw. Curious, Wyndham took a peek, peering over his shoulder.

"That's very good," he said. "Have you thought of doing this professionally?"

Strother looked up at him, blinking. He looked over at Lamon who was on the verge of tears with suppressed laughter. "Now and again," he said drily. "This is Ward Hill Lamon. He's the sheriff in these parts. This is Sir Percy Wyndham."

Lamon got to his feet and offered his hand. "Marshal, actually." Wyndham shook hands and signaled for a waiter. Strother, finally satisfied, closed the sketchbook.

Percy Wyndham sat down. "For Harper's, I presume?"

Strother nodded, and looked over to Lamon who laughed out loud.

"I inquired of our tailor about you, Mister Porte Crayon," said Wyndham. "I think I've actually read some of your work."

Strother nodded graciously.

Lamon laughed, "That was too rich. 'Have you thought of doing this professionally?' Very good."

Wyndham smiled, "It rivals some of the questions I've gotten from people at the War Department."

Lamon sighed. "I can believe that."

"Hill spends a lot of time there, these days," Strother said.

"You're a Provost?"

"No," Lamon replied. "Federal. Civil warrants and courts and that kind of thing."

"Oh, a barrister?"

"Lawyer. We don't make the distinction here," Lamon said. "Actually I work for the President."

Wyndham looked suitably impressed. "Doing what?"

"Whatever he wants me to do."

Lamon said this in such a flat tone of voice that Wyndham knew to ask no further. He turned to Strother, "What brings you to war, then?"

"A belief in the Union," Strother said seriously. "It must hold."

"It's not about the slaves then?" Wyndham asked.

"It is for some," Lamon said. "The Abolitionists want to make it about that."

"From your tone of voice, I gather that you don't much care for the idea," Wyndham said.

"Most people don't own slaves and don't care much about the issue," Strother said. "The war was imposed on us by fanatics on both sides. The Abolitionists have pushed very hard with their propaganda and activities like the Underground Railroad."

"Which is theft, plain and simple," Lamon said. "They try to make it about something else, but that's all it is."

Wyndham shrugged, "We outlawed slavery in England long ago, but no one ever proposed to fight a war over it."

"Five billion dollars," said Lamon. "That's the amount of capital you destroy if you free the slaves."

"Really?"

"In an agricultural society like the South, hard money is scarce. You have land and what it grows, and you have slaves to work the land, like any other beast. They are money, and credit. Without credit or money, crops would not be planted and the entire region would collapse and starve."

Lamon added morosely, "If you are going to free the slaves then you have to replace the money they represent. Given time, we could have found a peaceful way to do that."

Wyndham nodded, absorbing this.

Strother sighed. "Hill and I are from Virginia. We grew up in Martinsburg and still have kin there, not to mention old friends. This is not an easy time for us, and the choice to work for the Union has cost us dearly."

"So, you're not, as they say, 'Yankees'?"

Lamon shook his head. "That word is a term for a certain kind of business man. Yankees are hard-hearted and grasping, always looking for the most advantage in a deal. New York and Boston are the heart of Yankeedom."

"Most of the Abolitionists are not Yankees in that sense of the word," Strother said. "Far as I can tell, they're the children of the rich and some well-meaning Quakers."

Wyndham smiled. "Extraordinary. How do you mean?"

"The Underground Railroad is mostly a Quaker invention.

Philadelphia people run it. Rich people in Boston finance it," Strother said.

"It's not quite that simple," Lamon said. "The idea caught on. You get a lot of newcomers involved, immigrants, Irish, English, German. Some do it for religious reasons. Pinkerton is in it up to his neck, but that may be a way of doing business for him."

"How do you mean?"

"Pinkerton is a very sharp operator. He hires women and even Negroes to be detectives," Lamon said. "Whatever works."

"Seems like a practical man," Wyndham commented.

"Too much so," Lamon said mournfully. "He's crossed the line with some of what he's done. Thrown the Constitution away. Everyone has."

Strother looked equally unhappy. "I've been very surprised by the extreme positions people take. Passion overrules judgement."

A redheaded man about forty years old strode up to their table and said, very sharply, "There you are, Lamon. I've been looking for you. Have you a moment?"

His manner was so abrupt, and his head and beard such a bright shade of red, and his bright blue eyes so fierce in aspect, that Wyndham stood up quickly, as if he expected a fight. He watched the newcomer carefully, saying nothing.

Hill Lamon looked up, his irritation plain. "Oh, it's you, Baker," he said with a singular lack of enthusiasm. "What do you want?" He did not care for Mister Baker, that was plain.

"It's Baltimore."

Lamon sighed, drained his beer and got heavily to his feet. "Very well." Recalling his manners, he turned and said, "Do you know these gentlemen? This is Captain Strother and this is Colonel Wyndham."

Percy Wyndham offered his hand, "Sir."

Baker took it. "La Fayette C. Baker," he replied, and gripped it so firmly that Wyndham again looked surprised.

"I'll be back in a moment," Lamon said, and, taking him by

the elbow, led Baker away to an unoccupied part of the bar, waving off the bartender.

It was a conversation held in whispers, with Baker gesticulating fiercely. Finally, Lamon, poking his finger into Baker's chest, made a comment of his own. He gave an order and Baker, seemingly satisfied, walked off. Lamon, shaking his head, returned to where the other two sat and took his seat.

"Interesting fellow," Wyndham said drily. "Extraordinary manners."

Lamon sighed, "One of our more notable fanatics. Came here at the start of the war and went on some sort of scout for General Scott. This was before the battle at Bull Run. He's been made some sort of Army detective."

"Like Mr. Pinkerton?"

"Yes, but he's not one of Pinkerton's men. He's set up his own establishment. That's probably wise. Pinkerton is basically McClellan's man, and will likely rise and fall with him."

Strother smiled, "Fall? McClellan? The Little Napoleon? You speak heresy, Hill."

Lamon chuckled, "Abe ain't going to wait on him too much longer. Pinkerton is a good man and I'll be sorry if he goes. Baker's a teetotalling, bible-thumping thug. He was a Vigilante in San Francisco in the Fifties. Ain't much on due process, and admires the methods of Vidoc, the Chief of the Paris police."

"I've heard of that fellow," Wyndham said. "Been very effective."

"But at what cost?" Lamon asked. "It's a different system of law there. Napoleonic code. You're guilty unless you can prove yourself innocent, not the other way around. That's a bloody-minded way to go after people. We've got quite enough of that as it is, with all these oaths of allegiance and arrests without trial."

"War-time conditions," Wyndham shrugged.

Lamon sighed. "We've got the Constitution but we could lose it if this goes on. It's what this fight is really about, being one nation with laws that protect the weak against the strong. We're going to regret a lot of what we're doing because it sets a terrible precedent."

Wyndham nodded, trying to understand. "I'm just a simple soldier," he said. "I leave such things to the politicians."

"Everybody in this war is a politician," said Lamon. "It's the curse we suffer for our sins. Makes it hard to know who you can really trust."

"You trust Mister Baker?" Strother asked.

"Not hardly," Lamon said. "I read his report, which he just turned in. In one part of it, he describes an encounter when he was held prisoner by the Confederates and they sent a young girl disguised as a religious missionary to try and trick him into admitting he was a Yankee. Said it was Belle Boyd."

"The famous Rebel spy?" asked Wyndham, "That the newspapers go on about?"

"Pure libel, most of it." Strother frowned. "We're distant relations. Third cousins once removed or the like. She's a passionate young lady when it comes to the Confederacy, and did, in a clumsy, amateur way, try to get information to Turner Ashby when the Union invaded Martinsburg, but there's nothing against her since then. Not that can be proved. She's only seventeen years old, for God's sake! I don't find the idea that anyone would use her to do that on a regular basis very creditable."

Strother caught the quizzical look on Wyndham's face.

"Everyone in that part of the country are close relations to everyone else. I've known her all her life," he said. "Her parents are dear friends of mine, and her uncle, James Stewart, and I have been friends since boyhood. We had rooms together at New York University."

Lamon said. "I've another opinion about Belle. I think she's dangerous as Hell. She shot and killed a man last year and got off on self-defense. I have suspicions — but that ain't a crime here. Not yet, and not so much as people like La Fayette Baker might wish it so."

He looked at both of them. "Belle, in her own way, is as much of a fanatic as Baker or that old fool, John Brown. Reason don't enter into it, not for a moment. She's Sessesh, and that's the end of it. In the South it's the women who are most passionate for the Cause."

"Of course," Wyndham said. "But it's the men who do the fighting and dying."

"Belle would be in arms if they'd let her," Strother commented.

"Surely you jest?" Wyndham smiled.

Strother shook his head. "Not at all," he said. "I know these ladies. They are the most charming and agreeable creatures you'll ever meet, but they hate you and will do you in without a moment's hesitation or remorse, given the chance. They make the Sicilians look tame. Proceed with great caution when dealing with them."

Wyndham, taken aback, started to speak, then pursed his lips, shook his head just an instant and said, "Good advice. I will keep it in mind."

Lamon had brought a glass of whisky with him back from the bar. He took a healthy slug of it.

"I asked Baker how tall she was, this girl who tried to trick him, and what she looked like."

"And?" Strother was curious.

"He described her as dark-haired girl about five feet, six inches tall, quite pretty."

Strother shook his head. "He said that?"

Lamon nodded. "He did."

Wyndham looked at them questioningly.

"Belle is quite a bit taller than that," Strother explained, "And her hair tends to red-brown. She's a big girl, taller than most men. She's quite striking, but not what most would call 'pretty'. Rather strong-featured, actually."

Wyndham smiled. "So, Mister Baker is mistaken?"

"Given that I know that Belle was home in Martinsburg when he said it happened, not at Manassas, he's either a liar or a fool."

Lamon looked discontentedly at his empty whisky glass.

Wyndham looked sympathetically at his two new friends and said, "It must be very hard for you, having to go up against your own in a war."

"Hardest thing I've ever done," said Strother.

Lamon pushed back his chair. "Me, too. I have to catch a train to Baltimore. Baker wants to arrest the Chief of Police."

He went off. Strother and Wyndham asked for menus and, over supper, talked about Italy. Strother had spent three pleasant years there as an art student in the Forties, and was gratified to learn that the recent war had not damaged any really important art works. For a soldier, Wyndham proved to be remarkably knowledgeable about art.

CHAPTER SEVENTEEN

Northern Virginia, March 1862

David Strother was seen in Martinsburg, not just in the uniform of a Union Captain, but leading a company of cavalry. Belle was the only one not surprised at the news, which reached Front Royal overnight.

Alice Stewart wept when she heard.

Her father, normally a voluble man, found himself unable to speak, so depressed was he. "What am I to do?" he moaned. "I cannot meet him. I cannot see him or even look at him."

"You must not," agreed his wife, Belle's aunt, Frances. She was slightly younger than Belle's mother, but otherwise her twin in looks and attitude. Hard-headed and all business in most things, she was more passionate for the South than Belle and Alice, if such a thing was possible.

She looked directly at Belle, "Will the Yankees invade this far south?"

She's been talking to Mama, and I've told Mama too much, Belle thought, feeling a brief moment of panic. Then she realized that Frances Glenn Stewart could keep a secret as well as she could. So could her uncle. In addition to having been a newspaper publisher and now a hotelier, he was a lawyer. He kept many client secrets; so did his wife.

"Probably," Belle said. "Spring is upon us. Everything is thawing and mud makes most roads too difficult for large bodies of troops and wagons. As soon as things dry out, they'll move upon us."

"We can't just abandon the hotel," Aunt Frances pointed out. "It's a valuable property and most of our capital is tied up here."

"Besides, we're making money," Alice added.

James Stewart nodded glumly. "I have cases before the local court, but if the Yankees get this far, that will be the end of that."

"But will they?" Aunt Frances asked.

"They'll follow the railroads, and they take over the hotels and big houses," Belle said. "That's what they've done before."

"And pay us in worthless Union money, if they pay us at all,"

James Stewart grumbled.

"I can change that money for you," Belle said.

Her aunt and uncle looked at her, startled, but any questions they had died unspoken on their lips. If her mother no longer questioned Belle's comings and goings and her friendships with so many new and strange men, it was not their place to do so either.

"I can run the hotel," Alice volunteered.

Her parents looked at her, suddenly amazed. Her father started to object, but his wife answered, "I'm sure you can. But not alone."

"I'll help," said Belle.

"And what will the other people here make of that? Two young girls running a hotel? There will be talk. There's already talk about Belle," Aunt Frances objected.

"Ignorant, uninformed talk," Belle replied angrily.

"You're both just seventeen," said her uncle. "Hardly old enough to command respect from people here."

"The war has changed all the rules," Alice observed.

"Not all," her father said. "Reputation is still important." He looked at Belle. "How long do we have?"

"Not long. They've taken to moving troops by train rather than marching them," she said. "This is quicker and easier to supply. It also means that railroad towns like this one get invaded first. They can be here in force in a week that way."

Belle frowned. She was displaying too much knowledge, but this was her family. Thank God that Fannie wasn't there to hear all of this and recount it to Lucy Buck.

"How about Grandmother Ruth?" asked Alice suddenly. "She could chaperon us."

"She doesn't know the business," James Stewart said.

"Neither did I, six months ago," Alice smiled. "It's not that hard, as long as you make sure the rooms are cleaned and the meals are on time."

Eventually, it was agreed. Alice's parents and sister would go south, away from the Union Army. Belle liked that, because Fannie would no longer be gossiping with Lucy Buck. Alice would be more amenable to helping her spy on the Yankees. Eliza had already determined which of the Stewart servants could be trusted, and drawn other slaves from nearby families into the work.

A few days later, the girls' grandmother, Ruth Burns Glenn, arrived.

Short, slender, her hair still dark brown rather than gray, and with green eyes that held more laughter than tears, she was a formidable presence. Unbowed by a lifetime of hard work and exhilarated by her first train ride, she listened carefully as the Stewarts described the problem.

"I think you're being foolish, to run off just because you can't stand to see Strother anymore," she said to her son-in-law, "But you must do what you must." She sniffed. "Alice and Belle are women grown. Biggest risk you run is that we end up with Yankees in the family. 'Course, if Porte Crayon is a Yankee, then we already bear that disgrace, don't we?"

Her son-in-law winced. She smiled a bit meanly, "Well, you can be a lawyer anywhere, I suppose, but the Fishback Hotel is Glenn money. We have to do what we can to save it." She turned to Belle.

"Jimmy told me what you've been up to. What are your orders?"

It took Belle a moment to realize that she was talking about her son, Belle's uncle James Glenn. She was the only person in the world who could get away with calling him 'Jimmy'.

"Stay behind and watch them," Belle said. "I can do more that way."

Ruth Glenn looked at her and at Alice and shook her head. "Too young by far for such dangerous work. I'll say no more. Less I know about all that, the better."

Belle smiled at her. If her family was behind her, it didn't really matter what cruel lies other people told about her.

Within a week, James and Frances Stewart, with their

younger daughter Fannie, left Front Royal, a day ahead of the retreating Confederate Army. The day after that, the Union Army quietly occupied the town.

McClellan finally moved his troops into action, not in direct assault, but down the James River so that he could attack Richmond from the East. Belle was not privy to the plans of the Confederate Generals, but had a sense that the Union had far more troops and supplies than the Confederacy, because they were also advancing on this front as well.

Like the ponderous beasts Alex Boetler had described, the armies of both sides slowly began to move with deadly intent.

Belle got a message that ordered her to scout north. The only way to do that was by rail. Her cousins and uncle were still scouting for Ashby, but she had no idea where. She returned to Martinsburg on the pretext of seeing her mother, who was again trying to run the family store there. Two days later, Eliza beside her, she took the train north to Winchester, hoping to get permission from the Yankees, who held it, to get all the way home.

She carried several packets of letters. Regular mail service had been stopped between North and South, but if letters could be gotten across the lines, they could be re-mailed.

Letters to the border counties went by degrees, with whoever was willing to carry them. Sometimes money was exchanged for the service, and Belle received her train tickets and several Union banknotes as fees from a few businessmen.

With Winchester in Union hands, she made haste to deliver the packets of letters, and then applied to the Union commander, General James Shields, for a proper pass to travel on to her home in Martinsburg.

Shields was a charming Irishman who had done well in business and politics in Harrisburg, Pennsylvania, and had the knack of command. Large, ruddy-faced, and affable, he was a bit of a rogue who, after a few questions about what she had been doing, and some flirtatious replies on her part, allowed himself to be charmed into personally signing her pass. Belle enjoyed the exchange, and noticed with pleasure that her ability to excite the interest of Yankee officers had not diminished.

At the train station, it all went wrong.

She and Eliza had just taken their seats in an almost empty car when she saw Lieutenant Preston on the platform opposite. He waved pleasantly at her, but rather than come over to chat, stopped and spoke with another officer in charge of a detail of Confederate prisoners.

That officer marched the prisoners and guard detail across the tracks, formed them up nearby and left them charge of his sergeant. Then he made straight for Belle.

"Is this Miss Belle Boyd?" he asked sternly, standing over her.

"It is," Belle replied, suddenly very thankful that she had delivered all of the letters. "And you are?"

"Captain Bannon, miss. Assistant Provost Marshal for the Union forces in Winchester. An order was issued this morning for your detention. The train is about to leave, so I must ask you to get out because your case must be investigated before you will be allowed to proceed."

"Upon what charges?" Belle looked sideways at Eliza who held herself silent and impassive, waiting for any hint of what Belle wanted her to do. Belle, digging in her purse, found the pass from General Shields.

"You are suspected of carrying letters against the interest of the government, and of spying for the Rebels," Bannon said severely.

"But I have here a pass for my maid and myself allowing us to go home to Martinsburg. It is signed by General Shields."

Bannon took the pass hastily and examined it. He took another order from his dispatch case and read that. Spotting Preston across the way, he gestured urgently for him to come over. As the train headed south to Front Royal pulled out, Belle saw that it was full of Union Infantry.

"Lieutenant Preston reporting, sir," he said with a crisp

salute. Bannon returned the salute. "How are you, Miss Belle?" Preston asked politely, and nodded to Eliza acknowledging her presence.

"I am well," said Belle. "And you?"

"Got myself a staff job helping with the trains," Preston responded proudly as he examined the two documents that Bannon handed him.

"Yes," he said to Bannon. "A bit of a pickle, isn't it?"

"How would you handle it?" Bannon asked, genuinely puzzled.

"You can't go wrong bumping it up to the next level of command," Preston advised.

"I have to take these prisoners to Baltimore," Bannon said. "Can't you take charge of her?"

"Can't help you, sir. I've got to help make up three more trains — which is not anything I should be saying in front of her."

Bannon nodded and looked around, "Well, no time to resolve it here and now." He turned to Belle. "I hardly know how to proceed. Orders have been issued for your arrest, yet you have a pass from my commanding general allowing you to proceed. I will take the responsibility upon my own shoulders and convey you to Baltimore with the rest of my prisoners, and hand you over to General Dix."

"May my maid accompany me?" Belle said.

"No. She is not the subject of any order and I cannot convey her. She is liable to confiscation as 'intelligent contraband' if you do that. I will, however, convey her as a free woman as far as Martinsburg, if she can produce a ticket."

Silently Eliza handed him her ticket. He looked at it and handed it back. Lieutenant Preston tipped his hat and left the car, running back across the tracks to resume his duties. Bannon went to get the rest of his detail and prisoners on board.

"We kin git," said Eliza. "Git home some other way."

"That would make me a fugitive," Belle said. "And I have

done nothing wrong, nor anything they can try me for. Not this time. Someone we saw yesterday is a traitor to the Cause, or I was recognized. No, we will play out the hand."

"You want dis pistol?" Eliza had Belle's Colt .44 revolver in the large bag she was carrying.

"No, I'll be safe enough. Take it home with you. Hide it. They won't keep me long."

"You say so," Eliza sniffed. She settled into her seat, slumping down. Belle sat a little straighter, to show her figure off to best advantage. She had noticed that Captain Bannon's eyes sometimes slipped south of eye-level.

When the train pulled out of Martinsburg for Baltimore, Belle was alone. Eliza had left her, giving her only a quick hug and a promise to tell her mother everything. Belle squared her shoulders and looked brightly around. She spotted a merchant she knew from Martinsburg.

"Mr. Martin," she called. "Would you please sit by me?"

Martin looked up, and smiled with glad surprise. "Why certainly, Miss Boyd. Nothing would delight me more."

Captain Bannon glared at him and started to object, but Belle forestalled him.

"I am being detained by the Yankees," Belle said, "Along with these other prisoners, and have no friend to protect me on the journey."

Martin chuckled. "We all know how weak and helpless you are," he teased, nodded politely to Captain Bannon, and sat beside her. "With the good Captain's permission, I'll see you as far as the station."

Martin was a stout man, about fifty, with an eye for the ladies. He affected side whiskers, which he dyed to keep himself looking young, and was about Belle's height. His double chin was freshly shaved, as was his upper lip, which gave him a link to the older generation. He was careful about his suits, too, wearing homespun in Martinsburg, but fine black English wool when in the city, with a cravat around his neck. He had an air of confidence. Captain Bannon decided to leave him alone and permit him to converse with the prisoner.

On the short journey between Winchester and Martinsburg, Belle peppered Bannon with numerous questions, none of which he would answer. Knowing her reputation for charm and flattery, his responses had been so guarded that his jaw was now tightened up and a sick headache loomed. Martin, whose family had founded the town, was known to him as a respectable and responsible man who had signed the Oath of Allegiance.

"So, where are you coming from?" Martin asked Belle.

"Front Royal. We were stopping at Winchester, when some evil person accused me of being a spy and I was ordered detained. However, General Shields had signed my pass, so the whole matter has to be decided by General Dix, in Baltimore." She looked ahead to where Captain Bannon was in conversation with his sergeant. "Why are you going to Baltimore?"

"Business," Martin said, shifting uncomfortably in his seat. "One has to live."

"I see," Belle replied coolly. "Trading with the Yankees?"

"Not exactly," Martin was defensive. "Trading on them, more like. There is money to be made from this war."

Belle looked at him appraisingly, "How is that?"

"The Union spends money like water in Martinsburg, but those loyal to the South cannot spend it. If they don't take it, the Union quartermasters take what they want anyway. They cite the Legal Tender law, which says that if you refuse U.S. money, then you make them a gift of it. I exchange their notes for our own currency, and then take them to Baltimore, where I buy supplies."

Martin kept his voice very low, "We then smuggle them back south."

"Then you are a Rebel?"

"Most certainly, but many are for the Union. Have you heard

of Ward Hill Lamon? Lincoln's friend?"

"I know the man. He was once a friend of my parents," Belle said sourly. "He was at my hearing when I shot that Yankee who assaulted Mother. What is he to Lincoln?"

"One of Lincoln's law partners before the war, now his bodyguard. Virginia born, but for the Union. Lincoln made him Chief Federal Marshal of the District of Columbia, but he spends most of his time doing little political jobs. Recently, he's been organizing the Unionists in the western counties, trying to split them off from the rest of the state."

Belle pretended to be a bit shocked by this. "Does that mean that Martinsburg will be Yankee territory?"

"In all probability," Martin said unhappily. "I see no remedy for it, unless the Confederacy can put in an occupying army."

"Not our style," Belle said. "And even if it were, we haven't the men. Father is still in the field with the Second Virginia."

Belle gave him a look which made him blush.

"They also serve, who stand and wait," he said. "How is Ben?"

"Standing and waiting, as it happens. This 'gentleman private' nonsense has pretty much run its course. Men of ability are needed on the staff. He's been made paymaster with the rank of Captain." Belle smiled graciously, hiding her true feelings.

"Let me assure you I carry the Confederacy next to my heart," Martin said. Looking around to make sure no one was looking their way, he flipped back his coat lapel to reveal his inside pocket, where there was a small Confederate flag, of the new 'stars and bars' pattern designed by General Beauregard. It was mounted on a round wooden dowel.

Belle suddenly felt seized with mischief. "May I have that?"

Martin was cautious. "Why?"

"To embarrass these Yankees at the proper time."

Martin sighed, shook his head, and slipped the flag out of his pocket. Belle slipped it up the sleeve of her dress.

"Do you need any money?" he asked.

"I have some," Belle replied. "Yankee and Confederate."

Martin took a *carte d'visit* from his vest pocket, "This is my address in Baltimore. Send to me when you know what they plan for you. Anything I can do...."

"I may need a lawyer," Belle said. "To obtain a writ."

"Lincoln has suspended the writ of habeas corpus for the duration of the war," Martin said unhappily. "We are truly under the heels of the tyrant. There are Provost Marshals everywhere now, with little knowledge or concern for civil rights."

That gave Belle a fresh appreciation of the risk he was running. He could be arrested simply for having a Confederate flag on his person, and held without trial. She took his hand in hers and squeezed it gently. "Thank you," she said.

Still, she would not be cowed. As the train entered Baltimore and started its final run for the station, she stood up and started waving the flag that Martin had given her.

"Hooray for the Confederacy and Jeff Davis," she shouted. There were about forty Confederate Army prisoners. They took it up with a shout, and then broke into cheers and laughter. Bannon came over and snatched the flag away from her. He stared at her furiously, but she continued her cheer, which was now repeated, not just by the prisoners, but also some of the civilian passengers in the car.

His sergeant broke into laughter and applause, and the Union soldiers joined in, which defused the situation.

"It's a good joke on us," said the sergeant loudly, "That we should bring this detail in under a Confederate flag, and that waved by a Rebel lady!"

Bannon looked around, still furious, then rolled up the little flag and slipped it into his dispatch case. Martin, who had not joined in the cheers and laughter, shrugged when Bannon looked at him, as if to deny any responsibility.

CHAPTER EIGHTEEN

Baltimore, Maryland, March, 1862

Captain Bannon held the detail at the station while he sent a message to General Dix, informing him of Belle's arrest. Belle sat and drank lemonade purchased from a vendor for her by a young man she had never seen before, with Union soldiers standing guard on either side of her. Bannon, thirsty himself, made sure cold water was provided to the prisoners and his own troops. After an hour or so, the messenger returned. Bannon read the note and grimaced. He walked over to Belle.

"General Dix has no time to decide your case right now and wishes to send for details to Winchester. He has directed that you be held."

"At Fort McHenry?" Belle asked fearfully.

"No, at the Eutaw House," Bannon replied with disgust. "At our expense."

Belle couldn't help it. She giggled. The Eutaw House was only the biggest and best hotel in Baltimore, far beyond her own means.

"I am to take you there and detail men to guard you. You may not come and go as you please, nor may you send any letters or telegrams until General Dix can see you," Bannon said.

"You will see to my trunk?"

"Certainly," Bannon said, a bit put out. He motioned to his sergeant and sent that worthy off in search of it. The man returned a few minutes later, empty-handed. He whispered in Bannon's ear. Bannon walked back over to where Belle was sitting.

He was aware that passers-by were looking with curiosity at the young girl guarded by soldiers. Baltimore was Sessesh to the core and more than one riot had occurred for far less reason.

Bannon cleared his throat. He looked around, a bit desperately. "Your trunk was loaded off at Martinsburg, as it should have been. Buy what you need at the hotel."

"At the Union Army's expense?" Belle stood up.

"Of course," Bannon said and offered her his arm.

She smiled very becomingly and took it. "This is turning out better than I hoped," Belle said.

"It's becoming something beyond my worst nightmare," Bannon said, and then smiled, trying to make a joke of it.

"You're too kind," Belle said as she prepared to promenade her way to Eutaw House.

Once word got around that Belle was in Baltimore, and being held at the Eutaw House by a Union Provost Marshal, old friends began to visit. Most were former classmates from the Mount Washington Female Academy.

Bannon's men, more than a little dazzled by their femininity, beauty and charm, made little effort to prevent this. Indeed, they found themselves playing the role of equerries to a queen.

Belle would not have escaped if she could. Would not have dreamed of it. It was all too delicious! A dress-maker was summoned and three new dresses ordered, after much consultation with two of her friends as to the current fashion in Baltimore. Underwear, stockings, and cosmetics were also purchased, and while Belle had a fair idea of what it all cost, she never saw a bill.

One of her visitors was Harry Gilmour, neatly attired in a new suit. The last time she had seen him, he had been one of Turner Ashby's cavalry officers.

"My, you do look fetching, Miss Belle," Harry said with twinkle in his eye.

"And you, sir," Belle replied. "Have you given up your old ways?" This was an oblique reference to his status as a member of the Confederate Army.

Harry looked across the large sitting room of Belle's suite to where the Union Army guard was standing and watching.

"Not at all," he said easily. "Just visiting some old friends. Exploring some new ventures. Baltimore is my town, y'know."

"You still have friends on the police force?"

"Here and there. Why?"

"I was wondering what they might know about General Dix?"

Harry shrugged, "Not a bad man, for a Yankee. He's trying to defuse the situation here and keep civil order. Believes in the law, and doesn't much care for the excesses of the Black Republicans."

He leaned closer, "They arrested all of the police commissioners and the Chief, and sent them to Fort Warren in Boston," he said very quietly, "And replaced them with their own men."

Belle was shocked. "Goodness," she said after a moment. "What will you do?"

"I'm supposed to go up to Ohio to meet with some people." He frowned, looking at the guard, who seemed to pay them no attention. "Thought I could get a pass from someone on the force, but there are Pinkerton detectives everywhere."

"So you'll be going back?"

Harry nodded unhappily.

"When are you returning home?" Belle asked.

"Soon. Very soon," he sighed.

"You must be sure to give everyone my love and tell them I am well."

Harry looked around the room and laughed. "I'd say you are very well," he said, "And it's not like they can dispose of your case quietly. You're in the newspapers."

"Am I?" The notion gave Belle a strange feeling, somewhere between elation and being sick to her stomach. "What do they say about me?"

"Oh," said Harry, "It's mostly a bunch of trash about how you wrapped those Union boys around your little finger and made them tell you their secrets. Much exaggerated, I'm sure."

"Are you?" Belle felt a bit miffed by his casual dismissal, but then realized that it might be said for the benefit of the listening guard. She also wanted to ask for copies of the news articles about her, but thought that would be vain.

At the end of their visit, Harry gave her a kiss on the cheek and whispered, "Be strong. Admit nothing and demand to see a written charge first and foremost."

Belle nodded, and Harry took his leave, giving the guard one of his cigars on the way out.

The next day, Antonia Ford came to call. Belle greeted her with a glad cry and swept her into the room with a big hug. Belle's third dress had been delivered moments before; naturally she had to try it on. Antonia offered to help.

"If you would give us some room," Antonia said to the guard, "For decency's sake?"

"I ain't supposed to...."

"Oh, pshaw," said Belle. "We're on the third floor. What do you think I am going to do? Climb out the window and crawl down the fire escape in a hoop skirt?"

The boy blushed, picked up his musket and went out the door. Antonia made to lock it behind him.

"Don't," said Belle. "It will get him in trouble and they'll break down the door."

She held the dress up in front of her, looking at her reflection in a full-length mirror. "Besides, I can't wait to try this on." She waltzed a bit, and then laid the dress carefully on a chair.

Antonia smiled, put her purse and umbrella aside and walked over. "It's nice to see that you're still so much a young girl, Belle," she said. "I feared your recent experiences might have aged you."

She began to help Belle out of the dress she was wearing. Belle felt her cares lifted from her for a moment. "I have been working very hard, and have not had much fun of late," she admitted.

Antonia sighed. "No one has. You get talked about more than the rest of us."

"Really?" asked Belle, not at all happy to hear this.

"Yes, mostly about the nursing. Everyone has talked about that."

"And what do they say, besides the disgrace and scandal of it all? I don't need any more lectures." Belle pouted to show that her fun was being spoiled.

"Oh, you won't hear that from me," Antonia said. "I think you are very brave. I think that what you did will make it possible for other women to summon the courage to do likewise, and we will need them to do it. Certainly, my father would never permit me to do such a thing."

"But you're over twenty-one," Belle said, "And you're doing far more dangerous work."

"Still under his roof and 'guidance', and will be until I have a husband. That's just the way of it," Antonia said. "I pretty much get my way. Always have, as long as the proprieties are observed."

Antonia then grew very serious. "What I am about to tell you is for your ears only and cannot be told to another soul."

Belle nodded, as Antonia sat beside her and took her hand in hers. She picked up a small wooden stick and began to give Belle a manicure.

"These hands need a lot of work. They look like they belong to a field hand," Antonia said.   "Now, in the beginning, Colonel Jordan set up some groups of agents in Washington, even before the war was declared. You remember Betty Duvall?"

"Yes."

"Betty was the one who brought the message that alerted Beauregard to the Union movement towards Manassas. I was with her part of the way. She came through the lines disguised as a simple country woman, if you can credit that."

Belle giggled at the idea.

"Yes, it was rather amusing," Antonia said. "But she was recognized on the way back. She came from Mrs. Greenhow."

"My word! *The* Mrs. Greenhow?"

"Yes. A great patriot who did us a lot of good, but she has been captured by Union detectives and they've turned her house into a prison. Lily Mackall was with her and they were able to get some information out. Something happened to Lily, but I don't know the details. Mrs. Greenhow is in Old Capitol Prison now, and her little daughter with her."

Belle found herself unable to speak, this was so shocking.

Antonia licked her lips. "It has been easy for young women like ourselves — belles — to charm passes out of Union Provosts and go about as we pleased. Now, the Army detectives are beginning to look for us. They pick up any they suspect. So far, they don't suspect me, and most seem to be from the West, or even from England or Ireland or Germany. They are easy to fool, since they don't know our ways. Some are women, although I can't imagine what would compel a woman to go into that line of work."

"Perhaps, for the adventure. It's a real job, and they can be free and independent," Belle said.

Antonia regarded her carefully. "Perhaps," she admitted. "The idea is not without its appeal."

Antonia started to manicure Belle's other hand. "Be that as it may, women of our class do not do such things. One might as well become an actress or a...," she left the sentence unfinished.

"Matrons in hospital are accused of that," Belle said.

"I know," Antonia said. "You did your reputation some harm."

Belle started to make an angry reply, but Antonia raised a hand. "I'm not saying that you've done anything untoward, Belle, but that it doesn't matter to most people. There are rules. Appearances matter."

"It's in a good cause," Belle replied, fiercely, on the verge of tears. Antonia stopped what she was doing and gave her a little hug.

"I know, dear one," she said, "But there are other ways to serve the cause. You are needed in Front Royal, and I'm going home as well. Wait and watch; that's the game now."

Antonia picked up a nail file, "One of the advantages of the Secret Service is that it is secret, and always will be. No one will ever know I've done what I've done, and no scandal will attach itself to my name. I wouldn't do it otherwise. I do want a husband and children, after all."

"How is Tom Rosser?" Belle smiled.

"Very well. He's been made a Colonel now, and given his own regiment. He says it's because he shot down one of McClellan's spy balloons, but Jeb Stuart must think well of him in other regards."

"Does he copy the Stuart style?"

"Not at all. Strictly in homespun, like most of his unit. He's in the field now."

"Ashby doesn't go in for all that style. 'Course, he's still pretty torn up about his brother," Belle said.

"Cavalry is a dangerous life," Antonia said gravely. "Men will die."

"Oh, Ashby knows that and so did his brother. He once told me that neither one of them expected to survive the war, but to die gloriously in battle." Belle shook her head sadly.

"That's not good," Antonia said, after thinking about it for a moment. "From what I saw at Manassas, the real thing is pretty ugly."

"Is there any little thing I can do while I'm here?" Belle asked after a moment.

"No," Antonia said. "Don't risk it. You just try to get out of this and back to Front Royal. Colonel Jordan's spies in Washington have been mostly rolled up, and the real need is for military information in the field rather than the political material provided by Mrs. Greenhow. What the service most needs is women like us, who can ride well and can remember everything they see and who can play a variety of roles."

Belle sighed, "That I can do. I can't go about in disguise anymore. My height works against me. I'm too often remembered, but I can still do the rest, by God."

"And you're a good shot too," Antonia commented, raising an eyebrow. Belle looked at her, uncertain if she was being criticized or not.

Antonia smiled reassuringly, "I wish you would teach me. I'm not very good at it, and men just want to get their arms about me, rather than actually teach me anything."

"I will," said Belle earnestly. "It's not hard."

"Good," said Antonia. "You need to get out of this present difficulty first, of course."

"Shouldn't be that hard," Belle replied. "Since I haven't done anything. Not this time."

"Really?"

"I had some letters, but nothing of any real value. I was accused, but they have no proof."

"An accusation is often enough," Antonia said sadly. "But it's getting your name in the newspapers that has done this. It makes you a target."

Belle sighed. "Every time I think I've learned it all, I get another sharp lesson."

"It's good for you." Antonia finished the manicure and brushed her hands. She helped Belle finish dressing, and then looked at the small watch pinned to her shoulder.

"My train will leaving soon. I must go."

She and Belle hugged with real affection. Belle felt something odd under her hands.

"Have you gained weight?" she asked.

"Perish the thought," Antonia said. "I'm carrying 12 pounds of quinine under my corset. The Secret Service is also smuggling supplies through the land blockade. I'll hand this off when I get back to Fairfax Court House."

"If I get clear of this arrest, I would like to help with that," Belle said.

"Someone will be in touch," Antonia assured her, and then let the Union guard back into the room. With a smile and a wave, she was gone. Belle spun herself around, happy in her new dress. The guard looked at her with admiration.

When Belle was finally called to see General John Dix at his office two days later, the interview was a short one.

"You're rather young," Dix said. He was over sixty, clean shaven, his gray hair curling at his neck, full of face and with an air of authority.

"Seventeen, sir," Belle said, trying to keep her natural exuberance in bounds for once and play the modest maiden.

Dix shuffled some papers on his desk. "Well, it seems that your accuser is not willing to come here and testify against you. Indeed, I understand that there is no evidence against you since your interview with General Birney last July." He frowned.

"Have you been spying, Miss Belle?" Dix looked at her severely, suddenly anything but paternal.

Belle smiled as if the very notion of spying was beyond her understanding. "No, sir. I've been a nurse and matron at Front Royal General Army Hospital these past months, but was going home to recuperate. The work made me ill and a doctor urged it upon me."

Dix's expression did not change. If anything, he seemed perplexed. He picked up another paper. "Well, you've been well lodged and otherwise compensated for your trouble, I see."

"I have no complaints about my treatment, sir. I've had a wonderful time seeing my friends here in Baltimore." Belle smiled her sweetest smile.

Dix finally returned the smile. "Well, this is still a nation of laws, war or no war," he said, "And mere suspicion should never be reason enough to hold someone. I find no creditable evidence against you, Miss Belle, and therefore no charges will be laid. You are free to go." He picked up the hotel bill again and winced slightly. "I would very strongly suggest that you return to your family in Martinsburg. I know we can't afford to keep you in such style."

"It was your idea, sir," Belle reminded him. "And I am very grateful for the courtesy."

"Yes, my dear," said General Dix with good humor. "But all good things come to an end. I hope not to see you again in such circumstances. Next time it will be jail for sure. Much less expensive."

Belle smiled, nodded, and left. No Union soldier followed, so she felt free, but, as ordered, she went back to the Eutaw House, packed her new clothes in her new trunk and took the next train going west to Martinsburg. There were regimental camps everywhere along the rails, some quite large. The troops looked more orderly, and there seemed to be long trains of supply wagons and ambulances along the roads.

The Union Provost Marshal riding in the same car with her watched her carefully with cold, unfeeling eyes. There was no way she could keep track of all that she saw from the train. It was going almost thirty miles an hour. She smiled at him and turned her attention to two books she had bought at the train station. One was by William Howard Russell, an English journalist, and called "**North and South**". She had never heard of him, but thought it a fine bit of writing and it looked to be very informative.

But the book that held her attention was concealed inside that one. It was a more slender volume, a pamphlet really. On the cover was a drawing of a soldier in Union Army uniform, but the fair face and the way that the blouse fit over her breasts made it plain that the soldier was a woman, as did the title, "**The Lady Lieutenant**". The subtitle was even more compelling.

"A wonderful, stirring and thrilling narrative of the adventures of Miss Madeline Moore, who in order to be near her lover, joined the army, was elected Lieutenant and fought in Western Virginia under the renowned General McClellan and afterwards at the great battle of Bull's Run."

Belle leafed through this book quickly; the writing was crude and sensationalistic; pure melodrama, and probably entirely an invention of the writer's imagination. The idea itself she found fascinating and thought provoking. Was any of it true? If Confederate girls could follow their men, certainly Union ladies might do likewise, and she'd begged for such a chance herself, even after Dick Ashby was killed. Antonia Ford had managed to penetrate the Union lines at Manassas, which the Yankees wrongly called Bull's Run after a little creek that ran near there. Were things changing that fast? Would women someday be allowed to serve in the Army? She tucked **"The Lady Lieutenant"** away to be carefully studied later.

CHAPTER NINETEEN

Strasburg, Virginia, March 1862

For David Strother, the most interesting thing about the Army was all of the new friends he was making. Even New York City paled in comparison for the diversity of society.

One new friend was Thorton Fleming Brodhead, the colonel of the First Michigan Cavalry Regiment. "Call me Thor," said Brodhead, a small, handsome man in an immaculate uniform, who turned out to be the founder and co-owner of the **Detroit Free Press**.

"That's a good name for a military man," Strother replied with a laugh.

Brodhead smiled, "Well, I do mean to bring the lightning down on the Rebels," he said, "And I've drilled these boys into some semblance of cavalry. Of course, that might not survive the first contact with the enemy forces."

"You've done this before then?"

"Mexico."

Strother nodded respectfully, "You're not one of these political officers, then."

Brodhead replied, "I'm in the State Senate, but I like to think that my colonelcy is on merit. I was at Cerdo Gordo, so I've some experience of battle."

"And what does that experience tell you?" Strother asked.

"That it was a Sunday school picnic compared to this," Brodhead said, his face grim. He looked at Strother curiously. "That was a reporter's question. I employ enough of them to know all their tricks. Are you writing for someone?"

"No," replied Strother. "I've been making maps and drawings for the Army. My reports are for the generals, not the newspapers."

It wasn't entirely true. He was keeping a journal and making sketches, but for after the war. After the war, he would publish, if he survived. For now, he simply wished to see it won, and the nation reunited.

Brodhead held out a hand, silently asking to look at the

sketchbook he was carrying. Strother handed it over. Brodhead opened it carefully so as to not smear or damage any of the pages and gave a low whistle.

"This is very fine work, Captain. It looks like something from Harper's magazine." Brodhead turned the pages carefully, looking at each drawing in turn.

Strother didn't quite know what to say. He didn't like to brag. He wasn't much of a showboat. He let the work speak for itself. It had made him famous, or rather, it had made "Porte Crayon" famous.

"Thank you," he managed to say at last.

Brodhead suddenly looked up. "You've got a Virginia accent. I know this style, don't I? You're Porte Crayon."

"Guilty as charged," Strother admitted reluctantly.

"Well, this is a pleasure," Brodhead said. "I think I have all of your books, and well-thumbed they are, too. Very enjoyable."

"You're too kind," Strother murmured.

"I had rather assumed that you would stand with Virginia," Brodhead said after a moment.

"So did many others," Strother sighed, "Including most of my friends and family in Virginia. Perhaps I lived in New York too long. I'm for the Union."

"Not for freeing the slaves?"

Strother had to think about it. "In time, on some abstract level, I might be, but this isn't the way I'd choose to do it. Most people in the South don't own slaves. They've been seduced into this thing by radical elements that wanted to break up the country, and seized upon the activities of the Abolitionists as an excuse."

"And those same Abolitionists have stirred up the war fever on this side. Radicals on both sides have pushed this war into being. It could have been prevented." Brodhead gestured with his hands as if to indicate the futility of it all.

Strother nodded. "The rich and privileged wanted a war and the rest of us will pay for it."

Brodhead smiled. "Well, now that we've settled that, what brings you to our humble camp?"

"Staff work for Banks," Strother replied. "It takes me to many places I'd rather not see again. Strasburg, where we are now, is as stupid and dirty a village as you will find in this beautiful valley."

Brodhead looked around. "That's rather harsh," he said. "It seems like quite a pleasant little place."

"People here are just mean," said Strother. "I paid fifty cents this morning for a cold, weak cup of rye coffee."

"And that has put your temper awry?" Brodhead joked.

Strother winced. Thorton Brodhead, quite pleased with this effect, laughed and clapped him on the shoulder.

"What you need, Captain, is some real Army java, which we have here in abundance."

"I also need a tent and an orderly," Strother said unhappily. Both, he had found, were in short supply.

"Well, there's some extra room in my tent," said Brodhead. "You're welcome to bunk in with me."

"That's very kind of you, Colonel," Strother replied gratefully.

"Not at all. I'm starved for intelligent conversation," said Brodhead with a big grin. Somehow, in a few brief moments, they had decided they liked each other.

That night, Strother met some of the other officers of the First Michigan over a desperate supper of beans and hardtack, barely saved by real coffee. Brodhead said, with apology, "In the field, my staff eats what the men eat. We carry no mess chests here."

"Very virtuous," added a tall, lean elderly man in a somewhat shabby civilian suit with a clerical collar.

"This is the Reverend Doctor Hudson," said Brodhead, "Our chaplain, who tries to keep the men on the path to virtue."

"Something which would be far easier," Hudson said, his voice mild, "If the good Colonel would see fit to restrict the camp to the men themselves and exclude certain civilian elements."

Brodhead smiled at him. "Save the preaching for Sundays, Reverend. Sutlers are part of an army on the march. They carry many little things which the men need, and they have a right to live."

"Yes, sir. But they have no right to sell sin and degradation along with their other merchandise."

Brodhead looked at the other two officers seated at the table with them. One was a Major Charles Town and the other a Major named Angelo Paldi. Paldi was, like Brodhead, an older man. He spoke excellent English with a slight Italian accent.

"Mister Hudson, every army has camp followers, and they are needed. Especially for cavalry. Our men cannot lay about like the Infantry. They must see to their horses every day as well as maintain themselves. Having women who are willing to do laundry and cook makes us a stronger force."

"I don't know why I should take the word of a Papist," Hudson said, his voice still mild, "and if it were just laundry and cooking that these women sold, I would have no objection, but they sell themselves, as well."

Paldi frowned and muttered something in Italian. Brodhead, who had been watching the byplay with a tolerant smile, asked, "What was that, Major?"

"Your pardon, Excellency," Paldi said. "I meant to say that we have no proof such things occur."

Strother, whose Italian was still very good, had heard something entirely different, but he was a guest here and not inclined to make trouble.

Major Town asked, "Did that never happen in the Italian War, Angelo? Men satisfying their lusts with the women of the camp?" Town, Strother saw, had said this as a dig at Hudson rather than a challenge to Major Paldi.

Paldi regarded him a moment, and then spoke very carefully. "Indeed, it did. But we had a dispensation from the Holy Father so the sin was washed away. It was preferable to the alternative, signors, of rape and pillage."

Hudson turned pale and looked quite distressed. "We are marching in a holy cause, to save the country and carry on the work of the sainted John Brown...," he began, and then stared at Strother, who had choked and turned red in the face at those words.

They all looked at him curiously. Strother sighed, suddenly seeing his new friends in a different light entirely. He stared at Hudson angrily.

Hudson caught the look and lifted his chin proudly, frowning. "Is something wrong, Captain Strother?"

Formality. And his rank was used. Hudson was obviously not a man who liked having his opinions challenged. Nevertheless, Strother could not contain himself.

"I have a different opinion of Brown," he bit out, "And him being a saint is so far from the truth I hardly know where to begin. In a way, the whole war can be laid at Brown's feet. He was certainly the catalyst for what happened in Virginia."

Brodhead leaned back and stared at him a long moment. "I flatter myself on having an open mind on most topics. This view of Brown as a saint is part of the political religion of the moment, but I recall his deeds in Kansas and am open to the idea that he might not have walked with the angels. Do you have facts to support your position?" Hudson and the other officers waited for him to speak as well.

"I am a reporter, sir."

"As someone who publishes a popular newspaper, I must tell you that assertion does not inspire confidence. Every newspaper out there is attached to some political cause or another. None are the ideal arbiters of truth that they make themselves out to be."

Brodhead reinforced his coffee with a generous dollop of whisky as he said this, smiling, and then did the same for Strother's coffee, and passed the jug to Town and Paldi. Hudson primly placed his hand over his cup.

"I told you I was starved for intelligent conversation." Brodhead smiled encouragingly.

Strother relaxed a little. "Well, let me begin by citing my authority on the matter."

"Say on."

"It's me. I was there, by sheer coincidence, and filed reports under my own name for Harper's, which does hold itself to a higher standard than that glorified fish wrapping you put out."

Brodhead laughed heartily, "Oh ho! Now we're down to cases! Very well, Strother, the battle lines are drawn. Deploy your facts in the cause of truth."

Strother sipped at the doctored coffee, and felt a warm glow come over him. "I was preparing another of my travel books. Harper's Ferry is a wild and beautiful place, and I was doing a lot of sketches. I was staying with Alexander Boetler's family. He and I are second cousins on my mother's side, and he had just been elected to Congress and wanted to know how to deal with Yankees. Figured I had some experience in that line since I'd been up in New York all those years.

"When the news came that the Armory had been captured by Abolitionists and that they were calling for a slave rebellion, the effect on the town was electric. Alex is not excitable, but he had to ride over and see to the problem. Had to wire the governor to call out the militia. And the Army in Washington. Understand there weren't that many of them. Brown and his sons and a few more, but they had hostages and they were known killers.

"The Virginia militia at that time was basically a social club, mostly for those who couldn't get into the Masons and weren't well educated. There were all kinds of weapons in the Armory, so the big thing was to keep those out of the hands of the slaves.

"A lot of them were riding around, bullying the Negroes. The big fear, ever since Nat Turner's Rebellion, has been just that kind of thing. What Brown did was like jamming a stick in a big old wasp's nest. Telegrams were sent, and pretty soon here comes Mister Ashby and his Mountain Rangers, parading as though it was another tournament holiday. Other militia units start showing up, but no one actually wants to take Brown on. Instead they start looking for accomplices. So any stranger becomes suspect and arrested. There was this one fellow passing through on the train, a poor little drummer in ladies' notions. Jewish. Rosenblom, Rosenfeld, some such name, and they're ready to hang him just for being a Yankee. He's scared to death, naturally, so I have to intervene and carry him along with me wherever I go. And, all I'm trying to do, along with Alex Boetler and few other men of sense, is to keep the whole thing from becoming a riot."

"A riot?" Hudson looked alarmed at the notion.

"It could have come to that. Most of those boys were drunk to start with and now they're scared that the Negroes are going to rise up, and start burning their houses and murdering them and their families. That's been the big bugaboo down there for nearly thirty years. Men like Ashby, who is just another merchant when he's not riding around patrolling for escaped slaves, use that fear to get political power. Alex Boetler got elected on that fear."

"Was there any danger of that really happening?" Town asked.

Strother was thoughtful for a long moment. "I'd have to say, slim to none. Most Negroes ain't that displeased with their lot in life. '**Uncle Tom's Cabin**' was a masterful load of horse manure when it came to representing the usual situation. You don't abuse slaves, any more than you would a horse or a cow. It's not good business and people frown on it. House servants especially have an easy life. They become part of the family."

Hudson's lips stiffened a bit when he heard this, and he started to say something.

"Mind you," Strother added, "I don't hold with slavery. I think it's time is past. But I'd rather see it disposed of peacefully, through the political process."

"Too late for that now," Brodhead said.

"Yes," agreed Strother, "It is. And that's John Brown's fault. You might say he started this damned war." Strother leaned back and took another sip of the coffee and whisky.

Hudson stared at him a long time, condemnation in his eyes, and then asked, "How do you work out that it's Brown's fault?"

"I covered the capture, the trial and the execution, and I spoke with the son of a bitch more than once. He went to the gallows very calmly, knowing what he had done. It was a political act, not a military one."

"A demonstration?"

"Yes. He knew that the slaves would not rise up. Told me as much. He also knew the character of the local militia; that they'd be fighting each other before they took him on in any real strength. When the Federal Government got around to sending troops, under Colonel Robert E. Lee and Captain Jeb Stuart, our local lads pretended to be disappointed, but quickly got out of the way. Stuart led the charge and it was over in minutes. Not much of a fight to tell the truth."

"But it made news," Brodhead said, his face suddenly alive with comprehension. "The bastard did it for the publicity."

"Exactly," Strother replied, "And with that came the crisis. Political meetings in Virginia became rallies for the whole idea of breaking up the country, with hired bullies there to suppress anyone who tried to advance any notion of peace or common sense."

Chaplain Hudson smiled softly. "Have you read the lives of the saints, Captain Strother?"

"I've not had that pleasure. Isn't that a Catholic document?"

"Yes, but Old Church, before the Reformation. And I am not devoid of knowledge of Catholic liturgy, sir. My role as a chaplain requires me to minister to all faiths. Before we marched, I sought out a Rabbi of the Jewish faith to acquaint myself with their requirements. But that is neither here nor there. My point was that saints do extraordinary things beyond the ken of mere mortals. Often, they sacrifice themselves for the greater good. Is not that what Brown did when he gave up his life so gracefully? We are now washing away the nation's greatest sin in blood and fire. John

Brown's methods were deplorable, but his goal was holy and righteous." Hudson looked so smug that Strother wanted to hit him.

Everyone was quiet and thoughtful for a long time. Finally Strother sighed and said to Brodhead, "I will make other arrangements tomorrow."

Brodhead was startled. "But why? Because we had an intelligent conversation? Damn it, Strother, I like you. You give as good as you get and you don't hold back. This whole conversation has been very illuminating. You know things that others in this Army need to know. You know the ground here and the people, and I think you may have other talents than just making maps. No, I won't hear of it. You're welcome here."

Strother smiled with relief. "You're very fair, Colonel, for a politician."

Brodhead poured more whisky, again skipping Hudson's cup. "It's like I told you, Captain Strother," he said. "I flatter myself I have an open mind."

CHAPTER TWENTY

The Shenandoah Valley, March 21, 1862

Snow was still on the ground when Turner Ashby received orders to scout General Shields' lines near Kernstown. They came not just in the form of a written order, but from a briefing by Major Henry Kyd Douglas, newly appointed to Jackson's staff as an Assistant Inspector General.

The two men were hardly friends. Douglas was a lawyer, and from Maryland, both of which aroused suspicion and hostility in Ashby. He also thought Douglas too pretty and too popular with the ladies.

At the mention of the "strategy", Ashby turned on him, furious, "Don't you go High Hat on me, Harry Douglas! You ain't no West Point man!"

Douglas, taken aback, blinked, and chose his words carefully. "Colonel, it's my responsibility . . ."

"What? To tell me how to run my units and discipline my men?"

"If need be, yes."

Ashby flushed, his dark countenance becoming more so.

"Stonewall can tell me what to do, but not the likes of you!"

Douglas took a deep breath. He looked around. Ashby's officers were nearby, listening. He would have to make his points without the violence that passed for reasoned argument among the Chivalry, or give up his new staff job.

"I am here for Stonewall, as his agent — I won't cite the relevant regulations, since I doubt you've read them — if you can read."

That shot had Ashby staring speechlessly at him.

"Further defiance will end with your arrest, Colonel," Douglas added quietly. "Do not try me here — you have much more to lose than I."

Ashby made a visible effort to master his temper. He forced a laugh and drew Douglas off a ways.

"What is it then?"

"We need scouts sent towards Kernstown."

"Scouts are out," Ashby replied; "I'm not a complete amateur."

Although Ashby didn't know it, one of his scouts was in deep trouble. On the other side of Massanutten Mountain from Strasburg, on one of the low hills that overlooked the road, Belle Boyd rode a stolen Federal horse with a new McClellan saddle and gear. The sensation of being astride the young colt was not an unpleasant one. She had not done the like since her days as Dick Ashby's "squire" at tournaments when she was twelve. It was rather exciting, and the horse, who had suffered many riders over the past month, appreciated her light touch on the reins and reassuring soft voice.

The sensations she felt from the big animal between her legs eased other less pleasant ones from her close call the night before. Her breasts ached and her thighs were bruised. The memory of the shame and humiliation she had been subjected to made her face burn, and made her regret that she had left her big Colt revolver behind in Front Royal when she'd set out on this scout. Otherwise there would be at least five more dead Yankees to her account.

And one dead Confederate girl, came the unbidden thought.

The roads here were impassible, with mud that would have caused the beast to founder, and the woods sparkled with melting snow on every branch. Belle wore a stolen uniform as well, which fit rather loosely over her undergarments. Her simple homespun missionary's dress was tightly rolled in a blanket tied behind the saddle. It needed repair. The memory of rough Yankee hands ripping open the front, popping the buttons like a volley of musket fire, and exposing her breasts to the lewd gazes of the drunken men who'd assaulted her, brought tears of fury to her eyes.

They had laughed! Made crude jokes about her "hidden treasures". Belle spurred the horse forward through the dense woods. It would go hard with her if they caught her now.

The night before she had entered a Union camp on the road from Winchester, riding with Mr. Ames, a sutler, who had agreed to her passage when she offered to help with his wagon. Unlike the majority of sutlers, Mr. Ames did not carry tobacco or whisky, not even whisky disguised as medicine. He was as hard-shelled a Baptist as she had ever met, and could not seem to move without stopping to pray over the matter. For all of that, he did a good business in candy, stationary, and small items such as pen knives and scissors and needles and thread. Unlike most sutlers, he was enthusiastic about Belle's purported missionary work, and after trading quotes from the Bible with her, pleased to have her company.

Belle scouted the camp, going about with her religious tracts, engaging in conversation with soldiers rather than officers, and avoiding the provost marshals. It was that rare item, a cavalry regiment made up of regular army men. They were tough and coarse and, as she soon discovered, brutal.

As the night wore on, she found herself in serious trouble. Whisky was plentiful, and some drunken men herded her into a tent, "wanting a bit of fun." She had been outraged by their rough hands, which felt and twisted her big breasts as they laughed; one fellow dared to feel her thighs and between her legs. She might have been raped had an officer not intervened.

Rather than rage at them she had cried openly, to keep the character she had assumed and conceal her spying. Tearfully she put her plight as a religious sister to him and he offered her his tent for the night, undertaking to sleep outside, but nearby to protect her from further harm.

That he hadn't arrested the men who had assaulted her infuriated Belle, but soon an opportunity presented itself — a late night conference of the regiment's officers in which they planned their line of march in the morning. Belle was close enough to hear it all clearly.

The discussion had been a rambling one, over their own supply of whisky. The fire burned low and they fell asleep. Belle found a spare uniform that, for a miracle, fit her. She changed into it, rolled her ruined dress in a spare blanket, put it under one arm, crept out of the tent, relieving her host of his hat and pistol belt and moved silently to where the horses were picketed. They were still saddled, so no time would be lost if the camp was attacked.

She walked a horse as far as the edge of the camp and then mounted him, riding slowly around the perimeter until she found the road. With the pistol in her hand, and her heart somewhere close to her throat, she started down the road, which was still frozen, moving now at a trot, and found a vidette two hundred yards away. He was facing the other way, and turned, alarmed, saw the uniform she was wearing, and managed a salute as she went past him at a gallop.

Soon she was far enough away to leave the road. As the sun came up, she was able to get her bearings and moved cautiously towards Front Royal. She grabbed handfuls of snow and put them in her mouth for water and became aware that her breasts and buttocks were bruised from having been mauled by the men in the tent. They hurt. She had been pinched in other areas. Areas where no man's hand had ever touched her.

She focused her anger. She must find Ashby! She struck an old Indian trail and followed that around the base of the mountain.

About mid-morning she heard the cocking of a revolver's hammer and the soft words, "Hold it right there, you Yankee son-of-a-bitch."

She knew the voice. It was her cousin's: Billy Boyd Compton. She pulled back on the reins, slowly raised her hands and said, in a deep husky voice, "Oh, please Mister Rebel, don't hurt me."

"What the — Belle, is that you?" Billy uncocked the revolver and rode up next to her as she took off the officer's hat and the long hair she had stored there fell out.

"It is, Billy, and thank God I found you," Belle said, close to tears. "I've had a terrible night."

He looked her up and down and replied, "I don't doubt it. How did you...."

"We haven't time for that right now," she said urgently. "You must take me to Ashby at once. I have important information for him."

"But...."

"None of the rest is important, Billy. I beg you, never speak of this to anyone and take me to Ashby right away."

Billy bit his lip and then nodded, "You'll go as a Yankee prisoner. Better put your hair back up and give me that pistol."

Belle did so, and within two hours they were back at the farmhouse Ashby was using as a temporary headquarters. If he was surprised by her manner of dress, he didn't show it.

Belle recounted what she had heard the Union cavalry officers say the previous night, and added, "Henry. This is the same unit that killed Dick."

His eyes flashed at her. "Are you sure?" he asked, his voice tight, whispering low. "Are you very sure?"

"One of them bragged about it to the new officers. He was quite specific about how he only regretted he hadn't caught the other Ashby."

Turner Ashby nodded slowly. He went to a table where a map was spread out. "They are the advance guard for the regiment, you say, and they march to Warrentown Junction tomorrow?"

"That's their plan as of last night. It may change."

Ashby looked closely at the map. "They're trying to keep us from hooking up with Ewell. They pretty much have to go that way." He frowned, nodding. "Yes. I know what to do."

He turned to Billy Compton. "My compliments to Captain Thomson, and I will need that half section of six-pounders he has, sent to Warrentown Junction with as much canister as can be found. I need his company as well, in good order, before sundown. I will meet him with further orders." Compton saluted and left, running down the stairs and jumping on his horse. He rode off quickly.

Ashby turned to Belle, "You need to change out of those clothes," he said, cracking a grin. "We wouldn't want you shot as a spy."

"I have my dress outside, on the back of the horse I liberated, but I need a needle and thread to effect repairs," Belle said, "And some food and sleep would not go amiss."

"We'll find you something," Ashby said, and then looked at her with deep concern in his eyes. "Did anything happen...."

"Nothing that I can't handle," Belle replied briskly. "Let it go." Ashby stared at her a long moment, his cold black eyes assessing her. Here was no frail maiden but another soldier of his command. He had to respect that. He nodded.

"Ride with me tomorrow," Ashby said, "And you will gain a small measure of revenge. But, for now, leave me and get rested. I have much to do to prepare a welcoming party for our Yankee guests."

The light careless way he said this made Belle's blood run cold.

His eyes burned with unquenchable thirst for revenge.

"Blood oath," was murmured among the cavalry of his command. There was serious bloody work to be done.

The next morning, as the Union cavalry rode towards Warrentown Junction, they were set upon by bushwhackers firing from concealed positions in the woods. Five horses, with their troopers, went down. Dead, all of them. A troop immediately dismounted and charged into the woods to find the snipers. Despite a crackle of pistol fire, they returned empty-handed. The advance guard started out once more at a trot, came over a small hill and saw Warrentown Junction waiting for them.

It was a place that had sprung up from the joining of two rail lines, haphazardly laid out and indifferently cared for. Peeling paint and bare gray wood set the visual tone. One long street divided the town's commercial district with a few houses scattered on the rude dirt streets behind. No one was on the streets.

They proceeded carefully until the moment that a squadron of Ashby's cavalry dashed in among them, with terrifying yells, flashing sabers, and a few well-placed gun shots. One of those shots ended their commander's life, and the Union horsemen, now leaderless and enraged, pursued the retreating Confederates into the town. There were still more than eighty of them.

They discovered that the end of the main street was blocked with rubbish and bales of straw, as were those that led off the main street. Two six-pounders and their crews fired canister directly into them with deadly effect. Men and horses died, screaming in panic. Survivors sought refuge on the side streets, only to be shot down by men hidden on top of the buildings as they tried to surrender. The bales of straw burst into flame and poured a thick, cloying gray smoke over the entire area. The two six-pounders fired again and again. The entire company was wiped out. It was sudden, and over in less time than it takes to tell.

From the top of a nearby hill, Belle watched, first with elation and then with dawning horror. Despite the distance, she could see everything quite clearly. Little details stuck in her mind, such as one Union soldier's head flying off in a great spurt of blood, and how the horses screamed as the cannon disemboweled them. Some of the Union men tried firing back with pistols and carbines, but most, confused, just tried to run away from the sudden Hell unleashed upon them. Bales of flaming straw tossed into the street behind them prevented that. She was grateful when the smoke hid it all.

Turner Ashby rode up next to her and surveyed the scene with grim satisfaction. He wore a tight little smile. Belle supposed that his previous sentiments about horses not knowing North from South had been put aside. She found herself, hand over her mouth, biting hard into the fleshy part of her palm below the thumb to keep from crying out.

Belle turned to him and started to speak, tears in her eyes. He cut her off. "It was your information, but my responsibility that brought this vengeance on them. Go home, Miss Belle. You can do us as much good in Front Royal as anyplace else, and at less hazard."

"I don't fear the risk," Belle said.

"I do," Ashby replied. "I've risked you too much already. We must not assume that because the Yankees have been fooled before that they will be fooled again. What would I say to your parents if some harm befell you? How would I live with myself? Go home. That's an order. Find ways to spy on the Yankees that don't put you in such peril."

"I'll be eighteen next month," Belle said stubbornly.

Ashby sighed. "If you live that long. Go home, Belle, please!"

So she did, slipping back into town quietly, and again helping Alice Stewart with the management of The Fishback Hotel. A few days later she went to the Buck farm to buy eggs, and was welcomed into the parlor where Lucy Buck was excitedly recounting the way Ashby had trapped the Union cavalry at Warrentown Junction. The tale was fourth-hand from her brother, and listened to avidly by her sisters and her cousin Mary Cloud.

"How glorious it must have been," said Lucy Buck, "To watch the Yankee scum slaughtered so furiously." The others agreed happily.

Belle had to literally bite her tongue to keep from revealing her role in the fight, not from pride, but from sorrow. It was anything but glorious for her, and someplace mothers, sisters and daughters were weeping for the dead. *Maybe women are not made for war after all,* she thought, *if they can only talk a good fight.*

Lucy Buck would be horrified if she ever learned of Belle's role in the battle, and would either refuse to believe it, or take the lead in condemning her for her unladylike ways, especially if the near rape was revealed.

Belle felt no satisfaction at having her honor avenged. In the midst of all that blood and pain, her honor had been a small thing. A trifle.

Walking back, with four dozen eggs carefully nested in straw and secured in an old wooden box, she realized that she was no longer fit for polite society. As a soldier — and what else was she but that? — she was too hard for innocents such as these girls. Having taken this course, she had no choice but to see it through to the war's end.

"I can't even say that Mother didn't warn me," she said

mournfully, and wished that Antonia Ford were at hand to advise her. Only Antonia would understand it. There was no one else, not even Alice.

Eliza came to Belle two days later.

"Somet'in' you should see," she said, her face serious. Belle was finally learning to read the way that black folks held themselves. Eliza was worried, if not downright scared.

"What is it?" She was going over the accounts from the previous week.

"Strange men. Dey say dey Sessesh, but . . .," Eliza's voice trailed off.

"Tell me," Belle said, becoming concerned herself. She closed up the account book and put it back under the front counter.

"Come wid me," Eliza said.

Belle did so. Eliza walked out of the front door of the hotel and pointed across the street towards the train depot. There was a group of men, Cavalry, in gray uniforms.

An elderly black man in an old, worse for wear, black suit came up. Eliza leaned towards Belle and spoke softly.

"Dis Silas. He belong to de Reverend. Take care de church."

"Of course," Belle said, recognizing him from past Sundays. "How are you, Silas?"

Silas snatched off his hat and held it close to his chest. "I'se well, Missy Belle, de Lord be willin'."

"What am I suppose to be seeing here?" Belle asked softly, because, to her, the men near the depot looked like just another squadron of Ashby's over-sized regiment.

"Look de way dey set demselves," Silas whispered softly. "Look how dey looking everywhere, all around, and how dere hands ain't never too far from de pistols. Dey don't talk like our folks, and dey don't ride like dem either."

Belle saw that he was right. Each was a small thing, but together all the little details spoke volumes.

"Dey uniforms is new, too," Eliza said.

And a bit too uniform, thought Belle. No one in Front Royal had seen anything but homespun for making uniforms in some months now. These men wore some kind of machine-woven cloth.

"Jessie scouts," Belle said at last. "They're Yankees in disguise, and they're scouting Front Royal."

"You want me to tell dem get de horse saddled?" Eliza whispered.

"No," Belle said. As tempting as that was, she had no idea where Ashby was, and he had given her a firm order to stay put.

"A soldier follows orders," Ashby had admonished her. "He stays where he is assigned." That Belle was neither male nor a regular member of the force meant little. He expected her to obey and not go wildly off on her own.

"No," Belle said to Eliza. "Find someone who can pass easily through the lines and find Colonel Ashby. I will send a note. Otherwise, we'll let them be."

Eliza and Silas looked at each other guardedly. Silas shook his head, "Don't like dese Yankees coming in here. Dey's evil people. Evil."

"Who will go?"

"I get Moses," Eliza said at last. Moses was a frail old slave about seventy, who moved very slowly, at a walk. His prize possession was an old pocket watch, or rather the silver case of one, given to him by his owner as an ornament some years past. It could take half a sheet of foolscap, folded twice.

Belle called this her "underground railway" and was a bit hurt when Eliza didn't take the joke. Moses was slow, but he was also wily, and always found his way to Ashby's camp if it was anywhere close to Front Royal.

Belle decided not to approach the strange cavalrymen herself, but wait until they stopped by the hotel. They chose to go to Lucy Buck's house instead, where, Belle later learned, they had quite a long and pleasant conversation with her and her father, passing themselves off as members of Harry Gilmour's company.

Belle was not surprised that Lucy had been so taken in. It made her glad that she had never confided in her.

CHAPTER TWENTY-ONE

Edinburgh, Virginia, April 14, 1862

As a newly made Captain, David Strother found it prudent to listen rather than talk. Few of the officers elected to higher rank seemed to know how to manage the large units they were charged with leading. Problems abounded at every level.

On this day, he rode with General Nathaniel Banks, and several other members of his staff, from Woodstock to the nearby town of Edinburgh where General James Shields made his temporary headquarters.

Shields seemed able enough. More so than Banks, in fact, but both had what he considered exaggerated expectations for the cavalry under their command. When asked for his military opinion, Strother hesitated, and then said, "I firmly believe that cavalry, especially volunteer cavalry, should be trained in all the necessary maneuvers at a walk and not even permitted to move at a trot until they can do so," repeating something that Sir Percy Wyndham had told him.

Banks, knowing that Strother had no more real military experience than he, smiled politely, said nothing and moved on to the next officer. Banks tried not to seem totally at sea, but his lack of knowledge was severely at odds with his rank and responsibilities.

Banks and Shields were to combine their commands with Fremont's to keep Jackson and Ewell from joining the defenses near Yorktown. McClellan estimated he faced over a hundred thousand men even if this were accomplished.

"And we want to keep Jackson in the Shenandoah in any event," Banks rumbled, "Lest he make a move towards Washington."

Shields nodded, "We strive to capture their capital and they ours, a bit like that children's game we all played as boys."

"Capture the flag," said Strother.

"Yes, just so." Shields turned to two young men who stood attentively near by. "Allow me to introduce Captains Keogh and Keily, who have just joined us. They bring extensive experience from the Italian war."

The two men stepped forward and shook hands. Keogh was shorter, darkly handsome and well-turned out. Keily was balding, with a head shaped like an egg atop a lanky body. Both wore uniforms so new that vagrant threads hung from their sleeves. Strother noticed that Keily wore three medals on his chest, and Keogh two.

"Captain Strother, do you have a map for us?" Shields prompted. Strother spread it out on a table, and began to point out features of the land.

"You know this ground quite well," commented Keogh.

"I grew up here," Strother replied.

"This is very fine work," Keily said, examining another of the drawings that Strother had made of the Lurey Valley. Next to it was an elevated view showing the ground ahead of them in three dimensional perspective.

"Thank you." Strother felt his own curiosity growing about these two young men. "Where are you from originally?" he asked in what he hoped was still fluent Italian.

Keogh looked surprised, but replied in Italian, "Daniel and I hail from Waterford, in the north of Ireland. We've been adventuring, and wound up in the Papal Guard, in the Honorable Company of Saint Patrick."

"Wearing the most garish green and white uniforms," Keily added, "After Napoleon sold the Pope down the river."

"You know the Pope?" Shields asked, having caught that much from their conversation. His other officers looked confused, as if they might be talking about General Pope.

Keogh slid easily back into English, "Stood guard on his personal quarters every day, and in the audience room as well."

"Aye, that we did," said Keily, "But it wasn't garrison duty that brought us there. We'd come to fight for the Holy See and the Papal States. While t'was a great honor, garrison duty did not really appeal to us. When the Archbishop of New York showed up, looking for experienced officers for the Union Army with the promise that we would rank as Captains, why naturally we had to come along and help you out."

Shields was very impressed and could not contain himself. He was a devout Catholic. "What's he like, the Pope?"

"Oh, he's a grand fellow," Keogh replied, "Full of majesty and wisdom like you'd expect in his official life, but willing to come down to the guard's quarters at night for a drink and a game of billiards."

"He's a man like any other," Keily agreed.

At first Strother suspected that these two young Irishmen were engaging in a bit of the well-known sport of blarney, but not a smile did they crack nor was there a twinkle in their eye. Suddenly he believed them. Pope Pius IX was not a subject for humor.

Shields smiled, "They got those medals at the battle of Ancona. Tell them."

"Not much to tell," Keogh said, demonstrating a becoming modesty with perhaps a bit too much skill. "We mounted a vigorous defense. My tall friend there was First Lieutenant and I was Second. In the end, we had to give up the fort, but we marched out, under our own flag, our heads held high."

In other words, they had surrendered. There was silence as that realization sank in with the other staff officers. Shields suddenly became conscious of the business at hand. "Well, gentlemen, your recommendations."

"Well, if this map is true," began Keily, "And I've no reason to believe otherwise," he added, catching the look in David Strother's eyes, "Then we should send cavalry in force towards this town — Fort Royal."

"Front Royal," Strother said irritably.

Keily looked closer at the map, "So 'tis. Your pardon."

Continuing on, undeterred by his mistake and, with Keogh adding the odd comment, Keily seemed to create a plan for operations out of his head that was smooth, complete and comprehensive.

Banks and Shields looked at each other and nodded, satisfied.

This was the professionalism that their volunteer units sorely lacked. Strother caught the look and felt a sense of relief. He could get his ideas accepted if he could persuade these two young Irishmen to suggest them.

Later, over drinks and dinner, as Banks and Shields conferred with other officers, he cultivated Keogh and Keily, telling them about his own experiences in Italy almost two decades before.

"What made you take up drawing?" Keogh drawled. "It don't seem like a proper occupation for a man."

"Ignore this Philistine," Keily said. "He thinks the paintings on the ceiling of the Sistine Chapel are of no account."

"I've seen better," Keogh maintained stoutly.

Strother laughed. "I'd like to know where. That's Michelangelo's work. Would that I could paint a tenth as well."

"What made you take it up, then?" Keily teased, "If you fall that short of the mark?"

"I found it relaxing. My father indulged me at first, until John Chapman told him that I had a talent that could be developed. So I went to New York and studied with Samuel Morse...."

"Any relation to the telegraph man?" asked Keogh.

"The same, actually," Strother replied. "I began to work at little jobs, and then spent a year and a half going up and down the Ohio River doing portraits for rich land owners. In 1839, my father had a very good year in the hotel business, and sent me to Europe so I could study further. I tried an academy in Paris, didn't like it. Much too stilted and formal — but Italy...Italy. I left part of my soul in Italy."

"Oh, Italy's a grand place. Especially the women," said Keogh.

"Except being in the Papal Guard is like being a bloody Jesuit brother for all the good it does you that way," Keily said, his eyes rolling comically. The three of them laughed.

"How are the women here?" he asked after a moment. "These

southern belles I've heard about. How are they? Do you know any, sir?"

"The most charming, most beautiful ladies you're ever likely to meet, — and dangerous as Hell."

They stared at him, waiting for the joke, but he had none to offer. He was entirely serious, thinking back to Hill Lamon's assessment of Belle Boyd.

"Be very careful," he cautioned them, and was a bit put out when they laughed.

CHAPTER TWENTY-TWO

Martinsburg, Winchester, and Front Royal, Virginia, May 1862

Belle's eighteenth birthday passed almost unnoticed, even by her. Della, the cook, brought in a cake at dinner, mostly because her brother and sister expected it. Otherwise the day passed without ceremony.

She'd gone back to Martinsburg to help her mother close up the store, and to see what she could learn about Yankee movements along the railroads. Even with a pass signed by General Shields, traveling by rail was more difficult. Her extraordinary height made it easy for Provost Marshals to pick her out of the crowd and keep close watch on her.

In Martinsburg, Major Charles Walker, Provost Marshal of the Tenth Maine Infantry, took the precaution of re-instituting the sentries on her parents' house. The officers of that regiment, warned about her previous activities, politely avoided her, as did most of her neighbors. Martinsburg was now a Union town.

They would try to go to Richmond, her mother said, her jaw set in a way that signified that all arguments to the contrary would be futile. Mary was determined to get Belle and the rest of her family away from the continuing conflict between two great armies. Belle was equally determined to stick it out at Front Royal.

Mary pleaded with Major Walker for passes to take them as far as Winchester, where another Provost Marshal of the Tenth Maine, Lieutenant Colonel James Fillebrown, informed them that civilians were not allowed to travel from there to Front Royal.

"But what are we to do?" Belle pleaded. "We have no kin here we can stay with, and you Yankees have taken over all the hotels." She spoke in a low musical voice and leaned over him just enough that her bosom was directly in front of his face. Her best everyday dress had gotten rather tight lately, especially over her breasts, which moved slightly. That had the desired effect. He coughed and his face turned red.

Belle, with an air of utmost innocence, grasped his hand warmly, "Surely you can let us go as far as Front Royal. We are needed at The Fishback Hotel. If you would just talk to General Shields...."

"General Shields is not here," Fillebrown said. Belle hesitated. If Shields was not here, then where was he? She thought it impolitic to ask.

Fillebrown was uncomfortable, but his eyes kept scanning her figure. Not a boyish gawk, and he was as old as her father, but he was definitely not looking at her in a paternal way. Anything but.

Belle didn't know whether to be amused or indignant. Neither would serve her purpose here, so she simply smiled, licking her lips invitingly.

"You really must assist us, Colonel," she said, spotting the Masonic pin he wore tucked under his lapel. She reached over and touched it. "My father has one of these."

Fillebrown looked at her face. "Is that true?"

"Equality Lodge number 136," she whispered in his ear. "He's the Grand Master."

Fillebrown looked at her and then over where Mary sat, her face like a stone, watching the byplay between him and her daughter. He cleared his throat. "Well, perhaps I can do something after all."

Pawing through some papers on his desk, he extracted a schedule, and said. "We have a train for Front Royal departing at eight tonight. It is a troop train, but I can give you and your family permission to ride in the baggage car. You will have to sit where you can, and there are no windows, but, all goes well, you should be in Front Royal by three o'clock the next morning. I will detail Lieutenant Hasbrouke Reeve, who is returning from furlough, to accompany you."

"Oh," Belle said, "Thank you so much." She produced a small penknife. "May I have a memento of our encounter," she asked flirtatiously, and before he could respond, separated a brass button from his coat.

"You see," she said, "I have many such."

A number of military buttons were sewn on her dress and

made a sparkling display. "Quite a collection," he replied weakly.

"Yes," Belle replied, and fingered one in particular. "This is from General Shields himself."

Fillebrown was both annoyed and amused, "Then I'm in good company," he said briskly. "Now, just let me write you an order for transit, and then I have many other things to do this day."

Belle bowed her head slightly, watched as he scribbled out the order and handed it to her. She folded it carefully and put it in her bag. "Thank you," she said, still smiling warmly and moved to the door. Her mother followed closely behind her.

Once outside, Belle said, "Say it, Mama. I was shameless."

Mary shook her head, "No. It went quite a bit beyond 'shameless', Isabelle. I don't know quite what to think. That man is old...."

"Enough to be my father," Belle finished. "Oh, well I know — and he's married to boot, or did you not see the ring? However, we have not just a pass but an escort, and will be back in Front Royal tomorrow, instead of thrown on our own resources here in Winchester. Don't forget that it was the agency of some kind person here that led to my arrest and confinement in Baltimore."

Mary frowned, "Belle, I fear for you. You are much too bold, and if you're not careful you'll find yourself marrying some disgusting old man like Colonel Fillebrown because no one else will have you."

Belle considered this carefully, and then said coolly, "I suppose I could always take a lover."

Mary sputtered in indignation at the idea, and then Belle pointed at her and laughed to show it was a joke. Mary threw up her hands in exasperation. Looking behind them, she saw that two or three Yankee officers were looking at her daughter in open admiration.

"You are an impossible, difficult child," she scolded.

"I'm eighteen," said Belle, "And not a child at all."

Mary took her hand and squeezed. "You will always be a child to me, dear one," she said, suddenly almost tearful.

Belle felt her own composure slipping. "Hush, now," she said gently, "Not in front of the Yankees."

Hasbrouke Reeve was a young man of impressive looks. Well over six feet tall, and crowned with fine blonde hair, he was clean-shaven, with blue eyes and a face which betrayed all too well his love for the pleasures of the table. 'Strapping lad' didn't begin to describe him — he weighed more than 240 lbs, yet had the agility of a dance master. When he spied Belle, dressed to show her figure to maximum advantage, his lips pursed as if he might whistle in admiration, but no sound issued until he introduced himself very politely to Mary, and inquired if there was anything he might do to assist her and her family.

The way that he lifted Belle up into the baggage car made her feel positively dainty. She found herself genuinely attracted to him.

As it turned out, he was not a Provost Marshal but the First Lieutenant of Company L of the First Michigan Cavalry, which was stationed in Front Royal.

Belle, playing the simpleton once more, got him to volunteer much useful information about this unit and the rest of Shield's brigade. Mary watched balefully for some time and finally lay down on the floor of the car where some blankets were spread. William continued to watch the byplay between his big sister and the Yankee officer, at first biting his lip anxiously and then with increased boredom.

Belle took pains to collect a button from his uniform coat for her collection and encouraged him to call on her at the hotel. Why not? He was actually quite personable. If she had to consort with Yankees to do her work, why shouldn't they be handsome ones?

Her mother's probable reaction to this made her keep her own counsel. Part of her wanted to play with Reeve's fine blond hair, and wondered how those thick lips of his would feel against hers.

The train moved very slowly. Reeve explained that Rebel

bushwhackers sometimes shot into the cars. The slower they went, the more likelihood there was of detecting where the shot had come from and being able to return fire. Consequently, they did not arrive until after dawn the next day. Great confusion occurred as troops came off the passenger cars, while teamsters and laborers unloaded supplies.

The depot was full of supplies, as were two nearby warehouses. Front Royal was destined to play a major role in the next campaign the Yankees planned.

Lieutenant Reeve was helping her mother down from the baggage car when a Union Major came up, identified himself as Hector Tyndale, the Provost Marshal assigned to Shields' headquarters, and demanded to know why civilian passengers had been transported on a military train.

Reeve showed him the orders from Fillebrown. Tyndale looked at Belle, quite annoyed, shaking his head and muttering something that might have been a curse, probably on Fillebrown's head.

He allowed Reeve to escort Belle and the others across the street to the Fishback Hotel, sending an armed sentry with them despite the short distance. Guards were posted everywhere. Front Royal was under very strict martial law, with passes required at every turn.

Shields and his officers had taken every room in the hotel for themselves. Alice Stewart and her grandmother Ruth Glenn now lodged in a large two-story cottage formerly reserved for the servants of hotel guests.

Late that afternoon, having washed her face and changed her dress, she presented herself at General Shield's office and pleaded for a pass through the lines to Richmond.

Shields was jocular. Half teasing he said, "I would not expose you to General Jackson's tender mercies, Miss Belle." He paused to light a cigar and blow out the first refreshing cloud of smoke. "In a few days, his army will be destroyed and you and your mother can go where you please. In the meantime, I hope you'll honor us with your presence at dinner tonight. So many of the local ladies seem set against meeting my officers. That's especially hard on Captain Keogh and Captain Keily."

He gestured to where two young men stood, listening attentively. It was the older one, Keily, who caught her eye.

His neatly waxed mustache projected sharply from each side of his face, curling up at the ends, where Keogh's followed a more natural curve along his lip. Both had neatly trimmed van dyke beards, another thing which made them stand apart from the other officers, and both stood with the erect stance and natural ease of men who'd spent a lot of time at drill. Keily was far from handsome, but it was he that her gaze returned to again and again.

He, too, seemed entranced by her, and when she offered her hand, managed to take it with a very European flourish and the suggestion of a kiss. Belle blushed with pleasure.

Shields laughed, "You obviously learned many things in Italy besides the art of warfare, Keily."

"That I did, sir," Keily said, only slowly releasing her hand and staring deep into her eyes, "And not the least of that was how to treat a lady."

Belle was puzzled. The name was Irish, but his accent was almost German rather than infused with the brogue used by Shields or by Michael Kelley. He was wearing three military medals, the like of which she had never seen. Keogh had two of the same medals.

"What are those?" she asked innocently.

Keogh, who was by far more handsome, stepped forward and said self-importantly, "This is the Pro Petri Sede and this is the order of San Gregorio, both awarded by his Holiness, Pius the Ninth."

Shields, watching this byplay, said, "These men earned their spurs in the Italian Wars. They've come to show the rest of us the proper way to run a campaign."

Belle smiled her most gracious smile, "And what is that third medal for, Captain Keily?"

He looked down, his large forehead wrinkling in concentration, "Spelling?"

Everyone laughed. "It's something like that," he said, all wide-eyed innocence, "I'm sure of it."

He moved closer to Belle, who could not seem to take her eyes off of him. "You must call me Daniel."

"Daniel," she tasted the name in her mouth. She felt very odd. It was as if the room's temperature had suddenly increased by ten degrees. She felt faint for an instant.

"Well, General, if you will not grant me a pass, then I should go assist my cousin in getting dinner ready. If you gentlemen will excuse me...."

At that moment, a man in a civilian suit bustled into the room. He was wearing pince-nez glasses on a ribbon, holding a notebook and a pencil. Shields regarded him warily.

"Mister Clark, would you be so good as to wait outside?" Shields said.

"But, sir — are you aware...."

"Outside, sir, until I am ready to see you."

Shields did not raise his voice, but his tone was such that Clark stopped as if he had been slapped, turned on his heel and exited the room.

"Annoying fellow," Shields muttered. He saw the inquiry on Belle's face. "Mister Clark is a special correspondent for the New York Herald. He is traveling with us and filing his stories by telegraph wherever it can be found."

Belle smiled as if she hadn't a clue what he was talking about and murmured, "Well, I really must go, but it has been a delight meeting you all. Especially you, Captain Keily."

Keily nodded, smiling, while the other men in the room chuckled knowingly. "Allow me the privilege of escorting you, Miss Belle."

"From here to the kitchen?" she replied archly. "I think I know the way by now, Captain."

He nodded, his eyes bright. Belle felt short of breath, but managed a graceful exit. Outside in the hallway, the man Clark stared at her angrily, but said nothing. She passed him by with a nod.

William Clark resembled nothing so much as a malcontented walrus, with a mustache that fled from his upper lip to his jowls but a clean-shaven chin that had three folds to it. He was practically steaming from the ears by the time that Shields condescended to see him.

"Are you aware, Shields, that you have the most notorious spy of the Confederacy right here in Front Royal?"

"That's General Shields," came the rebuke, "And, last I heard, Rose Greenhow was safely lodged in the Old Capitol Prison."

Clark looked as if he might suffer an attack of the vapors any second. "I mean Belle Boyd, the so-called Confederate Cleopatra."

"Oh," said Shields. "Yes, the Provosts have been in and laid out the case before me. I don't find much there, and neither, by the way, did General Dix, when she was carried to Baltimore against her will and held there for a week. I find her quite charming, and, need I remind you, we need the good will of the locals if we are to prevail in our ambitions here."

Clark flipped open his notebook and started to write furiously. "You may not use any of that," Shields said sharply. "Put it out your mind."

"The people have a right to know, sir!"

"Not before time and not in such a way as will damage my operations," Shields replied, holding out his hand. Glowering, Clark ripped the page out and handed it to him.

Shields ripped it into tiny bits and threw them into the fireplace. "My officers are well aware of Miss Belle's reputation. I rely upon their discretion. We are not complete fools."

Clark looked at the other officers in the room, all of whom seemed to regard him with something approaching pity. "That will be all, Clark," said General Shields. Clark left quietly, his back stiff with suppressed anger.

Myles Keogh watched him go. "Why do you permit him to accompany us at all," he asked, "Sir?"

"It's an unfortunate part of our system of government," said Shields, "Guaranteed by the Constitution. Just try to not tell him anything that might compromise a movement. Be cautious."

"What about Miss Belle?" asked Daniel Keily.

"Well, I think most of the accusations of spying are simply romance. She's a young girl. Who would trust her with collecting military information? How would she even know what was wanted?"

Keily nodded thoughtfully.

Keogh said, "We really need to scout out this ground. These maps are — inexact."

Shields leaned back in his chair. "General Banks is coming over tomorrow. He's bringing Captain Strother with him."

"And he would be...?"

"Topographical engineer."

"You remember the man, Myles," said Keily. "We met him a few weeks past. The artist fellow who has been to Italy."

"Aye," said Keogh, "And he's from these parts. Knows the ground."

"That's the one," said Daniel Keily.

That evening Daniel Keily and Myles Keogh, being only Assistant Aides de Camp, took their dinners at the second table and admired the brisk efficiency with which Alice Stewart and Belle Boyd directed the servants performing the service. The food was excellent as well, and copious amounts of lemonade, beer, and wine were served, along with coffee drawn from army stores. The main course was a Virginia ham, with mashed potatoes and peas.

Keily thought that sitting among the junior staff was a good way to learn the unwritten miscellany of this new army he and Myles had joined, along with John O'Keefe, another veteran of the Papal Army who had joined them in Cork. O'Keefe had been doing detached service with the cavalry and had just rejoined them that evening.

It was less than six weeks from the day that the three of them had come ashore from the steamer *Kangaroo* in New York, under the escort of John Hughes, the Archbishop of New York. Privately, both Keily and Keogh thought that O'Keefe, who was a nephew of the Archbishop of Cork, had been sent, despite his tender years, to send reports back to his uncle about the state of the Union Army and the war. Reports that would then be forwarded to Rome for the edification of his Holiness, Pius IX.

The boy was a Jesuit spy, they believed, and this shaded their own dealings with him. Keily, for his own part, was falling in love with America and its wildness.

It was a tremendous opportunity for all of them, he and Myles agreed one night over bourbon whisky. Starting as Captains, they might quickly become Colonels or even Brigadiers, a rank which they never would see in Europe, as any number of fifty-year-old Lieutenants of their acquaintance could attest. Citizenship, by means of something called a "private bill" would be theirs as soon as Congress got around to it, Archbishop Hughes assured them. Wealth and opportunity beckoned, as soon as this troublesome rebellion could be disposed of. That would take, at most, he said, a year.

But the devil was in the details. There was much to learn, as O'Keefe told them over a post-dinner drink.

"The difference between Northern Cavalry and that of the South is enormous," he said, looking worried. "The Southern gentry, the Chivalry as they call themselves, seem to have been born in the saddle. The North uses horses to draw a plough or a wagon. There is little appreciation for the tactical ability to move men quickly and to scout enemy positions."

"Hard to believe that they have such poor maps of what is, essentially, their own country," Keogh said.

"The Rebellion did not occur overnight. There may have been maps, but they disappeared. Before the war, my uncle said, men with

Southern sympathies who worked for the Federal government wore a blue cockade in their hat, so they would know each other. There were many such. He said that such men began their treason long before the war started. The authorities weren't paying close attention to this because Washington is a southern city in its heart, and so is Baltimore. They've spent a lot of time securing those against capture from within as well as without."

Keily nodded, "Because if they don't, the game is up. What about the South? What is their position?"

"They came away with most of the best officers and much in the way of plunder, and they have good interior lines serviced by railways and telegraphs — in the East. With the fall of Island Number Ten, which was this tremendous fort they had in the Mississippi River, and then of New Orleans itself, they've been split in two. They are waging a defensive war rather than an offensive one." O'Keefe looked into the bottom of his empty glass and put it aside. Keogh refilled his glass and that of Keily's and offered the bottle to O'Keefe, who shook his head no.

Keogh shrugged, "That won't answer. Why won't they take the initiative?"

O'Keefe had to think about that. "It's hard to say. We're pressing them on two fronts before Richmond and, as I read the reports, they've concentrated most of their strength protecting their capitol. According to one report I saw, there's one hundred and fifty thousand men facing McClellan's army on the Peninsula and perhaps half that many here in the Shenandoah. Twenty-seven regiments of cavalry here alone. That's Ashby. Stuart has as much or more. And they're bold. Always ready for a fight. We had a minor skirmish with them when I was out with the First New Jersey. They descended on us, seemingly from out of nowhere, screaming like wild savages. It was quite unnerving." O'Keefe grinned, to show that he had not been particularly afraid. "They hit us mid-column, where the artillery was. A pair of six-pounders, so-called 'flying artillery'."

"And?"

"They killed or wounded the entire crew of one, and half of the other, but they didn't stay around for us to retaliate. Just ran off, still making those weird, rather terrifying cries."

There was a moment of silence. "That's a guerrilla tactic," said Keily at last. "How were they dressed?"

"Bits and pieces of uniforms, some of them Union blue, and civilian clothes. I couldn't see much from where I was."

"So they were not regulars?"

"Again, hard to tell. The South is hard up for uniforms, it seems. I saw some dead ones. Most didn't have shoes, much less proper boots or brogans. This lot could have been some kind of militia."

Keogh grimaced, "Militia? Militia don't attack columns and they don't know to go for the artillery crews as the hardest to replace."

Keily drained his glass. "This ain't a set-piece battle like we had in Italy. Different rules. Lots of damned amateurs."

"Which means we'll win in the end," Keogh predicted. "Give it a year, maybe two. Then we can marry some of the women, settle down and become proper Americans."

"My Lord, yes," said Keily. "Have you looked at these women? Our hostesses tonight were as fine as any signorina I saw in Italy."

"And not a proper Catholic among them," said O'Keefe primly, "All tied to the Luther heresy or worse. I actually saw a Masonic temple in one town. They practice that openly here."

He got up and nodded to his two older companions, "I'm riding out again in the morning, so I'd better make a night of it."

They watched him leave and then looked at each other.

"How old is he again?" said Keily.

"Nineteen."

"And raised by the Jesuits. I doubt if he's ever had a woman." Keily refilled his glass once more. "We should do something about that."

"Oh, I'd take him in hand myself," said Myles Keogh, "If I didn't fear he'd report every gory detail to the Archbishop."

"Aye, that's the nub of the matter. We'll leave him to his own devices. I'll not be accused of corrupting a priest, or a lay brother either, for that matter." Daniel Keily looked at his friend speculatively. "You see anyone you fancy?"

"Like to have a go at that Alice," said Keogh. "She seems to be a solid type and she's very pretty."

"I'll take Belle on, then," replied Keily.

"Welcome to her," said Myles with a shudder. "She reminds me of my horse."

Keily stared at him a moment, almost angry. "That was unkind. She has wit and charm."

Keogh grinned, "And a body that can only be described as heavenly or in terms too obscene for such noble company."

Keily's hand lashed out and stopped an inch short of his ear. "Careful," he said jokingly, "You may be talking about the woman I love."

CHAPTER TWENTY-THREE

Front Royal, Virginia, May 1862

The next morning, Belle joined Alice at the front desk of the hotel as the Yankee officers came down to breakfast. Alice introduced her to the ones she hadn't already met.

Belle, flirting and girlish, made a point of removing a button from as many of their coats as she could. The young men went along with the game, each flattered by her teasing attention in a town so hostile to Yankee blue.

Unlike the other young ladies in Front Royal, Belle and Alice made it their policy to treat Yankee officers with charming graciousness. While others wore heavy veils to conceal their faces when walking on the street, or turned their backs with deliberation and scorn as the Yankees passed by their windows, the two young ladies in charge of the Fishback Hotel welcomed them, not with open arms, of course, but with a grave courtesy tempered by a flirtatious manner, and the charm for which Southern women are widely famed. Belle, in particular, seemed eager to engage them in conversation.

As the last of them trooped by and into the dining room, Alice asked, "What's the button thing about?"

Belle smiled, and spoke quietly, "These are staff officers who perform various important tasks for General Shields. These little souvenirs help me remember them all."

Alice thought about that for a long moment. "While you were gone, I did ask that they all sign in, so that we would know what rooms they were in." She pulled the register, a large bound book covered in light green cloth, from beneath the counter.

Belle took it, flipped it open to the most recent page used, and sighed, "Oh, dear. Look at this. So untidy. I'd best make a clean copy."

The page was immaculate, with names and titles printed as well as signed, but Alice simply said, "Of course."

"I'll do that while I'm going over the books," Belle said.

At that moment, William Clark came thundering roughly

down the stairs. He stopped and glared at them.

"Ladies," he said gruffly, and passed on into the dining room.

Belle put her hand unconsciously over her throat. "What an unpleasant man."

Alice said, "One who fancies himself far more attractive to our sex than he really is."

Belle looked at her, alarmed.

"Oh, there's no real harm to him," Alice said dismissively. "A sharp word will keep him at bay. I worry more for the maids than myself."

"Has he...."

"Once, with young Martha, who is barely more than a girl." Alice frowned. "I was quite firm with him. I told him that if he adventured that way again, that I would not just complain to Major Tyndale but publish it so that all of his friends would know."

"I'm not sure he has friends," Belle said. "He's a reporter, after all."

"But one who wouldn't want his editors to know that he's developed a taste for 'coal'," Alice replied. "These Yankees are either fools or hypocrites when it comes to dealing with the Negro. To hear this lot tell it, none of them are Abolitionists."

"Yet they are here to finish the job John Brown started at Harper's Ferry," said Belle. "They exaggerate the colored folks' capacity and desire for freedom — those that want it find a way to buy themselves free."

That Alice knew for a fact. The last census just before the war revealed more free Negroes than slave in Virginia. It made one wonder why it had come to war.

Alice shrugged, and then said, "Mister Clark is particular about his room and his papers. Doesn't want anyone in there when he's not present himself, and doesn't want anything on his desk touched." Alice raised an eyebrow ironically.

Belle looked at her thoughtfully, "Did he say why?"

"Says he knows where everything is and wants it left so he

doesn't need to find it again when he starts to write."

"Sounds very reasonable." Belle smiled the same false brilliant smile she had used with the Yankee officers. "But perhaps there's another reason."

Alice raised her eyebrows again in silent inquiry.

"Perhaps he has something to hide. Perhaps he's some kind of spy," Belle whispered.

"For us?"

"Oh, certainly not," Belle said, still keeping her voice very low. "For them."

"He doesn't go out in the field very much. Him, a spy? I think not," Alice sniffed.

"Of a type," Belle said, "Of a type. There are those who lay in wait for other spies."

Alice's face registered alarm now.

"If such is the case," Belle continued, "He's not very good at it. He's already denounced me to Shields and been rebuffed because he had nothing more to offer than what's been said in the newspapers." She sighed. "For all of that, he's a dangerous man."

"Any reporter is. My father calls them the princes of lies — and him a lawyer!" Alice said unhappily. "How does the button thing work?" she asked.

Belle looked at her for a long moment, licked her lips and said, "It's a memory trick. I put them in different pockets, which allows me to recall if the officers who gave them to me are artillery, cavalry, or infantry, or staff or engineers. Some have different designs which designate the units they are with. I can make a better report if I keep them separate."

"And sewing them on your dress?"

"Allows everyone to feel comfortable playing my little game. You can't use this, Alice. I don't want to draw attention to it."

Alice smiled, "Why, I don't need it. I've gotten them to very kindly write it all out."

Belle smiled, "So you have."

She took the register away to copy the information from the page. When she returned about an hour later, she stopped short. Another party of officers, led by a Major General, was entering the lobby.

After a moment she realized it was Banks, who had been Speaker of the House of Representatives, and then Governor of Massachusetts not long before the war, but her attention was on the tall, bearded Captain who walked next to him.

It was Porte Crayon, the artist and writer, or, as he was now known here, Strother the traitor.

Tears came to her eyes. She wanted to flee to her room, but that was hardly possible. She needed a moment.

Strother's attention was caught by the two landscape paintings featuring Massanutten Mountain that hung in the lobby.

"These are mine!" he exclaimed. "The work of my youth!"

Banks and the other officers gathered around the paintings, making admiring comments. Strother, rather than flattered, was distressed.

"I gave these long ago to my dearest friend, James Stewart. How did they come to be here?" he agonized.

Alice came out from behind the desk, "They were hung, with much regard, by the owner of this establishment."

Strother stared at her, uncomprehending.

"Don't you know me, Uncle David?" Alice asked, almost in tears.

Strother's face changed, and he seemed on the verge of tears himself. "Alice?"

"Yes!"

He turned to where Banks, and now Shields and members of his staff, stood watching. "This is Alice Stewart, my friend's daughter." He seemed a bit choked. "And as dear to me as my own daughter."

"Then she's well met, and it's a happy day for you both." This was said in a very kind way by Myles Keogh.

It was far from the truth, but General Shields, in the avuncular way he had, pretended to agree, shook hands with Banks, and introduced his staff, including his two new Irish experts.

Belle, recovered her composure, and walked into the room in a very bold way that everyone immediately noticed.

"Mistah Crayon," she said in the exaggerated accents used in amateur theatricals, "Whatever are you doing heah?"

Strother turned towards her. He smiled, relieved.

"Miss Belle? I must turn the question back on you. What are you doing here?"

"Meeting fascinating men," Belle said, her eyes rolling around the room. "Gorgeous men."

The other men in the room chuckled in appreciation. Strother looked momentarily troubled, and then smiled. "Surely there's more to it than that?"

"Well, Alice and I, despite our tender years, have charge of this establishment, her parents being inconvenienced in Richmond. This certainly," she said, and cast a look particularly towards the two Irish officers, "Improves my chances of finding a beau."

Again there was laughter at her boldness.

Shields took charge of things once more. "We have an important staff meeting, gentlemen."

Strother looked over to Banks, who nodded. "We have a few minutes on preliminaries, Captain. In your own good time, as long as you're quick about it."

"Thank you, sir."

The rest of the Yankee officers crowded back into the dining room, where the remains of breakfast had been cleared away. Three servants remained to serve coffee. One of them was Eliza.

As the doors closed, Strother looked from Belle to Alice and asked, "How is that you're here?"

"When you Yankees forced Father out of Washington, we came here and leased the hotel. It seemed like a good business." Alice's voice was edged with anger now.

Strother nodded. His face took on an expression of deep longing. "Too bad he's not here. It would be so good to see him again."

Alice said nothing, but simply looked away. Strother's own face grew sadder, as he grasped the reason for her silence.

Belle, to break the mood, walked up to him quite saucily, and said, "You must let me have a memorial, Captain Strother." She produced a small penknife and, before he could react, cut a button from his uniform coat.

"Why did you do that?" he asked, taken aback.

"For my collection," Belle replied, her eyes dancing with mischief, as she pointed to the trophies sewn on her dress. "Here is General Shields', and here is Colonel Fillebrown's and this is Major Tyndale's assistant, and this Lieutenant Reeve and this...."

Strother laughed heartily. "Well, I'm in distinguished company," he said. "It is very good to see you both again; however, I am needed in that meeting." He leaned over to pick up the rolled maps he had brought with him. Both girls looked at them, realizing what they were.

David Strother's eyes were filled with grief even as he smiled that broad smile they knew and loved so well. "Ladies, always a pleasure."

"Will you be staying for dinner?" Alice asked, trying to be practical and business-like.

"No," said Strother regretfully. "We're going back to Strasburg at four o'clock." Without another word he went into the dining room, closing the door behind him.

Belle and Alice looked at each other, each with lips trembling, on the verge of tears. The room grew very quiet as they each searched for something...anything...to say. It was an impossible situation.

"Well," said Belle after a moment, "That's that."

"Yes," Alice answered firmly, "Just so."

On the train back to Bank's headquarters at Strasburg, David Strother seemed distracted. Nathaniel Banks and a newly made Brigadier, John White Geary, who had also gone to Front Royal, were having a quiet argument. It was polite, but intense.

"I don't trust those foreign officers very much," Banks grumbled.

"The Irish?" said Geary, with a smile. "Well, they've good experience in Italy, and since I'm of that tribe, I'm inclined to give them the benefit of the doubt. They seem likely lads."

Strother, who had been wondering miserably whether or not he would ever heal the breach with his family caused by his decision to fight for the Union, listened more carefully.

The word "experience" was ever so slightly emphasized by Geary and directed as a jibe at Banks, who had none. Everyone knew that he had used his political influence and friendship with Henry Wilson, the Chairman of the Senate Military Committee, to gain his commission, which ranked him only second to McClellan himself.

Geary, on the other hand, had led a Pennsylvania regiment in Mexico, and raised a brigade when Lincoln called for volunteers. He also looked like the popular image of a general, nearly six and a half feet tall, with a very full beard and sharp eyes that missed little. Known for a sharp tongue, he had been in the thick of the slavery issue since 1856, when he had been appointed briefly as the Governor of the Kansas Territory.

What is it about lawyers, Strother wondered, *that makes them think that they can do anything they turn their hand to?* Unlike his new friend, Colonel Thorton Brodhead, both men were fervent Abolitionists and wanted to make the war about slavery rather than preserving the Union. The difference between them, he saw, was that Geary was a soldier first and Banks was, always and forever, a politician. Their argument bore that out.

"See, here, General. We have an enemy before us that we dare not take lightly. McClellan's plan is to take Richmond from the east, by degrees, and for us to apply the same kind of slow, relentless pressure in the Valley. I want simply to assure we have a good base of supply of all kinds."

"If Shields can trap and destroy Jackson's army, then we won't need so much supply, and too much becomes an attractive target for the enemy, who will either try to capture or destroy it," Geary replied patiently.

Banks looked at him narrowly with eyes red-rimmed from lack of sleep, chewing on his mustache. "How would you know that?"

Geary favored him with a condescending smile. "Because that's what I would do if I were them. Have you seen some of the prisoners we've captured lately? Ragged and dirty, most of them without shoes, but still plenty of fight left in them. They're hungry, too. Our supplies will draw them like flies to honey."

"Jackson has twenty thousand men, by our estimates," Banks said. "That gives our friend Abe some problems. He worries, and rightly so, I say, about the safety of the capital." He shook his head. "McClellan says he's facing a hundred and fifty thousand east of Richmond."

"I doubt it's that many," Strother said suddenly.

Both generals turned and stared at him.

"And why is that?" Banks demanded.

"Virginia certainly couldn't field that many on its own," Strother said, "And regiments from other states are mostly engaged on other fronts, especially since we took New Orleans."

Geary nodded appreciatively. "That's the problem with a defensive war; you have to defend the ground from attacks from every direction."

"They've done that," Banks objected. "Triple lines of fortifications in every direction. The cost of overcoming such is high in both blood and treasure, as we learned to our sorrow at Bull's Run."

"But eventually," Geary said, "We will overcome them. They will run out of men. Why, they've even started a draft to fill the ranks."

Banks nodded sagely, "And we'll have to do the same. The bloom is off the rose with the glory of it all. People are beginning to have second thoughts."

Strother said, "Certainly the case here. Most of the population now realize that they've been played a nasty trick by the slave-holders. We're getting back the northern counties of Virginia. Elsewhere, the matter is less clear."

Banks, with unexpected sympathy, said, "This has been very hard for you, hasn't it, Captain?"

Strother suddenly could not speak. He suppressed the tears that came to his eyes and looked away. "The hardest thing I have ever done, sir," he said at last.

Banks patted him gently upon the knee and then got up. "A moment gentlemen, while I relieve myself. Too much army coffee."

One of his aides sprang to his feet when he stood, but Banks waved him off. "There are still some things I am allowed to do for myself," he said gruffly.

He made his way to the rear of the car. The train was going at a faster clip and rocking gently side to side.

Geary looked at him speculatively. "You don't think Jackson has twenty thousand men?"

Strother shook his head. "Ten thousand at best, and that's if some of the Louisiana regiments are with him."

"Why do you say so?" It wasn't a challenge. Geary genuinely wanted his views.

"I grew up here, General. I know these counties and I know these gentlemen who signed up. There aren't enough of them."

"And I know Jackson, from the Mexican War," said General Geary. "He made quite a name for himself. He was the only one of his West Point class who came out of the war a Brevet Major."

Strother looked suitability impressed. "He hasn't had much of a reputation since he came home to Virginia. Students at VMI call him 'Tom Fool'."

Geary chuckled, "He ain't much of a talker. I imagine that sitting through a lecture of his might qualify as a form of torture; but he does know how to fight. In Mexico he was famous for aggressive tactics." He leaned back, wriggling uncomfortably on the hard bench, which was too small for him. "One advantage the Rebels do have," he said.

Strother raised an eyebrow in silent inquiry.

"They have sense enough to leave the fighting to the generals and keep the politicians out of it. Even Jeff Davis ain't allowed on the field." He winked. "Nothing against my illustrious colleague, of course."

"You're a politician," Strother said.

"Just restless," Geary replied with a laugh. "Law practice bored me silly, so I went out to San Francisco to be the Postmaster, and got elected Alcade and then Mayor."

"Isn't that the same job?"

"It is. Different language and a different way of doing things. I did well, cleaned up the town, with some help from the local vigilance committee, so President Pierce decided I was just the fellow to calm Kansas down. He was wrong, unfortunately. Slaveholders controlled the legislature."

"You ever meet John Brown?"

Geary frowned, "That's a loaded question if there ever was one. I did meet the son of a bitch, several times, but he ain't no kind of holy martyr to me."

Strother didn't say anything at all. He reminded himself that he wasn't a civilian any longer and this man was a general officer. There were limits to what he could say.

Geary smiled. "What are you thinking?"

"How much I'd like to resign," Strother said frankly.

Geary nodded. "It's hard, this war, and very hard on people who want to do the right thing."

Strother nodded, sighed, and flipped open his sketchbook to a clean page. He took a pencil stub from his pocket and began to draw.

Geary watched for a few moments. "Why do you do that?"

Strother looked up and saw kindness in his eyes. "It relaxes me," he said. "It demands one's complete attention and careful observation. When I draw, I don't think about other things. I can't, and do it well."

"And you do it very well, I'm told."

Strother continued to lay down the bones of his sketch. It was of the lobby of the Fishback Hotel and the two paintings he had found there.

Banks finally made his way back to his seat. He had stopped along the way to talk to several of his officers.

Always the politician, Strother thought, closing the sketchbook.

Banks looked at Strother curiously. "The Provost Marshal tells me those two young ladies at the hotel are spies and whores," he said with unusual bluntness.

Strother blinked. He felt his temper rising. Banks was watching him carefully. He was being deliberately provoked.

"I've know them both since they were babes-in-arms," he replied with a far milder tone than he felt. "They come from good families. Alice's father was the friend of my boyhood and my roommate at college. Belle's parents are also numbered among my dearest friends. I am sure the Provost is mistaken in both particulars, especially the last."

I will resign, Strother thought.

Banks stared at him. Geary cleared his throat.

"Sounds like someone has been listening to bad gossip," he said, equally quietly. "See here, Banks, Miss Boyd shot a man in justified self defense when her home was broken into and her mother was attacked. We've all read the reports. She then probably undertook some clumsy work as a spy, but the case was never proven. She's a young lady with a lot of energy and charm, and newspapers love the idea of a girl spy, as ridiculous as it is. You and

I have both been newspaper editors in our checkered pasts...."

Banks looked at him, startled that he knew this.

"That means we should know bad, sloppy reporting when we see it," Geary continued. "If General Shields' overtures to the local population are to be effective, we can't be going around arresting people without sufficient cause. As I understand the customs here, Captain Strother is now entitled to issue a challenge to a duel in defense of his female relatives."

Banks turned pale when this was said. Southern gentlemen were famed both for bad temper and quick retribution. He had been present when Preston Brooks from the South had beaten Charles Sumner, a much larger man, so severely with a cane that he had nearly died. The brawl was sparked during a debate over slavery, of course.

"I apologize, Captain, if I have in any way offended you," he said hastily, and seemed contrite.

Strother summoned a reassuring smile, only because Banks was his superior officer. As appealing as the idea of duel might be to some, he was neither good enough a shot nor robust enough a brawler to carry one off with any profit. So he showed far more graciousness than he felt. Both Banks and Geary noted with alarm the small muscle in his cheek that continued to twitch.

"Dueling is against military law, but your apology is accepted anyway, sir." Strother's voice was soft, but dangerous.

How am I going to continue to be able to work for this fool? he asked himself.

"As you saw, Belle is an outrageous flirt. Some men take that wrong," he added after a moment.

Banks nodded. There was a breach between them now, and it was entirely Banks' fault.

Geary looked at them shrewdly, seeking a way to defuse the moment with humor. "Do any of us have all of our buttons?" he asked. Remembering Belle's souvenir collecting, they all laughed.

"See here," Geary said to Banks a moment later, "If I am to

defend the Manassas Gap and Winchester while we build up our supply, I'd like to have someone who knows the ground. Perhaps Captain Strother could come over and give me a hand?"

"Of course, General," Banks replied, quickly. "That all right with you, Strother?"

"Of course, sir. Wherever I'm needed." It was more than all right. Thor Brodhead's unit was part of Geary's command. He could continue to share Brodhead's very comfortable tent and seemingly endless supply of coffee. Just then the very sight of Banks raised his ire. He opened his sketchbook again and resumed work on his drawing, and did not look up for the rest of the journey.

Belle came to Eliza, as she and the other servants were clearing up the dining room and getting it ready for supper.

"Walk with me," she said. Eliza nodded, looked over to the others, who studiously ignored her, and left the room with Belle. Belle led her out to the barn, where Fleeter was tethered. A union sentry stood in the yard, but did not challenge them.

"What happened at the meeting? " Belle asked, as she patted Fleeter's broad head.

Eliza closed her eyes, trying to remember, "Dey after Jackson. Goin' to put a big store of supply heah, den move further south."

"They say where?"

"Dey ain't sure. Jackson been givin' dem de slip. Hard to find, and dey patrollin' with eighty, ninety mens in dere cavalry. Afraid of ambushes. Dey talk about how Ashby trapped dem at Warrentown Junction. Called it a massacuh."

Belle sniffed. "Cowards. That's too many men to do the work."

She had no intention of telling Eliza or anyone else about Warrentown Junction or her role in it. Eliza looked at her, questions in her eyes. Belle changed the subject.

"How are the local colored folks taking all this?"

Eliza paused, surprised by the question. "Dey mostly scared.

De ones at de Buck place, dey all happy the Yankees here, dink it means dey go free soon. Foolish niggers."

Belle pretended to look at Fleeter's teeth, gently forcing his mouth open. "Why do you say that?"

Eliza shrugged, "Dey got a good situation, fer one ting. Bucks ain't hard masters. Dey kind people. Black folks mostly waitin' fer de big Yankee to say de slaves go free. Den dey see what dey do."

"Big Yankee? You mean Lincoln?"

"Uncle Abraham, he de man decide all dis. Dat Yankee Fremont find dat out quick enough."

Belle turned and stared at her. Most white southerners hadn't heard about how Lincoln had reprimanded Fremont, yet her Negro maid, who could not read, knew the story. People talked in front of slaves as if they weren't there. She'd done it herself. She'd have to be more careful.

She needed Eliza's help now more than ever, so she let the matter drop.

"Please tell Moses that we need him later today," Belle didn't repeat her joke about the Underground Railway. The real thing was probably more active than ever — and spying for the Yankees.

"I will," said Eliza. "Ashby?"

"Yes," Belle said.

Belle let go of Fleeter's head, wiped her hands, and started out of the barn. Eliza followed.

"Dat Irish Yankee askin' 'bout you."

"Which one?" Belle asked. "They're mostly all Irish."

"De 'talian one wid de medals."

"The tall one or the short one?"

"De tall one."

"That would be Captain Keily."

"Yes'm."

As they walked back to the main building, Eliza said a surprising thing. "He big 'nough man fer you."

Belle stopped, turned, and looked at her. Eliza was brimming with suppressed mirth.

"What do you mean?"

"Tall, handsome fellah, and a soldier jest like you."

Belle felt herself flush. "Don't be ridiculous. We have nothing in common."

Eliza actually grinned at her, which Belle found very irritating.

"Don' mattah. He got de look and you got de look."

"What look?" Belle felt a little scared. Negroes saw so many things that white folks missed. They were always watching. Watching everything.

"De lubbin' look," said Eliza with satisfaction.

Belle shook her head. "I haven't time to fall in love," she said firmly, trying to stare Eliza down.

Eliza just kept smiling.

CHAPTER TWENTY-FOUR

Front Royal, Virginia, mid-May, 1862

Something was afoot with the Yankees. There could be no doubt. Lucy Buck was, it was said, in a continual simmer at various outrages committed by the Yankees at "Bel Air", as her father so grandly titled his farm.

To some degree, thought Belle, *this is his own fault.* He had inherited a grand manor house from which depended two large wings, and then failed to make enough children to fill all the rooms. His sons were off with Beauregard, and his oldest daughter Lucy, upon the death of his wife, assumed the duties of "Lady of the Manor". It was the kind of house that might well ornament a plantation of several thousand acres rather than the hundred that William Buck claimed as his own.

He was a prosperous merchant, and part of his business was a dairy, from which many in town bought milk, butter, cream and eggs. Half of the land was in wheat, and from this the Bucks made enough bread for themselves with some left over to sell every day.

The Yankees found Bel Air, so close by the main road, irresistible as a place to camp, disturbing the dairy cows in their pasture, and converting Mister Buck's fence rails to tent supports and firewood. This was done without leave, and to add further insult to the injury, Yankee soldiers did not hesitate to come into the house begging for a glass of milk or even demanding their supper. Mister Buck bore this with far more equanimity than his children, especially Lucy.

Mister Buck, with far more reluctance than he actually felt, agreed to let the Union General, Kimball, pitch his staff tents in the yard and even allowed that worthy, who was ailing, the use of some unoccupied rooms in the west wing of the house. In return Kimball personally went to try and get the ordinary soldiers to stop tearing down the fences and ruining the field of wheat by going back and forth through it, but to no avail.

Mister Buck also appealed to General Shields, who, anxious to gain local goodwill, sent down an order. This guaranteed that future thefts were carried out stealthily, under the cover of night, rather than openly.

Belle was amused by the pretensions that Lucy, who was only sixteen months older than she, assumed. Lucy's quietly controlled fury at the invaders, and towards those who dealt with them with even a modicum of grace, was remarked upon by the locals almost as much as Belle and Alice's excessive display of good manners.

No one disputed that the Bucks were imposed upon most grievously, but so was everyone else in Front Royal. Yankees paid with Yankee dollars, which were worthless now, and while William Buck made a show of refusing individual payment from the Yankee soldiers who dined at his table, saying that a Southern gentleman did not take payment from his guests and that there were hotels in town if they wished to contract for board, he was quick to accept the rather larger sums offered by Yankee quartermasters and provosts as payment for his goods and as reparations for his damages.

He knew that the Fishback Hotel, under the control of the gimlet-eyed Ruth Burns Glenn, would change Yankee dollars for good Confederate money.

The good Confederate money was provided by Belle, and the Union notes harvested by this operation sent to be disbursed to other agents of the Secret Service. Secretary Benjamin devised the plan, and trusted Belle and Antonia Ford, as the knowledgeable daughters of merchants, to oversee it.

Belle's grandmother readily fell in with the plan because there was quite enough attention directed Belle's way from many directions. Not just the scorn of Lucy Buck, Mary Cloud, and their friends, who viewed Belle and Alice as interlopers to their social scene, but also from two Union officers.

For the first time in her life, Belle was the object of intense romantic interest, not just from Daniel Keily, but also from Hasbrouke Reeve, who made a point of stopping by to see her if his duties carried him anywhere nearby.

Keily lived at the hotel and had the advantage. He was in the best position to express his ardor, and express it he did, daily with poems that praised her looks and other charms extravagantly, and with flowers.

Belle was amused at first, but could not help be impressed. Some of the poems were in Italian, which was close enough to French for her to decode. Keily was not a handsome man, but she had never expected handsome, since she herself was no classic beauty, and she found him more attractive than any of the others and puzzled aloud as to why.

Alice put it in perspective for her, "Because he's a man."

"What do you mean?" Belle asked. "They are all men."

"No," said Alice thoughtfully. "They are all male. Very few of them are men. There's just a boyishness about most of them. They are all having the time of their lives on a great adventure, which is this terrible war which is destroying everything we know and love."

Belle looked at her. They were going over the daily accounts. Officers at Shields' headquarters were obliged to pay for their room and board. Given the uncertain situation, Alice thought it wise to ask for payment daily, which would be simple enough but for the little extras they demanded. Most of these were bottles of whisky, Belle noted. The hotel had a good supply, but it was shrinking fast.

"We may have to get some of these boys to sign the pledge," she joked, and looked over again to Alice. "Why do you think Daniel more a man than the others?"

Alice smiled. "Well, he's a real soldier, not one of these volunteers who barely knows the craft of it, and he's proven brave if those medals on his chest are any witness, but mostly it's his attitude. I have yet to hear him speak of 'cowardly rebels' or similar blustering. He respects our men as worthy adversaries. And those manners. So refined."

"Myles Keogh acts the same," Belle observed.

Alice smiled softly, "That he does, and he's a sight better looking." Alice moved her hips unconsciously, just ever so slightly. "I'd try him at a dance."

"Has he written you a poem yet?" Belle asked, teasing.

"Not yet, but he will," said Alice confidently.

Belle smiled and shook her head. "These men are not husband material, you know."

Alice laughed, "I'm too young to be a widow anyway. These lads, as they call themselves, are apt to lead charges. But that's the least of it."

Belle finished making out the bills and closed the account book, "And what's the most of it?"

"Irish, Catholic, Yankee," said Alice slowly and distinctly, which said it all.

"Marry one and prepare to leave Virginia for the rest of your life," said Belle. "Totally unsuitable."

"But as a dalliance...," Alice said, still smiling.

"As if my reputation hadn't suffered enough damage," Belle replied, serious now.

"Oh, Belle," said Alice, a bit put out, "If not for the war, we'd both be young matrons in Washington Society by now. Your great friend Antonia said as much, and it certainly was my mother's fondest wish. Who knows who we might have ended up with, and there a Catholic, or even a Jew, is not out of the question."

"Looks like we'll settle for drunken Irishmen, then," Belle said, shaking her head.

"What do you mean?"

"These lads like, as they call it, 'a touch of the creature'. By this account, the touch is more like a slap. Seems they each go through about a quart a day."

Belle never drank hard liquor. Neither did Alice. Wine was sometimes served at dinners on special occasions, but they, heeding motherly advice, merely sipped and never asked for a refill. Hard drinking was something men did and women deplored them doing.

"Why will men put into their mouths a thief to steal their brains," Belle murmured.

"What's that?"

"Shakespeare. Othello, I believe. A play you'll never see in these parts."

Alice looked confused, "Why ever not?"

"It's about a Negro General in Italy who marries a beautiful white woman."

Alice was very shocked. "I should hope not. I can't imagine such a thing."

"He suspects her of adultery and murders her."

"Serves her right," Alice sniffed.

"No, she is blameless, the victim of a plot by another man, who wants to destroy his general. He gets another officer drunk and tells him lies and does other things to make it appear that they are lovers. All lies, but she's murdered anyway."

"What a terrible idea for a play," Alice said. "Who would watch such a thing?"

"It's over three hundred years old, so I imagine a number of people have seen it over the years," Belle replied thoughtfully.

"And a Negro general! What an absurd idea."

Perhaps, Belle thought to herself, but changed the subject. "So, should I agree to see Daniel?" she asked. "Won't people think ill of me?"

"They already do that, Belle," said Alice, showing that practical streak that Glenn Clan women were noted for. "You've got the name, you might as well have the game."

Another time Belle would have been hurt and stormed out of the room, but there was no malice in what Alice said. The sad truth was that her secret service demanded sacrifices.

I will simply have to bear up under the difficulty, she told herself, with a rising feeling of excitement and anticipation at what Daniel Keily might do, given the opportunity. She was feeling distinctly restless and in need of some fun.

Still, she did not make it easy for him. No belle would. Rather she played Lieutenant Reeve as her foil, allowing him to take her for walks in the evening. It did give her the chance to experience those rather full lips, and Hasbrouke was big and strong enough to make her feel dainty. But, he was also a bit of a boy, tentative, and almost like a puppy fearing a kick when he was with her. There was just so much she could do to build up his confidence. Certainly, he would not respond well to the kind of kiss that Jules St. Martin had given her that one afternoon.

She had not thought much about it since. It was too strange and unexpected, and had scared her a little. *Jules St. Martin was, if anything, a bit too sure of himself,* she thought, and upon reflection she found him less than attractive. He was a little too well used.

What was she to do, but accept Daniel Keily's rather extravagant courtship? It was done in spurts, because he was often absent on duty. On the nights he came to her, he bore the evening well, but always seemed to have a glass in his hand.

She allowed him to snatch a kiss in the alcove next to the kitchen one night. It left her feeling a bit breathless, despite the taste of whisky. She danced away from him, but not before he covered one breast with his large hand. He did this so softly that she didn't notice at first, and the sensation was far from disagreeable. She pretended not to notice, and felt a little wicked for not stopping him the next time. Her nipples stood up as if she had doused them in ice cold water, but she felt very heated. It was strange, and a bit wonderful.

By comparison, Hasbrouke was not as interesting, but she continued to see him as well, if only for the conversation. She suspected that Hasbrouke Reeve would never be so bold as to place his hands on her breasts, and that if he did, he wouldn't quite know what to do with them.

However, he had been drafted by Major Tyndale as an assistant Provost Marshal, and found the work interesting. Belle was genuinely interested in what he had to say about it.

She had learned the art of conversation well, and listened, bright-eyed and eager, to everything he told her, pretending ignorance often enough that he felt compelled to elucidate further, in detail. Evenings spent with him produced good reports for Turner Ashby.

But they weren't a patch on what she learned from Dan Keily, who, like most drinking men, rambled on about his troubles at great length. Since he and Keogh were charged with planning the next campaign against Jackson, Belle absorbed every word eagerly, often between kisses which grew ever more passionate.

Belle faithfully reported all to Ashby, although she was sure that some was very obvious. Jackson's edict to provide only hard information and not speculate on enemy intentions was ever in her mind.

That the Yankees believed the South well garrisoned became evident when Keily told her that McClellan faced a hundred and fifty thousand men before Richmond with only two-thirds that number.

"Going against such strong positions, you want at least twice as many men as those defending," said Keily.

"So he's two hundred thousand men short?" Belle said.

"So he thinks," Keily said. They were walking, side by side, in the outer yard. "I don't know where he gets such a number though, because, from what I've read so far, reports and the like, it doesn't seem logical that the South would have that many men there. My own guess is that the entire Southern army doesn't number that many in this area."

Belle was alarmed. Keily was a smart, experienced officer who knew his business. "What will you do?"

"Not my bailiwick," said Keily. "We've enough to do here, trying to trap Jackson."

It had been raining intermittently, for two days. The courtyard, well covered with gravel, gleamed wetly.

They were close to the barn and Belle could see that he hoped to draw her in under the eaves as he had two nights before. His kisses had been more passionate, and longer, and she had more or less swooned in his arms in sheer physical delight.

Suddenly, thunder cracked overhead, louder than any

cannon. Rain came gushing down on top of them. They ran for the barn, and slipped inside.

Belle was soaked to the skin and chilled by the rain, and Keily looked rather woebegone, his fine mustaches soaked and drooping down. It gave him a comical appearance and she giggled.

Outside, the rain thundered down in the kind of downpour country folk call a "gullywasher".

Rather than being hurt or offended by her laughter, Keily smiled and tried to push some of the water off his uniform with his hands. He looked at her speculatively.

"You should get out of those wet things," he said simply, as if it were the most reasonable thing in the world.

The words filled Belle with a thrill and a shock. The idea of being naked in front of him had never occurred to her. She licked her lips, confused.

"What about you? You'll catch your death of cold." She made one last attempt to rid herself of the crazy feelings that were taking hold of her. It was dark in the barn, except for a single lantern burning dimly in one of the stalls.

"Isn't there a sentry?" she asked suddenly.

"Not tonight," Keily said. "I made out the roster meself."

She gasped. *He planned this!*

Not the rain, of course, but a place where he could seduce her. She could smell a pile of fragrant, loose hay someplace nearby. And there was something else, the smell of him.

"Do we have time?"

"I don't think the rain will stop any time soon," he replied.

Suddenly she wanted him as much as she had ever wanted anything in her whole life. "Well, it's certainly cold in here," she said softly.

"Let me warm you," he moved to embrace her and then kissed her slowly and softly, nibbling at her lower lip, and then her neck and then her ear lobe. Belle felt reason slip away. She broke from him, staring at him across the dimly lit interior of the barn.

She began to unbutton her dress. He moved to help, but she held up a hand. "What's fair is fair," she whispered. "If you get to see me, I get to see you."

He nodded, and began to unbutton his own shirt, sliding his coat off. Belle let the dress fall to her waist, and he was barechested. He took a step, slid his arms around her and, rather than kiss her lips, bent his head to her large, firm breasts.

His fingers slipped her breasts out of the confinement of her chemise. Her nipples were so hard and rigid and so sensitive that she could feel his breath on them. His lips very gently took one, nibbling. She gasped from the sheer pleasure that brought.

She ran her hands over his balding head, encouraging him to give equal time to the other one. He did so, sucking gently and then biting her gently. Belle had never felt such sensations. Had never imagined them.

She began to kiss him tenderly on his bare chest. He groaned and seemed to tear at the buttons near his waist. His trousers fell away and he pulled off his boots, standing there in the dim light only in his stocking feet. She gasped when she saw the size of him.

She knew what it was, of course. Any girl who grew up on or near a farm learned early on what it was and what it was for. A cock. His cock.

She still had on her pantaloons and corset, as well as her boots. With his help, she got them off quickly, so she could be as naked as he. He tried to embrace her, but she stopped him gently, one hand flat against his chest. He cupped her breasts gently in his large hands and led her to the pile of hay.

Outside the rain thundered on as she sank to her knees, wanting to examine his cock. Never had she been so close to one, and, certainly, never had she been naked and free with any man. His hands rested gently on her shoulders as she reached out tentatively to touch it.

His skin is as soft as well-worked deerskin, she thought, *but the instrument it covers is as hard as a wooden dowel.* She put her hand all the way around it and suddenly the idea of it inside her had her gasping for breath. She kissed the head of it and a shock rippled through his body. A bit of liquid appeared on the end. She licked it. It had a salty taste.

"Oh, my gawd," he whispered, "Oh, don't stop."

She nibbled it, nipping sharply with her teeth. He groaned. "Sheet!"

Belle suddenly felt both in control and out of it. She didn't quite know what to do next, so she stood up and, cupping her hands under her breasts, offered them to him. He buried his head between them, and then trailed kisses down to below her waist. She realized that she was very warm and the part between her legs, to which she had never paid much attention before, was now radiating heat.

It was heat that he tried to douse with his tongue and suddenly her entire body shook. She cried out in surprise.

He took her gently in his arms then, and laid her down in the hay. Then she felt him at her nether lips, now wet with desire, and wondered of he would root at her the way Fleeter did when he was bred to a mare.

But he was slow. Torturously so. Because, she realized, he wanted to be gentle. And she was tight, tight around him, stretching to take him all in, and then he began to gasp, and then pulled his cock out of her, spilling his seed all over her belly.

"Oh why? Why did you do that?" she cried.

"You don't want a baby, do you, darlin'?" his voice sounded half exhausted and far away.

"I want you and I want you inside me. Now!"

He slid himself back inside her and for a wonder was still hard. He began a slow rocking motion that teased her to the edge of something she had never felt before. Her legs curled around his as she pulled him deeper still. Her body shook again and she bit his shoulder to keep from screaming.

Outside the rain slacked off. He collapsed heavily against her and she felt the weight of him sweetly crushing her breasts. They lay there, silently, barely breathing for a few moments.

"We'd better get back," he said at last.

"Back where?"

"Where we should be," he said, reminding her that she had crossed a line here.

I will not regret this, she told herself defiantly. *I will never regret this.*

He got up, fetched the lantern and collected his clothes. Slowly, she sat up and felt his fluid run out of her into the hay. Then, alarmed, not knowing how long they had been there, she heard the rain begin to taper off.

"Bring the lantern closer," she said.

He did so, whistling softly at the beauty of her form. She looked between her legs. He offered her his handkerchief so she could wipe herself.

"I didn't bleed," she said in a tone of wonder. She wiped herself and smelled the handkerchief. "There should be blood. As big as you are, there should be blood."

He was stunned. "Are you telling me I'm the first?" he croaked after a moment.

"The first and only, darlin'," Belle said, her voice coolly disappointed. "You surely didn't believe all those newspaper articles and camp gossip?" she asked, suddenly cold and angry. "All of those poems were simply a ploy; another military campaign?"

"No, not at all...," he stuttered.

She got to her feet and looked about for her clothes. "Help me dress," she said, her disappointment in him manifest.

He did so, with a skill and dispatch that told her that she was far from *his* first. She brushed herself off. Her hair was a problem, but that could be blamed on the rain.

Keily suddenly seemed shy of her. "I...," he began.

"Just hush," Belle said impatiently. "I'm eighteen and not a child. I wanted this as much as you. If this meant anything to you at all, and was not simply a lie for a lay, then you will stay silent about it and protect my good name."

He nodded slowly. "I would do no other."

"I certainly hope so."

Keily looked so woebegone that Belle felt a rush of real feeling for him. Still, she could not forgive his insulting assumption of her easy virtue quite so easily.

"Well, see me back to the kitchen door at any rate," she said. The rain had finally stopped.

He looked hangdog and confused as he said goodbye. So much so, that Belle felt compelled to grab his ears in each hand and kiss him for a very long time.

"Thank you for a lovely evening," she said, a twinkle in her eyes. He walked off, somewhat in a daze and obviously confused, to find the front entrance and go to his room to sleep.

Belle had no idea what time it was. The entire building seemed very quiet. There was a light in the kitchen. She went in, to find Eliza sitting there, shelling peas to pass the time.

Eliza looked up at her, her face impassive and her eyes concerned.

"Is there any coffee?" Belle asked.

"I make some tea."

"Tea will be fine," Belle said. Eliza got up and poured some hot water into a waiting cup. She slid the cup in front of Belle who wrinkled her nose at the smell.

"What is this?"

"'erbs. Special fer women. You drink it all down."

Belle tasted it and realized it was some kind of medicine. She looked a question at Eliza.

"Drink."

"Why?" Belle asked.

"So no baby come," Eliza said simply.

"How did...."

"You dink 'Liza can't tell when a woman be well fucked?" Eliza said, her teeth flashing whitely against her black face. She put her hand kindly on top of Belle's. "Dis slave secret. Woman git wid man she don't want baby from, dis de cure."

Belle felt herself flush bright red. There was nothing she could say. Their roles were reversed. Eliza would tell her what to do, and she would drink every horrid drop of the medicine because she truly did not want Daniel's child, no matter how much she wanted him — and she realized suddenly that she would let him have her again — and again — if she could.

She drank the tea. Eliza finished shelling the peas and put the bowl aside. "Best git to bed," she said.

"God, yes," Belle said, "I'm a wreck."

Eliza grinned at her, almost mockingly, "You git fucked pretty good, huh?"

Belle grinned, "I suppose I did." Her face grew troubled. "I didn't bleed. I thought there would be blood."

Eliza looked at her with a certain native shrewdness, "Dat happen. Happen slave women all de time. Dey work hard. Cherry break on its own, or master take it too early."

Belle shifted uncomfortably. Every southern woman knew about how female slaves were abused, but none of them knew what to do about it. Legally they were as much a chattel as any slave girl. The scandal of black children with light skin and a family resemblance was never, ever remarked upon. It was the way of the world.

Or was it? "This tea. A slave secret?"

Eliza smiled serenely, "You dink we give babies like we breedin' stock? Buckras don' always git dere way."

Belle had the sensation of hearing something very subversive.

"De bleedin' don't come when young lady ride horses much," Eliza said, with a glint in her eye. "Fleeter done already got yer cherry."

Belle gasped in outrage and then started laughing. It was a fine joke. Eliza was more than a servant, she realized. Somehow, despite all that was against it, they had become friends.

CHAPTER TWENTY-FIVE

Front Royal, Virginia, mid-May 1862

Belle tried to conceal her joy in the wonderful experience she'd had with Dan Keily, but it was hard. She was noticeably more vivacious, and even more charming towards the Yankee officers. She laughed more than she had for months.

At the same time, she was mindful of her responsibilities, and these were many and varied. At odd moments she would recall their passion, and catch herself singing snatches of favorite songs as she worked on the hotel's books, seldom a chore that she regarded with favor.

To her relief, her period began a few days after. She would keep careful track of it from now on. While she was positive that she did not love this man, she was entranced by the idea of him and the adventure of being able to explore the mysteries of his maleness. He was quite strong, yet delicate in the way that he addressed her body, and in that way he reminded her of no one so much as Dick Ashby, who, when she was twelve, she had found completely engrossing because he was so very kind and paid attention to her.

There was no possibility of marriage with Dan Keily. Not only was he Irish and a Yankee, but Catholic. It was not to be thought of. She was surprised that the risk of a scandal increased her excitement and desire.

She faced the world with a cool, knowing smile. Let others wonder. She knew her own heart and it was firmly for the South. The crude male expression she'd heard often about putting a certain body part "on the line" now had a special meaning for her, and made her smile often. She was, in her own unique way, making war on the Union. She would advance her campaign further in the days to come!

A few kisses were stolen here and there, but no opportunity presented itself for a second encounter. Not that it didn't rain copiously. So much rain fell that any major movement of troops became impossible.

He was not bolder with her and did not presume on her

affections, but maintained a nice discretion when others were nearby. He stayed careful of her reputation.

So this is what the great mystery is? Belle thought. *Little wonder that no one talks about it. Everyone would want to do it, all day long, and then how would any work get done?*

"What are you smiling about?" Alice snapped at one point, annoyed by her constant humming. "You look like the cat who swallowed the canary."

"Daniel," replied Belle truthfully, and then detoured into falsehood, "That last poem of his was really quite sweet."

"He's a lot on your mind now," Alice grumped. Poems and flowers from Myles Keogh were not so often nor so ardent. Keogh preferred a drink with other officers to the courtliness that Alice and Belle, and every other young lady of their class, considered their due from a beau. Not that he did not persist, but simply that his effort was intermittent and inexact.

Both officers were heavily involved in the planning for whatever operation Shields would undertake next. Ashby needed that information as well. Belle would have endured much from Dan Keily to get it, but found, delightfully, that being with him was anything but a burden.

Supplies stacked up in the warehouses and the depot. Union scouting parties went out daily. Keily and Keogh often went with them, to learn the terrain that lay ahead and where the passes were through the Blue Ridge and the Allegheny mountains that bracketed the Shenandoah Valley.

For their own part, Alice and Belle had a hundred things to do every day just to keep the hotel running. On top of that lay the problems that came with being spies. Belle had been openly accused by Clark, the reporter. Fortunately, he did not have much traction with the Union Army staff, who saw him as a risk to their own security, and an annoying pest to be borne rather than a valued colleague.

And pest he was, intruding at odd times upon Belle and Alice as they went about their work, trying to insinuate himself into the second floor sitting room that they reserved for themselves.

How could he think that they had not heard of his accusations against them? they wondered, even as he tried one more time, in a leering way, to impose himself upon them. His assumptions on the state of their virtue were hardly complimentary, but there was no male relative present to defend them, nor did any Yankee officer take up their cause.

They feared him, or rather the power he represented. In the political atmosphere of the Union volunteer regiments, Clark was flattered and courted, in hopes that he would return the gesture, in print, where it would be a political benefit.

Belle finally lost patience with him one day, got up from her chair, forced him to back out of the sitting room, closed the door in his face and locked it. This was very rude, but she and Alice had other concerns than his good opinion of them.

The Yankees used a lot of paper, and sometimes the clerks made mistakes and had to redraft an order or a list. Flawed copies were discarded in the trash and also sent to the outhouse.

Eliza was able to rescue some important documents from this trove. She could not read, but she could tell, by the way sentences were spaced, which were orders and reports.

Belle skimmed the take carefully and had most of it returned. She then passed on digests of what she found to Ashby. When it became impossible to find the time to recount it all, she took the additional risk of sending some of the documents themselves onward.

At this point, the "Underground Railroad" via old Moses' pocket watch ceased to function. There was simply too much paper.

An alternative presented itself as the campaign heated up. Confederate prisoners passing through the town were granted paroles and given permission to pass beyond the lines.

Alice and Belle visited these men as they arrived at the depot, bringing baskets of food. They were Southern women, after all, and not the only girls from the town who lavished small attentions on the prisoners.

Most were ill-fed, weary and not disposed to do more than return to their farms to resume a normal life. Very few could be trusted to take a message through the lines.

Belle looked particularly for men of Ashby's who had been paroled, and failing that, men who were sergeants or officers in Jackson's "foot cavalry", as his fast-moving infantry had taken to calling themselves. To these men, many of whom she knew from Martinsburg, Belle entrusted packets of salvaged Union documents and the occasional coded dispatch.

It was a slow, hit-and-miss proposition. She told these volunteer couriers to discard the packets at once if it looked like they would be searched.

To this embarrassment of riches was added another opportunity that Belle could not ignore. Yankee officers drank every bit as much as their Southern counterparts, and they were careless with their accessories. This was especially true of the junior officers. At the hotel, pistols and their belts, sabers and even the odd carbine or musket made their way into the lost property room, to be returned to their shame-faced owners the next day.

Some of these items simply disappeared for good, much to the distress of their owners who, having been seriously drunk at the time, could seldom recall where they had last worn them. To these young officers fell the embarrassment and expense of obtaining replacements.

Through Eliza, Belle put out a bounty on every piece of Union equipment that could be diverted this way. The servants in Front Royal, as resentful of the Yankees as their owners, and faced with a very uncertain future, responded with alacrity to the standing offer of a three dollar Union gold piece or ten dollars in Confederate notes. Hard money was never come by easily. Most chose the gold.

The collected weapons were hidden in that same barn where Belle surrendered her virtue to Daniel Keily with such enthusiasm, beneath the hay in gunny sacks. Soon there were enough to attempt a smuggling operation. Della's son, Nate, was selected to carry the prizes through the lines to Winchester. He was close to manhood now, having suddenly shot up to six feet and gained about forty pounds.

The gunny sacks were laid out on the bed of a farm wagon. A layer of boards was placed on top of them and then a heaping, reeking, mound of horse manure was forked into a pile on top of that. Nate hitched up a team and, on a morning when the sun had condescended to show itself, drove the entire rig calmly to where the Union pickets waited. He thought that city boys would not examine his load too closely.

He presented his pass to a red-eyed Pennsylvania sergeant with an obvious hang-over.

"What you got in the wagon, boy?" the sergeant asked harshly.

"Horseshit, boss!" said Nate, with a wide grin.

The sergeant, sure some disrespect had come his way, roared, "What did you say, nigger?"

Nate, blinking, smiling no longer, held out his pass. "Dc ladies, dey likes it fer dey flower gardens," Nate spoke more softly, but he met the sergeant's glare eye to eye. He wasn't going to be cowed by any damn Yankee.

The sergeant walked over to the wagon, wrinkled his nose at the smell, and then managed a grin.

"Load like that, boy, I should send you straight on to the War Department."

Nate laughed as if this was the most hilarious thing he had ever heard. The other soldiers joined in and even the hung-over sergeant, pleased at his own wit, managed a kindly smile.

"Go on with yez, now," he said, and Nate drove on. By nightfall, he was back, the wagon empty. With him he carried a letter from Alexander Boetler to Belle.

Finally, the gallant Captain Keily himself appeared early one afternoon to ask for permission to accompany her on a walk. They went out the front door, around the building, and slipped quickly up the back stairwell to his room. He pulled her inside, cautioning silence with a finger to his lip and locked the door.

From the ballroom below the sound of the Yankee staff in some sort of meeting came quite clearly. Belle knew the room. It was hers when she had visited here as a child. There was a hole that had been drilled in the closet floor for some reason. It provided an excellent view of the ballroom below and many was the time when she and Alice, as children, spied on the parties held there.

"I am assuming," he whispered, "That if we can hear them, they would be able to hear us, so, for the sake of both of our reputations, can ye be as quiet as a mouse?"

Belle stared at him, inwardly amused. "What kind of girl do you think I am?" she whispered back, pretending indignation.

Startled, confused, he actually blushed and began to stammer. She pulled him quickly down on the bed, landing on top of him, kissing him furiously.

Then, just as quickly, she sprang up and, watching him coolly through slanted eyes, began to slowly undress.

He sat up, a bit flustered until she pulled off her dress and carefully folded it and put it over a chair. He then, smiling now, took off his uniform sack coat and his vest and then his shirt. The sight of his bare chest excited her. He was built of slabs of muscle. His skin was soft and fair. The contrast fascinated her.

He pulled out his pocket watch and opened the cover. "We have forty minutes," he whispered.

Belle understood at once. More than that would be remarked upon. "Then let us make the most of them," she replied softly, and taking one of his carefully-waxed mustaches in each hand, pulled his face into her breasts.

They were back in the front parlor at the appointed hour, but just barely. Her mother and grandmother looked at her, looked at each other, and said nothing.

I have once more been well fucked, she thought, suppressing the big grin that tried to creep onto her face. She had seen new brides with a peculiar kind of glow about them the morning after their wedding night, and she had seen that look with other girls who had succumbed to their beau's entreaties, sometimes to have a first healthy baby born prematurely. It was a miracle that a child delivered two months before full term looked so healthy and well, other people said, and said no more.

Belle did not love Daniel Keily, and if that was true, it was more than a little wicked to let him use her so. But she got as much as she gave, and the necessity of keeping absolutely silent as waves of passion crashed through her body made it all that much more exciting. He was a tender lover, careful of her even as his cock ravished her again and again. There was a sweetness to him.

She raised an inquiring eyebrow at her mother and grandmother. Mary looked away, her face hard as a stone. Her grandmother, to her surprise, smiled kindly at her.

This is war, Belle told herself, *and I am a soldier. I offer my body in our cause, like any other soldier.* Never would she summon the nerve to say such things aloud.

Daniel Keily made light conversation and quickly excused himself, tipping his hat. He had early duty on the morrow, he said.

The next morning he found her early on. "I fear we'll have little opportunity for a rematch," Daniel Keily whispered, leaning over the front counter. Belle was looking once more at the register, ostensibly to total the day's bills.

There were a few people in the lobby, but none looked their way. "And why is that?" she asked, fluttering her eyelids flirtatiously.

"General Shields wishes to finalize our plans against Jackson," he whispered back. She could smell whisky on his breath. It had made him incautious — or she had.

"Perhaps there will be a surprise waiting for you," Belle replied softly.

His eyebrows raised a half-inch. "You'd risk that?"

"Perhaps not," Belle said, smiling mischievously.

"You're cruel to tease me so," Keily groaned.

"Serves you right for breaking our appointment."

"Ah, my love, 'tis duty and only that which keeps me from thee."

He was waxing poetic again, she saw, and she didn't want that, not just because it might be noticed and commented upon, but because he wasn't really very good at verse and she feared that she might laugh outright at his sentiments. It would never do to laugh at him. She wasn't done with him yet, not by any means, and men had their pride, as foolish as it sometimes was.

Since he was neither a Southerner nor a true Yankee, but a different kind of animal entirely, she was always anxious not to accidently offend him. His friend Myles Keogh had a noticeable set-to with another Yankee officer over a matter that everyone but he considered trifling. He had been ready to express his displeasure with knife, pistol or fist, as required. The quarrel had been smoothed over and blamed on drink. Keogh, recovering himself, had apologized and then suggested that they affirm their new friendship with another drink, cementing his reputation as a dangerous drunk.

Keily left her, brushing his hand against hers briefly. That sent an electric thrill through Belle's body. No, she was not done with him yet.

Still, duty first. If the Yankees were meeting in the ballroom, then Keily's room would be empty. The hole in the closet floor would be available to her. From there she should be able to determine their plans.

At seven, she pleaded a sick headache and went back to the cottage, allowing her mother to tuck her into bed and Eliza to bring her some soup from the kitchen.

At eight, she piled blankets and pillows into what she hoped was an approximation of her sleeping form and slipped out into the yard. The sentry, as was his habit at that time every night, was in the outhouse, so she gained the back stairway unobserved.

A few minutes later she was laying down on the closet floor of Keily's room, in the dark, her ear pressed to the hole. General Shields made some remarks, and introduced General Kimball, and Colonel Brodhead.

Followed was a long discussion of the supplies that had been accumulated at the Front Royal depot and how many days rations, ammunition and so forth this would provide for the campaign. The Chief Surgeon outlined where the ambulances would be stationed and where field hospitals could be established.

Belle's mind drifted. She was suddenly remembering how, when Keily had unbuttoned himself, his very erect cock sprang out and she had grabbed it in her hand, suddenly feeling its velvet thickness and realizing that he would put it in her very slowly because she was so tight. That would produce both pain and pleasure of an intensity she had felt only once before, with him. Suddenly she was gasping for breath, so excited was her memory, and felt herself becoming aroused.

What if he discovers me here? she thought, and forced herself to pay better attention. Daniel himself was speaking now. Jackson, he said, was at New Market, headed for Mount Jackson. This was the other side of Massanutten Mountain from Front Royal. They had only to send out two columns to trap him at Lurey. They would have to move quickly, far in advance of the supply train, with infantry sent down by rail to keep pace with the cavalry.

Belle was all attention now. This was a major departure from Banks' cautiousness, and that, it seemed, was because Shields' and Geary's divisions had been taken away from Banks and given to McDowell, who still looked for vengeance for his humiliation at Bull's Run.

Keily and Keogh were credited as the authors of the plan and it was a good one, Belle realized at once. She could visualize the movements on the map in her mind. So intent was Shields on trapping and destroying Jackson that he was pulling out every unit from Front Royal and bringing in a new Maryland regiment to hold the town. Only a thousand men rather than the five or six times that number that held it now. The depot and warehouses of supplies would hang like an overripe peach, ready to be plucked.

Belle thought hard. *It will take them two or three days to make all of this ready, but I cannot wait that long. Ashby has to be found and told at once!*

From old Moses, she knew him to be at a farm between Front Royal and Lurey. She knew the farm and the way to it. Fifteen miles away if it was a foot.

She had no time for another encounter with Daniel Keily this night! Quickly she got up, hearing the tread of heavy cavalry boots ascending the front stairs as the meeting broke up. She opened the door, peeked into the hallway and saw that Daniel and some other officers had paused on the stairs to discuss some minor point. She slipped out, locking the door behind her and went lightly as she could down the back stairs, glad that she had worn slippers rather than boots.

The sentry was back at his post but did not challenge her, since she went between the main building and the cottage a dozen times a day. She smiled at him and let her hips sway slightly back and forth, to which he offered a lewd grin but no commentary since she was always seen with officers and he knew that he had no chance with her.

Belle slipped back into the cottage. Everyone was sleeping. She sat, took a half sheet of foolscap and began, with very small printed letters, to encode a digest of the information she had heard. She had done this so much lately that she no longer had to consult a table. The letters came to her easily. Of course, the next time the key was changed she would be back to tracing the letters from the grid, but not, thank God, this night.

As she wrote, she pondered how to get it to Ashby.

Awakening a servant would draw far too much attention and it was far too important. There was nothing for it but to go herself.

She folded the paper into a leather pouch on her belt and picked out several Union passes obtained from paroled Confederate prisoners. She found her riding boots, drew them on, and then wrapped a thick cloak around herself and covered her head with a thick woolen bonnet.

She peeked out and saw that the sentry assigned to the yard was dozing. Silently she slipped out to the barn, entered, found Fleeter and saddled him.

"You must be entirely quiet," she cautioned him. He seemed to understand, for he made very little noise as they glided out of the yard and down the main road to an old tree stump, where she mounted and rode towards Lurey. The night was illuminated by a full moon, but the road was wet and uncertain, so she did not press him too hard. It was a tremendous risk. Her only thought was for Jackson. To save him she had to find Ashby. Nothing else mattered.

CHAPTER TWENTY-SIX

Near Front Royal, Virginia, May 14, 1862

Turner Ashby awoke instantly as a lone rider thundered down the road towards the farmhouse. *What now?*, he wondered, fumbling first for his pistol and then for his watch. *Past three in the morning!*

His host, Silas Martin, threw open the window of the upstairs bedroom and shouted, "Who are you? What do you want?"

Ashby struggled to collect his wits. He'd come to dinner, eaten and drunk too well, and laid down on a couch, telling Silas to, on no account, let him sleep past midnight. The Yankees now sent out parties of men disguised in Confederate uniforms to seek him out, to kill or capture him. He acknowledged the compliment by never spending the night in a house. These could be easily surrounded by a small force, leaving him trapped with no way to escape. Sleeping rough in the field was less comfortable, but much more secure.

The rider shouted something he could not hear clearly, and then the horse came clattering up the stairs onto the broad porch. *Unlikely to be Yankees*, he thought, *and not someone from my camp.*

The next words he heard startled him. "I'm looking for Colonel Ashby," the rider shouted up to Silas Martin in a high, strained voice. "Is he here?"

"Who are you?" Martin shouted back. "What's it about?"

"I'm Belle Boyd," came the reply. "I have important intelligence for Colonel Ashby." There was a hollow thump on the porch as she dismounted the hard-breathing horse.

"He's not here," Martin lied loyally. "But I will come down."

Ashby shook his head, trying to clear it. He had the musty feeling that comes with having slept too well in too many clothes. Silas Martin, well past fifty and afflicted with rheumatism, made his careful way down the stairs, a candle in one hand and a Colt revolver in the other.

Ashby moved to intercept him. "It's all right, Silas," he said,

"She's one of ours."

"Out at this hour of the night, in this weather?" Silas grumped like a disapproving father. "What is she thinking?"

"That whatever it is, it's deadly important," Ashby said quietly. He held out his hand for Martin's pistol, more to forestall an accident than anything else. Martin handed it over gladly. "Answer the door."

Martin opened it cautiously. Belle Boyd was talking gently to her horse, whom she had hitched to the porch rail. The horse was not breathing so hard now, but relaxed enough to make a large deposit on the planking. Martin hissed in irritation, but Belle simply pushed her way into the foyer and pleaded with him, "I must find Colonel Ashby. He must have this information at once."

Martin looked at her doubtfully, "His camp is about a mile down the road," he answered, careful not to specify a direction. "How have you come here?"

"I forced the sentries with a false pass," replied Belle impatiently. "Oh, I have no time to tell you the how or why of it. I must find Ashby at once!"

Ashby looked through the crack of the door at Belle. Her color was high and her jaw had a determined set to it. She would not be deterred or delayed.

He opened the door wide and stepped into the room.

"Miss Belle? Am I dreaming? How are you here, now?" His voice was weighted with sleep even now. He wondered if it were indeed a dream. Before the war he had never put much stock in the prophetic power of dreams, but he had seen his brother Dick die in one and that had come true. He had seen his own death in another and was determined to avoid that fate if he could.

Belle turned, saw him and smiled in relief. Tears came to her eyes. Whatever she had must be very important indeed.

"What is it?" he asked.

"The Yankees had a big meeting tonight and I was able to listen in from the room above," she said. "They have a plan to trap

Jackson and his whole army, and have assembled enough men and supply to do it."

Ashby came fully awake now. This was indeed the most important intelligence that Belle could obtain.

Belle fumbled at her belt and found a folded piece of paper. "It's all written here," she said anxiously, "The entire order of battle and direction. If you have a map I can show you quickly, but I must get back, if I can, before dawn, so I'm not discovered missing."

"Yes, of course," said Ashby, moving quickly to find his dispatch case. He pulled out and unfolded a large map of the Shenandoah Valley and spread it on a table while Silas Martin brought his candle closer to illuminate it.

Belle leaned over and said, "Shields will move here to here and Geary and Kimball from here to here. Fremont will come over the mountains here. They think Jackson is at New Market. They plan to trap him between the two forces like, they said, 'a hammer and anvil'."

"How many?"

"Ten thousand and eight thousand, plus Fremont's division," Belle said, "But they will detail about two thousand back towards Winchester. To protect their lines of communication."

Ashby nodded, thinking furiously. "Jackson must know of this. I will take it to him at once. How many will remain at Front Royal?"

"Less than they have now, but they plan to lock the town down. It will be almost impossible for civilians to move."

"I need you to go to Winchester," Ashby said, "To see Colonel Boetler."

Belle looked a question at him.

"To inform him of this and that Jackson will counter it. I cannot predict what action he'll take, but there is that old farm road we used between Strasburg and Front Royal that leads to the Gooney Manor Road. Say nothing of that to Boetler. He will have important information for you to carry back."

Belle nodded, a line between her eyes as she committed his orders to memory.

"Banks has suddenly found his boldness," Ashby said. "It's a good plan and might have worked. We'd be heavily outnumbered and on low ground."

"It's not Banks," Belle said. "Shields and Geary now report directly to McDowell."

Ashby said, "That's very important. Stonewall will want to know that, too."

"It's in my report," Belle said, "And now I must go."

"Do you need a fresh horse?" asked Silas Martin.

Belle managed a smile. "My, sir, wouldn't that give the game away? A strange horse in a stable we share with Yankee officers. Even the Yankees might take notice and ask questions — and my horse is equal to the task. I bought him from Colonel Ashby."

Ashby smiled. "So you did. And a very strong smart animal he is. Go, girl, and Godspeed."

Belle did not hesitate, but turned, went out the door, and unhitched Fleeter, leading him back down the porch stairs. Ashby and Martin followed, watching as she pulled herself easily into the saddle.

"Sorry for the mess on your porch, Mister Martin," she called as she turned and cantered out of the yard and up to the main road.

"Think nothing of it," Martin called after her. "It's in a good cause." They listened to Fleeter's fading hoofbeats for a moment. Silas Martin said, "So that's Belle Boyd."

Ashby said, "None other."

"And she really is a spy. Think of that."

Ashby looked at him curiously, "Why would you doubt it? It was in the newspapers."

"Oh," said Silas Martin, "I never believe what I read in the newspapers. Damn lies, most of it."

"You must not say anything to anyone," Ashby cautioned. "She's already under heavy suspicion."

"It's a shame that people don't know the truth of it. It's a scandal what people say about her in town, the names they call her." Martin shivered from the cold. He was in his nightshirt and the wind was coming up. He moved to go back inside.

"All part of the game, Silas," Ashby said. "Fooling the Yankees means fooling a lot of other folks."

"Your own kin talk against her," said Martin indignantly, "Especially that Lucy Buck."

Ashby walked with him, offering him a steady hand. Martin looked at the pile of horse manure left on the porch. "That will wait until morning," he decided.

Once they were inside he turned to Ashby and said, "She's a brave girl. You're lucky to have her."

"I am," Turner Ashby said, as he slipped on his overcoat and packed up his dispatch case. "Wish I had a hundred like her."

"You should set the record straight," Martin said reproachfully.

Ashby answered, "I will, after the war. For now, it must be a closely held secret. You understand?"

Silas Martin sighed, "I do. Don't much like it, but I understand."

Ashby shook his hand, collected his things and went out the door, and then into the nearby woods where his own horse was tethered and two of his men waiting.

By five Belle was back in Front Royal and by six she was in bed. Fleeter needed a good rubdown, which Belle did herself, and then inspected his hooves and fetlocks. She got by the sentry by pretending that she had been there all along, greeting him with her usual morning cheer.

Inside the cottage, her mother was waiting. Everyone else was already in the main building going about their normal routine. Belle tried to forestall her. "Don't ask."

Mary Boyd just shook her head. "I suspect I wouldn't like the answer. Good Lord, Isabelle, if you had to take up with one of those Irish boys, you might have at least picked the good-looking one."

"Mama!"

"I said last year that you were a woman grown. I'm not going to be one of those mothers who tries to act like a policeman with her children. You've been raised so I shouldn't have to do this."

Belle found this more-in-sorrow-than-anger lecture very unjust. Yet, what could she say? That she'd been on a thirty mile horse ride in the middle of the night? Her mother obviously assumed that she'd spent the night with Dan Keily, and as sore as she felt, she wished it were true.

"It will be all right, Mama," Belle sat down next to her and placed her hand over Mary's. Belle had never felt so tired. All she wanted was her bed. But something was wrong, she could tell from the expression on her mother's face.

Mary started to cry. "I'm not at all sure it will be," she said through her tears. "I've had a letter from your father."

That woke Belle up. "What is it?" she asked urgently. "What is wrong?"

"He's been given a medical leave. Something is wrong with his heart."

Belle just stared at her.

"He's going back to Martinsburg, and I will join him there. Della and Nate will go with me. And William and Mary. I hate to leave you and Alice short-handed."

"We'll manage," said Belle. "You'll need passes and I need to go to Winchester tomorrow anyway."

Mary looked puzzled. "Why?"

Belle looked away. "I can't say."

Mary's face suddenly relaxed into a relieved smile, "You weren't with him last night, were you?"

Belle stared back at her. "I wish I had been," she said with a touch of defiance.

Mary smiled and shook her head ruefully. "You never forget

your first," she said after a moment.

Belle was very surprised. "Wasn't Daddy your first?"

"No," said Mary, half whispering, "It was Hill Lamon. Why do you think I am so angry with him for being a Yankee?"

Belle sat back, a bit shocked. Mary got to her feet briskly, having said altogether too much, but far from enough.

"Well, you'd better get some rest. You look like you've been 'rode hard and put away wet', as they say. I will tell Alice to say that you have a nasty cold and will spend the day in bed."

Belle nodded. Mary gave her a kiss on the cheek, dried her own tears and went out the door. Belle removed her dress, boots and corset, and settled into her bed, pushing the extra pillows aside. She sighed deeply and within seconds was sound asleep.

CHAPTER TWENTY-SEVEN

Strasburg, Virginia, May 15, 1862

David Strother woke that morning still in the grip of melancholy. Thor Brodhead was briskly solicitous, but was preoccupied with his own duties as the brigade's Chief of Cavalry. He knew he was needed on his staff duties now. The campaign against Jackson was at the tipping point.

He'd suffered a nasty cold with a full menu of chills and fevers, but that passed. He'd used that to cover his despair and sense of loss. He hadn't touched his sketchbook in days. The encounter with Alice Stewart and Belle Boyd at the hotel in Front Royal haunted him. He had separated from his former life. Everything he did widened the gap between then and now.

Strother finally hired a servant, a runaway slave or "intelligent contraband" named John, who had belonged to the owner of a hotel in Winchester and was trained to service. He was practically Strother's shadow in the camp, very anxious to do well. Aside from the dollar a week he put in John's hand, not much had changed. John was, as they said in Virginia, "a likely boy". He wondered why he found that, of all things, depressing.

Two cups of good strong army coffee lifted his mood, and he dressed and wandered over to the large tent where Geary had his headquarters.

"Captain Strother," said Geary; "Feeling better?" He and Brodhead were looking at the map again.

"Yes, sir. Thank you for asking," Strother replied wearily. His two friends looked at each other. Strother shook himself and tried not to slump. He made an effort to stand a little taller and felt better for it. He smiled reassuringly at them as if to say, it will be all right — and hoped it was true.

Brodhead lifted a corner of the map and cleared his throat. "Perhaps you can tell us something about this terrain."

"Certainly." He sat and bent his head to look closely at the part of the map Brodhead pointed at.

"We've got some damned Englishman coming from

McDowell's headquarters to discuss cavalry tactics," Geary added.

Strother looked up. "Sir Percy Wyndham?"

Geary nodded. "Colonel Wyndham, yes. You know him?"

"Not well," Strother replied. "We've met. He's not a bad fellow. Seems to know his business. Fought in the Italian War."

"As what?" Geary asked, interested.

"Uh, Brigade Commander, I believe," Strother said cautiously.

Geary seemed impressed now. That was his current assignment.

"Well he's particularly interested in this fellow Ashby." Geary scratched his beard, his brow furrowing. "He's not a regular military man, and Wyndham thinks it should be easy to overcome him."

For the first time in days, David Strother smiled. "Yes, I can see how he might think that."

Geary and Brodhead looked at one another. "If there's a joke to be found here," Brodhead said, "By all means, share it. We could use a good laugh."

"It's not just Ashby, you know. It's his entire regiment, but the matter is a complicated one, so I'll save it for when Colonel Wyndham visits us."

Percy Wyndham showed up with a brace of young lieutenants in tow. Handsome young men with blonde hair who said little and followed his every gesture attentively. Strother took it upon himself to introduce them around. His fellow officers were cordial, if somewhat distant.

Over the evening meal, Wyndham asked about Turner Ashby. "Do you know anything about the man?"

This was directed to Strother. "A bit. We both come from Martinsburg. He's younger than I am, so I never had much to with him when I was a wild and foolish youth."

"You?" Brodhead was amused by the idea.

"I had my moments," Strother replied seriously. "Had a bad case of measles when I was twelve, from which I almost died. That let something wild loose in me. I drank and went to parties and was generally the despair of my parents until I started drawing."

He spoke so calmly that he had everyone's attention.

"Ashby made his mark as a militia captain about the time of the John Brown raid, leading a group of like-minded men who went out patrolling for escaped slaves and Yankee infiltrators. I don't recall that they ever actually caught anyone, but when Virginia started forming an army, he was the natural choice to lead the cavalry. He is rich and not without political power."

"Some sort of horse farmer, isn't he?" Wyndham growled, nodding. "That would make sense."

"He knows how to lead," Strother replied. "Men want to serve with him, especially the gentry, the so-called 'chivalry'."

"You means like the knights of old? Sir Walter Scott's "Ivanhoe", and all that fantasy?" Wyndham laughed scornfully. "That's very amusing."

Strother looked at him with great seriousness. "I would not discount it. They're from the same native stock as yourself."

"Oh? But not to the manor born, are they?"

"Scatter a handful of British dirt anyplace on this planet and a volunteer crop of aristocracy will present itself," Strother said. "In the North, these people have economic, and hence, social power, but they pretty much keep to themselves, and don't bother the rest of us."

Strother sipped at a cup of water and cleared his throat. Percy Wyndham still looked slightly amused and Strother wanted to be taken seriously. Wyndham discounted Ashby at his peril.

"In the South it is completely different," Strother continued. "The gentry don't have to scratch out a living, and devote themselves to politics and other recreations. Brute labor is provided by slaves, and what they grow, tobacco and cotton, has always made them wealthy enough to maintain the status quo. Less able white men envy them, but also seek to emulate them.

"They provide all of the warriors, statesmen, gentlemen and

office holders of the land, which perpetuates their grasp on power. The only path for outsiders is that followed by Mister Benjamin, who, being a Jew, may be considered the ultimate outsider. He went to the right schools, read for the law, and became both a merchant and a politician. He rose by sheer ability, and sits at Jeff Davis's right hand. It is a remarkable achievement."

"But Stuart, the other cavalry chief, I understand, has been to West Point and was a serving officer before the war," Wyndham objected. "Ashby is a horse farmer who pretends above his ability and station."

"You thought only the North had political officers?" Strother asked drily, causing general laughter around the table. "We're a democracy, Sir Percy, so the idea of 'station' doesn't enter into it, and Ashby does have some ability, and any number of companies of cavalry to back it up — and they are all from his class and known to him. They flocked to his banner not just from a misguided patriotism but from personal loyalty."

"Do tell," said Wyndham, smiling no longer. "He's leading an untrained mob, not a regiment. A tribe of Indians is better fit for battle."

"Ashby used to play an Indian at tournaments — and win. His men were born to the saddle, unlike your New Jersey farmers that you complain about. They are well trained. A true Southerner is a rural creature, and squirely in his taste and manners. He delights in horses, guns, dogs, and all exciting sports, especially games of chance. He is overbearing, opinionated, and easily provoked to violence, but also social and hospitable. He carries himself with the grace derived from an unconscious assumption of power, for he has only to say to his servant, 'do this' and it will be done, and to his neighbor, 'think this' and it will become the only opinion extant."

Strother sighed. "It is half of the reason we got into this fight. Those in power naturally sought to preserve their privileges, which they mistake for natural rights, and their aristocratic counterparts in the North seek, with equal zeal, to overturn those rights to save a people which neither seeks nor requires their intervention."

"Free the slaves, you mean?" asked Geary.

"Your passion, sir, with all due respect, not mine. It would have come of its own accord," Strother replied.

"Why do you say that?" Geary was both alert and interested.

Strother thought for a long moment as the others watched him silently, waiting. "Machinery," he said at last. "If you have machines, you don't need slave labor."

"How so?" said Brodhead. "You still need men to run machines."

"Yes, but say a machine can do the work of ten slaves or a hundred, then you don't need so many, and it becomes cheaper to hire free men than to maintain slaves. Slaves have to be very well cared for. They are a major capital investment and they are, for most, members of the family; not like a sibling, but certainly more than a dog or cat."

Wyndham was fascinated now. He was absently twirling one of his very long waxed mustaches with his right hand, like a villain in a melodrama. "Go on," he said.

"Look at how having railroads and telegraphs has changed the way we're fighting this war. It pulls everything closer together and makes movement possible that was not even dreamed of twenty years ago," Strother pointed out.

"Yes," Wyndham laughed. "Poor McClellan. Try as he might, he cannot escape the interfering politicians in Washington."

"They interfere because he fails to move," Geary said. "Lincoln sent down a message that if Little Mac wasn't using the Army he would like to borrow it for a bit."

Wyndham laughed loudly. "He fears making a mistake and with all the damned reporters hanging about the place, observing every move, he don't have the luxury of burying them. But he is a professional officer, West Point trained. That counts for something."

"He lacks boldness," Geary observed. "His caution borders on cowardice."

"Which is not Ashby's problem. He doesn't plan, but he does act." Strother stared at Wyndham, wondering again how to get his point across.

"But he lacks McClellan's intellect. Sooner or later he will make a error; a fatal one." Wyndham's voice was still smug and self-confident.

"I've always considered him a man of low intelligence, myself," Strother said. "But his passion must be taken into account. He and his men know how to fight — and they fight as well as any Indian war party."

"More to it than that, old fellow," Wyndham said smugly.

"He's a Scot," Strother observed.

"Well, I suppose he is," Wyndham said. "What of it?"

"Have the names of the men in the opposing camp have no meaning for you, Sir Percy?" Strother asked. "Stuart, and its variants, and Boyd and all the rest of the good Scottish family names? They are also a tribe of warriors."

Wyndham looked at him, obviously puzzled.

Strother was expansive now, almost happy. "I am the historian of my family. You recall the Revolution of 1745?"

"Of course. Bonnie Prince Charlie and that lot."

"Well, he was a Stuart and most of his kinsmen were dispossessed of their lands and titles. The chief of the Boyd clan was dispossessed of his head as well. He had been particularly troublesome. All of them came here and settled in, only to get caught up in another revolution a generation or so later, the one that made this nation of ours. They were born for this."

"And now they're thick in the middle of another one," said Wyndham slowly.

"Just so," said Geary. "Just so."

Wyndham shook his head. "I admire their fighting spirit, but superior tactics executed by a professional army will win in the end."

"But at what cost?" asked David Strother quietly. "At what cost?"

The next morning Thorton Brodhead walked up quietly behind David Strother, who was engrossed in making a sketch of the tent they shared. His impatience must have been felt by the artist, for he laid his pencil aside, looked up and asked. "What is it, Thor?"

"Sir Percy's already gone?"

"At the ungodly hour of five. Why?"

"They think they've caught Ashby." Brodhead watched with amusement as Strother stood up so quickly that he nearly fell over the camp stool he'd been sitting on.

Strother stared at him wildly for a second and then asked. "They think? Don't they know?"

"He's given another name, looking to be exchanged. None of them, he or the men captured with him, are wearing any rank. All in homespun."

Strother grimaced. "That don't signify, one way or the other. What name did he give?"

"Johnson."

"Hmmph. Might have been Smith or Jones."

"My thought exactly," Brodhead replied. "You know him by sight?"

"I do," said Strother. "I saw him just a few months past in Martinsburg."

Brodhead gave him a quizzical look. "How was that, old fellow?"

Strother looked uncomfortable for a moment, looked around, and despite the fact that no one was close enough to hear, lowered his voice. "Are you a member of the Noble Craft?"

Brodhead took his hand and exchanged the required handshake with him. "I am. What does that have to do with it?"

"Ashby and I are Lodge Brothers."

Brodhead looked surprised for just a moment and then nodded. "Will you have any problem identifying him?

"That's outside the Lodge."

"Come along then, and have a look."

They mounted their horses and rode over to a part of the camp where Confederate prisoners were held. Strother thought them all a scruffy lot, with not a complete uniform between any two of them. They were lean, ragged, dirty and looked hungry.

Brodhead spoke to the Union Captain in charge. "Point out the man you believe to be Turner Ashby."

"That one there," he replied, pointing to a tall, well-built man with a bushy black beard and a commanding attitude. "Claims he's First Sergeant Hiram Johnson."

Brodhead looked at Strother, who smiled ruefully. "If he says so, then he probably is. I can see how you might think otherwise. He has a very commanding presence and is certainly arrogant enough to be a general, but that's not Turner Ashby. Ashby is a good half foot shorter than that man, slight and mean looking, with skin so dark you might take him for a Negro."

Brodhead was disappointed. "I'd hoped we could have sent Sir Percy back. If we have Ashby then he's not needed. It would also be quite a feather in our cap if we captured him."

"That won't happen," Strother said. "He won't let himself be taken alive. No more than his brother Dick did. He died under his horse, slashing with a saber at any trooper who came near. They finally had to shoot him."

"That's serious fighting," the Union Captain said, admiringly.

"These Rebs are entirely serious," Strother replied. "Never assume otherwise. And never take them lightly."

On the way back to their own camp, Brodhead posed the question that troubled him. "You had a chance to capture Ashby and didn't?"

Strother looked at him, surprised. "It was a Lodge meeting, Thor. And I didn't hold a commission then as I do now. Just another civilian."

Brodhead sighed. "A great pity, then."

Strother studied him as if seeing him for the first time. "You do not hold that the Lodge is sacred and beyond politics?"

"My God, David, there is a war on. The worst the world has ever seen. My Masonic obligations stand second to the lives of the men under my command, and Ashby will kill more than a few of them before we are done."

Strother sucked his teeth thoughtfully. "That view of the matter had not occurred to me. I've known Henry Ashby all his life, and before he became the hero of the moment, he was never going to be in that Lodge, no matter how much money he had. Men of his class are never even asked, much less admitted. No, this was something that Alex Boetler and Ben Boyd cooked up between them. Pure politics, and Alex is the man who rules this county that way."

Brodhead suddenly grinned. "Back in Detroit, they often say the same about me. Maybe I'd feel different if it were my Mother Lodge. So Ashby's just an Entered Apprentice?"

Strother smiled sardonically. "Master Mason. Went through all the steps in a single night."

Brodhead blinked, very surprised. "A prodigy," he murmured.

"Politics. But the Brotherhood assembled and no one dropped the Black Ball on him, so it's done. From a military standpoint it would have been quite a coop to arrest everyone, except that I was there and Ward Hill Lamon, Lincoln's partner, was there. So it was quite impossible, you see, for anything like that. Hill would never have permitted it."

Brodhead stared at him, amazed.

"A Union raid would have left Jackson almost bereft of cavalry, Thor, with all of Ashby's company commanders there. But even if I'd had a commission, I would not have done it. I am already thought a traitor by my family. My Lodge? Such a thing would blacken my name for all time. I would never escape the shame of it. Once the war is over I may be able to make amends and overcome the present bitterness against me, but not if I did that."

Strother became aware that Brodhead was studying him very carefully. Strother stared back.

After a long moment, Brodhead spoke gently. "I've never put much faith in the no-politics-in-the-Lodge rule because the reality in Michigan is at variance with that, but I do hold that Masonic Brothers must rely upon one another even in war time. If one cries out for assistance, I will honor his plea. I find it ironic that Ashby is my brother."

"As do I. Absent this war, it never would have been," Strother said. "But that protection cuts both ways. Hill Lamon and I walked away that night from a meeting filled with men sworn to kill or capture us."

Brodhead nodded. As they were dismounting, he asked, "That thing you said about not taking the Rebels lightly — does it apply to the women as well?"

"Even more so. Why do you ask?"

"We had a patrol bushwhacked this morning. They stopped by a farmhouse and found only three women there. They asked for water and were told that they would find it out by the barn. Two of them were shot dead, right out of the saddle by someone hiding in that barn. The rest of the patrol took cover, then rushed the barn, but whoever did it was gone."

Strother looked distressed. "I hope it has not come to that. That would be very bad. In that kind of war, the Rebels have a tremendous advantage. They know the ground and they have a thousand places to hide everywhere you might look. They also hit what they aim at. This could get very nasty."

"You think that the women knew it was a trap?"

Strother looked at his friend sadly. "In all probability, yes. And whether or not it was some Rebel scout or pickets or some farm boy with his Daddy's squirrel rifle, you'll never find out. This is the war most of them want to fight."

"How would you handle it?"

Strother had to think for several moments before he answered. "Nip it in the bud, Thor. Go back in force , drive the women out of the house, and then burn it and the barn to the ground."

"That seems harsh." Brodhead was shocked at the notion. "Shields would never permit it. He wants the good will of the people here."

"He's not running for office, goddamn it!" Strother took a deep breath and let it out slowly. Then he tried to speak with reason he did not feel. "I know that I said that the locals here were fooled into this war by the slaveholders, but that does not mean that they have awakened from their illusion. Most of them still think they've been invaded by a hostile foreign power."

Brodhead nodded slowly, absorbing this. "Does that include those two charming cousins of yours in Front Royal?"

"More than likely. Belle is Rebel to the core. They are very distant cousins, but close family friends. Or were. I think I've lost all my friends here now."

"And are they..uh.. what General Banks said?"

Strother looked at him sharply.

"No offense intended," Brodhead said calmly.

"None taken," Strother bit out. "Certainly not the second, and I very much doubt the other. It is newspaper sensationalism and nothing more. They are young girls! The idea is absurd on its face. Belle might have played at it, but Alice hasn't the stomach. She's very shy. Belle has always been the bold one. I can't see Alice as a spy."

"Unless Miss Belle put her up to it," Brodhead observed.

CHAPTER TWENTY-EIGHT

Front Royal, Virginia May 16, 1862

She did not love Daniel Keily. Belle was certain of this, although she found his company more than agreeable.

He, alas, was in love with her. The daily presentation of flowers and poetry did not abate now that he had, as the saying went, "had his way with her". His ardor increased. He seized every convenient opportunity to press his suit upon her.

Belle welcomed his interest because he was particularly prone to sharing with her little tidbits about his day's work. That work involved the plan to capture and destroy Jackson's "Valley Army", so she paid very close attention, hanging on his every word.

And in their few moments of stolen passion she was equally attentive, because of the intense physical attraction she felt for him, for his well-formed, hard-muscled body, for the scent of him, and for the way he could be both tender and delightfully cruel as a lover, withholding himself from her until she felt like she might explode. In his own way, Daniel added to her education.

His attentions did not pass unnoticed, and affected the attitudes of his fellow officers, from the genial, avuncular smile directed her way by General James Shields, to the too-knowing look and slight smirk of Myles Keogh. William Clark now directed his attention to her in a very specific and crude way, with a leer and a wink, which she did her best to ignore. The ***Herald*** reporter was a persistent pest.

Hasbrouke Reeve also continued to woo her in his shy, awkward and endearing way. He brought neither flowers nor verse, but rather a puppy-like devotion which stared at her soulfully and said little, so that she was forced to draw him out. Because he commanded the cavalrymen assigned as the Provost Guard under Major Hector Tyndale, he was also an important source of information.

Alice was quietly furious with her over the surrender of her virtue to Keily. Myles Keogh assumed his pursuit of her would be met with equal favor. Alice's firm, hard slap across the face had not convinced him otherwise. In normal times, she would have satisfied herself by having nothing further to do with him, but these were, as Belle quickly pointed out, far from normal times.

"We need to keep him sweet," Belle said, so Alice, with very mixed emotions, continued to see him. He, too, liked to brag about his work. Myles apologized, with flowers and verse, but seemed to regard the episode as a tactical blunder in a long campaign of seduction. Alice maintained a public face of cheerful politeness, but confessed to Belle that she felt both attracted and repelled by Myles.

"I know just what you mean," Belle laughed, ruefully. "A year ago, neither of us would have looked twice at either of them."

"Oh, we would have looked," Alice smiled, "But not touched. Or been touched. Never that."

William Clark contented himself with the passing vulgar remark, which in other circumstances would have resulted in him being shown the door. Alice broke down one day and complained about this treatment to Lucy Buck, who was sympathetic, but quick to blame Belle as the instigator of it all.

Belle would have liked to set Lucy Buck straight, but this was a risk beyond calculation. Lucy was fervently for the South, but lacked both guile and discretion, and was all too willing to express herself vehemently to the Yankees at any given moment.

So she bore it all — the whispers, the sly looks, and the other hurtful things that people in Front Royal did and said; and she tried to give Alice as much cover as she could by being the bold one. It didn't help.

Even her little brother William had been drawn into the controversy. He had come home covered with mud one day, his clothes torn, and sporting a black eye. The result of a fight with Tom Ashby, the twelve-year-old son of one of Turner Ashby's cousins.

"You've been such friends," Belle said, as she helped him clean up. "What happened?"

William stared at her resentfully. "He called you a 'Yankee hoor'," he said.

Belle had stared at him a long moment before she could reply. He had done what any brother should: defend her honor.

It broke her heart that he had lost a friend for her, because this was an insult that could not be forgiven. Lucy Buck and her friends had caused this, with their gossip and loose talk. There was nothing she could do about it. This insult would have to be born with all the rest.

"Someday, when you are older," Belle said, "I will explain all this. It is in a good cause." William nodded, looking at her very steadily, and said nothing more.

All this drama was a minor distraction when measured against her urgent need to get up the road to Winchester and find Alexander Boetler. Most of Shield's Division was moving out, and Keily and Keogh with it. A Union regiment from Maryland was rumored to be coming in. Belle thought that surely there must be more than one, if only to protect the huge amount of supplies. No one seemed to know which regiment or who would be leading it.

Twice she applied to Major Hector Tyndale for a pass and was refused. Tyndale, having a wife he loved deeply, was immune to her charms. Charged with both the security of the village and scouting the roads ahead for Shields, he was a busy, impatient man.

While polite and mindful of Shield's general instruction to maintain good relations with the locals, he was strict about controlling movement in the town. There were sentries everywhere.

At "Bel Air", the Buck farm, one sentry had been placed between the pasture and the barn, which created a problem for the dairy maids in the Buck household. Cows had to be milked twice daily and were brought in from the pasture for that purpose.

A literal-minded sergeant assigned to the post kept the maids from going to the pasture, and also kept the cows from going to the barn because none of them had the required pass.

This petty revenge he exacted because he had been refused a second glass of milk. The Bucks were very much imposed upon with requests for free milk and meals by the Yankee soldiers who invaded their property. Mister Buck tried to set an example for his neighbors by gracious acceptance of these little robberies, but his efforts had as much effect as they would on a plague of locusts.

Belle, out of pure mischief, went to Hasbrouke Reeve, explained the situation and obtained from him, for the price of one long kiss, a pass that said, "These cows have permission to pass to and from the Buck pasture to the Buck barn for the purpose of being milked." Belle presented this document to Lucy Buck who accepted it with the kind of forced graciousness that only highlighted her resentment. It was displayed between the horns of the lead cow, causing much laughter at that sergeant's expense.

Belle no longer cared what Lucy Buck and her friends thought of her, and Lieutenant Reeve was, for a shy man, a particularly good kisser. She wondered why his kisses did not ignite in her the same overwhelming passion that Daniel Keily's did.

Finally, Major Tyndale relented and said that Belle might have a pass to go to Winchester the next day. Belle, thinking that Alice needed to get away from William Clark, who renewed his attentions after she slapped Myles Keogh, included her in the party, along with Eliza.

Word of the journey in the town naturally brought a number of requests to carry letters through the lines. Ordinarily, Belle would have been happy to oblige, but doing so could get her searched and detained and prevent her from reaching Winchester.

Lucy Buck, of all people, approached, a letter grasped firmly in her gloved right hand, as Belle sat in an open carriage going over the plans for the journey with Reeve. She leaned closer and whispered in Hasbrouke's ear.

Out of the corner of her eye, she saw Lucy Buck stiffen, quickly put the letter in her purse and pass by, her nose at a noticeable, disapproving tilt.

Stupid woman, Belle thought, *stupid, stupid, stupid woman*.

That night, Belle told Alice about this episode. Alice simply sighed and shook her head. Belle raised an eyebrow.

"What?"

"Perhaps, if we went to Lucy and explained," Alice said.

"No!" Belle cut her off. "Absolutely not. With that woman around, Front Royal has absolutely no need of a newspaper. If the Yankees find or even suspect that their plans are discovered, they will change them, and that will be very bad for us."

"If she knew it was for the Cause...."

"My nursing was for the Cause, and you saw where that got me."

Alice was almost in tears, "You go too far sometimes, Belle. Women of our class...."

"Will lose us the war, if they don't realize that everything has changed," Belle said heatedly. "The old South is gone, Alice, and for better or worse, a new one is rising in its place. With our best men in the field against the Yankees, we women can let these invaders run over us roughshod, or we can do our part."

Alice stared at her. "Was sleeping with Dan Keily your part?"

Belle blushed. "Yes," she said, and should have let it go at that, but Alice turned her head away. Belle's stomach filled with a disagreeable sensation and she felt herself suddenly on the verge of tears.

"Listen. I am already widely assumed to be in league as well as bed with the Yankees — and that is part of the job! Did you not read Fenimore Cooper's novel, 'The Spy' ? It is the way of these things."

Alice stared at her, "But the risk...."

"Is mine and mine alone, dear heart." Belle frowned. "I risk hanging, so the possible effect on my marriage plans pales in comparison to that grim possibility."

When Belle mentioned the trip to Winchester, Alice had her doubts. "Why should we both go?" she asked.

"To get you away from that man Clark, if for no other reason," Belle replied. "If Myles Keogh were here you could appeal to him for protection, but he's not. Besides, I need your help in Winchester."

"Because they watch you."

"Exactly. And there are places that Eliza cannot go."

Alice sighed, "All right. I'll go."

"Pack for a week. We won't be gone that long, but you never know."

"I don't look to Myles for any help with Mister Clark," Alice said sadly.

"No?"

"He thinks Clark a great jokester. Says it's all in fun."

Belle said nothing, but just looked at her sympathetically. Alice got up and poked at the fireplace of their private sitting room. "Not that I care, you know, but as a beau, Myles is something of a cipher. He doesn't know our ways here, but he's very well mannered when he's with me and in company."

"And when you're alone?"

Alice blushed. "He assumes too much."

"If he shares Mister Clark's bad opinion of us, that's not surprising."

"He hasn't said, one way or the other," Alice said unhappily, "But they drink together."

"And that makes them like brothers, I suppose, in that great fraternity of drunken men who lose their good manners sip by sip." Belle sighed. "Well, a few days away will do you good."

"I hope so," Alice said, still unhappy. "Why should I care at all about drunken Irishmen, even if they are handsome?"

At that very moment William Clark suddenly appeared at the sitting room door. Belle stared at him, scared almost to death. How long had he been there? What had he heard?

He leered at them suggestively, "Ladies...."

Belle got quickly to her feet went over, shut the door firmly in his face, and locked it. She could smell the alcohol on his breath. She turned and leaned back against the door, her heart beating wildly. A sudden thump shook the door as Clark hit it from the other side. She waited for his footsteps to recede and then went back to her chair and sat down. Alice was staring at her, eyes wide. They waited.

After several moments, Belle said, in a slow dreamy voice, "Alice, about Daniel."

"Yes?"

"You know how our mothers told us, when we were twelve, about the relations between a man and a woman?"

Alice nodded cautiously.

"What they didn't tell us," Belle said, grinning now, "Is how much fun it is."

Alice looked startled, "Perhaps they didn't know?"

Belle laughed, "Oh, they knew. They had to."

"Why did they keep it from us?" Alice asked, smiling slightly.

"Why do you think?" Belle laughed.

Alice laughed, too, and then grew more serious, "Because we're supposed to save it for marriage, for our one true love."

Belle sobered at that. "Everything's changed now." She leaned forward and took Alice's hand in hers. "When we were being presented in Washington, I seem to recall the aim of that game was to make a good appearance and find a proper match. Not once did the word 'love' enter into it."

Alice was disturbed. "That's true," she admitted after a moment. "But I did have hopes."

"If I am ruined," Belle continued, "And I rather suspect I am, for all sorts of reasons, not the least of which is my own love of the game, then it is because I sought to serve the nation. My peculiar form of duty may never be revealed or told, and I will never receive recognition or thanks for it. I knew that from the first, from having read Mister Cooper's novel. I am at peace with it."

Alice looked away suddenly, on the edge of tears. "My God, Belle, you are so brave! Where do you find this courage? This fearlessness in the face of so many enemies? How do you do it?"

"I don't know," said Belle seriously. "I never think about it.

I just do it as the moment demands."

"You should have been born a man," Alice joked, but Belle did not laugh.

"I can play the man," Belle said, "But no man could do what I am doing here, and it needs doing if we are to win this war."

"I'm sorry," Alice sighed. "I want a normal life. I want a husband and children and all of that."

"You'll have them," Belle said. "The war won't last forever."

"It's already lasted far too long by me," Alice said mournfully, and touched Belle's cheek tenderly with her hand.

"Poor Belle. You should have been a soldier."

"Darling," replied Belle, "I *am* a soldier."

The next morning they found that Major Tyndale was on a scout, at the head of a column of cavalry. Lieutenant Reeve relayed the unhappy news to Belle. Belle pouted and stamped her foot pettishly. "Well, when will he return?" she demanded.

"Not until tonight," Hasbrouke said, regretfully. Alice and Eliza sat in the closed carriage Belle had hired for the journey. It was still threatening rain.

"We must get on to Winchester," Belle said fretfully.

Hasbrouke licked his lips nervously but didn't say anything.

"Look here, Hasbrouke Reeve, you pretend to be a great friend of mine. Prove it and assist me out of this dilemma by passing us through the lines."

"I cannot," Hasbrouke said. "I have no authority to write passes. Major Tyndale reserves that for himself."

"Did you not have business in Winchester yourself?"

"I did. Do." Hasbrouke shifted his feet, almost like a small boy.

"Surely...."

"Get in the carriage, Miss Belle," he said suddenly.

"Pardon?"

"Get in the carriage. If I drive, we will be passed through the lines without question and without needing a pass."

Belle favored him with a large toothy smile.

"What a brilliant man you are," she said and touched his arm with her hand. "I won't forget this," she murmured in a low voice that held the promises of kisses and perhaps a bit more.

She got into the carriage and settled herself in the seat opposite Alice, who looked at her and then looked away and said nothing. Eliza, seated next to her, wore the same dark impassive face that served her when dealing with Yankees. The air was thick with their disapproval.

"What is it?" Belle asked as the carriage jostled forward.

"Sometimes, cousin," Alice said carefully and delicately, "You surprise me."

Belle answered after a moment. "Sometimes I surprise myself."

CHAPTER TWENTY-NINE

Winchester, Virginia, May 21-22, 1862

With Lieutenant Reeve driving and herself confined for most of the journey, Belle saw only bits and pieces of the Union Army. He was as good as his word, and got them through all the Union pickets between Front Royal and Winchester. As the day wore on, the rain stopped and Belle was able to see a bit more, but with Union Provost guards and officers present at every point, she tried not to draw attention to herself by obviously looking at the various units along the way.

At the edge of Winchester, the last picket point cleared, Reeve stopped, jumped down and told Belle that she would have to drive the rest of the way. He had business at a Union encampment nearby and would "catch up" with them in the morning.

Belle had wondered how she was going to keep him occupied and distracted while she did what she had come to do. She was relieved, but also a bit curious since Hasbrouke Reeve, normally the most open and readable of men, suddenly became sphinx-like in manner. She had no time to solve the mystery just then, but her curiosity was aroused.

She got up on the driver's seat, took the reins and drove the carriage a few short blocks to the address she had been sent in a letter a month before. There, to her surprise, Betty Duvall greeted her warmly. Another woman she had never seen before greeted her with open arms, a big hug and the title of "niece".

"It is so good to see you," Betty said, "And you, Alice."

Betty had been under a strain. Her normally beautiful face looked drawn and haggard. She no longer had the confident and superior manner which had been so condescending to Alice and Belle two years before when they were presented in Washington. It was now replaced by a trembling, humbled gratitude for their presence. It was a shocking transformation.

"I'm very surprised to see you here," Belle said.

"My doctor recommended a stay in the country," Betty said, her voice strained. "Washington has become a sink-hole of vice, degradation and Yankees."

Alice looked at Belle, and then at Betty. Belle looked out at the hired carriage, where Eliza was directing two male servants in the unloading of their trunks, and then at the woman whose house this was.

"Aunt...."

"Esther," the woman supplied in a low voice, "Esther Boyd."

"Of course, it's been so long," Belle smiled, her face smooth but inwardly very relieved. Boyd was a very common name in this part of Virginia and snooping Yankees would have as much trouble as the Boyds themselves sorting out the degrees of relationship between them. Aside from the fact that all were descended from the Boyd Clan of Kilmarnock, Scotland, whose leader had lost his head when the Revolution of 1745 failed, no one kept track. Belle, because of her height and manner, stood out, but the rest and their collateral kin in the Reed, Stephenson, Burns, Glenn and other family lines were a mystery even to themselves.

Belle saw a resemblance to her mother and aunts in Esther Boyd's features. She began to relax. Alice was still tense and as agitated as a hummingbird, but Belle, reflecting that this was her first time "in the field", simply laid a reassuring hand on her arm. "You're very kind to have us."

"Not a bit of it, my dear. Always a pleasure to see kinfolks. Can I offer you some tea?"

"Certainly," said Belle, picking up the cue. "Has anyone called with something for me?"

"No," Esther Boyd said, "But Mister Alexander sent word he would call this evening."

It took Belle a moment to puzzle out that she meant Alexander Boetler. "It will be good to see my old uncle again," she said.

Alice, watching, looked irritated and confused for a moment, but then turned to Betty Duvall and asked, "Is that a new dress?"

Betty seemed almost embarrassed. "Not that new," she said.

"I got it last year from Elizabeth Keckley."

"You'll be the envy of all the local young ladies," Esther said, as a tall black man dressed as a butler brought in the tea.

She watched him put down the tray and then served the tea herself. "So hard to get good help these days," she said. "My Hazel went over to the Yankees."

The butler, without a word, walked out of the large front room. "Some are loyal," Belle said.

"Yes, Justin is a jewel, but I had to buy him back from a Yankee Provost Marshal. Two hundred dollars. Quite a bargain really, were it not for the fact that he's already mine."

Belle, looking sideways at Eliza, could see that she was absorbing every word. She changed the subject.

"How is Missus Greenhow?" she asked Betty.

Betty perked up. "Still giving the Yankees fits. They have her close held in Old Capitol Prison now, and her little daughter with her, and no one can do anything about it. McClellan hates her, and blames her for all his misfortunes. It's all dreadful and quite illegal. She simply will not bend."

"And Miss Lily Mackall," asked Alice. "How does she fare?"

"You haven't heard?" said Betty, suddenly very upset.

"We read about Missus Greenhow in the Yankee papers when we can get them," said Belle, "But there's nothing about Lily."

Betty, with tears in her eyes, said, "She's dead."

There was a shocked silence. After a moment, Belle asked softly, "What happened?"

"She was raped by one of Pinkerton's savages, and got with child and died from it," Betty said all in a rush.

"Oh my God," Alice said in a whisper, her hand over her mouth.

Belle felt tears come to her own eyes.

There was a long silence. At last, Belle managed to say, "She will be in all our prayers."

"Yes," Betty said.

"And does the work go on?" Belle asked.

"Not by us," said Betty simply. "The whole thing's broken up. Most of us have gone South for fear of being picked up and put in the Old Capitol."

"You as well?"

Betty nodded. "I am going to Richmond if I can get a pass. Without Rose and Lily and Missus Phillips, we are a rudderless ship; totally without direction. And it's not just Pinkerton you have to fear. There is this new man, Baker, who is even more of a rabid Black Republican. He's like one of those priests who led the Spanish Inquisition. They say he has a thousand men."

"Catholic?"

"No, thank God," said Betty, "Or I should really fear him. But very unpleasant."

"No one to protect you?" asked Alice.

"How? They come in the night and take you away now, and lock you up without charge," replied Betty, "And no can get a writ to free you. Those who intervene risk prison themselves. Why, even Rose Greenhow's kin can do nothing for her."

"And we are just women, after all," added Esther Boyd. Belle felt her temper rising, but said nothing. For all the presumed kinship, she did not know Esther Boyd or her household. The less said, the better.

Again she tried to change the subject and lighten the mood. "Any beaus, Betty?" she asked.

"All in the Army," said Betty unhappily.

"Ours or theirs?" Alice asked suddenly.

"Both," Betty admitted sadly. "It's very confusing."

"Belle and I both have beaus," said Alice suddenly, with a high nervous laugh. "The only problem is that they're Yankee officers."

There was dead silence in the room at that.

"Well," Betty offered after a moment, "At least they're officers."

"It's in the line of business," Belle said, shooting a sharp look at Alice. She wanted no discussion on that score.

She got to her feet. "Aunt Esther," she said, "I think that we are rather fatigued from our journey. Perhaps if you could show us to our room, Alice and I could rest a bit before dinner."

"An excellent idea," Esther Boyd agreed with a generous smile.

Once they were alone, Belle whispered harshly at Alice. "What were you playing at in there?"

Alice looked at her wide-eyed, and then burst into tears, which made Belle throw up her hands and then sit beside her on the bed to comfort her.

Alice sobbed, "I'm sorry. I'm scared!"

"Of what?"

"Everything," Alice replied tearfully.

Belle put both arms around her and rocked her like a child for a few moments. Alice broke away, found a handkerchief in her handbag and dried her eyes. She looked at Belle and spoke with an unnatural calm.

"I found the news about Lily Mackall quite unnerving," she said.

"As did I," Belle said. "I think any woman would."

"Then how can you be so calm about it?"

"Because I must. We must always be calm, dear one. What they did to Lily was deliberate, performed with great malice, as an act of war. It is designed to break our will; to make us fear them."

Belle got up and found her own handbag. From it she took a small silver flask of brandy, unscrewed the top which served as a cup and poured a solid ounce, which she gave to Alice, who looked at it doubtfully.

"Drink it," said Belle. "You've had a shock."

Alice sipped at it tentatively and then tossed it off the same way she had seen the Yankee officers at the Fishback Hotel do so many times. Belle watched with interest as Alice's face flushed bright red and she gasped for breath.

"Better?" Belle asked after a moment.

"Different," Alice said, and then, perhaps emboldened by the alcohol coursing through her, said, "It's easy for you."

"Is it?" Belle asked. "Why is that?"

"You're never afraid."

Belle laughed. Alice looked at her uncertainly.

"I'm afraid every minute of the day, Alice."

"You don't act it."

"No, I don't. If I do, they win. It's not the fear, Alice. Everyone is afraid, if they have a grain of sense, because it's a war and people die — and have worse than that happen to them. You can't give in to your fear."

Belle sat again beside her cousin and held her. "It will be all right, but you must be brave."

Alice looked at her, wide-eyed. "I will try," she said at last.

"That's all I ask," said Belle tenderly.

Supper that night was an exercise in artifice and pretense. Nothing further was said about the work they were all engaged in. Instead, Betty Duvall held forth on the latest fashions in Washington and how difficult it was to even get an appointment with a dressmaker with all these Yankees and their women crowding in. Everything was so expensive.

Belle, who when men were present liked to exhibit her vivacious nature and be the center of attention, was content to let Betty claim that role. She ate silently and observed Alice, who was less nervous now.

Eliza helped with the service. While Belle and Alice were resting, she had gone into the town, on a kind of scout. As Belle was dressing for dinner, and Eliza was helping her with her hair, she related what she'd found.

"Big doin's wid de Yankees," she said.

"Yes?"

"Dis Missus Boyd, she really your aunt?"

"No," Belle said, slightly alarmed. "The name is a common one. She is probably some sort of relation, but it would go way back, maybe a hundred years."

"Dis nigger of hers, Justin?"

"Yes?"

"He spy for de Yankees. Missus Boyd takes people and goods ober de border. He run away, but dey hire him to come back and spy."

Belle was alarmed, "Does he know who I am?"

"He know," Eliza said, "But he doan know why you heah."

"You talked with him?"

"Yes'm. Man likes his drink. He brag. Think Eliza ignorant nigger like him. Dey make much of him. Give him de two hundred dollahs she pay to get him back. He like to bust a gut laughin' when he tell me dat."

Belle smiled. "That is amusing."

Eliza shook her head, "Not right. He a bad man." Her face, normally so smooth and passive, displayed genuine anger.

Belle was surprised. She stood up and smoothed the fabric of her dress. "Why do you say that?"

"You belong to someone den you part of dem. You want to go North and not be dat anymore, den you go. You don' sell dem out. Not if dey been good to you."

"And had my Aunt Esther been good to him?"

"He workin' in de house, ain't he? Best food, fancy clothes, not no damn field hand all broke down. Not like she whip him, but mebbe she should have done dat."

Belle felt herself once more disoriented by Eliza's frank exposition of what servants felt and did. It was a secret, a gesture of trust in return for the trust she had placed in her. She looked at Eliza and saw that she was quietly furious.

"Why do you say that?"

"Teach him some respect. Damn nigger got no respect."

Belle nodded, seeing the way of it. Eliza was a Boyd first and foremost, and the idea of one of her own betraying the family to the Yankees was something she could not abide.

"You didn't say anything to him? About us?"

Eliza was wide-eyed at the idea, "Cain't trust him no how, so why I do dat?"

After dinner, at about eight o'clock, Alexander Boetler came to call. Belle and Alice made much of him, and Betty Duvall and Esther Boyd greeted him with equal enthusiasm. After coffee was served and some light, inconsequential conversation, he and Belle were able to go into the parlor alone.

Boetler looked very tired, Belle thought. "I'm very glad to see you. I have some very important information, which you must get to General Jackson, Colonel Ashby or some other responsible officer." He reached inside his elegant gray frock coat and drew out a bundle of letters.

"These are of moderate importance and must get through." He handed them to Belle and then drew a small piece of folded paper from inside his vest pocket, "This is the most important item and should, on no account, be given up to the enemy. If you are taken, it must be destroyed or there will be terrible consequences."

Belle took the paper, turned it over in her hands, and said, "I can swallow it, if need be." She unbuttoned her dress and tucked it between her breasts. Looking up, she saw that Boetler was both interested and embarrassed, his face blushing a bright red. She smiled at him. "That's safe enough for now."

Boetler looked hastily away and cleared his throat. "How will you proceed?"

"I came without a pass, so in the morning I will need to get one from Colonel Fillebrown, the Provost."

"He's not your greatest fan from what I hear," Boetler said doubtfully. "How will you do that?"

"He's a man who can't be bought," he added, when Belle

raised her eyebrows and just smiled.

"He can be flattered. Besides I came here with a Yankee officer who kindly drove our carriage and passed us through the lines."

Boetler looked disturbed. "One of your lovers?"

His tone was disapproving, which did not sit well with Belle. "No," she replied coolly, "Not yet. Perhaps not ever. But he would like to be and I've led him a dance." Her eyes blazed with resentment as she said this, even as her voice stayed low and sweet.

Boetler said no more. No fool, he. He made his goodbyes and left. Belle pondered how to keep the larger bundle safe, and it came to her that Eliza was not just above suspicion in Yankee eyes, but almost invisible.

Eliza divided the bundle and padded her own waist with the letters. Belle kept the little note close to her heart.

Over breakfast, as they were getting ready to leave, Esther Boyd approached and said, "I have some letters to go to Front Royal and a tiny package."

Belle looked at her in surprise. Nothing had been said about this, and she did not know this woman. *On the other hand*, she thought, *she's treated me as well as her own and taken no small risk herself. She does not know that one of her own betrays her.*

Alice looked a bit scared, but made no objection when Belle said, "You've been so kind. How could I say no?

"By the way," she added, "Do you know a good florist?"

Esther Boyd was puzzled by the request, "Yes. Why?"

"We came without a proper pass. We need to get back and I thought that I would ask Colonel Fillebrown to help me out."

Esther Boyd shook her head and grinned. "That's bold," she said.

"That's Belle," Alice replied and they all laughed.

Early that afternoon, Colonel Fillebrown, who had been so rude to her and her mother a few weeks before, greeted her warmly,

"Miss Belle. How nice to see you again." He did not, however, rise from his chair nor ask her to sit.

"Colonel. I'm in a bit of a dilemma."

"And how may I assist you?"

Belle carefully did not even glance at the big bouquet of budding roses and irises in a vase on his desk. "Major Tyndale promised me a pass to come here, but he was off on a scout when we started out."

"So you came anyway?"

"Yes. I know I was not supposed to."

Fillebrown rubbed his balding head and looked at her over his drooping mustaches. "That is a very serious matter. Why did you come?"

"To see our aunt, Esther Boyd."

Fillebrown nodded. "Of course. War or not, social frivolities must go on."

"Oh, I know it was wrong, but my cousin Alice has been working so hard and we needed to get away for awhile."

Belle could see that he was not going to make it easy for her. She smiled boldly at him. "It did allow me to see you again, too, so it was not entirely a bad thing."

Fillebrown stared at her a moment. He smiled. "And , if I grant your wish, will I continue to receive such compliments as this?" He leaned over and smelled the bouquet she had sent him.

"Why not?" said Belle gaily, as her stomach clenched painfully.

Fillebrown looked bemused. He stood up, and looked over to where Alice and Eliza were standing. "Next time you must come alone," he whispered.

Belle smiled broadly, and rolled her shoulders slightly, making her breasts move under her dress. His meaning could not be clearer. Next time the price would be more than a bouquet of flowers. She played to his obvious lust.

"Certainly," she replied with a half-wink, and brushed her lips against his cheek. She was filled with both excitement and revulsion. He was too old and held no attraction for her the way that Keily and Reeve did, but she had some power over him and that was, by itself, very exciting. She blinked, fluttering her eyelids, but Fillebrown's eyes were on her breasts. He licked his lips and took a step away, and spoke almost angrily.

"Well, I have no more time for your importunities this day," he said. "Let Tyndale deal with you when you get back to Front Royal."

He bent down and scribbled out a pass for "Miss Boyd and her party, to be passed through to Front Royal."

IIe datcd it and signed it and handed to her without another word. She bowed and said, "Thank you," and left, with Alice and Eliza coming quickly after.

Alice said, "Next time...."

"There won't be a next time," Belle said quietly. "Not with him."

She climbed up onto the driver's seat of the hired carriage while Alice and Eliza got inside. The bundle of letters and the little package that Esther Boyd had given her sat in a small basket. As she waited for Alice and Eliza to settle themselves, she took a stub of pencil and scribbled "kindness of Lieutenant Reeve" on both.

When they met Reeve at the place where they had dropped him off the day before, he was both happy and nervous.

"Your meeting went well?" Belle inquired.

"Very well," he said, and looked away.

Something was going on with him. An open and honest man since she had known him, he had become secretive, something for which he had no talent.

"What was it all about?" she pressed him.

"Horses," Reeve said nervously. "We need remounts for the campaign."

Belle knew for a certainty that this was not true. Hasbrouke was not a quartermaster and his own unit was well supplied. She wondered why he had lied and how she might find out the truth of the matter.

Lieutenant Reeve offered her his hands with the obvious intention that she should come down and ride in the carriage. She smiled at him.

"It's such a nice day. Why don't we enjoy the ride together?"

"But without a pass...."

"But I have a pass, sir. From Colonel Fillebrown himself."

Hasbrouke looked surprised. Belle drew it from her handbag and showed it to him. He examined it carefully, shrugged, smiled at her, handed it back and then climbed up to sit beside her.

"It's a lovely day for a drive," Belle said.

Hasbrouke looked around, seemed to relax. Smiled back at her and said, "Yes, it is."

They had not gone two miles when the were overtaken by two men on horseback. They were wearing civilian suits and bowler hats and were both dark-haired and ill-favored with ragged mustaches and unshaven faces.

They rode up so quickly that Reeve drew his revolver, thinking them Rebels or bandits. One of them held up a wallet with a gold badge in the shape of six-pointed star.

"Army detectives," he shouted, and Reeve lowered his weapon and pulled the team over.

One of them stood off in the road ahead of the carriage with two revolvers in his hands while the other approached.

"Miss Belle Boyd?" he asked in a voice that was straight out of Manchester.

"I am," Belle replied. "What is this about?"

"You're under arrest," the detective replied.

Belle reached for her handbag. "I have a pass signed by Colonel Fillebrown," she said with spirit.

"Don't know anything about that," the detective said, "But you must come with us."

"On what charge?" Belle asked loudly, angry now, thinking that Fillebrown had set her up.

"On suspicion of having letters."

Belle felt her stomach drop. Letters she had, and more.

"But, Colonel Fillebrown said...."

"Don't know anything about that," the detective said patiently. "Don't much care. We work for Colonel Baker."

Belle shut up. She didn't know anything about Colonel Baker. Indeed, she had never heard of him until Betty Duvall had mentioned the name the day before. Next to her, Hasbrouke seemed agitated.

"Be calm," she advised him. "I'm sure this is nothing. We will soon get this straightened out."

Hasbrouke said nothing, but simply looked at her, his eyes wild with panic. *What has he been up to, to act this way?* Belle wondered.

"It will be all right," she assured him, although she was pretty sure that it wouldn't.

CHAPTER THIRTY

Winchester and Front Royal, Virginia, May 22-23, 1862

Belle's mind raced furiously as they were escorted to the camp that Reeve had visited the night before. The detectives made her take a seat in the carriage. She tried to decide how to play the forthcoming encounter with this new Yankee Colonel. Alice varied between being frozen with fright and drawing rapid shallow breaths.

I should never have brought her, Belle thought, *but what was I to do?* Eliza, sitting next to Alice, showed little emotion. Glancing at Belle, she took Alice's hand and squeezed it reassuringly.

"This is nothing," Belle said to them quietly. "We have done nothing wrong. Be calm."

Alice gulped and then nodded, finding fresh courage. Eliza gave her a fleeting smile and pulled her shawl around her so that the bulges made by the letters under her dress would not seem so obvious. Belle thought hard, not looking at them again until the carriage jolted to a stop.

Lieutenant Reeve jumped down from the box and opened the carriage door. Belle offered him her hand, and he, in a very circumspect way, helped her out. Four armed soldiers, holding muskets with fixed bayonets, arrayed themselves around Belle. Alice was left to trail behind and Eliza was almost forgotten in the detectives' haste to bring Belle into the tent where a Colonel was waiting.

He played the game of making them wait while he read some papers. This gave Belle a chance to size him up. He was about forty years old, but fit enough, compact, dark-haired and with an air of command. *Probably another politician, or lawyer (and weren't they the same thing?)*, she thought, *but one that has chosen to command fighting men. It would be a mistake to take him for either a weakling or a fool. He is playing a game which has worked for him before.*

Looking at Alice, Belle saw that the game had some chance of success. Eliza was also intimidated. Rather than wait him out, Belle cleared her throat, "Colonel Baker, why are we here, sir?"

He looked up, irritated, put the paper he had been reading aside, and said, looking severe, "My name is Brodhead, Miss Boyd. Thorton Fleming Brodhead, First Michigan Calvary. You are said to be carrying letters. That is a violation of military regulations."

"But I'm not in the military," Belle replied sweetly, with only the barest edge in her voice.

"Why are you here in Winchester, then?"

"We were visiting our aunt, Esther Boyd," Belle said.

"And you have no letters on you?"

Belle thought that if she denied it, he was perfectly capable of having her and Alice stripped naked, right then and there. That he might well welcome the opportunity to humiliate them. *Time to sacrifice a pawn*, she thought.

"Just these," she said and reached into her basket for the bundle of letters that Esther Boyd had asked her to carry. Brodhead pounced on them like a hawk on a pigeon. He immediately spied the inscription she had written on the outside of the bundle.

"Kindness of Lieutenant Reeve?" he roared. "Kindness of Lieutenant Reeve? Who the devil is Lieutenant Reeve?"

That unhappy man, who had followed them into the tent and was trying his best to become totally invisible, said, "Lieutenant Reeve, sir." His voice was miserable, like that of a small boy caught stealing apples from a neighbor's tree. He gazed steadily at his boots.

Brodhead turned on him, raging, "You? It's you, Lieutenant? How do you come to be here? You're detailed to duty in Front Royal!"

Reeve stammered, trying to reply as Brodhead ripped open the bundle of letters. He opened one and then another, and then a third, reading them quickly. He looked up at Belle, his eyes full of suspicion and anger.

"Why these are nothing but letters to cousins and aunts and sisters," Brodhead shouted, looking at the detectives, who seemed unwilling to argue the point.

Belle suspected that they were a great deal more, that there were messages hidden within the text or that invisible ink held others between the lines, but knowing they were lost, simply drew herself up, jutted her chin out proudly, and said, "Well what do you expect? You Yankees stopped the posts. How are we to get news of our families unless we resort to such subterfuge?"

Brodhead roared, "Is that all you have, then?" in such a loud and threatening manner that Belle took the small note given her by Boetler from her bosom. Like her hero Harvey Birch in Cooper's novel, **The Spy**, she was prepared to swallow it to keep it out of enemy hands.

But, at the very moment, Hasbrouke, obviously frightened, sweating even, took out the little package she had asked him to hold for her and threw it on Brodhead's field desk as if it were made of red-hot coals. He scooped it up and spied the writing on it.

"Kindness of Lieutenant Reeve, again!" he said, his voice now dangerously low, and looked up at Reeve with a dangerous smile. Hasbrouke looked at Belle who tried to intervene.

"Colonel," she began, "This is entirely my fault and none of his doing. I simply asked him to help me out of a difficulty...."

He saw the note in her hand. "What is that you have there?"

Belle looked down as if surprised to see it there. "This? Why this is nothing," she said, taking a step forward. "You may have it if you like." Another step and she would have to put it in her mouth and swallow it. Whatever was on it would be lost since she had not read it. If indeed, it were in any form that she could read, and not coded.

Brodhead tore open the package. Inside he found a carefully folded copy of "The Maryland News Sheet" a decidedly Rebel publication printed secretly in Baltimore.

Brodhead stared at the newspaper and then turned on the hapless Lieutenant Reeve, his face red as he shouted to the detectives.

"Put this officer under arrest. I want a full investigation of his activities here since he is assigned to Front Royal and not under any orders to be here in Winchester."

"And the women?" asked one of the detectives.

He swept the letters off his desk angrily. "I asked you for proof. This is not proof, and neither is the word of a nigger houseman!" Brodhead paused to get his breath.

"Let them go if they have a pass."

The two detectives looked at one another uneasily. Brodhead turned to Belle and asked hopefully, "You don't have a pass?"

"I do," said Belle firmly. She took the one signed by Fillebrown out of her bag and handed it to him. He examined it carefully, even looking at the back, as if hoping to find evidence of forgery, and then handed it to the detective that had arrested her.

"Did you even think to ask for a pass?" he growled.

"But she did have letters...."

"That's too thin. Letters is all she had — and there is no such crime as suspicion, not in any court in this land."

He looked at her balefully and then said, "Hold Reeve as absent without leave. Let the women go."

And so they were released. Belle took the reins and drove the hired carriage back to Front Royal. Once they were safely on the road, Alice had herself a good cry while Eliza made comforting sounds. When they were back at the hotel, and the bags were unpacked, Eliza handed back the letters she had smuggled under her dress.

In Front Royal, there were pickets everywhere. Belle tried to think of a way to get the messages she had out of town. It was no use.

Major Tyndale, infuriated at her "escapade", placed a soldier at her door, and that man matched her step for step everywhere she went. Eliza and Alice likewise had little leeway since the pass system was heavily enforced for everyone, and passes were not forthcoming for the staff of The Fishback Hotel.

Alice seemed relieved. Belle's frustration mounted. Yankee

officers now avoided her, and William Clark, half-drunk, renewed his campaign of innuendo against them both. The new Yankees came from Maryland, with two squadrons of New York cavalry. Belle had no opportunity to charm them. Once more, there was a sentry in the barn, so that a repeat of her midnight ride to Ashby was equally impossible. There was nothing to do but wait.

"I suppose you think me weak and silly," Alice said later. There was a coolness between them now, Belle realized. Alice had been terrified by her first contact with field work.

"No," Belle said, to reassure her. "You were very brave."

Alice started to tear up again. "I was so afraid," she said.

"As was I," Belle said quietly.

"You didn't seem so," Alice said, resentfully. "You seemed totally in control of yourself."

"It's not the same thing," Belle said softly.

Alice just stared at her, trying to comprehend. Belle let it go. Most women, she decided, simply were not made to be soldiers. Truth to tell, neither were most men, but they had little choice in the matter.

The next day, the noon meal having been cleared away and other chores dispensed with, Alice, Belle and their grandmother, Ruth, took their ease in the second floor sitting room they kept for themselves. Belle was reading aloud from the Yankee newspapers when there was the sound of feet running up the stairs, and young Martha burst into the room.

"De Rebels is comin'," she half screeched, "And de Yankees is making an awful fuss in de street!"

Belle held up her hand for silence and heard a great deal of noise suddenly, shouts and horses' neighs and the clatter of weapons and wagons. She opened the door to the hall cautiously and spied four officers running down the stairs as William Clark tore past them, charging upstairs to his room. She could feel Alice beside her.

"It's Jackson," Belle said. "It has to be. He's slipped the noose and turned it back on them."

"What about Clark?" Alice asked, excited almost to the point of glee.

"He's intruded on us so many times, perhaps we should return the courtesy," said Belle. "Give me your pass key."

They looked back at their grandmother, who shooed at them with her apron. "Time's a wasting. Do what you have to do."

Seeing no Yankees, Belle ran lightly on her toes, Alice close behind. Clark would run away, she was sure. She could lock him in and hold him, with his papers, even if it meant breaking off the key in the lock.

The door to Clark's room stood wide open, his own key in the lock. Looking in, they saw him gathering papers into a satchel. It was the work of a second to gently close the door behind him and turn the key. They slipped back down the hall, Belle pocketing the key ceremoniously and Alice laughing. They were almost to the first floor when Clark began to shout and pound on the door.

"Stay here," Belle told Alice, and went into the street. There she could hear the crackle of musket and rifle fire and the distant boom of a cannon. A shell tore into a Union position at the edge of town and exploded.

Men and officers ran in all directions in the street, filled with growing panic. She spotted an officer she knew from when Shields occupied the town, a quartermaster named McNab.

"Captain McNab?"

He stopped and looked at her, very surprised. He was about her father's age, portly, with the look of the storekeeper he had been in civilian life. She had talked to him about that business, she remembered.

"Miss Belle," he said urgently, "You should not be out here. It's going to get very hot. Too dangerous for you."

Belle managed to look lost and confused. "But what is happening? What is going on?"

"We are surprised. Jackson is upon us, sprung out of nowhere, he's driven the pickets in, and we cannot hold the town."

Belle's heart jumped for joy at the news. Outwardly, she was all concern for his problems.

"But Captain, what about your supplies? How will you move them?"

McNab laughed bitterly. "We won't. We'll burn what we can and skedaddle. The Rebs are as dark on the hills as flies on a dead dog."

"What about the bridges?"

"We'll fall back over them and then burn them as well, so stay clear," said McNab and, tipping his hat, ran on.

Colonel Kenley, the commander of the First Maryland, was trying to organize an orderly retreat. She looked where the pickets had been stationed, saw none, and realized that she could now move freely about the town.

The depot and the warehouse were full of all sorts of things that the Confederate Army could use. And she had Boetler's note to pass on. Somehow she must get someone to carry a message to Jackson or Ashby.

Quickly, she ran on, trying to find some loyal local man to do this, but it was no use. They were mere boys, or too old, or Union men, and all were intent on avoiding the field of battle, not running towards it.

She would have to go herself! Quickly she ran towards the sounds of the guns.

CHAPTER THIRTY-ONE

May 23, 1862 Front Royal, Virginia

As Belle ran closer to the battle lines she slowed down, not from caution but to avoid any Yankee who might try to detain her. Kenley's First Maryland was well deployed ahead of her to defend the town and discourage the Rebel advance. A battery of artillery pieces, six-pounders, mounted an effective defense by firing shells that burst right above the advancing Rebel soldiers.

Somehow, she had to get through! A vagrant musket ball whizzed by her head, making her duck low to the ground. Crouching, she crept behind a small house about thirty yards behind the Union lines, and surveyed the ground in front of her.

A small creek cut through the lines; it had flowed freely just a few days before when rain poured down, but was now almost dry. With a trickle of water at its middle, and a sandy path beside it, it divided two newly-built hospital buildings that the Union had put up the week before to treat the badly wounded of the coming campaign. Belle saw a safe low path through the lines — if no one looked out of one of the windows and saw her.

Her white bonnet was sure to be noticed. Pulling it off, she tucked it in her blue-gray apron and shook out her hair. Her blue dress was dark enough to blend with the green undergrowth. If she moved carefully and slowly, she might pass the Yankees unnoticed!

Crouching, she dashed from the corner of the house down into the creek bed. Using the cover of this narrow defile, she duck walked until she was about forty yards in front of the Union lines. Here the path narrowed and rose up, so that she was almost crawling on her hands and knees to avoid being seen.

There was a small grove of trees, which would have been a good place for Kenley to place an outpost, had he not been caught by surprise. She looked it over carefully before making another dash to gain its safety. She listened for any Yankee voices hidden in the almost overwhelming cacophony of musket and cannon fire. No one was there.

Hidden at the edge of the trees, she surveyed the Confederate lines. Finally, she saw what she was looking for: a group of officers on horseback, directing the battle. They were at least two hundred yards away, and uphill. Dead and wounded Confederate soldiers lay near the top of the ridge.

Was Ashby there? Was Jackson? She remembered the small but very important note that Alexander Boetler had given her and which she was still carrying next to her heart. Her breath came in deep, slow gulps, but she was perfectly calm.

Jackson, or whoever was there, needed that note. They needed to know about the weakness of the Union position and that the retreating Yankees planned to burn the supply depots and the bridges on the other side of the town.

Behind her came a shout and then a gunshot. She turned and saw that the upper windows of the two-story hospital buildings crowded with riflemen. Another shot whizzed past her, striking a tree trunk with an almost metallic sound — a solid clunk that frightened her far more than the whizzing musket ball had. She had seen the grievous wounds they made.

Suddenly, without further thought, she sprinted for the Confederate lines, as more bullets pursued her, splattering into the dirt near her on both sides. She ran as fast as she had ever run, pulling her skirts up with one hand to allow herself a longer stride. She began to wave her bonnet wildly with the other hand.

She felt surrounded by hornets, so many were the bullets now. One or two plucked at her skirts as she scrambled up the hillside. She began yelling, "Yoo-hoo!" as she waved the white bonnet. Ridiculous, but she couldn't think of anything else.

Finally, with a clarity she had never experienced before, she saw Jackson direct another officer to ride towards her. She reached the crest of the hill, and ran over the top and out of range of the Yankee fusillade.

Loud cheers rose from the Confederate lines as she ran the last few yards and then, suddenly, with fiendish yells and screams, a Confederate regiment rose up and charged the Union lines. They were Zouaves, she saw, wearing white and blue trousers with a vertical stripe — Major Wheat's Louisiana Tigers. Wheat, a huge man wearing a red sash and waving a sword, led them down the hill at a run.

Belle bent over almost double, her heart thumping wildly, as she tried to catch her breath, and then fell to her knees, barely aware of them as they surged past her.

Up rode her childhood friend Harry Douglas on a fine bay mare, wearing the epaulets of an aide-de-camp and the rank of Major. He jumped down to help her.

"Good God, Belle. You here? What is it?"

"Oh, Harry," Belle gasped, "Give me time to recover my breath."

"You could have been killed. What possessed you to...."

"I have intelligence for Jackson. I knew it must be Stonewall when I heard the first gun. Tell him the Federal force is very small," Belle said, now managing to stand erect. "First of all, the town is lightly defended. If Ashby can get cavalry around them it is ours for the taking. There is one regiment and a half company of Cavalry. The only artillery is what you see. They are trying to burn the bridges and the supplies — and there is a great deal of supply. Tell Jackson I know this because I went through the camps and got it from one of their officers. Charge right down and you can take them all."

Douglas looked at her, his eyes blinking rapidly as he absorbed this. "Wait here," he said, ran to his horse, swung himself up lightly into the saddle and rode back to the command group. Within two minutes Jackson, along with Ewell and a Louisiana general she didn't know and all their aides, were before her. They did not dismount, but leaned towards her, filled with curiosity.

Jackson looked at her kindly, a light in his eyes. "Now, my dear child," he said, "What do you have to tell us?"

Belle drew herself up, standing tall, and repeated what she had said to Harry Douglas. "There's more," she added, and unbuttoned her dress to retrieve the note that Boetler had given her.

The Louisiana general watched with interest and amusement as she did this, but Jackson, Ewell and their aides managed to find other places to look.

"From Colonel Boetler, sir," Belle said as she offered it to Jackson. "He handed it to me in Winchester two days ago."

Jackson took the note, unfolded it, read it carefully, and then looked right at her and asked, "Have you read this?"

"No, sir," Belle said. "Not my place. I'm just the courier."

Jackson nodded approvingly. "What is your impression of the disposition of Union forces?"

"Kenley has a thousand men in Front Royal. Banks is at Strasburg with four thousand. Colonel Brodhead's Michigan Cavalry is at Winchester, perhaps five hundred strong, but General White is at Harper's Ferry and can reinforce both by road and the railway. General Shields and General Geary are maneuvering to trap you from the East while Fremont is planning to do the same thing from the West." Belle rattled these off in the same manner she had seen Union staff officers make their reports.

"And the road between here and Winchester?" the Louisiana general asked.

"As of two days ago, Union forces were not apparent in strength," Belle said. "The road was clear."

"And the railway?" he prompted.

"There is no railway between Winchester and Front Royal," Belle said, a little surprised. "One must go by way of Manassas."

Jackson chuckled, "General Taylor is not from these parts, my dear. May I offer you a horse and an escort back to town?"

Belle was horrified at the idea. "My, sir, that would give the game away! No, thank you! I will go as I came, to protect what shreds of secrecy are left to me at this point."

Jackson was already turning away from her, his horse trotting back to the crest of the hill where he could better see the field of battle. "As you wish," he called back to her and then, to Taylor, "Come, we have work to do."

Harry Douglas lingered. "Are you sure? You have done us a valuable service."

"And if I'm to do more, the less show we make of it, the better," Belle replied, a little irritated.

Douglas looked at her as if seeing her for the first time. "You're Secret Service?"

Belle shook her head, and then smiled at him, "Those who say don't know and those who know don't say, Harry." It was what Freemasons often said of 'the Noble Craft' and its mysteries.

He continued to stare at her, trying to take it all in and unconsciously touched the Masonic pin on his lapel. He belonged to her father's lodge.

"My love to all the dear boys," Belle said. "I must hurry back. Remember, if you meet me in town, you haven't seen me today."

"I will see you in town!" he said and wheeling his horse around, rode off, leaving her standing there quite alone.

Belle suddenly felt quite tired and weak. She looked down the hill, over the path that she had come. The Union force had hastily retreated and the six-pound cannons were now under guard of some of the Louisiana Tigers. It was safe enough. She could see flames shooting up in the distance from the train depot. The Yankees had succeeded in torching some of their supplies.

There were at least three ragged bullet holes in the skirt of her long blue dress that would not lend themselves to mending. It would have to go for rags, along with the apron, now torn and badly soiled with mud. The white bonnet was still in her hand.

Slowly she put it back on and began the walk back, taking the longest possible way, hoping she would not be seen.

By the time Belle got back to the hotel, the battle was over. Front Royal was once more in Confederate hands. She slipped into the back door, ran upstairs, and almost fell into Eliza's arms.

"Quick," she said, "Help me change."

Eliza whistled softly at the condition of the dress and apron, and then went for warm water. By the time Belle had unbuttoned it, she was back with the pitcher, which she poured into a basin.

"Wash yourself," Eliza said. "You dirty everywhere, hands and face." She helped Belle out of the ruined dress and asked, "What we do wid dis?"

"Cut it up for rags," Belle said, "And bring me another one." The blue dress was almost a Fishback Hotel uniform, and she had two more. They were identical.

Eliza worked hurriedly, and asked, "You not hurt?"

Belle stopped and stared at her, "No, I'm fine. Why do you ask?"

"Dat Jimmie, from Buck's, he say you got shot by de Yankees."

Belle smiled, "Close, but no cigar, as they say." She peered into the mirror and looked at herself critically. "There's more to do."

"Bunch of yo' Yankee friends held prisoner outside de door," Eliza said with a sniff. "Didn't put up much o' de fight."

Belle, now satisfied, started to go out the door.

"Wat 'bout Mistah Clark?" Eliza asked.

"What about him?"

"He bangin' on de door somethin' terrible. Offer me fifty Yankee dollahs to let 'em out."

Belle looked at Eliza, whose eyes were dancing with amusement and laughed, "Why didn't you take it?"

"I don' wan' dat man's money, Miss Belle. He mean and he always after de young girls. 'Sides, Miss Alice said you got de key."

Belle laughed, "I do."

She was tempted to let Clark out, but then thought if her suspicions of him were correct that he should be held for investigation by a Confederate Provost Marshal.

"You just leave Mister Clark right where he is. Tell him that we're making up his bill."

Eliza found that very funny indeed. "I go tell 'em now," she said, laughing. "You a caution, Miss Belle."

"Aren't I just?" said Belle, as she put a fresh bonnet on, tucked in a random bit of hair and then went out of the room and walked slowly, almost elegantly, down the stairs and across the yard. Seeing no sentry at the back door, she went through the kitchen toward the lobby. Alice was behind the desk, and smiled at her.

"Where have you been?" she asked, her voice betraying a little anxiety.

"I had a call to make," Belle said. "What are you doing?"

"Since our Yankee guests are checking out, I'm making up their bills," said Alice, grinning now. "Some of them are out front."

Belle smiled brightly. "Let me see to it," she said. Alice handed her several half-sheets of foolscap. Belle impulsively leaned across the desk and kissed her cheek and then went out the front door, picking up a bouquet of roses that was on a hall table as she passed by.

"Make up Mister Clark's bill, too," she called over her shoulder, "But no charge for today."

Behind her Alice laughed out loud.

There were half a dozen Union officers under guard on the walkway before the hotel and a like number of Confederate officers. Both groups were from regiments called the First Maryland and all seemed to know one another and to be in good humored conversation. A hour before they had been trying very hard to kill one another, but now treated the entire affair as a game. There was an almost festive air about the meeting, with many joking comments and laughter. Belle was greeted cheerfully and began to present each officer with a rose for his lapel.

Belle also handed the bills to the Yankee officers, who looked, shrugged and then dug into their pockets. "Yankee dollars still good?" one of them asked. "Considering?"

"We'll find a use for them," Belle said sweetly. "We're always short of paper in the outhouses."

There was general laughter. Just then, Harry Douglas rode up. Belle smiled and called to him. "Harry! Harry Douglas! Don't you know me? It's Belle!"

Douglas stopped his horse and swept off his hat, playing his part in the drama. "Why Miss Belle, imagine finding you here. Why aren't you in Martinsburg?"

"I found the climate too hot," Belle replied flirtatiously. "It's so good to see you."

Douglas walked his horse over to her and leaned over. "Do you have anything else for us?" he asked in whisper. Several of the Maryland officers from both sides were calling his name — friends, if not always comrades.

Belle thought for a moment. "Are you any kind of Provost?" She took the last of the roses and pinned it to his lapel. *How handsome you are*, she thought.

"I'm a deputy Inspector General for Jackson," he replied, sniffing at the flower. "Why?"

"There is a reporter for the New York Herald — he calls himself a 'special correspondent', whatever that means; I suspect him of being some kind of spy. We have him locked in his room upstairs. He's been bothering us quite a bit."

"Us?"

"Me and my cousin Alice both. And the maids. Irish but no gentleman."

Harry Douglas looked thoughtful. "Is that all you have against him? Special Correspondents are not generally regular employees of the papers they represent. Paid by the column inch rather than given a salary. It's a common arrangement on both sides."

Belle started to speak, but heard a noise and looked upward. The window to Clark's room was open, she saw, and that worthy, with shoes and satchel in one hand, was attempting to climb out.

"That's him now," Belle said, and pointed upward.

Douglas looked up and murmured, "The guilty flee when no man pursueth." He slowly drew his revolver and cocked the hammer. Aiming carefully, he fired a single shot, deliberately missing Clark but breaking the glass in the window. Clark jumped in panic, almost fell, but caught himself in time.

"You, sir!" Harry Douglas called. "Stay as you are. I will send men to attend to you presently."

Clark nodded, clearly frightened. Belle blew him a kiss with her hand and had the satisfaction of seeing him turn bright red.

"Sorry about the window," Harry Douglas said. "Do you have a key? I'd hate to break anything else."

"Certainly," said Belle, "And we'll add the cost of the glass to his bill."

"Which you will present personally?"

"If I may," Belle said hopefully.

"Certainly," said Douglas, "But you might want to let it go. These reporters have a long memory. They can hurt you." His tone was that of an older brother.

"Oh, you're no fun. Besides, he's a common Irish ruffian. Not even the Yankee officers respect him."

Douglas nodded. "I'll get a detail."

Major Wheat, still holding his sword as a standard, and marching at the front of his remaining men, came into view.

Shortly thereafter, Belle watched as William Clark was helped back into his room by two of the roughest-looking men she had ever seen. Members of Wheat's Louisiana Tigers, they were previously 'wharf rats' from the New Orleans docks. They carried large Bowie knives rather than pistols, and Belle did not doubt that they were expert in their use. Neither did Clark. He was obviously frightened of them, all the more because they were so gentle and polite.

When Belle presented the bill to Clark he started to sneer at it until one of the Tigers cleared his throat and wagged a finger at him. "A gentleman always pays his debts." He had a thick Irish brogue, which Clark found even more unsettling.

Clark found his purse quickly and handed it to him. The man counted out the amount required in hard money. Belle pocketed the gold coins and smiled at Clark. "Thank you for staying at The Fishback Hotel," she said, trying not to break into gales of laughter. The Louisiana Tiger, who wore the chevrons of a Sergeant on his sleeve, handed back Clark's purse to him.

Clark pocketed it and smiled meanly at Belle. "It's your doing that I'm prisoner here. I will have my revenge."

The larger of the Tigers clapped him hard on the shoulder, almost driving him to his knees.

"That's no way to talk to a lady," he said quietly, and turned to Belle. "What would you prefer, miss? Break both his legs or just throw him in the river?"

Clark looked at her wildly, as if she might actually order one or both of these choices. Belle thought it a joke, or at least hoped so. She smiled at him with better grace than she felt, because she *was* a lady, and replied, "Neither seems appropriate for being a blowhard, which is all he is. No, Mister Clark should just prepare himself for a long stay in Libby Prison."

Clark managed not to say anything further as they took him away. Belle was glad to be rid of him. "Good riddance," she said to herself, and went to see what help Alice might need. If Yankee officers were checking out, Confederate ones would be checking in.

There was more to do. The battle for Front Royal had been quick and decisive, but several of Ashby's officers had been killed and several of his troopers wounded as they flanked the Union lines. There had been a fierce fight for the bridges.

Suddenly, Belle found herself taking charge of the wounded. Jackson's surgeons worked side by side with their Union counterparts. Colonel Kenley was rumored among the Union dead, but then turned up in the makeshift ward of the Fishback Hotel ballroom, gravely wounded but alive.

Belle gave him special attention, partially because he looked something like her own father, and because he had been, during their brief acquaintance, a perfect gentleman.

Several of the young girls from the town came in to help nurse, and were genuinely surprised when Belle told them that Union and Confederate wounded were to be treated alike.

"It's because we want their side to do the same," Belle explained to one girl who objected. "And we do whatever the doctors tell us to do, no matter how unpleasant or disagreeable." The young girl, whose name Belle did not even know, gulped, but did as she was told.

She was happy to see Alice pitch in this time, but looked in vain for any sign of Lucy Buck or her clique. Belle went out into the street to watch the regiments of Jackson's army march by. Kenley's command was destroyed, and the entire force was now pursuing the Yankees towards Winchester.

A young baby-faced Lieutenant from Jackson's staff rode up, dismounted and handed her a note.

It read:

"Miss Belle Boyd,
    I thank you, for myself, and for the Army, for the immense service that you have rendered your country this day.
    Hastily, I am your friend.
        T. J. Jackson, C.S.A."

Belle folded the note carefully, with tears in her eyes. The young Lieutenant looked at her curiously.

"Thank you," she said quietly.

"Any reply?"

"Only that this makes it all worthwhile," Belle said, "And thank you with all my heart."

The young man nodded, mounted his horse and rode off. Belle sat on a chair in the hallway, clutching the note to her breast for a long time, until Alice came and told her that she was needed in the ward.

She showed the note to Alice, who was amazed.

"From Stonewall himself," Alice said reverently. "Think of that."

"Yes," Belle said. "Think of that."

CHAPTER THIRTY-TWO

May 23, 1862 Strasburg, Virginia

"Hello, David," Thorton Brodhead said, when Strother entered the large front room of the hotel that served the officers of General Nathaniel Banks' headquarters. "What news?"

Strother unhooked his sword, put it in the corner and sat down heavily. A Negro servant rushed forward with a pot and a cup.

"Coffee, boss?"

Strother nodded, and stretched his long legs out. Brodhead said, "I'm having a spot of that English concoction called 'tea' in a bit."

"I hope, Thor," Strother grinned, "That you're not going to pick up all of Percy Wyndham's bad habits."

"What's wrong with Sir Percy?"

"He doesn't think much of Ashby. Thinks 'proper' tactics will defeat him. He's advanced a proposal to headquarters again."

Brodhead shrugged. "Maybe he's right. He does have the professional experience."

"Maybe," Strother agreed, "But he doesn't know the ground, and he rides parade-ground formations with insufficient flankers and scouts out. Ashby may not have the experience, but he does have the passion, especially since his brother was killed. And he's nobody's fool. Warrentown Junction proved that."

Brodhead frowned. "Are you sure he was the one behind that? That was murder, not war."

"Yes, I am," Strother replied. "Ambush, with no surrender, is the very tactic that he and his ilk advocated from the beginning. It was spoken of even as John Brown was being led to the gallows."

"According to the few who survived, they did not hoist the black flag." Brodhead shook his head. "Even war has laws and rules of conduct."

Strother considered that for a long moment, staring into his cup of coffee as if the answer might be found there. "You're a civilized man, Thor," he said at last, "And you expect that level of morality from our adversaries. Those trained to the usages of war will oblige you, but Ashby is a Red Indian at heart, and just as savage. His men are more of a tribe than a regiment. He used to delight in playing an Indian, who was also a knight, at tournaments, riding half naked, with incredible skill."

Strother stared at his friend, whose face still expressed some skepticism. "You'd be well advised to keep scouts out at all times," he said. "Warrentown Junction was very much within Ashby's character, something which our friend Percy disallows. Said the commander of our troops there should have been courts-martialed for carelessness. It was Ashby, I'm sure. He swore blood feud against that regiment. They killed his brother. He's clever and resourceful and he has spies everywhere."

"Here, you think? Now?"

Strother motioned towards the scene outside, which they could both see clearly through the window. "There are sutlers and other hucksters, dealers in horse flesh and those who criminally appropriate same, clothiers, merchants in contraband medicines, and Negroes of all descriptions, and, I can assure you, more than one Rebel spy taking our measure. Added to which is a troop of strolling players. What they are doing here...."

"How would you find the spies?" Brodhead pushed back from the table to let the Negro waiter deliver the sliced breads, jam, and scones for the tea.

"You probably wouldn't. I was put to interview some prisoners we took yesterday from a picket post. Simple country lads, each and every one, who had been told that, if we caught them, they would be executed. They were very relieved to learn that it was not so and quite forthcoming. Jackson's force is still at New Market as of two days ago. What plans he might have, these fellows were not privy to. Jackson is a close sort of man. Not even his staff knows his intentions until the moment he issues an order."

"Still, it's good intelligence," Brodhead said.

"I'd feel better if we had the same facility with spies that Ashby does," Strother said. "Of course, our General Fremont's

'Jessie Scouts' give him very good service." His tone was ironic which caused Brodhead to look up from his food.

"They go as Confederates, right?"

"Yes, but it's a dangerous business. If caught, they'll be hanged. We need men who can blend in to play that game."

"What about those new cavalry regiments forming for West Virginia?" Brodhead asked.

"An excellent idea. They are native to the region and have men who can act and talk like the enemy," Strother said with a rueful grin, "But not well received from a mere Captain. It will wear better from someone of your cloth."

Brodhead chuckled, "You are becoming a devious man, David. You should be careful or you might be tempted to undertake a career in politics."

Strother grimaced and lowered his voice, "I've seen enough of that, thank you." He looked around, as if Nathaniel Banks might enter the room at any moment.

An orderly sprinted into the room, stopped before Brodhead and saluted. "Telegram from Front Royal, sir."

"Yes?" Brodhead half rose from his seat, already alarmed.

"The Rebs have taken it."

Brodhead and Strother looked at each other.

"Impossible," Strother said angrily.

Brodhead was already buckling on his sword and throwing money on the table to settle the bill. "Maybe, but my place is with my men. I must return to Winchester this very moment. Tell Banks, will you?"

"I'd better get up to headquarters, and see what this is all about," Strother said, finding his own sword and hat.

A few minutes later, he entered the main tent of Bank's headquarters to find only clerks and orderlies, all on the verge of panic. General Banks and General Crawford, with all their aides and staff officers, were already out.

Half an hour later, as Strother was looking at his maps once more, and realizing that the road discovered by Major Tyndale the week before would indeed give Jackson a shorter route to attack Front Royal, a Negro came in and was challenged by a clerk. After a few moments of conversation, he was referred to Strother.

"What is it?" Strother asked, not unkindly but with a certain impatience. "What do you have?"

"Yessah. I'se just come from Front Royal and de Rebels hab it, Captain. Dey come in force and Colonel Kenley fightin', but fallin' back. He goin' burn de bridges and supplies. Rebels comin' in hard. De Louisiana Tigers wid de funny uniforms leadin' de charge, and dey yellin' and shoutin' and got dey big knives out. Dey break de Union line."

"You saw this?"

"Some of it. Dey's panic in de town."

"And who are you? Who's your master?"

The Negro, who was about thirty years old and well set up, looked around, saw that no one else was listening, and whispered, "My name is Bob Howard, sir, and I am no man's slave. I'm from Chicago and I work for Mister Pinkerton."

Strother was struck dumb for a moment, not just by the perfect English pronunciation, but by the fact that one of Pinkerton's agents was working so far from McClellan's headquarters, and was, in fact, a Negro — a very smart one at that.

He recovered himself. "I see," he murmured. "Do you have any proofs?"

"Only that I saw it with my own eyes and that Front Royal is surely lost by now."

The Negro looked around, suddenly nervous. "I needs to git on, boss," he said falling back into the concealment of slave patois.

Strother, tempted to call the Provost guards outside the tent and have him held, nodded instead. "You're right. You're not safe here."

The Negro nodded, grinned and walked out of the tent.

Strother looked at the map again. It was possible that Jackson had surprised Kenley with a small force, marching down that road, he realized, especially since Tyndale had been relieved as Provost there and sent to re-join Geary. Kenley had either not been properly briefed, or lacked the men to cover all the possible approaches to the town. Jackson had, once more, been lucky.

When General Banks and General Crawford and their staffs returned from a useless ride down the road towards Front Royal, Strother pointed out where he thought Jackson's forces might be.

"Not at New Market?" Banks asked, his temper showing a bit.

"It would seem not, but this has got to be a small force. We have only to send a brigade to Front Royal to counter his movement," Strother said.

Crawford waved a telegram that had just been brought in, "Jackson is reported, at the head of twenty thousand men, to be advancing on Winchester."

"The officer who sent that is a coward!" Strother exploded. "Jackson's entire force numbers no more than six thousand by all previous reports. This man is simply trying to cover up his own failure to do his duty by exaggerating the number."

Banks pursed his lips and looked over to Crawford, "General?"

"Be that as it may," said Crawford, "If he is advancing on Winchester with any sizeable force, then we are in danger of being cut off. He can then attack from both Front Royal and Winchester and destroy us in detail."

"Just so," said Banks. "Order the trains and wagons loaded for a movement to Winchester. We have the better path and can beat them there."

Strother could not hide his distress.

"Sir, may I suggest that we at least send a scouting party towards Front Royal to determine the enemy's strength and condition?"

"But who...."

At that moment a young Captain of Dragoons stepped forward, "I'll go, sir."

Banks looked at him and shrugged, "As you wish. Take a few of your men with you."

"Yes, sir."

Banks looked around the room. "Prepare to move to Winchester at first light."

Crawford and all the staff officers saluted and hurried away. Strother and Banks were left standing alone, except for a few clerks.

"What would you like me to do, sir?" Strother asked, a bit nervous.

Banks frowned, "You stay right here, Captain Strother, and wait for further reports. In case Jackson has more surprises for us."

"And where will you be, sir?"

"I'm going to bed," said Nathaniel Banks sourly. "Wake me at your peril unless attack is imminent."

"Yes, sir," Strother replied unhappily. Banks stomped off to his quarters in the big tent a few yards away. Strother sighed and went over to look at the map again. It was impossible that Jackson would have so many in his force, and if he did, how could he move them so quickly from New Market?

The next morning the young Dragoon Captain was back with news. Five thousand men and a baggage train were coming down the road from Front Royal.

"In addition to the so-called twenty thousand headed for Winchester?" Strother asked skeptically. "My pardon, Captain, but that seems unlikely."

"We counted twenty-seven regimental flags for cavalry alone," the young Captain replied, "And there seem to be Louisiana companies in the advance, as well as Virginia."

Strother grabbed a pile of telegrams off the field desk. "Why is our first information from Winchester, some eighteen miles away, and we have no fugitive officer or soldier from Front Royal, which is just twelve miles away? Winchester is twenty-two miles from Front Royal. Why are they not already at our throats here? There may be a Rebel force driving towards Winchester, but its size is monstrously exaggerated."

The young captain looked at him doubtfully. "How can you be so sure?"

"Because, my young friend, I am from these parts. I am native to Martinsburg and know all the ground around here very well. The roads will not support movement on that scale, and I'll bet you my horse and saddle that they have nothing near twenty thousand men near Winchester and another five at Front Royal. Jackson's entire force is no more than six thousand."

"It's not just Jackson, sir, but Ewell and Taylor. We picked up that much from one of the men who escaped the battle yesterday. He heard Reb officers bragging to one another."

Strother threw up his hands. "We should hold our position here."

The young captain looked out to where the loaded wagons were beginning to move off. "Can you not persuade the General?"

"I lack the *gravitas*," Strother replied bitterly. "Like you, I am only a Captain, and presumed not to possess the wisdom magically conferred by higher rank."

The young captain looked around, making sure no one was near and said in a low voice, "Banks ain't much of a general, is he?"

Strother saw where this might lead and said sharply, "He's the one we have, Captain. See to your men. I am sure they will be needed to guard part of the supply train."

Without another word, the young captain saluted and left. Strother began to gather his maps and papers.

Two hours later he was riding by Nathaniel Banks' side, as the wagons trundled down the road from Strasburg to Winchester. Mixed in with the Union Army wagons were dozens of civilian carriages and wagons, occupied mostly by Negroes and the other people who had made Strasburg such a colorful place the day before. It rained from time to time, adding to the misery as the crowd jostled along; accidents became common. Some of the civilian wagons, driven in haste, overturned. This aggravated the growing panic of those behind them, who tried to maneuver around and became stuck in the mud themselves.

"Why are all these niggers out here with us?" Banks growled.

"Fear, sir, of the Rebels," Strother replied wearily. "They ran away from good homes to be free, and now fear that Jackson and Ewell will put them to the sword."

"Would they?"

"I very much doubt it," Strother said. "A slave is valuable property and one does not kill them carelessly, any more than one sets fire to barns and houses or tears down fences or tramples crops."

"Our men have done all of that," Banks observed.

"Yes, sir, and that's why more of the local people have not rallied to our cause. We come at them as tyrants and oppressors. Even the most low-born white man in the South is possessed of a stubborn Scotch-Irish pride — and the women are worse!"

Banks looked back at the long stream of wagons coming out of Strasburg and said, "Well, perhaps it's just as well that they come along with us." Black smoke marked the fires which were consuming the supplies that had been left behind for lack of wagons to carry them.

"They will hinder us, sir," another officer objected.

"What would you have me do, Captain? Order the cavalry to drive them off with swords? We have better use for those swords."

A large overloaded wagon came tearing down the side of the road towards them, driven by a fat, bearded white teamster, wild-eyed with panic. He screamed, "The Rebs are attacking the head of the train!!" Parts of his load flew off as he passed, creating additional dangers.

"See what that's about," Banks ordered an aide. The young Lieutenant galloped off the way the teamster and his wagon had come.

Strother and Banks watched as other Union officers struggled to get the wagons moving again. Some of them drew their swords and threatened the already hysterical civilians.

This is a rout, not a retreat, thought Strother unhappily.

The aide that Banks had sent forward returned. He stopped his horse in front of them and saluted, "Rebel Cavalry, sir. They raided in force and made off with the extra horses. They set fire to some of the wagons and killed some teamsters and Dragoons."

"Ashby?" asked Strother.

"Seems so, sir," answered the Lieutenant.

Banks looked up ahead, where smoke from burning wagons was beginning to appear, and then back over his shoulder to where the burning supplies in Strasburg were pouring another tall black column of smoke into the morning air. It began to rain again, a steady light drizzle that darkened the already grim mood.

A wagon belonging to the troop of strolling players passed them, driven by an older man with a determined look on his face. His fellow actors, many still in costume from their performance the night before, made a bizarre sight even for this multitude.

Banks sighed and looked at Strother with a raised eyebrow. It was a sight that defined the moment. He took a small silver whisky flask from his coat, uncapped it, took a good swig and passed it to Strother, who took a drink himself and passed it back.

"It seems that we were mistaken in our calculations," said Banks gently.

The words half-destroyed Strother, who still believed that the reports of the enemy strength were exaggerated, but knew that he had lost the confidence of his general. He stared at Banks and then looked away. "It seems so, sir."

"Go see what you can do to get us moving again," Banks said.

Twelve miles away, in Front Royal, Major General Thomas Jackson looked at the note that had been brought by a courier and exploded in anger. "Damn him!"

Major Henry Douglas and Major Reverend Dabney, looked at one another in alarm. Jackson never swore.

"What is it, sir?" Douglas asked.

Jackson's eyes burned with fury. "Ashby raided Bank's supply train and made off with the extra horses."

"That's as planned, sir, is it not?" asked Dabney.

"Yes," said Jackson, "But they are now dividing the spoils and absenting themselves to take those horses away to their farms and plantations. Ashby has done nothing to prevent this, and suddenly he has an effective strength of seventy men, not seven hundred."

Douglas frowned. "We could make good use of those horses here. We have much Yankee supply to carry off."

"It took Banks weeks to get it here," said Dabney, "And it will take weeks to remove it all."

Jackson, not given to violent displays, just stared at them. "That's the least of it, gentlemen. We have an opportunity to destroy Banks's whole army, as we destroyed the command here. That would force the Union to pull troops away from Richmond, lest we move on to Washington. Ashby has permitted Banks to get to Winchester today, when he could have kept raiding and destroyed that entire train."

Jackson suddenly kicked a camp stool so hard that it flew several feet away. Seething, he growled, "This is why I do not like partisans and amateur officers. No discipline. No appreciation for strategy, and a selfish manner that makes them little better than bandits."

Resigned, Douglas asked, "Shall I prepare orders for Colonel Ashby's arrest?" This was Jackson's usual response when a subordinate commander failed to carry out his plans.

Jackson shook his head. "Who would I replace him with? His best company commanders were all killed or wounded yesterday when we took this town, and we need to move on and exploit our advantage. I need Ashby to reform his command immediately. Until then, Colonel Flourney and the Sixth Virginia will have to carry his load, and they are too close to Winchester to attack Banks' column today. So Banks escapes!"

Jackson paced up and down as Douglas, Dabney and all the other officers and clerks waited, almost holding their collective breaths. Finally, he walked over to where the map was spread out. He stared at it and then sighed. "We cannot get before their advance in any strength. Banks will not stand and fight. His will be a retrograde maneuver at the quickest possible pace."

Jackson pulled out the little piece of paper he had received from Belle Boyd the previous day. He read it again. "Let us press on to Winchester with all possible speed. Perhaps we can drive them to Martinsburg and Harper's Ferry. Colonel Boetler has prepared them a warm welcome of his own."

Douglas made bold enough to say, "But I thought you did not approve of partisan forces."

Jackson stared hard at him a moment and then smiled gently, "I try not to fight on the Sabbath either, Major, but I must work with the tools that the Lord has provided. Send word to Colonel Ashby that he is to report to me at once."

Dabney came over and drew him and Douglas aside, "Perhaps we should not be too harsh with Colonel Ashby."

Jackson, disconsolate, took a lemon from his pocket and cut in half with a pocket knife. "Why not?" he asked.

"Because I have word from Richmond that Ashby is to be promoted to Brigadier General next week."

Jackson nodded, "His friends have politicked for it hard enough, and Boetler most of all. Unfortunately, he is popular. I oppose it, but they will have him the equal of Stuart. I fail to understand why Jeff Davis, who aspires to be a general himself, would make one from such poor cloth."

Douglas said, "Politics, sir."

Jackson looked at him, his face grim. "I know nothing of such things, except that they may cost us this battle, and likely this war, if the civilians in Richmond do not get out of the way and let us fight it properly. We must exploit every advantage. Men like Ashby...," Jackson did not finish the thought.

"Drive Banks back as far as we can. Give him no rest." He stared at both of them with the fiery eyes of a biblical prophet. "We must destroy them. Otherwise they will invade this valley again."

CHAPTER THIRTY-THREE

May 24-25, 1862, Winchester, Virginia

Several messengers were sent to the Union forces in Winchester. None returned. Had all been captured by Rebel scouting parties? No one knew.

When, after four hours, Brodhead also sent no word to Banks' "headquarters in the saddle", David Strother, as tired as he was, volunteered to go ahead. It was a way to redeem himself. Banks now politely disregarded all of his suggestions.

He rode alone, down the turnpike road towards Winchester, wary of possible ambush, and so disappointed and angry at his own failures that he would have welcomed an encounter with a Rebel scout. But the road was eerily empty, as if the world had ended and was bereft of all living signs of humanity.

Brodhead welcomed him cheerfully, but asked, "Are you sure you wouldn't just like to lay out in an ambulance and get some sleep?"

The offer of an ambulance only meant one thing, Strother realized — that Brodhead thought the retreat would continue.

Strother shook his head. "No. An ambulance is the last place I want to be. The Rebel attack that created all the confusion outside Strasburg was on those carrying the wounded from Shield's division. There were about thirty of them, but they raised havoc."

"Ashby," Brodhead said grimly.

"They made another demonstration at Newtown. But only that. We have no idea where Ashby's cavalry is."

"Troops are ordered out from Winchester to protect our flank," Brodhead said.

"Which will further confuse and hinder our escape," Strother said, yawning. "Pardon me."

Brodhead looked at him oddly. "Escape. Interesting word, that," he said; then, shaking his head, "You should not push yourself so hard."

"What choice do I have?" Strother answered wearily. "What choice do any of us have?"

Brodhead nodded sadly, and said, "At least you're among your own here. If you're captured...."

Strother cut him off, "I have no intention of being captured. It would go very hard with me, because I am so well known here. By them, I'm a traitor to Virginia. My father was arrested and jailed simply for being a firm believer in the Union."

Half an hour later a messenger caught up with them with the news that Banks' rear guard had been cut off by Rebel cavalry and fifty more wagons lost. Minutes later another arrived, to tell them that the column had been struck by artillery fire at Middletown, trapped between the stone walls on either side of the turnpike, and broken in two. Another hundred wagons lost and perhaps three hundred men. Wholesale slaughter, the messenger said.

Strother sucked his teeth, thinking hard, trying to visualize the map in his mind. "If they had followed up with cavalry in strength, they would have broken us utterly. Something is missing."

"Ashby?" Brodhead asked. "Where is Ashby?"

"I don't know," Strother admitted. It was humiliating to say. His job was to know.

The Tenth Maine Infantry was still in garrison, with three companies of Provost guards on alert to support them. The lead wagons of the remainder of Bank's army could be seen cresting the hill on the turnpike from Strasburg.

A scout rode up, saluted Brodhead and handled him a note. Brodhead read it and laughed.

"David, the locals here are cooking cakes and pies for a banquet to welcome Jackson and his men on the morrow."

"Doesn't say much for their confidence in us, does it?" Strother grinned. All they could do was laugh about it.

Brodhead said, "If we establish ourselves here in strength, we can spoil the party."

Strother yawned hugely and suddenly almost fell out of his saddle. Brodhead caught him and pushed him back up.

"Sorry," Strother said.

"Get some rest, David," Brodhead said. "I'm going to make that an order."

Strother nodded. "I'll be at the Taylor House. Tell my man John to make sure my horse is seen to properly. He's back in the train with the rest of the headquarters servants. Send an orderly to wake me if anything occurs."

"I will," Brodhead assured him.

Slowly, as every muscle in his body screamed in protest, he dismounted and led his horse up the street. He had to sleep, if only to have a clearer head on the morrow. Maybe then he could figure out where Ashby was.

Strother slept that night like the proverbial log and woke much refreshed. He listened carefully, heard nothing unusual, and then turned over and slept some more. When his stomach growled sufficiently to wake him, he decided to seek his breakfast. He had slept close to fully dressed and needed only to pull on his boots, coat and hat and buckle on his swordbelt and pistols.

The hotel was oddly quiet as he walked down the stairs. He spotted the landlord and asked, "Breakfast is in the dining room?"

The man, ruddy-faced and fifty, with a salt and pepper beard and hair, looked up and said, "I'm sorry, sir. All of our Negroes have run off. That includes the cooks and the waiters. We will endeavor to have something for y'all shortly." His tone indicated that he somehow blamed the Union Army for his problem.

Strother walked into the dining room and saw three doctors from Banks' medical staff at one table and a quartermaster he knew at another. Some sergeants talked together at a third table.

The landlord came in with a large china pot of coffee, followed by his wife with a basket of rolls and some butter and jam. "You gentlemen will have to serve yourselves," the landlord said. "A dollar each. Eat all you like."

The price was outrageous, but the Union officers quickly lined up to get a cup of coffee and a roll with butter. Strother sat down and sipped the coffee, which was real and surprisingly good, and nibbled at a roll. From outside came the sounds of distant small arms fire, but, since no one else seemed alarmed, he relaxed and had another roll and more coffee.

A soldier entered and leaned over the table next to him, speaking to an officer from the Tenth Maine. "Sir," the soldier said quietly, "They've driven our men off the hill."

Strother sighed, got up, and walked out, leaving a dollar on the table. He continued on to the stable, where he found his mare saddled as she had been when he had left her.

"Here," he called to the hostler, "Why was not my horse taken care of last night?" His disgust was plain.

The man, who looked like, and probably was, the landlord's brother, said, "She was, sir. I gave her a good rubdown myself, and a bit of bran and corn along with her hay." He came over and laid a hand on the mare's neck, "She's a beauty."

Looking closer, he saw that his horse had indeed been taken care of. "Why did you saddle her before I came for her?"

"Oh, that wasn't me, sir. Your man did that, about an hour ago. Said you would be along."

"John?" Strother asked. "Where is he?"

"Took flight, with the others. Afraid that the Rebel Army would do them harm." The hostler shook his head woefully. "Hard to hold them back when they've got their wind up."

Strother looked around. The stable was almost empty. The hostler's comments could be more generally applied.

"Well, I'd best get on," he said casually, trying to conceal his anxiety, and flipped a coin to the hostler, who caught it and made a short bow.

As he led his horse into the street and admired the bright, fair weather, Lieutenant Pendleton, one of General Banks' aides, rode by. Spotting Strother, he shouted, "Mount, Captain, mount and ride for your life, for you have not a moment to lose! They are in the town!" Pendleton's voice was edged with panic.

His intelligence was confirmed by a ragged volley of musketry nearby. Strother swung up into the saddle, and then cautiously trotted along behind the hotel down the alley to Main Street. Several stragglers hurried along towards the Martinsburg road.

Further on an infantry regiment was being shoved into marching order by its sergeants and officers. Strother started towards them. A crackle of pistol shots sounded loudly from nearby houses on both sides of the road. Here they built close to the property line, so the Union soldiers were caught as if they were in a narrow canyon. The volleys came from every window he could see.

Strother, with great clarity, saw a soldier who had stopped to drink from a fountain near the town square, stiffen, and then fall prone in the street. Other men clutched parts of their bodies and began to fall, either wounded or dead. The pistol fire became general.

Horrified, Strother realized that this came not from a Rebel unit, but from the citizens of the town. The regiment forming up to march began to run down the street. Puffs of gunsmoke showed the locations of the shooters, but there were so many that a counter-maneuver was impossible. As he spurred his horse to ride out of the ambush, he saw that many of the dead and wounded were officers and sergeants. This was no spontaneous impulse on the part of those with Rebel sympathies, but something that had been organized to sow further panic and disorder among Banks' retreating formations.

Another regiment was half-a-mile away, towards the sound of a developing battle at the other end of town. He spurred his horse, wheeled around and rode quickly, pulling up in front of the Colonel commanding.

"Colonel Gordon!" Strother called. "Why are you in retreat?"

Gordon frowned and replied, "Jackson is on our heels, with twenty or thirty thousand men, and the people here are against us."

Gordon waved his arm to where several more men were receiving fire from nearby houses. "I will not hazard a stand here, Captain, not with civilians shooting at us as well."

Strother could see Rebel skirmishers entering the town less than a mile away. They came down the hill at a run, so many that the ground seem to ripple like water on a lake.

Throwing Gordon a hasty salute, he wheeled his horse around again and galloped back down Main Street, braving the steady gauntlet of pistol fire, hoping that Banks and the headquarters party were someplace up ahead.

Their only hope now was to get the entire army further down the road, in good order of battle, rather than being picked to pieces by continued raids and guerrilla attacks. Regiments were beginning to retreat without orders. Unless a general retreat was ordered, there would be panic and the Rebels would destroy them all.

He slapped the saddle in frustration and ducked as a pistol ball buzzed by his ear. Outside the town the fields were covered for a mile or more by running stragglers, infantry and cavalry mixed together, along with various camp followers. Many were Negroes, each with a bag or handkerchief full of plunder, all panicked by the rumor that Jackson would kill them for "desertion".

Safely out of pistol shot range, Strother pulled up, turned his horse around and saw Banks' army pouring out of the town by every available road. What few remained were in good order, the infantry in four short columns with artillery in between and flanked, in the approved style, by a column of cavalry.

My God, Strother thought, *we're down to less than five thousand men who can fight. No wonder Banks continues to run. It's the only way he can save us.*

A rippling motion the other side of the town caught his eye. He pulled out a pair of field glasses and took a closer look. Rebel infantry poured through Winchester so quickly that they threatened to overrun the rear guard again.

More small arms fire crackled. The Union troops moved faster. Union Army stragglers tossed knapsacks, canteens, overcoats and even muskets aside in their haste to get away.

Strother put his field glasses away, turned his horse again and trotted along with the rest, trying to find the headquarters elements. Finally, he found General Crawford, sword in hand, trying to stem the panicked tide of stragglers, with the help of a few other officers. Relieved to find something to do rather than run, David Strother drew his own sword and joined the fray.

In Winchester, at the office of the Provost Marshal, Lieutenant Colonel James Fillebrown gave final orders for evacuation and the burning of his files.

A gray-haired portly older civilian, Al Butler was the name he recalled, walked calmly into the middle of the chaos and inquired, "Why, Colonel Fillebrown, whatever is the matter? Are you retreating?"

Fillebrown recalled that the man was rumored to have been in Congress before the war and thought better of his first impulse, which was to have him thrown out of the tent bodily.

"Yes," said Fillebrown, straining to be polite, "In some haste."

The man lit a cigar, very calmly, as if he were at his club, and asked in a very reasonable tone of voice, "How did you get in such a predicament?"

Suddenly, Fillebrown spied the bouquet of flowers sent to him by Belle Boyd.

"There is your answer," he said angrily.

"The flowers?"

"Yes," said Fillebrown, with just a touch of self-loathing, "The sender of that bouquet is responsible for all our difficulties. Her name is Belle Boyd."

Fillebrown watched as the man walked over, smelled the bouquet, smiled at him, tipped his hat and walked away. "I doubt she was solely to blame, sir," he said mildly as he exited.

"Who are you?" he called after the man.

His unwanted guest didn't break stride, nor did he answer, but his shoulders seemed to shake with laughter.

Fillebrown, hearing small arms fire in the next street,

shouted, "That's all, men. Get out, and ride for your lives." He ran to where his own horse was waiting, mounted, and followed his own good advice.

Strother hoped that the retreat would stop at Martinsburg, or, if not there, then Harper's Ferry, but Banks opted for Williamsport, the other side of the Potomac River, in Maryland. Jackson's force remained on their heels, at a pace that no one believed they could maintain. Yet maintain it, they did.

At Martinsburg, ladies of the Union persuasion came out in strength to press coffee, tea, and sandwiches on the officers and men who marched by so wearily. These ladies were brave and cheerful, but their eyes betrayed despair to Strother.

"Don't worry," he told a small group of them who insisted on loading items into his saddlebags, "We'll be back."

"But, when?" one asked tearfully.

"Soon," said Strother, "Very soon," and knew it was true. Once the rout was stopped, the regiments reformed and re-supplied, it would be easy enough for them to march back the way they had come. The trick was to stop the Rebels before they got to within striking distance of Washington. If he was right about Jackson's true numbers, it would be easy enough for Fremont and Geary, with forty thousand men between them, to combine behind him and execute the trap that Shields' young Irish officers had laid out originally.

He was not privy to the higher councils of command, but he suspected that Jackson's dramatic advance had ruined McClelland's campaign against Richmond. He would never have the men he wanted now. McDowell, Geary, Shields, and Fremont would all be pulled back to defend Washington against Jackson, Ewell and the other Confederate commanders.

Strother tried to excite Banks with these thoughts, but Banks, weary and obviously scared, continued to treat him with perfect kindness, as one might a close relative with a mental defect.

A general trained in the military arts, who had experienced

previous battles would know that perfect anticipation of the enemy's intentions was as rare as dandelions in winter. Banks was a politician, first and foremost, and knew only power, its exercise and preservation. His defeat was total and humiliating. His purpose now was to shift the blame.

Strother knew he would be the scapegoat. He had failed to discern Jackson's intentions and the price paid was a heavy one. Over a million dollars in supplies lost. Hundreds of men killed and thousands wounded. And, if Banks was bitterly disappointed with him, he was more disappointed with himself. His very career was at risk.

Thor Brodhead advised, "You would have more influence if you could find a commission at a higher rank." This was over whisky the first night in Williamsport.

"I have to get my wife and child situated," Strother said. "And, to add to my troubles, my pay warrant has been refused because I am not properly ordered to this headquarters."

"You're a rich man. You don't need the money," Brodhead said.

Strother shook his head. "Not so. I took leave from Harper's when I took on my topographic researches. My family has been ruined by the war, and my books are all out of print. My purse grows thinner by the day."

Brodhead considered this a minute. "Your best course is to go to Washington and straighten it out. You might see if there is a spot for a Major in some regiment you like."

"Then I will take Mary Ellen and Kate to Eutaw House in Baltimore and lodge them there, and go to Washington by train and see to my pay. I'll need leave."

"I can see to that," Brodhead said agreeably, "But you need to stay here a day or two."

"Why?"

"Colonel Wyndham has received permission to try and capture Ashby. He seeks your counsel."

"When?"

"As soon as he can travel over here. His thesis is that any well-trained company of cavalry will do, so he seeks to borrow one of ours to add to his own regiment."

Strother nodded, and sipped at his whisky again.

"Eutaw House, eh?" Brodhead said after a bit.

"Yes."

"Rather expensive."

Strother looked at him calmly. "One must maintain a certain style, Thor. My wife expects it, and so does my public."

"Then why not take them along to Washington and stay at Willard's?"

"Because Willard's is now the province of generals and congressmen, and the neighborhood is foul with vice. My family does not need to be exposed to that," Strother replied unhappily. "It is a sad thing to see. My father owned that hotel before the Willards took it over."

Brodhead looked surprised just for a moment. Then he returned to the business at hand.

"Well, expect Sir Percy tomorrow or the next day, give him a good briefing and then go along to work out your problem with the War Department. I'm sure that you'll find a better situation."

"God," said David Strother, "I hope so."

CHAPTER THIRTY-FOUR

May 30-31, 1862, Front Royal, Virginia

Belle was quietly furious. The 12th Georgia Infantry, brought in to defend Front Royal, retreated rather than fight the Union Army when it came marching back into town, triumphant, bands playing and flags waving. Jackson's brilliant victory squandered!

She swallowed the bile in her throat and went to help Alice make sure that all the rooms in the hotel would be ready to receive their new guests — or, rather, their old ones. She could tell from the unit flags that the Union forces were the same that Jackson had driven from Strasburg the week before. Shields was back. The people of the town, ecstatic the week before, were now hopeless and depressed.

Lucy Buck fretted and wrung her hands, while her cousin Mary Cloud wept openly and cursed the Yankees as they marched by. Lucy's father watched grimly as Union teamsters turned six hundred mules into his meadow, trampling the lush grass that would have fed his shrinking herd of dairy cows through the whole summer.

The only resistance by the Confederate forces was to burn the captured supplies they had not removed. Fire roared through the warehouses and depot. Thick gray smoke pervaded the town, making it difficult to see. The volunteer fire company mustered to pump water, not on the flames, but on nearby buildings so that they would not burn as well.

Belle and Alice watched all this from the hotel's front balcony, which faced the train depot and warehouses. "That's a three hundred thousand dollar bonfire," Alice said, agonized. "Why did they run?"

"Easy come, easy go," Belle replied sarcastically. "Still a passel of Yankees out there. Jackson can't allow himself to be cut off and trapped. He won't be pleased that the Georgians made it so easy for them."

Alice raised Belle's opera glasses to her eyes and examined the Yankee column marching in. "It's General Shields' boys. I recognize that blond officer."

"Who is it?"

"Lieutenant Preston, the Deputy Provost Marshal."

"I knew him in Martinsburg last year. He's very sweet and polite." She sighed. "People will be besides themselves. We'd better go make sure all the rooms are ready for the general and his staff." She started for the stairway.

"Captain Keily on your mind?" Alice inquired bitterly.

Belle turned and looked at her in surprise.

"Actually, I hadn't given him a thought."

"No?" Alice frowned in disapproval. "You won't seek his company — or his bed?"

Belle stared at her, hurt on her face. "I might. In the line of business."

"What business is that, cousin?" Alice rejoined angrily.

"Spying, of course."

"That's not what other people here think."

"I cannot be responsible for what other people think. You and I know the truth."

Alice looked away, tears in her eyes.

Belle stepped back towards her and rested a long slender hand on her shoulder. "What's all this, then?"

Alice started to cry. "Lucy Buck is a friend of mine, but she makes me so mad sometimes. She had word of your bold run to Jackson last week."

"And?"

"She doubts that it's true. She challenged me to find one person who saw you do it."

Belle took Alice into her arms. "Were you bragging about me, cousin?"

Alice nodded. "Perhaps a bit. I know I shouldn't, that it's a secret, but she provoked me."

"How?"

"By asking me if it were true." Alice wiped away a tear.

Belle sighed. "You must not speak of this, Alice, to anyone. It *is* a secret. I tried not to be seen by people in the town. I doubt if

I managed it perfectly, as I had other things on my mind just then. Like not getting shot or killed. Surely you understand the less said about it, the better, especially now that our Yankee guests have returned. Do you want me arrested?"

"No!"

"Nor I you," Belle said, hugging her fiercely and then holding her at arms length. "Now, let us go prepare for this new Yankee incursion."

They were all smiles and courtesy as the Union officers from Shields' staff appeared one by one to claim their old rooms. Daniel Keily was especially glad to see her.

To her great surprise, Michael Kelley also appeared at the desk to ask for a room. He now wore the rank of Major and the badge of an Inspector General.

"Miss Belle!" he said with genuine warmth. "So good to see you again."

Belle let a big smile light up her face, "Michael! How wonderful to see you. It's been months." She turned to Alice, "This is Michael Kelley; Major Kelley I see now, who was so kind to me in Martinsburg last year. This is my cousin Alice Stewart."

"Miss Alice," Kelley replied, with a slight nod of his head. "A pleasure."

Alice looked up from the register, a bit worried. "Yes. Of course. You may have to share...."

"There is Mister Clark's old room," Belle reminded her.

"Yes," said Alice with a relieved smile. "Mister Clark will not be back any time soon." She chuckled and looked sidewise at Belle, who had a sly smile of her own.

Kelley saw the amused smiles they were unsuccessfully trying to hide, and asked, "And why is that, me' darlin's?"

"He was captured and sent to Richmond," Alice said innocently.

"Ah, is that the way of it?" Kelley smiled. "You know,

reporters are non-combatants. I think he was passed through the lines the next day."

Alice's face fell. "They let him go?"

Belle's heart beat quite a bit faster. Anxiety settled on her like a bad cold.

"Aye, that they did. But for all of that, I doubt he'll be back, so ye may as well let me have that room." Kelley watched their faces with a solemn expression, his eyes intelligent and alert, his smile quite gone, still the police detective.

Belle summoned her courage. "Why do you think he won't return?"

"You'd be well within your rights to shoot him, if he did," Kelley said, and he pulled a folded newspaper from the inner pocket of his coat. "He's written scurrilous things about you."

Belle took the newspaper and unfolded it. There, above the fold, in the first column, was her name in large bold type. Also the word "spy". Dazed, she walked over to the bench in the hallway and tried to read the news story. Alice came over and looked over her shoulder, and then gave a small cry of dismay.

She pointed at the bottom of the column, to the next-to-last paragraph. There another phrase leaped out at them — "accomplished prostitute".

It referred only to Belle, but Alice would suffer the libel as well. Belle felt her temper rising.

"Damn him!" she shouted. "How dare he?!" She stood up and looked at Kelley, who regarded her sympathetically.

"Ah, well," he said kindly. "I wouldn't give it too much mind. No one likes the fellow anyway."

Alice was trembling. "Do you know the character of this man? He constantly sought to impose his drunken company upon us without regard for our feelings or sensibilities, we each spurned his advances, and he swore to be revenged upon us!"

"I rather suspected it was something like that," Kelley replied with equanimity. "General Shields said as much."

"Are you investigating this?" Belle demanded angrily.

"I am," Kelley said calmly. "Part of me job, y'see."

Belle was so furious that she couldn't find words. Kelley said, "He's done you quite an injury, Miss Belle. Clever bastard, he is."

Belle tried to calm herself. "What do you mean?"

"Well, the source of the story is not the New York Herald, but rather the Associated Press. It's in all the papers in the North, and the Southern ones will copy it soon enough. He's not signed it either, the coward, so you can't even be sure whether it's him or some other reporter."

Belle felt her heart sink. She felt nausea and a headache coming on. Tears came to her eyes.

"What am I to do?" she moaned.

"I don't know," Kelley said.

"I do," said Alice.

Belle looked at her in surprise. "You do?"

"Yes," said Alice firmly. "You must refute it. You must make a statement for publication."

Belle looked at Kelley, who nodded. "Fight fire with fire, I always say."

Belle's defense of her good name was delayed, first because there were no reporters riding with Shields' headquarters that day, and because Major Tyndale, once more taking up his position as Provost Marshal for Front Royal, ordered her under close arrest and confined to the cottage she shared with Alice.

"General Kimball ordered it," Tyndale explained, making no secret of his agreement with the decision. Belle's appeal to Michael Kelley was met with an enigmatic smile and a shrug.

"Now, Belle, darlin'," Kelley said lightly, "It's not me place to tell General Kimball he's wrong."

"Well, where is he? Let me talk to him," Belle demanded. Her eyes flashed from one to the other, and the two officers looked genuinely embarrassed for a moment.

"General Kimball has taken up his old quarters at Bel Air, the Buck place," Tyndale answered.

Belle stared and then made a sound of disbelief and amazement, a wordless expression that carried a fair amount of disgust as well.

But it was true. Kimball had even shown his appreciation for the Buck's hospitality by going again, pistols in hand, down to the meadow to stop some men in his brigade from tearing down and burning the fence that Mister Buck had just had built to replace the one Kimball's troops had destroyed on their previous visit.

Belle knew that Kimball would not be amenable to her pleas. She wondered if Lucy Buck knew or cared what was happening. Not that it mattered. Lucy had no influence. Her hatred of Yankees failed to keep them off the Buck family property.

So Belle was confined to the cottage, with a sentry at the door, but Eliza was in and out with meals, and with news gathered from the other servants. Alice sent in the hotel register and the accounts for Belle to work on. These were carefully examined when they were sent back out, but Belle once more extracted the Union division's order of battle and officer roster, which she then encoded and gave to Eliza, who passed it on by way of a certain silver pocket watch.

General Shields returned, taking up his old rooms. Belle sent him a note appealing her confinement. Alice took the note to him herself, watched him read it and added, "It is very hard to run this hotel without her help, sir."

"Really," said Shields in his genial, avuncular way. "It seems equally hard to prosecute a campaign with her at large and charming my officers." He smiled, "If you and she can bring yourselves to be less inquisitive about our movements and stop asking so many questions, I will parole her. She must not leave the hotel grounds without an escort, nor can you."

Alice sighed, "As you wish, sir, but we have been grossly libeled in the newspapers by your man Clark, and...."

"Not my man, Miss Alice, not at all. I neither approve of

Mister Clark's actions nor do I believe the trash he has printed. He is a snivelling poltroon of low character, but he is not a member of the Army and we cannot take responsibility for his actions. If you feel that you or your cousin or this fine hotel have been defamed, then I suggest you consult a lawyer and seek redress in the civil courts. It's a civil matter, not a military one."

He looked over to where Michael Kelley was standing, listening attentively. "Is that not so, Major?"

"Yes, sir," Kelley replied, and smiled at Alice. "Your father is a lawyer, is he not?"

Alice was hard put to keep her temper. "He is, but he is not present, nor are other members of the Bar. The courts are not in session and we live under your rule, not theirs."

Shields spread his hands in mock helplessness, "But what can I do, Miss Alice? It is hardly our fault that the Rebel government retreated in such haste. That the courts are not open. Our quarrel is not with them."

Alice stared at him a moment, her face growing redder and then said resentfully, "We will accept your conditions, sir." She turned on her heel and left the room, her anger obvious.

Paroled, Belle found herself once again under siege by reporters as she went about her work at the Fishback Hotel. The new ones were polite enough and treated her with respect, but Belle found their questions ridiculous.

Finally, at her request, Shields assembled them so that she could refute the lies in William Clark's story. They listened patiently. Then the questions began.

"Is it true that you directed the fire of the Confederate artillery in the battle last week?" asked one, a weedy, consumptive youth who had been found unfit for military service by the Union surgeons in his native Philadelphia. In compensation, he had grown an over-sized military mustache that did nothing to hide his weak chin and thick spectacles.

Belle was startled by the question. She laughed: a lady-like tittering. "Who told you that?"

"I heard it in the town," the reporter replied, pencil poised over his notebook for her reply.

"It has been published," said a second reporter, a short, fat man of about forty who was well-dressed, but untidy and too big for his clothes.

"Where?" asked Belle, still smiling.

"It was in the Beacon."

"And was the reporter for the Beacon anywhere about Front Royal during the battle, or is this more rumor and supposition?" Belle asked sarcastically.

"He was at Strasburg," said a third reporter.

"So, the answer is no."

Belle smiled, while trying to keep her temper in check. "Don't you see how ridiculous that is? I'm just a girl. What would I know about artillery?"

"But you espouse the Rebel cause," the first reporter said.

"Yes, of course," Belle replied patiently. "You Yankees have invaded us, seeking to keep us in what the South views as a very bad marriage. Rather than grant us a civil divorce, you seek to batter us into submission."

All of the reporters shifted uncomfortably at this analogy. Belle smiled more widely, and then tried to charm them with sarcasm. "One of your papers credits me with sustaining our generals when they waiver in their councils. As if men like Jackson, Ewell, and Taylor need advice from the likes of me! Another has me, sword in hand, leading the charge on Front Royal last week. Excuse me, you honorable gentlemen of the press, but where do you find such trash? This is all lies — pure sensationalism invented to sell your newspapers to a gullible public."

"You wear a pistol in your belt sometimes," the fat reporter said mildly. "That evinces a martial spirit."

"That," Belle said, "Evinces the sad fact that many Yankee

soldiers are thieves, housebreakers and worse, and that we have no men here to protect us from their depredations. My cousin and grandmother have no skill at arms, nor do our servant girls. Your Provost Marshals would spend their time better if they controlled your men and prevented their drunken antics against innocent civilians rather than harassing us over trifles."

A reporter who had not spoken before said, "Is it true that you are personally acquainted with General Ashby?"

Belle blinked. "You mean Colonel Ashby, of the Seventh Virginia?"

"No," the reporter said. "He's now a Brigadier and reputed to have charge of the Second and Sixth Virginia as well."

"That's news to me," said Belle drily. All of the reporters laughed. "I've known Henry Ashby all my life. We are both from Martinsburg. There are very few men serving in those units whom I do not know personally. My own dear father served as a paymaster."

The reporters scribbled in their notebooks and looked at her, waiting for more.

"You see how ridiculous these stories are?" Belle asked. "And now one of you has, with considerable malice, put me, my cousin and our business in a false light that is very hurtful to our reputations."

"You are said to be very friendly with Union officers," the first reporter observed, speaking in a flat voice that invited her anger. Instead of exploding at him, Belle took a deep breath.

"How should I be? I am a Southern lady, first and foremost. I was brought up to be polite and friendly to everyone. We have a word for this that you Yankees seem unfamiliar with."

"What is that? " asked the first reporter, rising like a trout to the bait.

"Manners," said Belle. The man flushed red as his colleagues laughed at his embarrassment.

"I asked General Shields to make sure that I would be able to refute these absurd lies that are being told about me," said Belle,

"And I thank you for your time, but I will not pretend that I am not a proud Southern woman devoted to the Confederate cause."

"One last question," said the fat, untidy reporter. "Do you deny that you ran out, under fire, to warn Jackson last week?"

Belle smiled at him as if he were mentally defective. "Really, sir. Do I look like I could do something like that? I'm just a girl." She bowed and went out the door to the front lobby, leaving them there.

No one noticed Eliza had stayed behind and was now collecting their glasses and coffee cups, listening so that she could tell Belle later what was said.

"What do you think?" the first reporter asked his older colleague.

The fat reporter shrugged, "Beats me. A woman like that can do as she pleases. Not a great beauty, but such verve, such charm."

"Such a fine figure of a woman," the first said with a grin.

"Think her a whore as Clark said?"

The first reporter sucked at his teeth thoughtfully. "Naw. Clark never pays, cheap bastard that he is. He wouldn't know, and Shields got Banks to bar him from the whole campaign over that story."

"You know that for a fact?"

"No. It's another rumor. But he ain't here, is he?"

"Probably afraid he'd be shot by Miss Belle."

"She did kill a man in Martinsburg last year, and that is a fact," said another reporter who had been listening to them.

The reporters looked at one another, silent for a moment. Then, without another word, they went their separate ways to write up their stories.

Myles Keogh stood in the back of the room, taking notes for Shields as Belle spoke to the reporters. He delivered his report and then went to find Daniel Keily.

"You've got to give her up, lad," were the first words he said after he found Keily in his room.

Keily looked up from the scouting reports he was studying. "Who? Miss Belle?"

"You should have seen her, Dan. Cool as a cucumber. Butter wouldn't melt in her mouth. Didn't admit to any of it."

"Aye, I'd expect no less."

"Are ye daft, then? She's used you."

Keily shook his head slowly. "There's no proof against her. Mister Clark was annoying her and Alice both. You know that."

"I know that she's had you."

"But all we did was fuck," said Keily reasonably, "And I was her first."

"Augh! You're not falling for that old game, are ye?"

Keily started to become angry. "She's a good girl!"

Myles Keogh looked at his friend with pity. "She'll ruin you, Dan. She's the enemy."

"Perhaps not. Perhaps I'll conquer her."

Keogh's mouth fell open. "Say you were her first," he said after a moment. "You can't be thinking...."

"That I'd make an honest woman of her? I rather thought I might." Keily looked perfectly calm and rational as he said this.

Myles poured himself a drink, tossed it off, and then said, as reasonably as he could, "She's not even a Catholic."

"She can take instruction. I spoke to Father Doyle about it."

"Her family and all of her friends are Confederate to the core."

"Not all. Captain Strother is a close friend and some sort of cousin to her."

"You're right. Confusing war, this, but it doesn't matter. You see how Strother is hated by his own now. Do you, for a moment, believe that she'd marry a Yankee officer?"

"After Mister Clark's savage attack on her character, do you think any Confederate officer will marry her?" asked Keily with a charming smile.

Keogh stared at him. "Tactics, is it? Did you have anything to do with that article?"

"I might have said a word or two about how we were together. I've never had better." Keily smiled slyly.

Keogh was disgusted. "So you've ruined her and now you're going to make a complete bollocks of it by ruining yourself as well? You're quite mad, you know."

Keily leaned forward, placed a hand on his arm and said, "If you breathe a word of this to anyone, I'll cut your heart out, old friend. I aim to win her. This war will be over soon enough, the North will win, and she will need a man to stand by her."

Keogh just stared at him. "You've lost your bloody mind, Dan Keily, but I'll not say a word, for who would believe it?"

Keily relaxed and sat back, grinning. "Well, you've got part of the truth there. I'm mad for her. I've never known such a girl. She's no great beauty, it's true, but she's strong and agile, and has wit and style." He smirked. "And then there's the other," he said with a wink.

Keogh just shook his head, said nothing else, and went to get drunk.

That night Belle sneaked into Keily's room, unobserved by the sentry in the hall. That worthy was distracted by Eliza and Martha's request to help them put Myles Keogh to bed in his room on the floor below. The Irish captain was dead drunk and combative, singing loudly in bad Italian.

Keily and Belle made love feverishly, quickly, and then snuggled tenderly, their hands exploring each other's bodies for a long time. Belle was shocked at how her body had shook when he put his long cock in her. "My God, you're deep," she whispered, wrapping her long legs around his waist to draw him further in.

"You've never felt that before?" asked Keily.

"You're my first and only, darling, despite what you might read in the newspapers," Belle said mockingly and bit him hard on the shoulder. He thrust into her again, making her gasp.

"You like it?"

"Very much."

"I can go deeper still," he said softly.

"How?"

"I'll ride you like a stallion," he whispered.

"What do you mean?" Belle said.

He withdrew, causing her to groan. "Turn over," he said, "And get on your knees."

Belle was momentarily confused and doubtful.

"Like a mare?" she asked, suddenly grasping his meaning.

"To my stallion, yes," he answered.

Belle did as he asked, feeling exposed, ridiculous and very vulnerable. His body covered her as his hands squeezed her large breasts, kneading them, so that she groaned loudly with pleasure.

"Quiet," he urged her with a harsh whisper, as the head of his erect cock, slid into her slowly and probed so deep that she bit her lip to keep from screaming aloud. Her body shook again.

Still he was not done. He began to slide in and out of her, first slowly, and then quickly, varying the pace between a slow walk, a cantor and a gallop. Her body shook a third time and then a fourth, and after that she lost count. Her head rested on her arms and her nipples brushed the wrinkled sheets, sending fresh waves of sensation through her. "I never...," she gasped.

She had once had a dream like this about Dick Ashby, but this was no dream, and he was doing things to her that she had never imagined. Finally he shot into her like a fountain and collapsed on top of her, sliding out as she slowly sank into the mattress.

"Oh, Daniel," she sighed. She felt wonderfully sore and well-used, and warm and protected. She curled up in his arms, completely happy for the first time in months. All tension was gone from her body. She slept deeply beside him.

The first crack of dawn awakened her to reality. She cleaned herself with a small towel of his, dressed hurriedly and slipped out into the hallway. The sentry was back, but half asleep and barely saw her as she slipped, bare-footed down the stairs, her boots in one hand.

It was not until she had pulled on her boots, sitting in the kitchen and drinking the special tea that Eliza had set out for her, that she realized that he, as she was distracted by passion, had mentioned marriage. By playing stallion to her mare he had been trying to breed her, to get her pregnant.

That frightened her. "That will never do," she said to herself, and wondered what to do next.

CHAPTER THIRTY-FIVE

June 3, 1862, Front Royal, Virginia

From the hotel balcony, Belle could see Lucy Buck and her family returning, in a farm wagon, from where they had fled to a few days before. Making the Yankees welcome had bought them no safety and some hazard.

For a few days they feared their family estate would become the center of intense combat. Rumors of a Confederate counterattack ran rampant through the Union Camp. No one bothered to inform Mr. Buck or his family exactly what was happening — if, indeed, anyone knew. Artillery fire was much in evidence, although none landed close to the Buck house. Volleys of musket fire crackled through the air as entire regiments discharged their weapons to clear them preparatory to forming up and marching out to meet the Confederate forces. Finding discretion to be the better part of valor, Mr. Buck loaded up his family and skedaddled.

Belle had a quiet appreciation for the irony of the situation. That the Bucks had been so inconvenienced was their own fault. They had two sons on Beauregard's staff. Despite that, Mr. Buck sought to make up the losses imposed upon him by the Union troops that had ruined the place, and rented parts of his large, rambling house to Union generals and their staffs.

Lucy, as the lady of the house, learned to make herself agreeable to these unwanted guests, and had actually been seen in lively conversation with some of the younger Union officers.

Yet, she was regarded as a paragon of virtue by her neighbors while Belle was the object of scorn, despite her heroic dash to report to Jackson ten days before.

This was very unfair, Belle decided, although she conceded Lucy the home town advantage of having been born and raised in Front Royal and having many more friends than she and Alice enjoyed. She sipped her cup of coffee and looked sideways at the sentry in the doorway. She was having an hour of solitude, but was hardly idle. The hotel daily accounts rested on the wicker table beside her, as did her opera glasses. Half-sheets of foolscap were also handy, on which Belle added columns of numbers from the hotel accounts.

From time to time, in full view of the sleepy, bored sentry, Belle would pick up the opera glasses, look at something in the street, remark upon it gaily, and then write something down. What she said and what she wrote were two entirely different things.

The opera glasses allowed her to read the regimental flags as the Union troops marched through town, and to more accurately count the large number of wagons, ambulances and artillery pieces that followed them.

The sentry was a dull fellow who could not read, and had no wit or conversation. He jumped every time Belle spoke to him, having been warned how dangerous she was. Belle tried to charm him, but quickly gave it up as a bad job.

Jackson was now back down the Valley, headed for Cross Keys. The Union forces, smarting from their humiliation the previous week, followed.

Too cautiously, Belle thought, *but, Lord, there were so many of them!* Belle was stuck, not even allowed to leave the hotel, but that didn't mean that she couldn't do good work.

While Alice was also closely watched and suspected, Eliza was invisible. None of the Union officers realized that she was Belle's servant, and talked freely in front of her. Even Michael Kelley did not make the connection, despite the number of times he had visited her home in Martinsburg.

Union officers who were fervent Abolitionists said things in front of Negro servants that they would never have in front of any white person from the town. They had a sentimental regard for the Negro slave that was not returned, nor could it be. Black or white was not their concern — their first loyalty was to family.

"Dey don' see us'n," Eliza said when Belle queried her on the matter. "We all de same to dem. Buckras, dey know ebbryone, dey always lookin' out fer us, suspicious. Yankees, dey nebber look, no more dan if we be a horse er a dog."

Eliza had the ability of being able to repeat, word for word, several hours later, conversations she heard. She was learning what was important to listen to. With her help, under restrictions she had never suffered before, Belle was still able to spy on the Union Army staff.

She wished that she had someone within the Buck household, but Lucy she regarded as both a fool and a hypocrite. She and all her crowd.

Belle was more sympathetic to Mr. Buck's position. He was simply trying to survive an on-going catastrophe. Not that he lacked shrewdness. The last time he had come to her with a wad of Yankee dollars to exchange, he had asked for a discount.

Belle had been very surprised, "Why?"

"The Confederate dollar does not buy what it did," he replied.

Belle frowned, "There is a war on, sir. The deal is one to one. If you do not like it then I suggest you change these bills elsewhere, or simply buy what you need from your Yankee tenants."

Buck looked at her oddly. "Is that what you do?"

Belle saw the trap, and said nothing. If she said anything at all, she would be criticized, and the last thing she could say to him was that she used the money for secret service. For all she knew, he was getting some of these Yankee dollars by informing to them. He had been called in to smooth over problems in the town for them several times. Belle wondered what Lucy Buck would say if this collaboration were brought to her attention.

Belle would not do it, nor would she let Alice or anyone else point out the inconsistency in Mister Buck's actions. Like herself, and everyone else under Yankee occupation, he was simply doing what he must to survive.

Belle's money changing was simply a sideline to her real task, and that was going all too well. Her problem now was that there was no way to get the information out. Jackson had retreated beyond easy range. The positions between the contending armies were so fluid that she dare not use any of the secret mailboxes in the countryside, even if she could get to them.

And she had another problem. Daniel Keily continued to pay court to her in a most aggressive manner. The continued presentation of flowers and bad poetry put a nice gloss on the fact that they were fucking like rabbits every time they could steal an hour alone, sometimes with all their clothes still on. Belle knew she should be more discreet, but found, in his arms, a release from the constant tension that set her jaw to clench so hard as she slept. The artifice, the too bright manner she used to engage the Yankees in conversation made her feel very much like an actor on some deadly stage. One where the audience would reward a bad performance with a bullet rather than rotten eggs.

Fortunately, Keily was a responsible officer who put his duty first, so there were not too many such occasions. Belle, if anything, flirted even more outrageously with the other Union officers, but the situation was unnerving.

One way to get her information out was to simply get a pass through the lines. When General Banks came back, with his staff, she applied to him for one. He was still the highest ranking commander on the Union side except McClellan. A pass from him would carry her a long way.

The problem was, he knew it.

"Where would you go?" he asked. His manner was kindly, but while he was more politician than general, he was far from stupid.

"Why, to Louisiana, where my aunt resides," Belle replied, trying to flirt a bit. She had no aunt there, but Banks could hardly know that.

Banks grunted, frowned, as if he suspected that she would make a bee-line for Richmond instead, and then answered with his own considerable charm.

"But what would Virginia do without you?"

Belle blinked, still smiling. "What do you mean, General?"

"We always miss our bravest and most illustrious. How can your native state do without you?"

Belle laughed. "You are too kind, General."

He gave her a becoming smile. "I read the newspapers, too, Miss Belle, and while most of it is trash, you've never made a secret of your true affections. You do not love us, except perhaps one."

Belle actually blushed. "Sir...," she began.

"I do not believe everything I read, Miss Belle. I spent too many years in Congress for that. If I did, I would be quite upset with you for giving me a nickname which I'm not likely to live down."

"What is that?"

"'Commissary' Banks." Nathaniel Banks looked at her steadily, smiling all the while. "But, then I would be forced to believe all those other remarkable things written about you, Miss Belle, and then I would have to face the undeniable fact that I was taken in by a girl younger than my daughters. I would have to act upon that, and sacrifice a very able staff officer who is all too fond of you."

Keep smiling, Belle commanded herself. "Oh, sir!" she said, managing an idiotic giggle.

Banks seemed genuinely amused by his predicament. "That would not serve me. I prefer to think that Mister Jackson played a mean trick on me. He deceived me and did not present himself in a professional manner. So my officers with European experience assure me. There are rules to the game which were not observed, or so they say." His tone was ironic and his smile, if anything, wider, showing his large white teeth. He chuckled. "I can bear the current bad weather, Miss Belle. Like all political storms, it will blow over. The pursuit of Jackson and his cronies is now up to General Fremont."

Belle tilted her head, trying to size him up. *Is all this a game to him?*

"You do believe in the Union?"

Banks nodded slowly. "With all my heart. Like your cousin, Captain Strother, I believe that a terrible fraud has been perpetrated upon the people of the South by a few selfish men who seek to protect and preserve nothing more than their own fortunes. I believe that the rebellion must be put down and the rule of law restored. I do not believe that, to save the Constitution, we must first destroy it, and, if I were still in Congress, I would be very vocal about this. There are those in Washington who already seek your arrest, based upon those newspaper stories. But that is not proof. Not under any law I know."

Banks pulled out his watch from a vest pocket, snapped open the elaborately engraved cover and looked at the time. "I have a staff meeting shortly," he said. "I am always happy for your company, Miss Belle, because you are so agreeable and charming."

Belle bowed her head slightly, with a flirtatious, charming smile. "Sir."

"Your request for a pass is regretfully denied."

Belle took it with good grace. She walked out of the sitting room Banks had taken for his private office, nodded to the sentry who was detailed to follow her and went back to work.

CHAPTER THIRTY-SIX

June 3rd to 6th 1862, Northern Virginia

In Martinsburg, David Strother gathered information for a general who no longer entirely trusted him. Rumors about atrocities committed against citizens by Confederate troops in the town the week before had been published in the newspapers.

Talking to some of the same ladies who had stuffed his saddlebags with food and drink ten days before, he quickly found it was not so.

"No," said one who was a longtime friend of his father, and whom he regarded almost as a favorite aunt, "They were fairly well behaved. They took sugar and salt and coffee, especially that last, but only from stores, and they left worthless pieces of paper in payment."

"Better than nothing," Strother said with a rueful grin.

She looked at him severely. "It is the thought that counts, David." She poured him another cup of tea. "You know Mister Macklin, at the edge of town?"

"Yes, I remember him well."

"Well, he was a firm Union man. Then some boys from one of the Pennsylvania regiments came, took all of his eggs, and chased down and slaughtered most of his chickens and his two remaining pigs. They destroyed in an afternoon what he spent years building, and for what? So they wouldn't have to eat hardtack and beans that night."

Strother dismayed, murmured, "I see."

"Macklin no longer favors the Union. He isn't for the Rebels either, you understand, but simply wishes that both sides would go to...ah...the devil as quickly as possible." She stared accusingly at Strother. "You officers must control your men better. I give the Rebels that much. They don't steal, and they don't break into people's houses."

It was not the first instance Strother had heard of where Union troops robbed and pillaged. The day before, in Strasburg, he had watched as Union troops devastated a store on the main street.

He had called to the Captain in charge of the party. "What are you looking for?"

The Captain, quite a young man, looked at him in annoyance until he saw the General Staff badge he wore. "Weapons and ammunition. We don't want another ambush like we had in Winchester," he replied, self-righteously.

"And this gives your men the right to remove all the tobacco?" Strother asked sarcastically.

The young Captain had the grace to look embarrassed, but made no attempt to restore the merchant's goods to his premises. Further on, Strother saw another squad of men emerge from a house, carrying, among other things, several fine lace petticoats.

With a weary heart he went on to Winchester to find his friend, Thorton Brodhead, and to complain, "This looting must stop. It is costing us the few friends we have here."

Brodhead shrugged. "The Rebels are worse."

Strother grimaced. "You, of all people, should know not to believe what you read in the newspapers. The Rebels took supplies, but at least offered payment."

"In a devalued and worthless currency," Brodhead sneered. "They certainly show no hesitation about robbing our supplies and our sutlers when the opportunity arises."

"A legitimate tactic of war," Strother replied. "They are hard pressed. Even so, they do not annoy nor molest the local population."

"The local population seems to be another Rebel regiment, given what happened in Winchester on the 25th," Brodhead said angrily.

"I was there," Strother reminded him, "And count myself lucky to have escaped with my life."

"There have been arrests," Brodhead said after a moment.

"Oh?" Strother asked, "Who?"

"One was a twelve-year-old boy and the other a Methodist minister, about sixty years old."

"That is all?" Strother was incredulous.

Brodhead looked at him curiously. "What's the problem?"

"We received fire from every house. From many more than two shooters."

" Could the Rebel infantry have gotten so far ahead of us?" Brodhead asked, "It doesn't strike me as likely."

Strother nodded grimly. "You are correct. I am sure of it."

"Who were they, then?"

"Who else?" Strother said. "The women and children. Most of the wounds were from pistols, not muskets or rifles. A woman can fire a pistol without much difficulty and very little training, and so can children as young as eight. I think the mystery of so many missing sidearms is solved."

"What do we do now?" asked Brodhead, frowning as he looked at the rain-soaked street already ankle deep with mud.

"Short of burning the town," Strother said, "I don't know." He looked to where detritus discarded during the Union retreat still littered the main street.

"This was a sorry business," Strother declared. "The worst defeat inflicted on our army in its history, and I am thoroughly ashamed to have been mixed up in it."

"Don't take it so hard," Brodhead advised him. "Sir Percy and his less-than-merry men were through here yesterday, transferred to Fremont's division. A company of the Fourth New York went with them."

Strother tugged at his beard absently. "What of it?"

"He's still determined to trap your friend Ashby," Brodhead replied, lifting an eyebrow.

Strother looked away for a moment, and then turned his gaze directly upon Brodhead. "He is my friend, you know," he said sadly. "We've known each other since childhood, and we are Masonic brothers. He's a man of limited intelligence — more ruled by passion than intellect. Like most Southern gentlemen, he is prone to act first rather than hold back and think a matter through. He is fighting for his homeland. What is Sir Percy fighting for?"

Brodhead thought a moment. "His professional standing?"

"Now that's a cold thing, isn't it?"

"Perhaps," Brodhead agreed, "But Sir Percy is a cold kind of fellow. Icewater in his veins. He drills his men under fire."

"What do you mean?"

"There was an action where his regiment failed to execute the wheeling turn to his satisfaction. He had them repeat it until they got it right, as Minnie balls were hitting all around them."

Strother gaped at him a moment. "How did his men take it?"

"Oh," grinned Brodhead. "They love him all the more when he does some fool thing like that. He has them convinced that strict discipline is the way they will win battles — and so far he's not been wrong. Part of it is his undeniable style. He looks the way people think a soldier should look."

"I'll bet on Ashby," Strother said thoughtfully. "For all the reasons mentioned above. Ashby isn't pretty, nor is he my idea of a military genius, but then, neither is Sir Percy."

"How much?" Brodhead replied with a grin.

"Five dollars."

"Done."

Brigadier General Turner Ashby looked back towards Harrisonburg and then up the road to where the Union forces were advancing.

Harry Gilmour, whose company was closest, rode up and said loudly, "It's him."

Ashby permitted himself a brief smile. "What do the scouts say?"

"First New Jersey and one company of the Fourth New York. They're riding as if they were on parade. Colonel Wyndham and two of his company commanders lead the advance."

"They're sure it's him?"

Gilmour laughed. "You can't miss him, General. Those

mustaches of his flutter in the wind as he rides."

General. The word was sweet in Ashby's ears. He had strived for it, politicked for it, mostly for pride's sake. But, for the first time since John Brown's raid at Harper's Ferry, he felt unsure. Providing a rear guard for Jackson's retreat was easy enough. The presence of Colonel Sir Percy Wyndham was another matter. It offended him.

"Harry," Ashby said slowly, "This man has bragged for months about the superiority of his methods to mine. General Jackson has ordered me, quite directly, not to challenge him to combat without regard to my higher duty to the Army."

Gilmour looked at him oddly. "Yes, sir, but *he's* pursuing *you*, and has been quite disparaging about our tactics."

"Any word from Miss Belle about what is coming down the road behind First New Jersey?"

"None, sir. She's quite cut off." Harry Gilmour shrugged, "I'm not sure that camp gossip would be that useful."

"Intelligence, sir, intelligence," Ashby consulted the map he held across his lap. "This defile here."

Gilmour leaned over and looked, "Yes, sir?"

"A logical place for us to camp. What is it like?"

"Heavily wooded. At least next to the road. Nice camping spot about four rods in, a little meadow with good fresh grass for the mounts."

"We'll make camp there tonight. Send word to Colonel Funston. How would we also let Colonel Wyndham in on the 'secret'?"

Gilmour smiled, "I can always find one of the boys who's willing to defect to the Union lines. Some private who'll get paroled in a few days."

Ashby favored him with a gentle smile. "Make sure he tells them the truth about where we plan to camp. Then take your company off a ways and make sure that the scouts that Colonel Wyndham sends get back to their own lines okay."

Gilmour looked at him, amused. "You have something in

mind?"

Ashby shrugged. "I will keep my own counsel, Captain. I've learned something from our master, General Jackson. I need you to scout and make sure that Colonel Wyndham does not have another regiment operating independently that might flank us."

Gilmour pursed his lips. "I wouldn't have thought of that," he confessed. "I guess that's the difference between generals and the rest of us."

Turner Ashby nodded. Inwardly he glowed at the compliment. Outwardly, he simply looked at the map again. He was south of where he had operated before and did not know the ground. He did know that Percy Wyndham was fond of charging with his entire regiment, much like the doomed brigade in Alfred Tennyson's poem. Perhaps he could use that against him. Perhaps he could think like a general, despite Stonewall Jackson's open doubts on the matter.

Jackson's lecture to him after the debacle of his men deserting almost en masse to take Union horses as prizes of war embarrassed and enraged them both.

Only the Reverend Major Dabney was present, and that man was not given to gossip, something for which Ashby was thankful.

"If I had my way," Jackson growled, even before he could salute, "I would have you shot. It would save a great deal of trouble."

Ashby froze. Jackson, not raising his voice, continued, "You are perhaps the worst officer who has ever been imposed upon me or any other commander in this army."

Ashby bridled. "If that is the way you feel, name your seconds and we'll have an end!"

Reverend Major Dabney cleared his throat. "You're not helping your case here, Colonel, with such talk. Dueling is forbidden by regulation, and even a challenge to a duel adds to the many charges likely to be lodged against you."

Ashby recalled that Jackson had a habit of arresting and charging subordinate officers who displeased him. His very career was at risk. He kept silent for once, as Jackson rose from his chair and advanced.

"Stand to attention!" he said and Ashby reluctantly did so. Jackson then used his hands to correct Ashby's posture. Ashby flushed with humiliation.

"I despise amateur officers and so called partisans," Jackson said quietly, "But I have no choice. I must use the materials the Lord has provided me. You managed to get your most able cavalry commanders killed with a too hasty flanking maneuver last week. We send scouts in the advance just to prevent such things. I cannot replace you, given that you have so many friends in Richmond, friends who do not heed my counsel that you not be made a Brigadier, because you are simply not fit. Over my strong objections you are to become one."

Ashby was taken aback, but then said, "I must have done something right all these months."

"Much more luck than skill," Jackson replied, seething, "Like all your ilk, you are selfish and have little regard for our strategy or the overall campaign. You seek glory. But glory and victory over the foe are two different things entirely."

Ashby said in a hurt voice, "Selfish? I have sacrificed everything and stand ready to give up life itself for the Cause."

"Yet, you let General Banks remove his army, rather than destroy it. You failed to impose sufficient discipline on your men to prevent the theft of horses we need here to remove all these Yankee supplies. Your men are bandits, plain and simple. Selfish, without regard for the greater good."

Ashby turned pale. "Some of those horses were ours to begin with, removed by Union quartermasters from our farms and plantations."

"But not all," said Dabney.

Ashby looked embarrassed. "No," he admitted. Horse thieves were normally hung, and the war was a poor excuse for what his men had done. Sutlers wagons had also been plundered with great glee.

"Every ton of supplies is another day this army can fight," Jackson said. "Every horse is another man we can mount or, multiplied by four, another artillery piece or wagon we can pull. But that is not the most serious offense."

Ashby simply waited for the blow to fall. Jackson stared at him for a very long time. "You have no idea, do you?"

When Ashby looked away, unable to answer, Jackson continued, "If we had totally destroyed the Union force, it could not have been easily replaced and they would have had to shift their other divisions to protect Washington. It would have kept them away from this valley for a year or more, maybe forever. It would have relieved the pressure on Richmond. Wars are won or lost by such actions. Now they will reform, resupply, reinforce and come back on us with a vengeance."

Ashby muttered, "I'm sorry."

Jackson stared at him. "Yes , you are. But I am stuck with you and you with me. Against everything I hold dear as a soldier I am forced to accept your continued presence in my army. You have one chance to redeem yourself. One more such episode and I will have you arrested and court martialed and hung as a traitor."

Shaken, Ashby turned to go.

"I did not give you a dismissal, Colonel Ashby."

Ashby turned back. "Surely, there is not more?"

Jackson looked at him sourly. "I have your report from Warrentown Junction. A famous victory."

Ashby was puzzled. "It was."

"How little you understand this business," Jackson said, half amazed. "It was banditry pure and simple. You gave no warning and accepted no surrender, without orders and with no clear strategic advantage. For personal vengeance."

Ashby was unable to speak. He shook his head.

"My brother...," he began.

"Deserved better at your hands," Jackson said sharply.

"You've stained his memory with bloody cowardice. In the future your personal vengeance must be put aside. You can no longer lead charges of one regiment but must direct three. This is what being a general means, Ashby. You bear a heavy responsibility now, to use the lives entrusted to you wisely and to not be spendthrift with them against the Yankees. They have many more men than we do. We must husband those we have, or we will lose this war."

Ashby went down on his knees to beg Jackson's forgiveness then, and it was reluctantly granted. But the interview seared his memory and made him uncharacteristically self conscious and unsure of himself. There was more to being a general than met the eye. He knew that now and it scared him.

The next morning, Colonel Sir Percy Wyndham rode proudly at the head of his regiment, his aides on either side of him and two of his company commanders within eyeshot. The road ahead was clear. It was not quite dawn.

"We will catch the Rebels napping," Wyndham assured his officers. He had questioned the defector from Ashby's cavalry himself quite closely, and sent scouts to confirm the information.

At last I've found you, old fox, Wyndham said to himself, feeling elated. *Capturing Ashby will be quite a feather in my cap. A general and brigade commander. Which is what I should be.*

He chaffed at both his own lack of advancement and the inability of Union generals, from McClellan on down, to grasp how this war should be fought. McClellan he now regarded as a coward, although he was careful not to say so aloud, or to disparage the man in any way. McClellan had, after all, gotten him his commission. Moreover, he was entitled to Wyndham's tolerance and protection because he, too, was a Freemason.

I am a soldier, he thought, *and the political situation here confounds me.*

As they neared the point in the road where Ashby was reported to be camped, gunshots rang out. Two of his troopers fell out of their saddles and onto the ground.

"Steady!" Wyndham drew his sword as he pulled hard at his horse's reins. To his gratification, the entire regiment stopped in good order.

"Where did that come from?" Wyndham asked one of his aides.

The young man, who was comely and blonde, looked at him, and looked around, confused. "From there...."

Another shot rang out and his aide's head exploded bloodily. Rage seized Wyndham. He stood in the saddle, looked at the woods to his right, saw a rough road where a company of Confederate cavalry was milling about, aimlessly, he thought, and said, "Bushwhackers. Ashby's camp is just beyond."

To the bugler he shouted, "Sound assembly, then sound the charge."

His other aide and his company commanders looked hesitant. "Come now," Wyndham shouted to them sarcastically, as the entire regiment wheeled to face the right side of the road, "Do you want to live forever? Show some spirit, First New Jersey, and follow me!"

He spurred his horse and was gratified those nearby followed, as he had trained them to do. The Confederate cavalry broke and ran, and he shouted, "After them!" The lead elements of the First New Jersey thundered behind him.

The pine woods were thick and slowed the advance on both flanks. Wyndham and his command group broke through into a clearing, but rather than a camp of sleeping Confederates, he found the meadow empty and brightly lit by the overhead sun. Arrayed before him were two regiments of Confederate cavalry, flags flying, swords drawn, carbines leveled.

"Reform!" Wyndham cried, and wheeled his horse around, to see only about seventy men still with him. The rest of the regiment had fallen back to the road. He saw the two company commanders, his remaining aide and several other officers; almost his entire staff but very few troopers.

Behind him another regiment of Rebels on horseback filed out of the woods on each flank, too many to fight.

With a sinking heart, he realized that he was cut off from most of his command. He had fallen into a trap. Wyndham found himself staring into the muzzle of a Colt Dragoon pistol held by a Confederate private on horseback. He stared at it a long moment.

"What is your name, fellow?" Wyndham said finally, his voice high and tight.

"Holmes Conrad, sir, at your service," said the Rebel private.

Wyndham reversed his sword and handed to him. "Well, Holmes Conrad, accept my surrender and my sword, for I will not use it to lead cowards such as these!"

Private Conrad, amused, holstered his pistol and took Wyndham's sword by its grip. "Your servant, sir."

Wyndham did a remarkable thing. He jumped down from his mount and began kicking violently at the dead pine cones and brush on the ground, apparently in the throes of a rather impressive tantrum. His aide, another blonde young man, jumped down and approached with a soothing word, at which point Wyndham turned furiously and slapped him as hard as he could with his open hand. Shocked, the young man turned away, holding his cheek and burst into tears.

From between the regiments assembled on the other end of the meadow came a single rider on a fine black horse. Silence fell, with only a few gunshots in the distance heard as everyone, a thousand men or more, seemed to hold their breaths.

Wyndham, aware of the sudden silence, managed to get control of himself. He watched curiously as the rider, a short, ill-favored man with a bushy black beard and a dark complexion, wearing a new uniform with general's stars, trotted the horse up to where Wyndham stood.

"Colonel Wyndham, I presume?"

Wyndham recovered himself enough to give a proper salute, which the man returned in a careless, almost casual manner.

"I have surrendered to Private Conrad," Wyndham said.

"And the rest?" the man asked mildly.

Wyndham nodded. "Yes, of course." He turned and called loudly, "All First New Jersey, here present, stand down! We are surrendered." Wyndham could not help but wince as he heard swords, pistols and carbines fall to the ground behind him. He turned back to the Confederate general. "May I know your name, sir?"

A wide grin split the man's beard. "You already do, Colonel. Turner Ashby at your service."

Wyndham was shocked. He said, surprised, "You are reputed to be much taller."

"And you were reputed to be the man who would take me," Ashby laughed. "But I have taken you."

Wyndham nodded, still inwardly furious, but his face under strict control. "And what lies ahead?"

"Would you like to meet General Jackson?" Ashby asked, almost merry.

"Very much so."

"Well, he wants to meet you. Mount your horse, Colonel. We're sending you up the line."

Wyndham walked over and swung easily into the saddle and then looked around at the men and officers who had been captured with him. Not one could meet his eye.

"Let's go then," he said, and spurred his horse gently forward.

CHAPTER THIRTY-SEVEN

June 6, 1862, Front Royal, Virginia

Belle looked carefully along the line of settings on the large table in the hotel's small dining room, making sure that everything was aligned just so, and that all of the silverware, glasses and plates matched each other as closely as possible. General Banks wanted a small dinner party for his senior commanders, a place where he and his subordinate generals could relax and talk openly while enjoying good food and drink.

The menu requested stretched the Fishback Hotel's immediate resources, and if it had not been for the profits from Belle's money-changing operations they would have been hard pressed to pull it off.

It was hard to say which was more outrageous: the prices charged by local merchants in Confederate dollars, or the prices charged by Union sutlers in Yankee currency. Fortunately, there was plenty of both on hand, and they were able to provide not just turkey, roast beef and ham, but a full selection of cooked vegetables, fresh fruit, cheese, and, most importantly, liquor and wine. For her own purposes, Belle wanted the Yankees well-lubricated.

Belle fingered the once-fine linen tablecloth and wished that a replacement could be found. This one was too obviously mended in too many places. The Bucks had some new ones, along with some sheets and pillow cases, that they were selling. The thought of asking Lucy Buck for anything galled her more than she could bear.

She and Alice had discussed it with their grandmother and the old lady had been firm. "Go to them and the whole town will hear of it," she said. "It will be said that we had to beg them for help. They are already charging us too much for butter and eggs. To hell with them!"

The unexpected profanity startled Alice and Belle, but the sentiment matched their own. They would make do.

Delicious odors wafted from the kitchen. Belle consulted her seating plan, making sure that precedence of rank would be properly observed. All of the big fish would be there — not just Banks, but

Geary, Kimball, Shields, and Fremont.

Fremont was a particular problem. A lesser general, but a former Presidential candidate and a heroic figure in his own right, because of the unique role he had played in opening the West. Belle finally placed him at the other end of the long table from Banks, facing each other. Did this make them equals or place Fremont below all the others? Belle wished that famous hostess Rose Greenhow were handy; she would know immediately what to do.

Belle had planned to place Eliza immediately behind Banks, so she could catch anything important that might be said to him by the others, but the Yankee general had surprised her by inviting her and Alice to be present. He read the surprise on her face with uncanny accuracy.

"You may safely presume that this is a social occasion rather than an official one, and that we will not, as the parlance goes, 'talk shop'." He smiled at her in a most genial way.

"So you feel safe to invite us, who are said by your newspapers to be enemy spies," Belle laughed, trying to find a way out of a situation that now appeared to be a trap.

Banks chuckled. "I never believe what I read in the newspapers. Please be there, Miss Belle." Phrased as a request, it had the force of an order.

"Of course," she murmured. When she told Alice of the invitation, Alice was equally taken aback.

"Why do we have to be there?" Alice asked, exasperated.

"To make them behave. If ladies are present, then they will be more circumspect," Belle said.

"It drives a further wedge between us and the people here," Alice complained. "If we consort with Yankee generals at a party, the gossip will never stop."

"Then you must tell Lucy Buck that we were commanded to appear; that we felt we had no choice. She's hardly in a position to criticize us, given that she has more general officers in residence than we do."

Belle smiled a bright, false smile and fluttered her eyelids. It would have fooled a Yankee. Alice just laughed out loud.

"We have another girl in the party," Belle added.

"Who?" Alice asked, slightly amazed. "Who would be so bold?"

"Missus Annie Jones will be joining us."

Alice frowned. Annie Jones was a pretty Massachusetts girl of 17, who had come to them for help when the Union forces had retreated. Her tale was a sad one. She was married, she said, to one of the Michigan boys in Hasbrouke Reeve's cavalry company, and had been left behind in the hasty retreat.

Saying that, as Belle and Hasbrouke were such great friends, she begged Belle to help her, since she was alone and abandoned in a strange town. Belle and Alice had welcomed her as an act of charity, given her food, shelter and clothing, and allowed her to help them a little in the hotel. When the Union forces came marching back in, Annie Jones had gone right to Kimball and denounced them as dangerous Rebels.

She quickly bid them adieu and moved to Bel Air, where she was given a room paid for, not by her husband, whom she said had been killed in the retreat, but General Kimball. Was this kindness, or had Annie Jones found comfort in Kimball's arms?

Alice said, "We should cut her dead."

"This is not school," Belle replied. "The woman is an obvious snake in the grass. Nevertheless, we shall make her welcome. We shall be diplomats."

"You'll change your mind if she makes a play for Daniel Keily," Alice said sourly.

"Oh, I'll claw her eyes out," Belle agreed. "But I very much doubt she will. Annie obviously sees her future above mere Captains. She won't look twice at anyone of lesser rank."

Alice was shocked. "Even for her, that's a harsh thing to say, Belle. You make her out to be no better than a common whore."

"Generals do not sleep with common whores, Alice. I'd say

she has a way about her that far surpasses such base considerations."

"I don't like being forced to endure her company," Alice complained.

"But endure it we must," Belle said. "Have a little sympathy for her, too. General Kimball as a lover is a cross not easily borne, I suspect. Her path is not an easy one."

Alice shuddered. "He's an old goat. What can she be thinking?"

"What everyone is thinking, in one way or another," Belle replied sadly. "How to survive all this."

So Belle and Alice greeted Annie Jones as a long-lost sister, and she responded to this false kindness with good humor and better manners than they expected. She was careful not to gloat or to be too obviously General Kimball's companion. Indeed, her bright blue eyes seemed aimed towards fresh conquests. As her short marriage proved, men, even generals, get killed in war time.

The conversations between the Union generals were fascinating, but devoid of any real intelligence value. Most of the conversation seemed to be about the new Transcontinental Railroad and the telegraph line that was being built alongside of it.

"Sell your shares in the Pony Express now," General Geary advised. "Once they hook that line up, the need for it will disappear."

"Seven minutes to send a letter rather than seven days," General Kimball agreed. "But buy shares in that railway. It will do much good and the profits will be enormous."

General Banks nodded. "It will change everything."

Geary said, "It already has, sir, especially in how we fight a war."

"What do you mean?" Banks asked.

General Fremont spoke now, and everyone listened carefully because he was famed as 'Pathfinder', the great explorer who had scouted the West and who had stolen California from Mexico. "When we were in Mexico fifteen years ago, there were no railroads and no telegraphs. Everything went by wagon over very bad roads or no roads at all. Couriers had to be sent in threes, each by a separate route, to make sure that orders would get through, and there was a point beyond which it was useless to send anyone because the situation would change before the orders were received."

"Yes," General Geary added, "With the telegraph and the railway we can compress time and distance."

"Yes," agreed General Banks, "Pity we don't have them everywhere."

"Well, as we campaign on, it will become easier," Fremont said.

"Why do you say that?" Banks asked, looking at him shrewdly.

"The South has very good interior lines. Especially with railways that allow them to move men, horses and supplies quickly from one part of their perimeter to the other. It gives them defensive superiority, but, once we breach their rails and roads, we will turn that to our advantage." Fremont said this in a self-satisfied way that gave everyone pause.

Silence settled over the room as glasses were refilled. The men in the room were all reaching that golden state of half-drunkenness where great plans are proposed and quickly forgotten.

Fremont became careless enough to mention how spread out his division was and how the bad roads and the mud hindered quick communication, but a sharp look from Geary and a nod Belle's way were enough to turn the conversation back to their shared experiences a decade before in California.

The evening was a revelation to Belle, who quickly appreciated that this was the way that powerful men routinely dealt with each other. The comments about the railways and telegraph were equally fascinating, because during her short life, these things had always been. She had not realized how new and novel they were, and had accepted them as everyday commonplaces.

Sitting next to General Banks, she noticed that he regarded

Fremont with thinly veiled contempt. Was this political enmity, or something to do with Fremont's difficulties controlling his division? Fremont's comments about the difficulties of the Mexican campaigns were mirrored by his current situation. His division was spread over a wide mountain range with very poor roads and no telegraphs or railways to speed his orders or maneuvers.

"General Fremont," Banks said at last, "I'm only an armchair general, but I question your thesis." Uneasy laughter rippled across the room and Fremont, drawing himself up, prepared to be offended.

"It seems to me," Banks continued mildly, "That as the Rebel commanders are beaten back, that they will burn bridges and tear up rails, and do whatever else is necessary to deny us the use of their railways and telegraphs."

Fremont smiled and relaxed. "Precisely. But they will be hard-put to replace them. Already they are cannibalizing what they have, pulling up rails in one place to use them in another."

"And how can you know that?" General Shields asked irritably.

"I have very good scouts," Fremont replied.

"Ah, yes, the famous Jessie Scouts," Geary said sarcastically; "And do they report such a thing happening?"

"Indeed they do," Fremont smiled condescendingly. "In two places, with Negro labor. Nor is it hard to say why this is being done. Steel rails require special manufacturing facilities of which the South has none. Come to that, they have very little in the way of making steel itself. They are also short of horseshoes."

"Really?" Geary looked at him with real interest now. Unshod horses were of little use for cavalry or hauling artillery or supplies. Shields and Kimball looked at one another and nodded, impressed.

"This is a war of resources, gentlemen," Fremont said. "The South is running a very good bluff, but in the end we will overcome them because we have more men and material."

Banks frowned. "So we are spending millions to free a people who may not want freedom and who are ill-prepared to handle its consequences, and destroying this beautiful country in the bargain. It seems like a great waste."

Fremont relaxed into the easy posture of a man who has had just enough whisky, and leaned forward towards Banks. "You may recall that I was called a rabid Abolitionist in Missouri for proclaiming the slaves free."

Banks smiled at him. "It was a foolish, impolitic thing to do, sir, if you will pardon my candor. You almost sent the entire state over to the enemy side."

"I'm not a politician," said Fremont.

"Which is why you ran for President as a Republican," said Banks, causing the other men at the table to laugh outright.

Fremont smiled tolerantly and continued.

"It was a legitimate act of war."

"What do you mean?"

"My scouts report one thing that has caught my attention. The Rebels have not much armed their slaves to fight us, but they use them quite extensively to build fortifications, run the railroads, as teamsters and boatmen, and as nurses in their hospitals. Every third face on the other side is a black one."

Fremont tapped his finger on the side of his head. "Resources, gentlemen. If the slaves are proclaimed free, at least some of them will run off and the Rebels' ability to resist us will consequently be diminished."

The other generals looked at him silently, amazed by this revelation. Belle wondered how they would run the hotel if all of their servants ran away to the North. The thought chilled her. Obviously, they would be forced to close.

Kimball slammed his hand on the table and glared at Fremont. "With all due respect to my learned friend," he said angrily, "We cannot fight the war this way. We must overcome the Rebels in open combat. Our honor demands it! Despite our overwhelming numbers and supply, we are being outmaneuvered and outgeneraled at every turn. Just today, we have a dispatch that

Colonel Wyndham, advertised to us as a paragon of military wisdom and leadership, has been captured by Ashby."

Everyone started talking at once. Banks motioned for silence.

"This is rather important news! Why didn't you say anything earlier?" Banks asked mildly.

"I didn't want to spoil the party," Kimball confessed.

"Wasn't Wyndham under your command?" Banks asked Fremont pointedly.

Fremont frowned. "Colonel Wyndham seems to be operating on his own authority, under McClellan. He rushed in rather impetuously to capture Ashby and fell into a trap. Fortunately, most of his command lagged behind and escaped."

Geary laughed until tears came to his eyes. The others joined in, except Banks who smiled at them indulgently.

"So much for the superiority of European methods," he said drily.

"A toast to General Ashby," said Geary, "For putting that pretentious fop in his place."

All the men raised their glasses, and Belle, whose own glass held only well water, was bold enough to join in.

"It's no sin to acknowledge a worthy adversary," Geary said cheerfully.

"Yes, poor Ashby," Fremont said sadly.

Everyone paused in mid-toast and stared at him.

"What do you mean?" Banks asked.

"Oh, he was killed later. I had a report just before supper."

Everyone began talking at once. Belle and Alice stared at him, unable to believe what they'd heard.

Fremont held up his hand and everyone fell silent. "Ashby's brigade was too powerful for First New Jersey, which was reorganizing because most of the staff and two company commanders were captured with Colonel Wyndham. They fell back. Ashby brought his brigade back into a rear-guard action against my division which was on the advance. His horse was shot from under him and he took the field with two fresh regiments of infantry to, I presume, widen his lines."

Fremont paused soberly and took a sip from his whisky. "One of my colonels had an opportunity to have him shot. It would have been easy because he was in full view, but my colonel thought, and rightly, I believe, that a man like Turner Ashby did not deserve to die that way, so he ordered his man not to fire." Fremont sighed. "It only allowed Ashby a more glorious death. He was at the front of these fresh troops as we advanced, and mounted on a fresh horse. Again, as we charged his lines, his horse was shot from under him. He rolled to his feet, drew his sword and called, I think, for a counterattack — and, at that instant, fell dead."

Silence pervaded the room. Belle felt tears coursing down her cheeks. She stood up suddenly, murmuring, "You must excuse me...," and then, half stumbling as great sobs began to rack her body, rushed out of the room. All of the men and Annie Jones stared after her, shocked.

Alice, herself in tears, stood up slowly. "Do you not understand?" she cried with a low angry voice that claimed their attention like nothing else had that evening. "There is no one in our army who is not a brother, a father, an uncle, a dear friend or a cousin! These are our families you are killing!"

She stood up and slowly made her way out of the room. General Banks held out a hand to her, but she brushed it aside. Banks looked around at his fellow generals and his ruined evening, and then said sadly, "I believe that decency requires that we bring this to an end."

CHAPTER THIRTY-EIGHT

June 6, 1862, Harrisonburg, Virginia

Colonel Sir Percy Wyndham was ushered into the sitting room of the large plantation house that Jackson was using as his headquarters that day. He had been escorted by his captor, Private Holmes Conrad, and another trooper, his horse led, and his hands tied with a rough bit of twine to his saddle horn for most of the trip. It was getting dark and he was later than planned. The delay had been occasioned by a chance meeting with Major Robideaux Wheat, commander of the Louisiana Tigers, who had served as one of his fellow brigade commanders during the Italian War.

"Bob Wheat!" Wyndham shouted when he spotted him and jumped down from his horse.

"Sir Percy!" Major Wheat responded joyfully. The men of the 7th Virginia and Wheat's own battalion watched, highly amused, as the two rushed into each other's arms and danced a caper as they whirled each other around, while trying to pound each other on the back violently. Wheat even, in a moment of excessive esteem, kissed Wyndham on the lips and then pulled his mustache.

"Don't you ever trim this?" he laughed, as Wyndham pretended to clout him on the ear.

"Damn, Bob, it's good to see you," Wyndham shouted. "I'd heard that you were on the Rebel side, but had no hope we would meet again."

Wheat grinned at him, "Oh, I was pretty sure we'd run into each other, Percy. I'm sorry we had no chance to fight each other."

Wyndham grinned back, "You still want to settle that old bet, do you? Get me paroled and you may yet get a chance."

"Not up to me, old son. I'm just a battalion commander."

Wyndham looked at Wheat's Zouave costume and then at some of his men standing nearby. "Gawd, Wheat, what a motley looking crew. What brothel did you find them in?"

Wheat laughed, "You're not far wrong. Most are from the New Orleans docks. They ain't pretty, but savage in a fight."

"That's all you need," Wyndham said.

"Where are your men, Percy?"

Wyndham scowled. "Back there. What came with me. Truth to tell, Bob, I feel a little let down. Drill, discipline, all of it disappeared like so much smoke when the moment came."

Wheat nodded sympathetically. "That's hard." Then he looked at Wyndham slyly. "Still, you seemed to have misjudged the situation."

Wyndham took a huge breath and blew it out slowly. "I am chagrined," he admitted, "To have been done in by a horse farmer."

Wheat turned to Holmes Conrad and said, "Where are you taking this prisoner?"

"To General Jackson, posthaste," Conrad replied.

"I'm sure that Stonewall won't mind if two old friends catch up over a spot of lunch. You may sit with us as well." Wheat waved his hand to include all those standing nearby. "Come on."

Wheat turned, took Wyndham by the arm and led him to where a camp table was, under a shady tree. A lunch had been set out under the supervision of a Negro chef, complete with a tall white hat. The wooden table, covered with a fine linen cloth, was loaded with fine china and gleaming pots and utensils. Wyndham found the scene fantastic, but was suddenly ravenously hungry.

"Help yourself," Wheat said happily. "We're very democratic in our mess." Two of his men were handing out the food, cutting bread and meat and laying it on bone china plates. The cook was serving braised fish and rice.

Wyndham looked at him slyly. "I'd been wondering if a man who fought for Garibaldi would own slaves. I've heard that Rebel officers bring their servants with them to battle. I was rather looking forward to seeing that."

"Not my boys. None of them own slaves, nor hope to." Wheat kept smiling, but it was obvious to Wyndham he had struck a sore point. "These boys have their own view of the Negro and regard him mostly as competition for the best jobs."

Having procured a dish for himself, Major Wheat nodded

towards his chef.

"That man is no slave, but a free born Negro who used to grace the kitchens of the finest eating establishments in New Orleans."

Wyndham made a slight bow in the chef's direction, which was gravely returned by that worthy in a manner that would pass muster in any court in Europe.

"Remarkable," he murmured. "How did you get him to come along?"

Wheat smiled, patting his ample belly, "Oscar says when I am absent, his business suffers — so he followed me. I only pay him a Colonel's wage."

Wyndham smiled and shook his head as he dug in. "My word. This is wonderful."

Wheat sighed, "Life is short, Percy, and this is my last campaign. I plan to indulge myself with the finer things."

Wyndham saw that Wheat had changed since the Italian War. He was less jolly, more thoughtful, and carried himself now with an air of resignation. "What's wrong, Bob?" he asked quietly. "Are you somehow ill?"

Wheat shook his great head and gave him a sweet smile. "I've waited a long time for this war, is all. I've filibustered, invaded, and all in support of a right I do not claim myself — to hold another as my slave — I have none and want none — and it matters not. I fight for the South."

He leaned over and whispered, "I will not last the year, Percy. I will fall in battle, as I was born to do — and they will bury me at that very place — it's all arranged."

The finality in Wheat's voice was unnerving. Wyndham shook his head, clearing it, and changed the subject.

"Damn, Bob, it's good to see you again, even if we aren't on the same side this time. Say, do you remember the time that...."

Colonel Wyndham and Major Wheat spent the next two hours regaling the others with anecdotes of when they fought together in Italy. Half the time they were helpless with laughter as they recalled the good times they'd had in that campaign. The other men were fascinated by the *joie de vivre* of these two hardened professional soldiers who, it turned out, had saved each other's lives on more than one occasion and cared deeply for each other.

After an hour of this, a young man well turned out in the uniform of a Confederate Major came riding up. He was so handsome that Wyndham stared at him as if he had seen an apparition.

Holmes Conrad sprang to his feet and waved. "Harry!"

The Major waved back.

Wyndham turned to Wheat, "That's a bit informal, isn't it? The man's an officer."

Conrad, hearing this, turned. "He's also my brother-in-law." As the Major rode up, Conrad shouted, "I've got a real prize this time, Harry!"

"Have you? It wouldn't be Colonel Wyndham by any chance?"

"It is!" Conrad was excited now, "And he surrendered his sword to me!"

The Major dismounted and Wyndham rose to greet him.

"Sir Percy Wyndham," Conrad said, "May I present my brother-in-law, Major Henry Kyd Douglas, General Jackson's Inspector General."

Douglas smiled briefly. "Deputy Inspector General." He took the hand that Wyndham extended, shook it and then stepped back and rendered a proper salute, which Wyndham returned.

"We had begun to worry about you, Colonel. Stonewall sent me to find you."

"I am a prisoner, sir. I go where I'm told, and my old friend Wheat here wished to give me a proper meal before you put me on bread and water."

Wheat laughed. "Hardtack and beans, Percy. We ain't that hard."

After a few moments they were mounted and on their way. One did not keep Generals waiting.

Wyndham went under stricter escort afterwards, but thought the encounter worth the inconvenience and humiliation of being trussed like a fowl. By the time he arrived at Jackson's headquarters, he was relaxed and confident once more, the humiliations of the morning almost forgotten.

Stonewall Jackson, rail thin, with eyes that burned like those of a biblical prophet, dressed in a uniform so shabby that Wyndham would have scorned to use it for rags, rose to meet him when he entered the room and motioned him to a seat. Wyndham immediately saw there were two other Rebel officers present.

"This is Major Dabney, my Adjutant, and you have already met Major Douglas," Jackson said as Wyndham seated himself. Jackson resumed his own seat, casually took a pen knife from a pocket, a lemon from another and used the one to halve the other. He leaned back, sucked hard at one half of the lemon for a few seconds, swallowed, and then began, "I've heard a lot about you, Colonel Wyndham. You are a stranger here, are you not?"

"Very true, sir," Wyndham said, keeping his face as still as possible. Jackson did not strike him as a man susceptible to a winning smile.

"Why then have you come and involved yourself in what is essentially a family fight?" Jackson asked this in the mildest of tones, but his accusation was plain.

"It's what I do, sir," Wyndham spoke slowly and carefully. "In my time, I have been a revolutionary in France, served in the French Navy, and in the Eighth Austrian Lancers. Currently I am on leave from the Italian Army."

"How did you come to be knighted by the Queen?" Douglas asked. "Crimea?"

"I was not present in that campaign, sir," Wyndham replied testily. "My knighthood is Italian, from King Victor Emmanuel the Second."

Jackson raised his eyebrows. "Too fancy for me," he murmured.

Douglas said, with just a touch of scorn in his voice, "So you are a mercenary, a hired gun."

Wyndham looked perplexed, as if he didn't quite understand the question. "Soldiering is my profession, yes."

"If we were to offer you employment," Douglas asked, "What terms and command would you want?"

Wyndham was stunned. He stared at Douglas a long moment, and then turned to Jackson. "This man is a civilian, isn't he?"

"Most in our army are," Jackson said, his face expressionless, watching Wyndham very carefully.

Wyndham regarded Douglas coldly. "Having accepted employment with the Union, I would sooner die than change sides, especially for something as trivial as money and position. I hope you did not mean to insult me, Major. If you did, then name your seconds."

Douglas was flustered. "No insult was intended, Colonel, and I beg your pardon very sincerely if it sounded that way."

Wyndham glared at him. "This has been a most trying day, sir. Most trying. Let me explain this as I would to a child of six years old. Arms is my profession. I enjoy a reputation that travels far beyond Europe, and applications are made for my service fairly damn often. That reputation is the most valuable thing I possess. Why would I sully it by switching sides on an employer? Who would then employ me if I were such a treacherous fool?"

Jackson nodded, his face grave. "You are perfectly correct. Please pardon us. No insult was intended. Perhaps a little conversation over dinner...."

"If you want to hear about my experiences in the Italian campaign, that will be fine," Wyndham replied coldly. "If you plan to pump me about Union Army plans or intentions, then I shall be like the Sphinx in Egypt."

"I would expect no less," Jackson said with a gentle smile. Just then, a young Lieutenant entered the room. He seemed on the verge of tears and Jackson, obviously recognizing him, stiffened as if expecting a blow.

"Lieutenant Thomson, sir," said the young man.

"I know who you are," Jackson replied. "Have you come with a report from General Ashby?"

"No sir, with a report about him." Thompson drew a deep breath and blurted out, "He's dead, sir. Killed in battle."

Jackson's face froze. "Are you sure?"

"I was with him, sir. This is his blood on my coat, not my own."

Jackson got up, and without another word walked into the adjoining room, closing the door behind him.

Douglas let out a huge sigh. "How did it happen?"

"His horse got shot as he was leading those two regiments you had Ewell send up. He rose up, drew his sword, as the Yankees began their charge and cried out, 'For God's sake men, charge!' and then, the fellow next to him, startled by this, dropped his musket, or it went off, I'm not sure, but the bullet entered his heart, killing him instantly."

Douglas groaned and held his head in his hands. "What horrible luck! This is a terrific blow!"

"Yes," said Major Dabney. He was thoughtful, his gaze and voice remote as he added, "We must prepare a statement for General Jackson to make. The newspapers will expect it."

"It should not be too glowing," Douglas cautioned him. "Stonewall won't go for hearts and flowers. He did not like the man."

"Oh, something like 'as a partisan officer I never knew his equal'," Dabney replied slowly, sounding it out.

Douglas nodded. "That has the sound of truth. Write that down."

Dabney scribbled and then looked up at Thomson. "You're excused, Lieutenant. Thank you for coming so quickly."

"Who...," Douglas began as Thomson left the room, so that Wyndham, realizing that they had forgotten that he, an enemy officer, was present and were about to discuss vital plans, cleared his throat and said, "Excuse me. I'm very sorry for your loss. He was a most worthy adversary. If you would have someone show me to my tent and a bit of supper, I won't trouble you further." He stood to attention.

Both Douglas and Dabney got to their feet and offered their hands. He shook one and then the other with equal firmness.

"Thank you for coming," Douglas said meaninglessly, his voice and eyes dull with the shock of the terrible news. Wyndham nodded politely, put on his hat, and seeing no point in further conversation, stepped outside the room and walked a short distance away so that he could no longer hear what they said to each other.

Unopposed, he walked out to the veranda of the plantation house where Confederate Army staff officers huddled together, talking quietly, and some wept openly at the loss of a hero. Wyndham lit a cigar, and said nothing. No one seemed to pay him any mind. He looked around.

No one was watching him now. It would be easy to escape, had he not given his parole. How long it would be before he would be exchanged for a prisoner of equal rank?

An image of Turner Ashby from that morning came to mind: cocky, arrogant, and perhaps enjoying Wyndham's discomfort a little too much. And the strange premonition that had settled on his friend Wheat. Wyndham had seen that look of terrible resignation before — death would likely fulfill the ambition to die in battle quickly. But Ashby had been very much alive. So full of life, and he had been struck down without warning — it was a mystery.

"*Sic transit gloria,* " Wyndham muttered quietly to himself.

CHAPTER THIRTY-NINE

June 8th 1862, Front Royal, Virginia

Belle simply cried her heart out for a day. She had Eliza tell everyone that she was deathly ill, and sat in her room to let the grief wash through her like a winter thunderstorm.

She did not weep and wail copiously, but showered tears gently on her supply of lace handkerchiefs, suppressing the heart-broken sobs that occasionally racked her body. Weeping and wailing were simply not an option.

She had to get it over with, she knew, and dared not be too public about how close she felt to Henry Turner Ashby, lest some bright-eyed, intelligent Provost Marshal like Michael Kelley begin to wonder, and make the connections needed to build a case against her.

Those Yankees who were men of the law were rather circumspect about acting against her without definite proof. Her task was to not give them any.

Henry and Dick Ashby had taught her to ride, and so much more, and while it was Dick she had set her sights upon as a possible husband when she was just coming into womanhood, she had loved Henry as much, as a friend. Working with him against the Yankee invasion was simply the most exciting and most important thing that she'd ever done.

Eliza brought her herbal tea to calm her. This allowed her to think through the problem that now confronted her. Ashby had never written down the details of his network of spies and she knew only that part of his network that concerned her own operations. Few, even of his staff, had been told of her role. She did not even have a honorary commission to show anyone, like Antonia Ford. Harry Gilmour had, to her intense irritation, treated the whole thing as a childish fancy, an indulgence.

There were records in Richmond that would confirm her employment in the Secret Service, but the more immediate problem was who in Stonewall Jackson's command knew what she was doing, and how could she get her information to them? The only person who she was sure knew her role was Jackson himself.

The Yankees had consolidated their position in Front Royal so well now that she was entirely cut off. Information collected and ciphered into a quick report was discarded after a few days because of the constant changes. It rotted like over-ripe fruit. Old units marched out to be replaced by new ones almost every day.

New officers had to be cultivated, and because her run across the fields outside town on the 23rd to alert Jackson had now been published in the Yankee newspapers, they were not as easy to charm. They were polite, even engaging, and some were terrible flirts, but they had been warned about her and Alice, and kept their mouths shut.

Belle felt the strain of being outwardly agreeable and flirtatious when, in her heart, she quite hated them all. There was a constant tension which could have been alleviated by a good gallop on her horse, but permission for such an excursion was not forthcoming, even if she could have found one of these new officers willing to escort her.

A good mindless romp in bed with Daniel Keily might have answered. Unfortunately, the Irish officer was off with Shields, who was, once more, trying to trap Jackson's army. Belle half-convinced herself that Keily was not really a Yankee at heart. The entire political situation seemed to mystify him. For all of that, he was a man of principle. Having made a contract with the Union Army, he would honor it, even at the cost of his life. While this galled her more than she could say, she admired his sense of honor and duty.

About mid-day Eliza brought in flowers sent by the generals at that unfortunate party where she had learned so cruelly of Ashby's death. Belle stared at them and thought that it was a strange war indeed where the enemy showed such kindness. It did not make her hate them less.

There was nothing to do but to go on. Ashby would expect nothing less of her. She had been left in Front Royal for a purpose. It would dishonor his memory if she failed to do her best to accomplish her mission.

Alice came in, disgruntled at having been left on her own all day to deal with the Yankees. "Are you feeling better?" she inquired in a too-sweet tone that barely concealed her edginess.

Belle looked up at her and took another sip of the herbal tea. "I am now," she said. "I'm sorry to have been absent, but I had to work through this, and not where Yankee eyes would see how much Henry meant to me. Has it been too horrible?"

"No," said Alice after a moment, "Not at all. They are all damnably kind and considerate, which is worse since it robs me of the chance to rage at them."

She poured herself a cup of the tea, sat in the other chair and sipped it, finally relaxing. "The peculiar thing is that they seem almost as broken up about Ashby as we are. They genuinely admired and respected him. That tale about the Yankee colonel holding his fire when he had a clear shot is true, it seems. They wanted to beat him, not kill him. They are such little boys!"

Belle managed her first smile of the day. "Before the war," she said, "Remember how Henry, Dick and their friends held tournaments, like those in the novels by Sir Walter Scott? Henry was the best at that game where they would try and snatch the small black ring with the point of a lance at a full gallop. Dick was pretty good, too. Dick would carry my favor sometimes."

"Favor?"

"A scarf which he would tie to the lance, or sometimes a single red rose on his chest. It was chivalry, playing at being the knights of old and their ladies. This war is more of the same. They are playing at it, like some terrible deadly theatrical event, where it's the Yorks against the Lancasters, all over again, or under Cromwell with the Roundheads against the Cavaliers. And you're right. They are boys, hardly men."

Alice squinted a bit, trying to take that all in, and returned to the more important question. "Did it mean anything? The 'favor' I mean?"

Belle considered this and spoke slowly, "I was a gawky, willful child of eleven or twelve. He was a handsome young man who was kind enough to make sure I was not left out of the party. I had some fancies about him when I was at school, but I don't think he ever really saw me that way, not even after I got my full figure. Besides, my mother had other ideas, as did yours."

"Yes," Alice smiled ironically. "We were going to take Washington society by storm and hang the expense of it all. We were to make good marriages and become women of substance."

"I did love Dick," Belle said sadly, "And I admired Henry almost as much as Porte Crayon."

"Let's not talk about him," Alice said.

"No," Belle agreed. "It's too sad, and I am sad enough."

They sat together in silence for a number of minutes, and then Belle said, "You know, Alice, Henry once told me that he did not expect to live to see the war's end. Neither did Dick, he said. At the time, I thought it just more of all that posturing and bravado all the boys were doing when the war started, but now I see how brave and reckless they both were to know that, and still go on."

"And us?" Alice asked. "Will we survive all this?"

"Yes," said Belle. "That I am sure of. We must go on until the end and beyond it, come what may."

She looked at her cousin and saw how the events of recent weeks were wearing on her. Alice now looked much older, and more tired than Belle had ever seen her, and she supposed the same was true of herself. She smiled at Alice fondly.

"What have you learned, while I have been indisposed?"

"We have Union artillery in residence tonight. A battery is camped in the courtyard. I have the names of the officers who took rooms. We're giving them a good dinner and plenty of whisky." Alice grew angry. "I'd just as soon light a match and blow them all to Kingdom Come!"

"And us with them?" Belle asked, smiling. "That would never do. Our information will be needed when Jackson comes back up the

Valley. It would be pleasant to take a more direct role, the way those women in Winchester did, but...."

Belle stopped, thinking hard.

Alice looked at her curiously. "What is it?"

"Any small thing we do against the Yankees aids the cause, does it not?"

"Yes," Alice agreed. "Of course."

Belle smiled, mischief in her eyes, "Does old Saul, the carpenter, have a short saw in his tool box?"

"I suppose so. Why?"

"I know a thing or two about artillery. Major Bier, from Jackson's staff, taught me."

Alice was grinning, "What are you up to, you scamp?"

"The spokes on the wheels of a gun carriage are made of hickory, a very hard, well seasoned wood. This allows the wheels to carry the great weight of the cannon. If the wheel breaks, on either side, the cannon is useless. It cannot be deployed. For that reason, the wheel is so designed that, if one spoke breaks, it will continue to roll easily. In fact, two or three can break and it will still be mobile — unless they are right next to each other." Belle raised her eyebrows significantly.

"What are you going to do?" Alice asked anxiously.

"Cut them part way through and let nature do the rest. If they break here, it's no big matter. If they break when they are part of a column then it can disrupt and delay that part of the Union movement."

"But, if you get caught?"

"I won't. If the saw is sharp, it will be the work of a minute. There is plenty of mud handy to conceal the cuts." Belle said with more assurance than she felt, "Just get me that saw."

CHAPTER FORTY

June 12th, Front Royal, Virginia.

Alice came into the cottage and up to her room at a run, her face flushed with excitement. It was six in the morning and Belle was still dressing.

"I have word of Hasbrouke Reeve," Alice said.

Belle turned and stared at her, apprehensive. They had not seen Reeve since his arrest that fateful day in Winchester three weeks before.

"He has returned?"

"No," said Alice, smiling, "He is being court-martialed and dismissed from the service."

Belle shook her head sadly.

"That's a shame. He's a good fellow and I did not mean to get him into so much trouble."

"It's nothing to do with us," Alice said cheerfully. "It seems he was selling Union horses and pocketing the money."

Belle blinked. "Really?"

Alice nodded, grinning now.

"How disappointing," Belle said at last. "I had thought him better than that. Why, he's no more than a common thief."

"Yes, isn't it wonderful?" Alice said, causing Belle to look at her oddly, and then to give a short, sharp sound midway between a laugh and a cry.

"You mean because it can't come back on us? I suppose that's one way to look at it. I'm sorry to hear of it, anyway, because I am rather fond of him."

Alice looked a little shocked. "You didn't...?"

"No more than the occasional kiss," Belle said.

"You make it sound like a kiss is nothing," Alice protested.

"In the larger scheme of things, it's not all that much," Belle assured her, causing a shocked Alice to turn angrily on her heel and walk out of the room, down the stairs and out into the yard.

Belle sighed. How could she explain it? It would be like trying to describe a sunrise to a blind person. Alice had permitted

Myles Keogh to kiss her just once. The experience had not been an agreeable one. Belle had puzzled about that, because the kisses she exchanged with Daniel Keily rocked her to the soles of her boots. Myles was far more handsome and personable. It should have been easy for Alice, yet it was not.

This was a mystery, Belle decided, that she would not solve any time soon. She finished dressing, making herself as presentable as possible, went outside, nodded to the sentry who would follow her everywhere, and walked over to the hotel to begin another day.

Walking from the cottage to the hotel she saw that a new tent had been set up by the Union Provost Marshal. When she saw Lieutenant Preston standing there, flirting with Alice, she asked him the purpose of it.

"It's not much," Preston said, "Just a table and two chairs. We have a great many Confederate prisoners who will be paroled and allowed to pass through the lines to the South."

"Pity," said Belle, "That I am not permitted to leave with them."

"It's just that we admire your company so much," Preston said with a smile and winked at Alice, then walked off whistling. Alice and Belle stared at each other for a moment.

"If you say a word, I will...," Alice began.

"What could I possibly say? He is a very personable young man. I knew him in Martinsburg." While Alice was trying to work that one out, Belle smiled, patted her on the shoulder and walked on to the back door of the hotel. She went inside, through to the lobby and then behind the desk, pulled out the register and looked at the list of lodgers present that day.

Alice came in and just stood there, saying nothing.

"I take it that Lieutenant Preston suits your book better than Captain Keogh," Belle said, her voice flat.

Alice blushed. "He's a man I wouldn't mind kissing," she admitted.

"No mustache?" asked Belle. "Is that the difference?"

Alice thought about it. "Perhaps. The one Myles wears is stiff and rough. It made my mouth feel sore. But I think there's something else, too."

"Yes?"

"He doesn't stink of whisky. He's moderate in his habits and clean. I quite like the way he smells." Alice looked down, speaking very softly as she said this, so as not to be overheard.

"You can not play the game if you criticize me. That's not fair," Belle said mildly. She didn't want an argument and neither, it seemed, did Alice, who just nodded.

Just then, some of the Union officers clambered down the stairs, on their way to breakfast. Most were hung over, Belle noticed. She made a mental note to order more whisky.

New Yankee newspapers had been left behind in the dining room. Eliza collected them and brought them to the front desk, carefully smoothing them and folding them for later use.

Belle scanned the front pages quickly and was gratified to see that Jackson had handed Fremont a heavy defeat at Cross Keys, and Shields another the next day at Fort Republic.

Belle wondered if Jackson would head up the Valley now or fall back to Richmond. Union forces were stronger than ever around Front Royal. She would have to prepare another report in cipher shortly. Fortunately, she had done this so many times using the last key she had received that it was something she could do in her head without preparing a code table.

Unfortunately, that key was likely out of date, and the message might not easily be decoded by whomever received it. If the Union forces changed very much this report would go in the fire, like the last three.

About two hours later, Myles Keogh, dusty from a long hot ride, ran into the front lobby and said urgently to Belle, "Lass! You've got to come at once!"

Belle was startled. "What do you mean? What is it?"

"It's Daniel. He's been bad hurt, shot in the face. He's asking for you."

Belle felt her heart sink. "What happened?" She was alarmed as conflicting emotions washed over her. She did not love Daniel Keily, but she liked him very much, and not just as a lover. He was a Yankee and she hated Yankees passionately, but she...loved?...him. This unbidden thought made her head hurt. Feeling trapped, she sought a way out. She couldn't just run off to tend to a wounded Yankee — or at least she shouldn't. Keogh looked at her impatiently, tapping his boot on the floor.

"I'm under tight restriction," Belle said, nodding to the sentry standing near-by. She tried to think what to do, aware that both Alice and Eliza were watching her intently. "I'm not allowed to leave the hotel grounds."

"I'll see to that," Keogh said, and addressed the sentry directly. "Get the Provost Marshal now."

"But, sir," the private protested, nodding at Belle.

"I'll make sure she doesn't run off," Keogh said wearily. "Go find the man. On my responsibility, Private. And hop to it!"

The Union soldier, trailing his musket in his hand, walked quickly out of the room.

"Do you think you'll be able to persuade him?" Belle asked.

"Oh, yes," Keogh tapped the badge that identified him as a staff officer. "He'll let you go as long as I escort you. You must give me your parole, Miss Belle, for if you disappear it will go very hard with me."

Belle saw there was no avoiding this. Moreover, she felt a sudden anxiety about Keily's welfare. Was he hurt very badly? Might he die?

"You have my parole, Captain Keogh. I hope you are prepared to ride hard and fast." She looked at Eliza and said, "Eliza, please go out and have someone saddle my horse." Eliza slipped out of the room quickly. "I take it on faith that you will be able to get permission, Captain Keogh, and I will not embarrass you. While we wait to sort it all out, please tell me how Daniel was injured."

Keogh drew a deep breath. "I wasn't there, but the old son is up for another medal. We were falling back, in good order, when the Rebel artillery came slamming in. One of our six-pounders lost its wheel, and right in the middle of a short bridge at that. It was blocking the retreat. Ol' Dan thinks that this creek can make a natural trench and line of defense and that, if he can move that gun just a bit, he can counter the Rebel cannon fire, so he jumps down from his horse, and gets about a dozen men to lift the thing by brute force when he gets hit."

Keogh sighed. "The lads panicked then, and carried him away, abandoned the position. His face was all bloody and they thought him dead for a time."

Belle felt tears welling up. "Oh my, where is he?"

"House outside of town. He was moaning something terrible, and they left him there, along with a Rebel officer who was also shot. No one told me about it until today, and he's not been seen by a surgeon."

"Then he may still be alive," Belle said, now thinking hard. "How did the gun carriage break down?"

"As I told you, the wheel came off. Three spokes splinted together, right next to each other. Some of these damned, greedy government contractors will burn in hell, if there's a God in heaven," Keogh said angrily, and then realizing that he had used foul language in the presence of young ladies, said, "I beg your pardon."

Belle and Alice looked at once another, suddenly realizing that there might have been another cause: Belle's sabotage. Belle decided that she would rather not know what had caused the wheel to break. Her sense of irony did not stretch that far. She felt suddenly as if she had shot Dan Keily herself.

"I will need to change," she murmured and walked out of the lobby. It was far from a perfect opportunity to escape, she thought, since she was too tall, too recognizable. Besides, she needed to see Daniel. A few minutes later she returned, in her smartest riding habit, carrying a leather satchel.

Keogh looked at it and at the pistol she was wearing on her belt. "What's all this?"

"I am a nurse, sir. This is medicine and bandages."

"And that?" Keogh pointed to the pistol.

"A present from a Union officer, for my protection."

Lieutenant Preston was now present. Keogh looked at him questioningly and received a nod in return. "That's true. It's a privilege granted to her last year in Martinsburg and has never been revoked," Preston confirmed.

Keogh shrugged. From his red face, Belle could tell that he had helped himself to "a touch of the creature" as he called it. "Then let's go."

Fleeter nickered a greeting and jumped slightly as Belle lifted herself into the saddle and took the reins. She took off at a gallop, leaving Keogh to mount and ride after her. Fortunately, he was a very skilled horseman and quickly overtook her.

Belle suddenly realized that she had no idea where they were going, so let him take the lead and was surprised a few minutes later when he led her to the Ashby house just outside of town. This belonged one of Turner and Dick Ashby's cousins, and the lady of the house, Mary Ashby, was a cousin and close friend of Lucy Buck's.

With no time to stand on ceremony, she pulled Fleeter up sharply in front of the house, slid out of the saddle and recognized Tom Ashby, the boy who had been her brother William's friend until he had called Belle a whore and caused a fight between them. He stared at her and then at Keogh, who was just then tying his own horse and Fleeter to the porch rail.

"Where is the Irish officer?" Belle demanded.

Tom Ashby just gaped at her.

"The Union officer, who was wounded, where is he?" Belle asked again, speaking more kindly than she felt.

"Top of the stairs to the right," Keogh said. Belle rushed by the Ashby boy, into the house, past a startled Mary Ashby and ran up the stairs. Keogh was close on her heels.

There lay Daniel Keily, on top of a bare mattress, still in a dirty, blood-soaked uniform. He was half conscious, but tried to smile when he recognized her. This hurt so much that tears came immediately to his eyes.

"Don't move," Belle said, quickly removing her hat and riding jacket. She placed the medical satchel at the foot of the bed, and sat next to Keily. Sensing Keogh behind her, she said, "Get me some hot water and some rags."

He just looked at her.

"Until I clean the blood and dirt away, I can't see how bad it is," Belle said. "Please do as I tell you."

Keogh nodded. "Aye," he said, "You look like you know what you're about." He walked out of the room and went down the stairs. Belle heard him in loud conversation with Mary Ashby. Or perhaps at her, since she did not seem to respond to his questions.

Belle leaned over Keily and permitted herself a moment of tenderness. "Daniel, I am going to help you. You must be brave, because it's going to hurt quite a bit. It's a very serious wound. You are lucky to be still alive."

Keily tried to say something but it came out as incomprehensible mumbles.

"Don't try to speak," Belle said, and dug into the medical bag until she found a packet of white powder. "I'm going to give this to you a little at a time on your tongue," she said. "It's morphine. It will lessen your pain."

Keily managed to nod slowly and let Belle drop a little into his open mouth. He grimaced.

"Yes, it's very bitter," Belle said, "But you will feel better for having it."

Keogh returned, carrying a pitcher of hot water, a bowl and several towels. "The milk of human kindness runs thin here," he observed. "I had to find all this myself. The lady of the house would not even look nor speak to me."

"Ever hear the name Ashby?" Belle asked drily.

"The Rebel general? Yes, of course."

"These people are closely related to him."

Keogh looked startled. "Oh, dear God. I had no idea."

"That's the problem with you Yankees," Belle said as she moistened a cloth and then used it to begin cleaning some of the blood and dirt from Keily's jaw, "You never do."

"I'm not really a Yankee," Keogh said after a moment, as Belle stopped and gave Keily more morphine powder on his tongue.

"No," Belle agreed. "You're worse. A mercenary. A hired gun whose only interests are rank, pay and personal glory, plus whatever virgins you can despoil."

Keogh flushed bright red. "Now, see here...."

"Kindly shut up," said Belle, "And let me work."

Keogh did so. Belle continued to wash Keily's face and neck, using a bar of yellow soap from the bag and a fresh towel, until everything was clean and she could better see the bruises on his face. The bullet had hit him on the left side of the jaw and exited behind his ear. Both the entrance and exit wound had scabbed over. Belle was careful not to dislodge either scab and start the bleeding afresh. She leaned over and smelled closely at the wounds. To her relief there was no smell of decay or infection. She took thin gauze from her medical satchel and used it to pack the wound.

His wound might be all her fault. *Was the caisson he tried to move when the bullet struck him the same one that I sabotaged?* Belle wondered. *Whoever said that God lacked a sense of humor? If it were anyone else, anyone at all, I would not care half as much.*

She looked at his eyes. His pupils were very large now. The drug was taking effect. He lapsed into a semi-slumber. Belle washed her hands in the bowl, dried them and began to probe at Keily's mouth. He moaned loudly.

"I'm checking for broken teeth," Belle said, without turning to look at Keogh. "If he were to swallow one, it could create other problems, even choke him or kill him." She moved Keily's jaw carefully. "The bone is broken, in more than one place. It must be splinted and that is beyond my skill. You will need to get him to a surgeon for that."

Belle probed with her finger under Keily's tongue. He was unconscious, breathing heavily by this time. She found a broken tooth, and then another, pulled them out and placed them on the table next to the bed. She probed again and came away with several small fragments of tooth. Peering inside the mouth, she made a noise, dug once more into the satchel and found a small pair of pliers. These she used to extract two more teeth, which came out easily.

"They were very loose anyway," Belle said, "And would have been removed by the surgeon. He's probably going to take out the rest of the teeth on that side when he splints the jaw."

She turned to Keogh, "You must find an ambulance and have him moved, Myles. He's not safe here."

"No?"

"If he were, they would have tended him. In hospitals, all wounded are tended alike. It's a moral necessity and a practical one. We have their wounded and they have ours. In a private home, those rules are seldom observed. These people are mourning Ashby. You're quite fortunate that he's still alive."

Keogh nodded. "You people make the Sicilians look small when it comes to blood feud. I'll tend to it as soon as I return you to Lieutenant Preston."

Belle looked around the room and realized, from the furnishings and things in it, that it must belong to young Tom Ashby. She wondered where he was sleeping.

"I might stay with him a while — but I'd better have a word with the lady of the house." Belle put her jacket back on, looked in a mirror, tucked up a few stray hairs and went downstairs.

Mary Ashby would not meet her eyes at first and listened resentfully, her head down, when Belle spoke to her and then offered to see to the Rebel officer as well.

Mary Ashby's head came up and her eyes blazed with quiet

hatred. "That won't be necessary," she said in a low, tense voice. "He's been taken care of."

"But you let Captain Keily just lay there and suffer?"

"He is the enemy!" Mary Ashby ground out furiously. "I never asked to have him here!"

Belle shook her head sadly. "But, humanity requires...."

"And what would you know about it, you tramp?!"

Belle was taken aback.

Mary Ashby didn't raise her voice, but her words were like a shout in Belle's ears. "You, with your circus riding and your playing of the game of flirt. You only came here because this Irish bastard is your lover! Everyone knows about you and the way you shamelessly use men!"

"That's unfair," Belle started to say, and then stopped. What could she tell this angry, bereaved woman that would not be spread all over town the next day? Certainly not how closely she had worked with Turner Ashby as a scout and spy. That was a deep secret.

She started again, "I came as a nurse...."

Mary Ashby poked her in the chest with an angry forefinger, "More indecency. The very idea of a young woman of your class doing something so intimate with strange men. Well, Missy, you do your nursing and your whoring someplace other than my house!"

Belle was close to tears. It was so unfair to have to suffer this abuse, to be so misunderstood. It took her several moments to recover herself. Finally, raising her chin in a spirited gesture, she said, "I will see that Captain Keily is removed from your care. I dressed his wound and gave him medication. Until he is removed, I hold you responsible for his safety."

Mary Ashby, still in a simmering rage, just stared at her.

Belle looked at the other woman straight on, her chin still lifted proudly, and spoke plainly and calmly. "Anything happens to him," she added coolly, "And I'll have the Yankees burn your house down."

She had the satisfaction of seeing Mary Ashby go pale when she said that, but immediately regretted it. If that were repeated and spread around, people would never believe she was fighting for the Confederacy.

She went back upstairs, put on her hat, picked up her medical satchel and said to Myles Keogh, "He's safe enough for now. Take me back and then get him that ambulance."

"Aye, I will," said Keogh, "And thank you."

"Don't mention it, not to anyone," she said. "Please."

CHAPTER FORTY-ONE

June 1862, Front Royal, Virginia.

General Shields fell back again to Front Royal and re-established himself at the Fishback Hotel along with his superior, General Banks, despite the best advice of Michael Kelley and other members of his staff. He liked his comforts, the service and food at the hotel were first rate, and he simply did not consider Belle a serious threat.

The fact that she had ridden out to give medical treatment to one of his favorite staff officers gave him hope that the tall, graceful and charming young woman might finally be seeing the errors of her ways. Belle was careful not to disabuse him of the notion.

Keily was treated for his wound by Doctor Paul Bogardus, one of those distressing Virginia Unionists, like Porte Crayon, who'd joined the Yankee Army. Bogardus was young, only about ten years older than Belle, handsome, with dark brown eyes and hair and a clean-shaven, olive complexion. Like Keily, he was taller than she by several inches and made her feel more like a girl when they were together.

He set Keily's jaw, praising the preliminary work that Belle had done, and telling her that it had been a near thing, that Daniel Keily was lucky to be alive.

Belle not only found him very attractive but, as Chief Surgeon, more than worthy of her attention. She set out to charm him, even as Keily lay semi-conscious in the hospital. Belle volunteered once more to nurse the wounded, and this permission was quickly given because of her obvious skill. This provided the added benefit of daily contact with Doctor Bogardus.

Flirting soon became evening walks together, and, because Bogardus did not wish a sentry to dog their every step, that inconvenience was soon dispensed with. Belle saw no reason not to reward him with a kiss. She quite liked the sensation of his bare, smooth face on hers and the way he strongly, but gently, held her in his arms.

Because other officers were still avoiding her and Lieutenant

Preston was often busy with his duties, Alice was a bit jealous of Belle's new relationship, until a Mister Jefferies, a well set up man about forty, began to pay attention to her. Jefferies walked with a severe limp and used a cane. He had been wounded at the battle of Bull's Run, but no one seemed to know which side he had been on. He had a southern accent, but seemed to hold Abolitionist views when with Union officers.

Belle was wary of him. "Don't tell him anything," she said to Alice.

"Of course not," Alice said innocently. "What would I tell?"

Belle wondered if Jefferies would reveal himself by sign and countersign as an agent of the Secret Service, or if he were a Pinkerton man or a Jessie Scout or sent by Detective Baker. Perhaps he was simply the commercial traveler he claimed to be. It was a bothersome mystery.

She continued to visit Daniel Keily in the hospital, bringing flowers to brighten his room, and to walk out with Doctor Bogardus. The good doctor, she found, was very willing to talk about his work, which, among other things, included making tallies of the Union casualties from the recent battles. Dead, wounded and sick, each represented one less man that the Union could use against the South; important information that Jackson and other Confederate commanders needed. Belle listened carefully, trying to appear alternately fascinated and slightly bored, and kept him off balance with amorous looks and tender kisses which she enjoyed for their own sake.

Still, she led him a dance. She sensed that if Bogardus and she went the full distance to a bedroom, he would lose interest. He was as much in the hunt as she was. She let her mind rule her body where he was concerned.

The inconvenient fact was that she still had some feelings for Daniel Keily. When she confessed this, in pretty confusion, to Bogardus, he quickly arranged to have Keily transferred back to the central Army hospital in Washington for further treatment. Belle admired the smooth skill with which he disposed of his rival, but kept him at the same distance.

She softly objected when he touched her breasts. "It's all right," he said, "I'm a doctor." Belle felt like laughing out loud at this disingenuous ploy, but simpered and giggled like the little fool she was not. His attentions were not unpleasant, but she played the blushing virgin to the hilt and did not let it go too far. It was a terrible tease, she knew, and left her tense and a bit irritable, but it paid other dividends. She did not have to ask him too questions. So intent was he on impressing her that he told her everything quite freely.

All of this information was useless if she could not get it out! Belle, now granted the greater liberty of walking about the town, spent more time ministering to the needs of some of the Confederate prisoners, looking for officers or even sergeants from the Seventh Virginia or the Louisiana Tigers who could be trusted to act as couriers.

Prisoner exchanges, especially of the seriously wounded, were the most common opportunities. Belle managed to get out three dispatches in the care of sergeants who accompanied wounded comrades. Once it went wrong when a delirious patient had a seizure and the packet fell off the stretcher he was being carried on. An alert Provost Guard picked it up and turned it in, and for about a week every exchanged prisoner, no matter how ill or disgusting, was carefully searched. Belle was more carefully watched after that.

Belle knew the risks she was running, but when Alice cautioned her, said, "It's only a matter of time before they catch me, dear heart. If my impulsive nature does not do me in, the newspapers will. The only thing that has saved me so far is my youth and my sex. People simply do not believe that a woman my age can be a spy."

"It would be easier on us if they did," Alice said sourly.

"But then," Belle said with a winsome, eye-fluttering false smile that reduced her cousin to helpless laughter, "We would not be so effective."

When Alice recovered herself, she said, "There is a clerk staying at Lucy Buck's place who might be worth cultivating. Little Ambrose. He coordinates all the orderly reports."

"Oh, yes," Belle said, "But since Doctor Bogardus is resident there, it could be difficult."

"He's a shy boy, but Lucy seems quite taken with him, says he's not bad for a Yankee." Alice looked at her speculatively.

Belle frowned. "I will not bring Lucy into this work. She's an idiot and lacks all discretion."

"She can be useful," Alice observed. "That lack of discretion can work for us. She was telling me her latest take on Yankee lying. Doctor Hendricks told her that the Yankee killed and wounded at Cross Keys and Fort Republic were less than eight hundred men, but Little Ambrose had a different figure."

"Which was?"

"More than eleven thousand."

Belle pursed her lips in a silent whistle. "That's very important." She thought for a moment. "So Doctor Hendricks gave her false information, which means that they suspect her of being a spy, or at least a blabbermouth. For her sake, we dare not press her or this clerk, Ambrose, for details. But, perhaps we should be more social with Lucy, while playing our own cards close."

"There's more," Alice said, her eyes bright with suppressed mirth.

"Is there?"

"Last month, Jeb Stuart and twelve hundred of his cavalry probed McClellan's flank and ended up riding around his whole army, doing quite a bit of mischief in the process. Because of this, and because of what Jackson did here, Richmond is still safe. The entire Yankee army is being reorganized."

"And how does Lucy know this?" Belle asked. "It sounds like just more camp gossip."

"Her father has to deal with these Yankees he's boarding.

They've about ruined Bel Air, but they're out to impress him and convert him to their cause, so they brag, especially when they've been drinking." Alice was triumphant at having information that Belle did not.

"Why will men put a thief into their mouths to steal their brains?" Belle murmured, quoting Shakespeare, not for the first time. Alice nodded.

"Well, how are we to play this?" Belle asked. "Lucy quite hates me and thinks me a bad, immoral person. She barely speaks to me and is usually 'not at home' to me when I call."

"Then leave her to me," Alice said. "We're actually quite good friends, although she worries that you've led me astray and ruined my reputation along with your own."

"Lucy's big mouth has more to with that than anything else!" Belle interjected.

"Yes, of course," Alice continued, "But she is a famous gossip and may be able to help us fill in some of the blanks in our reports." She smiled at Belle. "Lucy will suffer your presence for my sake."

"How kind of her," Belle said sarcastically. "And I will suffer hers, for the sake of the mission."

So, Alice, with Belle in tow and accompanied also by Mister Jefferies, whom she was using to keep Lieutenant Preston both off-balance and interested, started calling on Lucy Buck. There were jolly evenings of singing, with Lucy playing the piano. The conversation was not so glittering as it might be in the salons of Washington or Richmond, but Belle profited by it. She was learning that odd bits of apparently useless information could be assembled to make a quite useful whole.

Doctor Bogardus and Belle, not wanting to discuss military or medical matters in such company, began to compare notes on their families. When Bogardus mentioned that his mother was a Katherine Glenn, Belle realized that they were, in fact, probably first cousins. Katherine was the name of one of her mother's younger sisters and Glenns were not all that common. All thoughts of taking him as a lover stopped at that point. That was incest, and worse even than him being a Yankee. He seemed eager to continue despite this, but she tactfully dissuaded him.

Bogardus became even more ardent. In time-honored tradition, he sent flowers, but not poetry. He contrived to meet her on the street and came to the hotel so often that Alice inquired if he wanted a room. He was a man inflamed by that which he could not have — Belle began to feel like a hunted animal. And his constant presence impeded her own work, at the hotel and otherwise.

Finally she came up with a clever solution, using a ruse worthy of Harvey Birch himself. Using the hand taught to her at school, she sent an anonymous letter to La Fayette Baker himself — in it, she exposed Bogardus' romance with her and denounced herself as a spy. It could have come from a malicious gossip like Lucy Buck or Mary Cloud. She slipped it into a Union courier's dispatch case and hoped for the best. It was a bold move, but she could think of no other way to dissuade Bogardus; perhaps the Union Provost could do it for her.

She heard through Alice that he had complained, quite upset, to Lucy Buck, about her inconstant ways. Soon he suggested that her services as a nurse at the hospital be discontinued.

This left Belle with time on her hands, and, still needing to find exchanged prisoners to take out messages for her, she started to stop by and engage the unwounded prisoners in conversation.

One tall young cavalry trooper seemed particularly interesting. She asked Lieutenant Preston about him.

Preston knew who he was at once. "Lieutenant Smitley, of the Rebel Fifth Virginia. He was captured at Cross Keys."

"He seems like a good fellow," Belle said. "Would you introduce me?"

Preston looked at her speculatively. "Gone off Yankee Blue, Miss Belle?"

Belle smiled sweetly and said, "My position is well known. I much prefer gray to blue, and simply seek to redress the balance between the two. Besides, he seems unhurt and will probably not be here long."

"True enough," Preston smiled back. "He has given his parole and is due to be exchanged shortly. I'd rather have you squired by a Rebel than one of us. Much less compromising."

Belle was suddenly a little short of breath. Like Michael Kelley, Preston was simply waiting for her to make a fatal error. Both had known her since that unhappy day in Martinsburg when she had shot and killed the Yankee soldier.

"Oh, Lieutenant," she simpered, "How you do talk! If I'm such a danger, then move General Shields to grant my request to go to Richmond."

"Would that I could," Preston replied frankly. "Smitley is staying with Doctor Gilmour. Come back at four and we will walk together to that house, where I shall make between you a proper introduction."

Doctor Gilmour was a elderly distant relative of Harry Gilmour's, Belle knew, and his daughter Hattie spent as much time cultivating Yankee officers as she did. Hattie had acquired the same dubious reputation in Front Royal as she had, of being an outrageous flirt and a serial kisser, but with another purpose entirely. She wanted to live in New York City, with its glittering lights and society, and sought only a rich husband to be her collaborator in this ambition.

Belle only hoped that Hattie had not already sunk her hooks into Lieutenant Smitley, but reflected that it was unlikely, since Smitley, whatever his estate before the war, was likely poor, and too dedicated to the Rebel cause to run off with the likes of Hattie Gilmour. Privately, Belle had more regard for Annie Jones. She was more honest.

At the appointed hour, Preston did indeed escort her to the Gilmour house and, with all due ceremony, introduced her to Smitley, who came from a farm near Harper's Ferry. He was poor, he said, but Belle saw at once that he was well brought up, had elegant manners, and a confidence about him that was very attractive. His beard was clean and well groomed, reddish brown, and he had beautiful clear blue eyes.

"What was your position with the Fifth?" Belle asked, still flirting girlishly while she tried to size him up.

"I was simply a squadron leader," Smitley said. "Nothing very important."

"Done any scouting?"

"Some, not much."

"Perhaps you know my uncle, James Glenn, or my cousins Stephen Boyd, or Billy Boyd Compton?"

Smitley frowned. "The names are familiar, but I don't think I've had the pleasure. My unit is usually part of the reserve, so we don't have much to do with scouts."

Belle smiled. "Any friends in the Seventh Virginia?"

"I knew Harry Gilmour when we were boys, before he moved up to Baltimore," Smitley said.

"Really," Belle smiled. "Harry and I are dear friends from when I was at school in Baltimore."

Smitley returned the smile. "He's a good fellow. You wouldn't like Baltimore now. The Yankees have the whole city by the throat. Detectives everywhere you turn."

"I was there in March," Belle said. "General Dix was very kind to me. Put me up at Eutaw House."

Smitley raised his eyebrows at that. Belle found herself telling him the whole tale, leaving out Antonia Ford's visit, but mentioning Gilmour's.

"So Harry was spying?" Smitley said this lightly, but the question alone was enough to make Belle draw back and speak with more caution.

"I wouldn't say that," Belle said. "Smuggling more like, to get things through the land blockade."

"Lot of money in that, I suppose," Smitley said.

"Some," Belle laughed. "But it's not done for the money. It's done because we need drugs like quinine and morphine."

Smitley smiled and nodded, and did not press her further. If he had, Belle would have been more on her guard with him.

Hattie Gilmour came in and told them that she had arranged a party for that evening and would be so happy if Belle would honor them with her presence.

"More officers will come," Hattie admitted, with a frank generous smile. "There will be no chaperons to dull things down." She winked. "Close combat for those so inclined."

"So you mean to use me as a Judas goat to lure them to the slaughter," Belle laughed.

"Oh, that's so cruel of you to say that," Hattie rejoined. "It's just that you seem to attract all the really handsome ones. They follow you like small boys."

Belle leaned over, and whispered, "Well, aren't they?"

Hattie laughed. In dim light she and Belle were sometimes mistaken for each other because they were equally tall and had the same spectacular figures, but Hattie was far prettier in the face, and knew it. Belle did not resent this, but hoped to use it to advantage.

"I will come, on one condition," Belle said.

"Name it," Hattie replied, her eyes dancing.

"That Lieutenant Smitley will be my beau tonight. I am weary of the company of Yankees."

Hattie licked her lips and gave her another large, generous smile. "More for me. How could I say no?"

Smitley laughed and said, "Don't I have a say in this?"

"No," Hattie and Belle said as one. He laughed again and raised his hands in mock surrender.

"Besides, Charlie," Hattie said, "You are like a brother to me."

"I must go home and change, and tell Alice and Lieutenant Preston where I will be," Belle said, rising from the bench where she and Smitley were sitting.

"Oh, bring them, too," Hattie said. "I want a big party. I've engaged some Negro musicians to play, and there is the piano. You must sing for us, Belle. You have such a beautiful voice. Wear your best gown and let us dazzle them."

"My goodness," Belle commented. "Will anyone not be there?"

"Yes," said Hattie firmly. "Lucy Buck."

When Belle told Alice about the party, she was quite excited. "Oh, it will be like old times," she said happily.

"Hattie sets a good table. It won't be any of that 'starvation party' nonsense they have in Richmond," Belle said.

"What is that?" Alice asked.

"Everyone pretends there is food and drink, but all they serve is bread and water. Charlie Smitley told me about it. Of course, they all stuff themselves at home beforehand."

"I would hope so," Alice said, "Else how would they survive the dancing and singing?"

Eliza was helping Belle into one of the new gowns she had bought with Union Army money in Baltimore. "Hattie will be so jealous," Alice said, "That you've a new gown and she doesn't."

Belle said drily, "Surely you don't think her so vain and shallow?"

Alice laughed and nodded.

"I've already promised to leave the field to her," Belle explained. "Tonight I shall be dancing with Charlie Smitley and no other. Trading Yankee Blue for Confederate Gray."

"That should confuse everyone. Myles won't be there?"

"No, but what if he is?"

"He might say something to Dan Keily."

"What if he does?" Belle asked coolly. "Captain K. is yesterday's news. I am a young girl in need of a good time, and I mean to have one tonight, the war notwithstanding. I advise you to do likewise."

Alice nodded happily. "Lieutenant Preston is a very good

kisser, for a Yankee."

Eliza made a deep rumbling laugh and started to walk out of the room.

"Where are you going?" Belle asked.

"I gots to make sum of dat tea," Eliza said. Belle tried to hide her smile and Alice looked at them both in confusion.

The party was the most brilliant affair held in Front Royal that year, talked about for quite some time after. Belle was the unwilling center of attention at first, but firmly deferred to her hostess. There was not much room for dancing, and most of the party gradually collected around the piano where a Yankee officer played. Mostly it was the younger officers from the new Union Virginia regiments who had come, and they were reserved at first, especially around Smitley, but soon everyone relaxed.

Belle tried to stir things up by singing the new Rebel anthems, 'The Bonnie Blue Flag' and 'Maryland, My Maryland,' but everyone just joined in on the choruses. The words were treason to the Yankees, but the music was engaging and no one was looking to spoil the party with a dispute. When Belle realized no one was actually listening to the words, tears of frustration began to come to her eyes.

"Let's sing 'The Bonnie Blue Flag' again," Smitley proposed.

"Yes, let's," Hattie Gilmour said, anxious that there not be a scene that would spoil the party.

Belle blinked her tears away and said, "Something that stands for Virginia. Yes." She nodded to the young officer at the piano and started the first stanza when he began to play. Three of the Virginia Yankees joined in, but she felt especially gratified when Smitley rose, very boldly and sang the Confederate parts in a beautiful baritone.

There were many more men than girls at the party, and most continued to play and sing, drinking all the while. Hattie Gilmour was suddenly absent and so was a handsome Captain from one of the New York regiments. Belle noticed that Alice and Lieutenant Preston were likewise missing, but probably somewhere in the big house.

Then Charlie Smitley took her hand and drew her part way down the hallway.

"Would you like to see where I am staying?" he asked quietly. "It's quite a nice room."

Belle smiled and let herself be led inside. It was a large, well-furnished bedroom with bright moonlight streaming in through the windows. Smitley closed the door behind them.

"Sir!" Belle protested softly as he slid his arms around her waist and drew him to her, and then said no more because he was kissing her and she was responding with a hunger that she had not known she had. She decided to let him continue, simply because he was so skilled and his fingers were so nimble. To be seduced in such comfort, at such a leisurely pace, was a new experience and one which she relished. Soon he was kissing her breasts and teasing her bare nipples and then she felt his hand slide gently between her legs, seeking her sex through the vent in her pantaloons. She felt a finger slide up easily and realized that she was wet and ready for him. She rolled over, hiked up her skirts around her waist and pushed him back on the bed, unbuttoning his fly.

He stared at her, but said nothing as she drew his cock out of his pants, made sure it was at maximum stiffness with her hand and then sat herself down upon him. Feeling him inside her, she took his face tenderly between her hands and kissed him, feeling him inside of her.

Disappointment washed through her. He was too quick and not the man of parts that Dan Keily was. She felt a bit cheated, and bereft any corresponding physical reaction. Her smile became fixed as she gazed at him, trying to think of what to say.

"We must be quick," she said, "Before our absence is noticed." Smitley simply nodded, and when she slid off him and rearranged her skirts and buttoned up the top of her dress, found a towel and cleaned himself before rebuttoning his pants.

Belle, feeling flushed, primped herself in the mirror, tucking up stray hairs, and made sure all her clothing was straight before nodding to him. He held the door for her and they slipped out into the hallway, then drifted down to the parlor, hand in hand.

The Yankee officers were singing some dreary Irish dirge about battle's end and Alice was curled up quite comfortably on a couch, in Lieutenant Preston's arms. Hattie and her Captain were nowhere to be seen.

Smitley was not allowed to leave the house after curfew, so Lieutenant Preston saw them both home, holding Alice's hand all the way. Belle made sure that Alice, too, had some of Eliza's bitter tea. Alice blushed bright red when Belle explained the purpose of it, but drank it eagerly. Two cups.

The next day, when Smitley, still on parole, came to call with a bouquet of flowers for her, Belle went for a long walk with him.

After some flattering preliminaries, Belle got down to business.

"When are you being released?" she asked him.

"Tomorrow," Smitley said, smiling regretfully, "Perhaps...."

Belle interrupted him. "You know the Yankees think me a spy?"

Smitley nodded, "Everyone has heard that. It's been in the newspapers. Everyone wonders why you are not arrested."

"They have no real proof," Belle said, "So I must be very careful. I need a dependable officer to carry a message to General Jackson or some other responsible officer. Actually, I have quite a bit of material that must go."

Smitley was distressed. He frowned and shook his head.

"Miss Belle, I have given them my parole."

"So have I, sir. I violate it all the time. That is a necessity of war. There would be no purpose in my staying here if I did not."

"So you are a spy?" Smitley looked genuinely surprised.

"Would I be so friendly with these Yankees were I not?" Belle smiled. "What do you take me for? One of Hattie Gilmour's ilk?"

Smitley looked properly distressed, "No, not at all! Last

night...."

"Will not be spoken of again," Belle said sternly. "I need a reliable man. On your honor as a Confederate officer and a gentleman, will you accept this mission?"

"Yes, of course," Smitley said gravely. "I am honored that you asked."

"I will give you the packet tonight," Belle said. "Tell no one."

"Of course not," he replied. Belle gave him a quick kiss on the cheek and let him walk her back to the hotel. Glancing sideways, she saw his expression was perplexed, and a bit angry, like a man who suspects he has been cheated at cards.

CHAPTER FORTY-TWO

July 18th-23rd, 1862, Front Royal, Virginia

"Miss Belle, who dat man you talkin' to?"

Belle looked questioningly at Betsy, the slave who was the hotel's chief cook. Betsy was part of the hotel personal property when her uncle had leased it, along with the other cooks, the laundresses and the maids who took care of the rooms.

She was about forty years old, Belle knew, and while she had been open and friendly with Eliza, tended to be silent and sullen when Belle or Alice spoke with her. Belle was always cautious around her since her feelings about the war might not accord with those of her owners.

"He's a Confederate officer on parole," Belle said after a moment. "He's going South."

Betsy's eyes widened. "You gib him anything fer...?"

Her face became very grave and she leaned forward and spoke in a lower voice, aware that others might hear what she said, but spoke urgently nevertheless. "Miss Belle, dat man ain't no rebel. I seen him wid Yankee officers last month — near de depot, in Yankee uniform! Eben dough he got Sessesh clothes on, he ain't no Sessesh! Dat man a spy. Cain't fool Betsy that way. Dat man a spy! Please God he is! Dat man a spy!" Betsy's large dark face shone with moisture and her eyes were filled with concern and alarm.

Belle tried to gauge this against her previous behavior and decided that it was as Eliza had told her — most slaves, connected to a family as servants, put that family before all other concerns. Especially if they were well treated. She searched for the right words.

"I'm sure you're mistaken, Betsy," Belle replied. "I've found him to be a very good fellow, very loyal to the South."

Betsy looked at her with pity, "Den you not thinkin' wid de head but sumtin' lower down." She walked away, shaking her head, muttering to herself.

Belle watched her go, not knowing whether to laugh or cry. Betsy was right about one thing, she hadn't been using her mind where Charlie Smitley was concerned. That Betsy had spoken so boldly to her and with such obvious concern was the most startling thing that had happened to her since — well, since she found herself making love to Charlie Smitley. She had not intended that.

Truth be told, she hadn't enjoyed him all that much. It was as if she were scratching an itch. It had been quick and close to brutal, and not satisfying. She felt more affection and involvement when she rode Fleeter at a hard gallop. Recalling the encounter depressed and confused her, and she fended off his efforts to arrange a second tryst. That was easy enough, given that both of them were supposed to be under guard.

The night before her grandmother had presented her with another problem.

"The Yankees have passed a new law which we must take heed of," Ruth said to both Belle and Alice as they dawdled over tea in their private sitting room. "That new Provost Marshal made a point of presenting me with a copy."

Belle and Alice both looked at her with concern. She passed over the printed pages and they read it carefully, sitting side by side.

"What do you make of it?" Ruth Burns asked, frowning.

Alice, being a lawyer's daughter who sometimes clerked for her father, spoke first, "Well, it's hard on treason, but that requires a trial. The parts where they take property from those who support the Rebel cause does not. That's under Lincoln, which means the Union Army can do as it pleases if they find evidence that you've supported the South in any material way."

"In any way at all," Belle added. "That 'aid and comfort' portion seems elastic enough to stretch around any case they might care to bring."

"Legalized theft, then," sniffed their grandmother, "But they need cause."

"You're worried about losing the hotel, Grandma?" Belle asked.

Ruth nodded grimly and sighed, "The lease is in Jimmie's name, but it's Glenn money that bought it and Glenn money must be protected and paid back. If the Yankees take it, then we'll owe Mister Fishback for the whole thing, lock, stock and chattels."

"I will have to leave," Belle said, "And Eliza with me. It's me they are after."

Alice began to cry quietly. "Oh, Belle, what will I do without you? I can't run all of this by myself."

Belle smiled, "Nonsense. Grandma can do books as well as I, and you'll be less troubled by Yankees if you continue with Lieutenant Preston as a beau."

Ruth looked at Alice sharply and then looked at Belle and said tightly, "If that's the way it is, then it's all your fault, Belle!"

Belle nodded, but Alice said, "Not entirely, Grandma. I had a little bit to do with it."

Ruth just frowned and shook her head. A muttered curse passed her lips.

Belle said, "Well, we can't just sit here and wring our hands. We must act. I am under close supervision by the Yankees. I can't go back to Martinsburg and I can't stay here. While I've enjoyed being a fly on the wall at Yankee headquarters and there was much profit in it, I don't want any of us to get swatted or dispossessed."

"The hotel should be safe enough," Alice said, "None of us are owners. You and I are not legally old enough to sign contracts. Grandma must do it for us. And the lease is actually owned by Father," she added. "Since he's not here, they can't make him responsible for our transgressions."

"Actually they can," Ruth said, "And it would be a matter for civil court, none of which are in session. We are under martial law. Yankees can do as they please and devil take the hindmost."

"Which is why I must go, to protect both of you and the family's interest," Belle said. "I have teased them repeatedly about being sent South, beyond the lines. They temporize, not wanting me to carry off information against them." She sighed, "I must provoke them into doing it."

"Lieutenant Preston is certainly in favor," Alice observed,

"And so is his immediate superior. It's Shields and Kimball who want to keep you here."

"I have a plan," Belle said after a moment's reflection. The other two listened silently, making no motion nor expression.

"I have asked Charles Smitley to carry a message for me to Stonewall," Belle said slowly, "But last night Doctor Bogardus came to me, in a jealous rage, and told me that Smitley is a Yankee spy — a Jessie Scout or the like. Being a silly young girl, I laughed at the idea. Charlie is a man of the South, born and bred and he speaks the native dialect of the Virginia Piedmont."

"So does Porte Crayon!" Alice broke in, exasperated.

Belle smiled. "So he does. Smitley is a bit too smooth and willing to break his parole. He has played me well, and now I will play him back."

"How?" Ruth spoke calmly, but her expression showed that she didn't like what she was hearing.

"I shall write a long friendly letter to Stonewall Jackson, but not in the usual code. It shall have enough information to make them send me South."

Alice looked very alarmed. "They might attribute some of that to me."

Belle smiled, "Not if I write about how difficult it is to work around you and your servants, and how I dare not confide in you since you are such firm friends with Lucy Buck, whom I do not trust. Bogardus can confirm some small part of that. Thus, we expose Smitley and his game, secure my release to Richmond, and protect the family interest. At the same time, I secure your innocence."

Ruth said "But the spying, smuggling, stealing of Yankee weapons and accessories, even the money changing — that all ends. They will be watching too closely for us to continue."

"No huge loss, Grandma. We are too closely watched to attain important information. What we've been doing can be done equally well by one of Harry Gilmour's scouts with a spyglass and a pencil and paper. As for the rest, they were crimes of opportunity and we are just about out of Confederate money."

"That which isn't false or suspect, yes," Alice agreed.

"It's time to think about shutting up shop entirely," Belle said. "We should sell out to some Yankee speculator."

Ruth Burns shook her head. "That won't be easy. Have to be a buyer who can pay cash. Gold at that."

"How fond of you of Lieutenant Preston?" Belle teased Alice.

Alice blushed, but admitted, "I could bear to part with him. He's a Yankee, after all."

"You must plead with him not to send me away," Belle said.

Alice blinked, "But, you want to go...."

"Yes, but they will suspect you less if you play it that way. The calumny that William Clark laid against me cannot attach itself to you, dear heart. You must remain here."

"To spy?" Alice looked doubtful.

"To run the hotel with Grandma. We'll get a better price if it's a going concern," Belle replied, with a smile. "Your secret service is over for now."

Belle went to her room in the cottage and wrote a six-page letter to Stonewall Jackson. She made it seem like the kind of chatty, non-consequential missive that a young girl might write to a favorite uncle, but was careful to mention significant details about the Union Army and its commanders. It was the same kind of letter that had gotten her into trouble in Martinsburg the year before, written in the same broad formal hand she had learned in school.

She prepared a short note, written in code, and told Eliza to get it to Harry Gilmour or one of his scouts, by way of a certain silver pocket watch. The note was about Smitley, in case he should choose to continue his masquerade South by actually delivering her letter to Jackson.

Smitley took the sealed letter from her and put it carefully inside his butternut-colored coat.

Belle smiled and said, "I cannot thank you enough. When will you go?"

"On the morrow, about six in the morning. I will have until the noon hour to get beyond the pickets." Smitley returned the smile and touched her cheek tenderly. "I'm going to miss you, darlin'."

Belle shot a glance sideways.

"Perhaps we can go for a walk later."

Smitley's eyebrows raised slightly, and he looked thoughtful. "Perhaps we can."

That night Belle favored Charlie Smitley with luxurious kisses and permitted him to briefly fondle her breasts, but demurred to go further because of the chance of being discovered 'in the act.' She encouraged foolish talk on his part and made it seem that she was quite enamored of him.

Early the next morning, she went to see him again, at the Gilmour house as he was preparing to leave, and said, with tears in her eyes. "They say you are a Yankee spy, Charles Smitley. Oh, tell me it isn't so!"

The tears began to course down her cheeks as she began to cry openly. Another man in Confederate Army uniform nearby looked at them both sharply as Smitley led her off a little ways.

"Dear God, Belle, don't even think such a thing! My life will be worth nothing if these other fellows think that true. They will wait until we are past the lines and most likely murder me. Do you want that?"

"No!" Belle wailed. "But, the cook said that she saw you in Yankee uniform last month near the depot."

"And so she did," Smitley said smoothly. "I was scouting the town. It was a reconnaissance for Ewell."

Belle looked at him doubtfully. "It was? Truly?"

"Yes!" he replied urgently and drew her letter from inside his coat. "Look, do you want this back? If the Yankees catch me with it my hope of parole will vanish like last night's biscuits."

Belle pouted, hoping that she looked like a simpleton.

"No, Jackson must have what's inside. No, I believe you. Oh, kiss me before you go, lest my heart break!"

Smitley took her into his arms and did just that, causing the other men nearby, Union and Confederate alike, to turn away and grin at each other.

Belle, knowing it was time to exit the stage of this little play, threw her arms around him, wiped the tears from her eyes, smiled like a fool and then ran off, back towards the hotel. Behind her she could hear the other men roughly teasing Smitley about his conquest of her.

Well, she thought, *if that doesn't get me to Richmond, nothing will.*

As she went about her daily duties at the hotel she found herself worrying about whether or not Daniel Keily would hear of her public embrace of Smitley. She was angry with herself. Daniel was an Irishman and a Yankee, totally unsuitable as a beau. Were it not for the war, they would have never even met, much less become lovers — and yet she found herself wanting his strong, sure touch on her bare skin, his muscular soldier's body against hers. Neither Smitley nor Doctor Bogardus, she knew, were half the man that Dan Keily was. She wondered where he was and how he fared.

Daniel Keily looked up and tried not to smile when Myles Keogh came into the room. He was dressed only in a loose-fitting linen shirt and uniform pants, barefoot, with an apparatus on his lower face placed so that he could not move his jaw at all. This was so the bones would knit back up and he would once more be able to consume something other than porridge.

It simply hurt too much to smile. He was allowed two bottles a day of laudanum, a mixture of grain alcohol and opium, for the pain. It was not yet noon and he was well into the second bottle.

"Hallo, Mumbles," Keogh said cheerfully. In reply, Keily made an obscene Italian gesture with his left arm.

"Now, don't be that way, lad. I've come with news about your lady love." Keogh wasn't smiling though, which caused Keily to raise his eyebrows inquiringly.

"It's not good, Dan. They've finally caught her out. They sent a scout in Confederate uniform, from the Fifth West Virginia he was, to trap her. She asked him to deliver a written message to Jackson."

Keily groaned.

Keogh nodded. "In that fine girlish hand she wrote down a pretty accurate order of battle for all of our units in and about Front Royal. The scout took the whole thing right to General Schneckt."

Keogh spotted a nearby wooden chair, pulled it closer and sat down. Keily had the look of a man in more than physical pain. Keogh leaned closer and spoke in a very low voice.

"You've been a fool, Dan, plain and simple. She played you, didn't she?"

Keily shook his head back and forth angrily.

"Ah, Dan, Dan, the woman's a spy! The story about her run to Jackson is true, and word is she gave her report to him like a staff officer on parade. And, for all your heroic acts at Fort Republic, sooner or later some nosey Provost Marshal is going to ask what you told her and when."

Keily made an emphatic gesture with his hand, indicating his strong disagreement.

"Well, I've wondered meself, old son. Jackson surprised us at Front Royal and rolled the lines back sixty miles. He wasn't able to hold, but maybe that wasn't his intent. McDowell got pulled back to protect Washington, which put paid to McClellan's campaign against Richmond. He won't do it now, and he was but five miles from the city. Richmond is safe, for now." Keogh shook his head sadly, "Our master, General Shields, is not a total fool, but he's been gulled by Miss Belle, as have we all. He's too much the politician to do anything but find someone else to put the blame to."

Keily, dazed, pointed a finger at himself, his eyebrows raised in question.

"Oh, yes. You made quite a display of your affections — even talked of marriage, didn't ye?" Keogh pulled out a cigar, bit off the end and lit it before continuing.

"Ye can get shut of it. Go to New York and see the Archbishop, see what influence he has. Stay on convalescent leave as long as you can manage, and when ye return, get into another unit entirely. It's a very large Army with more than a hundred generals ye can serve — or get yerself a command, but please, God, not in this valley."

Keily looked at him, almost on the verge of tears.

"Forget this woman, Dan," Myles Keogh advised him. "She's the enemy and she's near ruined you. She had the scout, too, by his account, so all the loose talk about her being a whore may not be so far off. Shields finds time to think about it, and you'll be under arrest for certain. Your best shot is him thinking you were a bigger fool than he."

Keogh drew on the cigar and blew out a ring of smoke. He watched it dissipate. "And one thing more, Dan. John O'Keefe and I have agreed to seek other positions in the army — so this stink you've made don't attach itself to our careers."

Keily wrote a brief note on a piece of foolscap and handed it to him. Keogh read it and crumpled it angrily, "You love her? Have ye not heard a word I said?"

Keily nodded slowly, almost on the verge of tears.

Keogh looked at his friend with pity. "And none of it matters, does it? You want her still. You bloody fool."

Alice heard from Lieutenant Preston that Richmond would be Belle's new home. They would send her beyond the lines. This was the intention of his superiors and it lacked only the proper arrangements to be done. Eliza had already packed her trunk.

When Bogardus taunted her about Smitley being a spy sent to trap her, Belle screamed at him until the Union doctor retreated.

It was a nasty public scene that got the attention of everyone within earshot, which was what Belle intended. She was equally gratified when Alice later told her of Bogardus's complaint to Lucy Buck about her, and how he had said it didn't pay to keep company with her.

Belle decided that it would be a relief to get out of Front Royal and down to Richmond, where things were not so confusing.

CHAPTER FORTY-THREE

July 30, 1862, Front Royal, Virginia

That morning she reread ***The Lady Lieutenant***, the trashy novel she'd bought at the train station in Baltimore, once more engrossed in the vital question of whether or not Madeline would win her lover Frank in the middle of the Battle of Bull's Run.

She knew it was a preposterous tale, despite the assurance on the cover that the story was "true and authentic". Yet her own adventures would give Madeline's a run for their money. Not to mention Harvey Birch's in the novel that had set her on this course, Fenimore Cooper's ***The Spy***. She drew courage from his example which was noble, self-sacrificing and had the ring of truth.

She was living on borrowed time. Michael Kelley was once more present, his brogue and genial joking manner running cover for his cold policeman's heart. He was immune to flattery and flirting, and the last thing Belle would have ever done was send him a bouquet, as she had Colonel Fillebrown. His light green eyes often looked like a pair of gun barrels aimed her way. Belle smiled and tried to flirt, but felt like a bug about to be squashed when he looked at her that way.

She did not share these feelings with Alice, who was still shaken and confused by her romance with Lieutenant Preston. Alice didn't mean to like the Yankee, and swore she did not love him, but Belle saw the soft looks she cast his way since they had become lovers.

Perhaps it is for the best that I go now, Belle thought, as she washed her face and combed out her long hair. Soon enough they would come for her and she would be passed beyond the lines to Richmond. Shields himself, at supper two days ago, had made a joke about her giving: "My best regards to Jeff Davis."

The mission had gone on too long and her judgment was compromised. The night before, seeing a large party of Union cavalry ride out to the west of town, she had conceived the notion that they were out to surprise and trap Harry Gilmour's company from the Seventh Virginia. She had hastily scribbled a warning and dispatched the old slave Moses, with the large silver pocket watch, to find him.

Moses had not yet returned. Harry's exact whereabouts were always a mystery to her, so she was not greatly worried. Yet she had been nervous all morning.

She heard a small commotion outside and went to the window of her room just as Eliza entered with a steaming cup of Yankee coffee and a fresh roll, hot from the oven, on a tray. Below, in the courtyard, Belle saw a detail of eight Yankee soldiers march to the barn where she had lost her virginity to Daniel Keily, and begin to open the wide doors where the hotel's carriage was stored.

Eliza set the tray on the little table below the window and looked over Belle's shoulder. "What dey doin?"

"I don't know, " Belle said, sipping at the coffee, trying to shake off the sleepy feeling that had come over her. She nibbled at the roll. "Why would they want the carriage?"

Eliza looked at her, eyes widening with alarm. "Fer you?"

Belle returned the gaze calmly. "Why? I can ride as well as any of them. Better than most, truth be told."

Eliza shook her head. "I go see what's what." She left Belle alone and went down the stairs.

Belle continued to sip her coffee and eat her roll as the Yankee soldiers, under the direction of a sergeant, took wads of cotton and began to clean the dust off the carriage's wheels and body. It had not been used in several months.

A noise attracted Belle's attention. Turning her gaze, she saw a number of Union cavalry ride into the alley that divided the hotel from the cottage and dismount. They stood about in twos and threes, relaxed, talking quietly, some smoking, yet obviously on duty. There was no joking or horseplay among them.

A pair of bay mares were led up and put into harness to draw the carriage. Belle thought wildly and briefly of making a run for it, but it was impossible. Every door would be guarded, every avenue of escape blocked. There was nothing to do but wait.

Eliza came back up the stairs and into the room, her face funeral-solemn. "Miss Belle," she said, "de Provo' Marshal wish to see you in de livin' room and dere's other men wid him."

"Yes," said Belle and put on her bravest smile. *I will not beg or plead*, she told herself. Holding herself in the manner she had seen that great lady, Rose Greenhow, display at a ball that now seemed as if it had happened a hundred years ago, she descended the stairs.

Waiting for her were five men. Lieutenant Preston and his immediate superior, Major McEnnis, and a tall Cavalry officer, another Major. Michael Kelley stood apart, his back to the rest, looking out of the window at the cavalrymen outside. The fifth man was a civilian, short in stature, ill-kempt, with an uncombed beard and a dirty neck and mean little eyes that glared at her suspiciously. She was immediately repulsed by his looks and manner, not just because he was obviously immune to her charms, but because he stared at her with utter contempt and a sneer on his lips.

Belle involuntarily put her hand to her throat. All of the men, save Kelley, looked at her steadily. Preston and McEnnis looked embarrassed, while the tall cavalry officer looked pleasantly curious and expectant.

No one seemed to know what to say, so Belle, speaking calmly and with a big smile, asked, "What can I do for you gentlemen?"

McEnnis started, cleared his throat, motioned towards the tall cavalry officer, and said, embarrassed by his words, "This is Major Sherman of the 12th Illinois Cavalry. He has come to arrest you."

Belle decided to play out the hand. "Impossible," she said in a loud, firm voice. "Whatever for?"

The little civilian looked irritated when this was said, and self-importantly drew from his pocket a half sheet of paper.

"I'm the arresting officer," he said sharply, glaring at McEnnis and then Sherman and then at Belle. "Alfie Cridge, United States Secret Service," he continued, loading each word with heavy significance.

Belle smiled because she found his Cockney accent comical. "You don't much sound like a Yankee."

"Neither do I," said Michael Kelley mildly, still looking out the window, but so that everyone could hear him. "Neither does General Siegal, but here we are, defending the Union." He put particular emphasis on the last three words.

Major Sherman stepped forward. Belle found him immediately attractive because he was almost six and a half feet tall and well-favored. He did not lack for charm either, as he took her hands gently in his and spoke.

"Miss Belle, this is a painful duty for me. You are a young girl and no doubt these charges are exaggerated; however, the order is plain and comes from the Secretary of War himself."

He held out his hand for the paper that Cridge held. Cridge stared at him a moment. With a growl, he surrendered the document. Sherman handed it to her.

It read:

"Sir: You will proceed at once to Front Royal, and arrest, if found there, Miss Belle Boyd, and bring her to Washington."

It was signed by Stanton himself.

Belle read it carefully and as slowly as she could, her mind racing as she tried to think what to do next. Behind her she could feel Alice and her grandmother come into the room.

With so many soldiers in the room and about the house, resistance was futile. Neither would she give them the satisfaction of arguing the matter. It would do no good. They were soldiers and had their orders. She had to respect that. But it was important to delay them a few minutes. Already Eliza had disappeared from the room, ghosting up the stairs to find her papers and get them safely burned in the kitchen stove.

Cridge said, "I must search the house."

Belle felt a thrill of fear go through her. There was evidence to be found here, she knew. Enough to get her hanged.

Ruth and Alice immediately posted themselves behind her, blocking the way to the stairs.

"Gentlemen, you must allow me to retire and my maid to prepare my room, which is in great disarray," Belle said. "And I must prepare my garments for the journey."

"I have no time fer yer geegaws," Cridge sneered.

"You ruffian," Alice cried angrily, "She's a young lady of good breeding and family. She goes nowhere without a proper trunk!"

Cridge started to push past them, but was restrained by the firm hand of Major Sherman on his arm. "Sir, you must give her leave. For decency's sake."

Cridge shook off his hand and grinned evilly. "I've heard all about her decency."

Belle regarded him coolly. "What kennel have you sprung from to be so unmannerly?"

Cridge started to reply, when Michael Kelley cleared his throat and raised his eyebrow. Cridge looked around the room and saw that the other men were against him on this point.

"One trunk," he grumbled. "No more — and I must search the house."

Belle inclined her head graciously, "Very well, I will retire now and make ready to go."

She turned and started up the stairs, but Cridge bulled his way past her. "Sir!" she protested, "Will you not wait until my room is in a suitable condition for you to enter?"

Cridge snarled, "No, yer don't! I'm coming with yer. Yer got some papers yer want to get rid of." And with that he proceeded into the room ahead of her. He proved to be a very through detective.

Cridge fell upon her trunk's contents like a man possessed, pulling each dress out, examining its seams minutely, turning it inside out, and then dropping it on the floor. Eliza made a wordless sound of protest, to which he paid no heed as he went on to the next dress and treated it with equal violence and disdain. Then he started in on Belle's other garments, including her underclothes. He looked under the bed and into the closet, pulling out the clothes she had intended to leave behind as too heavy for summer wear. Finally, he spied her desk.

Belle realized that her portfolio, which contained the code tables and ciphers was gone. She looked at Eliza, raising an eyebrow, and understood from her maid's gestures that its contents were now in the kitchen stove, being consumed by fire. A noise of triumph from Cridge told her that a few of the tally sheets she had been using to count up the Union troops, horses and supply wagons had been discovered. He favored her with a leer and then opened up the desk drawers. He positively crowed with triumph as he drew forth the Colt Dragoon pistol and belt that had been sent to her by a Yankee officer in Martinsburg.

"Excuse me," said Belle, "that's mine, and Major Kelley will tell you as much. He was there when it was given to me."

"That so," Cridge grinned tightly, "Well yer won't need it where you're bound, Missy. I'll just take it along, along with the papers." He turned and pointed at a cabinet in the corner of the room. "What's in there?"

Belle looked and said, "My uncle's law papers, which he will need when the courts are back in session."

"Where's the key?"

"I have no idea," Belle said, honestly confused, for she was telling the exact truth for once. "I presume he has it."

"And he'd be where?"

Belle shrugged. "Richmond, the last we heard. That was in March."

Cridge sneered at her again, gathered up the papers and the pistol and belt and went out of the room and down the stairs. "Yer can pack up that trash again, if yer want to take it along," he said over his shoulder.

Eliza, trying not to show her considerable anger, began to pick up the clothes. Belle bent to help her. When Eliza protested, Belle smiled at her and said, "I'm going to have to do for myself for awhile. I might as well start now."

Eliza was genuinely distressed. "Dey goin' take you and not me?" she cried indignantly. "Dat ain't right!"

Cridge bustled back into the room, a large pry bar in one hand, walked over to the tall wooden cabinet and attacked the door with vigor. It groaned loudly, the wood splintered, and the door popped open.

"You've ruined it!" Belle cried out, indignant. It had been a fine piece of furniture, hand-crafted of oak and cherry. Now it was beyond repair and would have to be thrown away.

Cridge ignored her and picked up some of the papers. Latin was not a language he was familiar with, she suspected, and there was enough on the papers and pleadings that he obviously assumed it was some sort of code. He grinned unpleasantly at her, bundled all of the law papers together, and, tucking them under one arm, said, "I've the rest to do. Yer got the half of an hour to pack." He walked out of the room, strutting with self-importance.

It was a hour before Belle, now dressed for travel, came regally down the stairs, her purse and parasol in one hand. Behind her, two Privates struggled with the trunk, which was rather heavy. Had Detective Cridge examined it more closely he might have found the secret compartments where Belle hid her money. Her money changing operations had left her with the incredible sum of twenty thousand dollars in Union greenbacks. Some of this she had slipped to Eliza to give to Alice later. One compartment held her stash of gold coins. Those she would take with her. Wherever she was bound, bribes would have to be paid.

Cridge was too busy talking to Major Sherman, making some sort of point to him, to notice anything about the trunk. Her grandmother and cousin pleaded tearfully with Major McEnnis and Lieutenant Preston. The latter seemed to be particularly bothered. His face was flushed from his hat to his collar, and he kept shaking his head sadly. Michael Kelley leaned against the wall, near the front door of the cottage, very detached from it all.

Alice and Ruth turned to Major Sherman, piteously pleading that Belle, who was only a young girl, be spared. Cridge, having seen that the single trunk was secured on the back of the carriage, came back into the room and took her roughly by the arm. Eliza, wailing in distress, knelt and threw her arms around Belle's knees, begging to go with her. Cridge, growling, started to strike her, only to find that Michael Kelley had interposed himself quickly and was restraining the detective's arm with his own rather strong hand. Kelley put enough pressure into his grip that Cridge gasped and turned white with pain for a moment.

"I suggest that you go outside and let me sort this out, old son," Kelley said, his brogue thickened by anger. Cridge started to bluster, but then thought better of it. Rubbing his arm, he went out the front door without another word.

Kelley then helped Eliza to her feet, handling her as gently as if she were a child. Everyone stared at him.

"Oh, Michael, can't she come along?" Belle said, wanting nothing more than Eliza's company at that moment.

"No," Kelley said, "We cannot permit it. She's not the subject of any order." He smiled at Belle kindly. "Besides, it's Washington where yer bound. Slaves are no longer the fashion there."

Belle nodded slowly and then took Eliza to her with a sisterly hug. "We must be brave, Eliza. I will miss you."

Eliza looked at her steadily. "And I you. You take care, y' heah?"

Belle laughed. "I will do that." She moved over and hugged Alice and then her grandmother. "It will be all right," she said, far from certain that it would be.

Michael Kelley offered her his arm. "If I may escort you to your carriage, Miss Belle?"

She took it, acting regal. "Certainly."

Cridge was already seated in the carriage as they came out the door. The street, Belle saw, was very crowded, not only with cavalry, but people from the town who had heard about the arrest and come to gawk. A murmur went through the crowd as she appeared. Belle looked carefully at them. Front Royal was not her home and she did not know many people here. Most seemed sympathetic and obviously distressed that she was being carted off. Some, however, seemed to look at her with a kind of triumph. She spotted Lucy Buck and her cousin Mary Cloud, not in the front rank of the spectators, but wearing mean little smiles and whispering to each other with something approaching glee. She made a point of bowing slightly in their direction. She had the satisfaction of seeing them stop and look back at her, alarmed. It was tempting to call out to them something that would cause them great difficulties with the Union authorities, but she was better than that.

As Kelley handed her into the carriage, she said, with some alarm, "You're not going to leave me unattended with Mister Cridge are you?"

Kelley chuckled. "No, indeed, darlin' — I'll be seein' you to the train meself."

Belle looked up and down the street and saw that there were quite a few more cavalrymen than she had observed from the window of her room. "Michael? How many are there in my escort?"

He smiled at her as she settled into the seat across from him and the disgruntled Cridge. "A full battalion. They fear a rescue by the Seventh Virginia. About four hundred fifty, altogether."

Belle stared at him in disbelief. She was both flattered and alarmed that the Union would take such measures.

"They say yer status in Hell is measured by the size of yer guard of honor, Belle," Kelley said with a twinkle in his eye.

Belle was unnerved by the joke. She grasped for words.

"Really, sir, you do me too much honor!"

He drew from his vest pocket the large silver pocket watch case she immediately recognized as the one belonging to old Moses. Belle looked at him with alarm.

Michael Kelley returned her gaze with perfect seriousness, as Major Sherman called out a command and the carriage began to move forward slowly. He waited a moment and then spoke with great deliberation.

"No, lass, we've finally taken your true measure."

— **To Be Continued** —

ACKNOWLEDGMENTS

The road from inception to final draft of this novel has been long and complicated. It really began in the early 1980s when I was one of about 4,000 people working on the revision of the *Encyclopaedia Britannica*'s *Micropaedia* volumes. Belle Boyd's short biography was one of 93 articles I completed for that project. So the first person I should thank is Bruce Felknor, my editor, for introducing me to her story.

It was not until 1998 that I had the opportunity to follow up and begin researching her story in earnest. This was at a time when I decided that I'd had enough of trade magazine journalism and wanted to return to my roots in fiction and drama. I was taking a few classes at Los Angeles Valley College and discovered in their library a very extensive collection of books about the U.S. Civil War, which provided me a rich array of historical personalities on which I could build my characters. I also gleaned valuable insights into the culture and political situation of the time, which gave me a framework on which to hang my narrative. I discovered more sources at the Oviatt Library at California State University, Northridge, and online at the "Documenting the American South" project at the libraries of the University of North Carolina, Chapel Hill, and the "Making of America" project jointly owned by the University of Michigan and Cornell University. Added to that were the 200 or so other books on Civil War topics and personalties I purchased and/or read as the novel developed.

The story changed, as stories will, and I found myself writing not just about Belle Boyd, but Rose Greenhow and her spy ring, about Antonia Ford and about Loretta Janetta Valezquez. All of them were secret agents for the Confederate Government and all did remarkable service for "The Lost Cause".

The original novel grew too large and unwieldy, because while many fine details were absent and needed to be filled in, there is considerable historical record as superstructure. The process of getting to this first of five planned novels in a series has been aided by a few discerning readers.

Most important of these in the early stages was the late

Gerald Pearce, a fellow writer whose sense of story never left him even as the details grew up like kudzu around him and who was able to keep me pruning those very interesting but ultimately irrelevant details that sink so many works of historical fiction. He was a great friend as well as a great writer, sorely missed by all who knew him.

My constant companion in this venture is my long time editor, assistant, and best friend, Leigh Strother-Vien, who has been involved in every stage of development and who introduced me to her distant relative, David Hunter Strother, who became the primary counterpoint character in this particular story. Without Leigh, this book would never have been finished. She has been my mainstay throughout and involved in every stage from first draft to setting the type for this edition.

Readers of various drafts include Mike Glyer, editor of *FILE 770*, the science fiction semi-prozine, who gave much valuable feedback, and Janet Olson and Anne Morell, who urged the original text be subdivided as too unwieldy. Other readers, those who resisted the impulse to sit down and edit like a high school English teacher, added other insights but wish to remain unacknowledged. So they shall.

The final walkaround in the Shenandoah Valley also took us to the Belle Boyd House in Martinsburg, West Virginia, where Don C. Wood was very helpful, and to the Belle Boyd Cottage in Front Royal, Virginia, where the way that Belle lived there is faithfully reproduced. Their researcher Chuck Pomeroy was also a great help.

The penultimate version of this novel is presented as a 14-part serial on Amazon Shorts at Amazon.com. This garnered some encouraging reviews and commentary from several people and helped us in the decision to go forward with this series.

Finally, an old friend from Tamalpais High School, Elizabeth Jones, (nee "Beth" Mason) suggested that we add the map and the list of principle characters to the front of a book for readers like her who are not as familiar with the Civil War. It was a great idea, which we embraced at once.

Greg Hemsath, of Way To Go Maps (waytogomaps.com), dedicated many more hours than he had originally intended to that map, which is drawn from contemporary sources.

The artwork on the cover is also based on actual photos of Belle Boyd and is by David Martin, a well known illustrator who lives in New Mexico.

The map background is a found object, from Henry Kyd Douglas's book, *I Rode With Stonewall*, and is said to have been used by Jackson himself. The pencil marks are his.

The cover design is by George Mattingly (email: george@mattinglydesign.com), who also designed the Brass Cannon Books logo, and the souvenirs we offer at CafePress.com and from our own Brass Cannon Books web site. George and I have been friends for over 37 years and his advice and experience as a publisher as well as a designer were instrumental in getting the book to the stage you see here.

Our web site, BrassCannonBooks.net, was put together by Bill Bice, of PC Pal, Frazier Park, California. (Tel: 661-245-0100)

ABOUT THE AUTHOR

Francis Hamit is an internationally recognized journalist, author and playwright who once served in Military Intelligence. His past work includes articles on Intelligence and Espionage for the *Encyclopaedia Britannica* and other publications. He is a member of the Association of Former Intelligence Officer and the National Military Intelligence Association, as well as the Military Writers Society of America. He was a member of the U.S. Army Security Agency during the Vietnam War and is a Vietnam veteran. He is also a graduate of the Iowa Writers Workshop.

His other works include the stage plays, *MARLOWE: An Elizabethan Tragedy* (1988), and *Memorial Day* (2005); the non-fiction book *Virtual Reality and the Exploration of Cyberspace* (1993, SAMS); the novella *Sunday in the Park With George* (2005) and hundreds of magazine articles, columns, reviews, essays and blog entries. Etc.